THE CLONE REBELLION

ALLIANCE

ALSO AVAILABLE FROM STEVEN L. KENT AND TITAN BOOKS

The Clone Republic
Rogue Clone
The Clone Elite (May 2013)
The Clone Betrayal (June 2013)
The Clone Empire (July 2013)
The Clone Redemption (August 2013)
The Clone Sedition (September 2013)
The Clone Assassin (October 2013)

STEVEN L. KENT

THE CLONE REBELLION

ALLIANCE

TITAN BOOKS

THE CLONE ALLIANCE
Print edition ISBN: 9781781167175
E-book edition ISBN: 9781781167335

Published by Titan Books
A division of Titan Publishing Group Ltd
144 Southwark Street, London SE1 0UP

First edition: April 2013
1 3 5 7 9 10 8 6 4 2

This is a work of fiction. Names, characters, places, and incidents either are the product of the author's imagination or are used fictitiously, and any resemblance to actual persons, living or dead, business establishments, events, or locales is entirely coincidental. The publisher does not have any control over and does not assume any responsibility for author or third-party websites or their content.

A CIP catalogue record for this title is available from the British Library.

Printed and bound in Great Britain by CPI Group Ltd.

This book is dedicated to Dustin, Rachel, and Dillan, mostly because I cannot come up with a more appropriate way to thank them.

SPIRAL ARMS OF THE MILKY WAY GALAXY

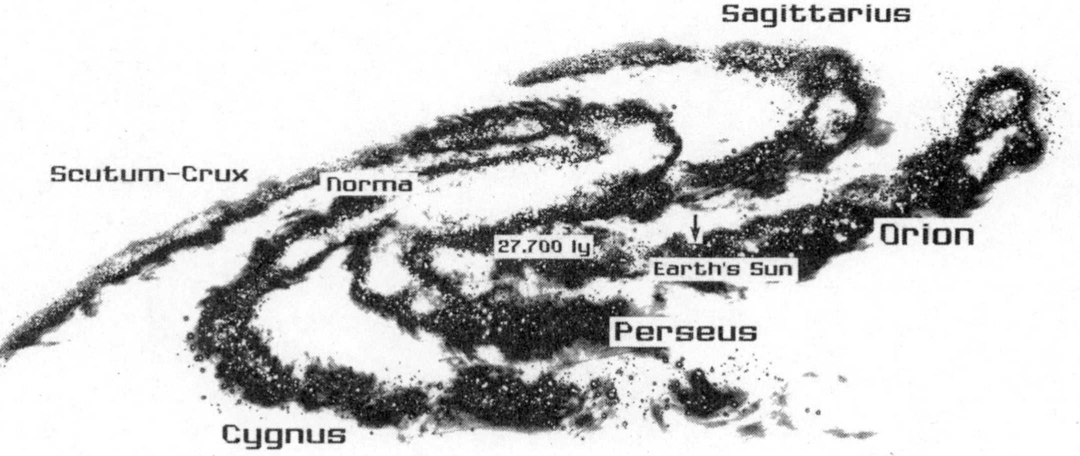

Map by Steven J. Kent, adapted from a public domain NASA diagram

Extremism in the defense of liberty is no vice,
and moderation in the pursuit of justice is no virtue.

BARRY GOLDWATER

PROLOGUE

I held the grenade in my left hand and fingered the pin with my right. I stood in the shadow-filled belly of a military transport. They called this the kettle. You could cram a hundred Marines into a transport like this, but I was alone… almost alone. Ray Freeman, my partner, lay unconscious on the bench that ran along the wall.

A tough bird like this transport would survive the grenade. The blast would not do the ship much good, however. The shrapnel would shred cables and piping. The force of the explosion would dent the walls, but the shell would remain intact. The insulation around the fuel tank would protect it from the explosion. The thick bulkheads around the cockpit were made to withstand a lot more than a grenade. Ray and I, on the other hand, would be nothing more than juice splashed along the walls. They would identify us by our DNA and wash us out with a hose.

If he had been conscious, Ray would have wanted me to pull the pin. He would probably have shot me and pulled the pin himself if he saw me hesitating. That was our agreement. "No going back." "No slow death."

Ray would have put an end to this, no doubt about it. But Ray was a natural-born. I was a military clone. Most of my thoughts were my own, but some of my psyche was hardwired into my brain through neural programming. I always knew about the violence that was programmed into me. They built me to kill. What I never realized was that they also programmed my kind to survive.

If I pulled the pin, I would die in an instant. I wanted that. If I turned the transport around, I would starve on the long flight back to Little Man. If Ray woke up, he would shoot me. I wouldn't mind dying, but I didn't want him to think that I lost my nerve when it came time to pull the pin. I didn't even need the grenade. If I opened the hatch, we would get sucked out to space. Without protective suits, our bodies would burst. Just press the button...

But I couldn't make myself do it. Could not pull the pin, could not press the button. Programming. Sliding doors don't swing. Mathematical engines don't spell words. Liberator clones do not kill themselves.

So I would try to fly this bird back to Little Man and take the slow death instead. I had one week's worth of food, six weeks' worth of travel, and a ship that had been taken well beyond its limits more than a month ago. On the bright side, maybe Ray would wake up and shoot me.

PART I

MODERATION… NO VIRTUE

1

EARTHDATE: SEPTEMBER 12, A.D. 2512
GALACTIC POSITION: SCUTUM-CRUX ARM

A book.

When we left the colony on Little Man, one of the Neo-Baptists gave me a gift. By its shape and size, I could tell it was a book. Since all of the books on the little farming planet were of the religious sort, I did not bother unwrapping the package.

After pretty much ignoring me for the months that I lived with them, the Neo-Baptists suddenly cared about my salvation. How touching. But why should they care? I was, after all, a clone. As far as they were concerned, I was a living being without a soul.

Ray Freeman, my partner, and I had come to this planet after the fall of the Unified Authority—the Earth-based empire that populated and controlled the galaxy. These Neo-Baptist colonists were his people. He had grown up among them, then abandoned their fold as a teen. I do not know how religion fitted into his psyche, but he now made his living as a mercenary. Killing came easily to Freeman.

Killing came naturally to me, too. What did not come naturally was living among religious farmers. We spent months trapped on Little Man, then Freeman got an idea that would either get us back into society or kill us. Either option sounded better than life on Little Man. He wanted to adapt a short-range military transport for pangalactic travel. We might as well have tried flapping our arms and flying the one hundred thousand light-years to Earth.

The colonists gave us a glib, "Thanks for coming," and handed me a gift wrapped in a swatch of pearl white cotton cloth. They said good-bye and walked off without a backward glance. That was also how Freeman and I left their planet—without a backward glance.

"Think there's any chance this can work?" I asked Freeman, as we entered our transport through the "kettle"—the windowless cargo and passenger cabin.

"Does it matter?" he asked. That was Freeman, always cutting to the heart of the matter. Conversation did not interest him, so he had hit the proverbial nail on the head. It made little difference to either of us whether our plan worked or we blew up in space, so long as we got away from the Neo-Baptists.

The military shuttle became the instrument of our passive suicide—a short-range ship made to fly distances of twenty thousand or thirty thousand miles at a maximum speed of two hundred thousand miles per hour. We were going to crank up the speed, preferably to a respectable ten million miles per hour, as we flew it to a satellite approximately four billion miles from this planet.

In the unlikely event that we made it to that satellite, we would start the next phase in our suicide. We would attempt to adapt specialized equipment used for transferring ships across the galaxy to work on our transport. Imagine taking a submarine and gluing wings and a rocket engine to its chassis. Your submarine might have wings and a rocket engine, but it would not work in space. That just about summed up what we wanted to do with our transport. Even if we outfitted it with a broadcast engine, that would not mean we could use it to broadcast.

I had no interest in opening the gift that the Neo-Baptists gave me when I first boarded the transport; but traveling with Ray Freeman left me lonelier than traveling alone. I knew I would need some sort of distraction even before I entered the cockpit and watched him silently working the controls.

Freeman ignited the engines, and we took off in an arc. Haze gave way to blue and soon blackness as we left the atmosphere, then Little Man was gone.

The first thing we needed to do was pick up speed. Transports routinely traveled at two hundred thousand miles per hour. Commanders used transports like this to ferry Marines and soldiers from battleships to planets during invasions. The ship had incredibly powerful shields but no weapons. As far as amenities went, the only padding in the entire transport was on the pilot's seat.

It took us less than a minute to fly from the surface of Little Man to outside the atmosphere, and I already felt lonely sitting beside Freeman. I left the cockpit and climbed into the all-steel kettle. It was a dimly lit cavern with steel walls, a steel ceiling, and a steel floor. There I sat down on the wooden bench that ran along the wall and unwrapped the book. The cotton cloth square slid back revealing an all-black cover made of leather. I was looking at the unmarked back cover of the book, but I recognized the Bible even before I turned it over and saw the gold letters.

A hundred years back, every major church signed the Religious Accordance of 2391, a document that stated that clones were created of man, not God, and therefore did not have souls. Not having to worry about favorable placement in the afterlife, I had abandoned religion altogether. I counted myself among the true nonbelievers, and I knew I would have to be pretty damned desperate before I would crack this book.

"Harris," Ray's voice called to me from the intercom station in the wall.

I left the Bible on the bench and went to the station. "Everything okay?" I asked.

"I'm going to have a look at the engine and play with the fuel," Freeman said. "Think you can keep an eye on the controls?"

"I've never flown one of these birds," I said.

"You won't be flying," Freeman said. "I just need you to tell me the speed."

"On my way," I said.

I climbed the ladder and stepped into the cockpit. Freeman left without saying a word. *Four hundred hours*, I thought to myself. That seemed like a long, long time. Then I realized, it would only be four hundred hours if we could coax the ship into flying fifty times faster than it was meant to fly. Otherwise, we might have a twenty-thousand-hour flight ahead of us. The good news was, I would not need to last twenty thousand hours. I would starve to death first.

I sat in the pilot's seat and watched the little red-lighted display. Ray had us cruising along at two hundred thousand miles per hour. The ship started to sputter. I don't know what Ray did to the engines, but the transport shook and convulsed, then slowed down. We had dropped to below one hundred thousand when he did something new, and the speed started to build.

"How fast are we going?" Freeman called over the intercom.

"What did you do?" I asked. "We're at five hundred thousand and climbing." Gravity in space is based on acceleration. At this rate we could have shut off our gravity generator and gotten on fine.

"We're up to a million," I called. I felt elated. My time stuck in the transport with Ray had just been cut from twenty thousand hours to four thousand. We'd still starve to death at this speed, but we'd die closer to the broadcast station.

"We're up to two million." A minute later I reported three million miles per hour. Unfortunately the speed topped out at four million miles per hour. That meant one thousand hours, a six-week trip with four weeks' worth of food.

Once he got the transport flying at a couple million miles per hour, Freeman spent most of his time toying with the electrical system and trying to figure out how he could splice parts from a broadcast station into the systems on the transport. We seldom spoke to each other. To keep from losing my mind, I started reading the Bible that the Neo-Baptists had given me. I originally decided that I would not read the book. I got desperate and read it several times. The Baptists would have been proud.

I did not like the New Testament. It made no sense. The idea that an all-powerful being sent his son to die for people who did not listen to him had no logic to it.

The Old Testament resonated better. I read it four times and had a religious awakening after a fashion. As long as I accepted God as a metaphor for government, the Old Testament of the Bible made perfect sense. God took a small nation and made it a big nation by saving citizens who followed his laws. Some of the kosher laws struck me as extreme, but every government has its peculiarities.

When Freeman worked in the cargo bay, I took that Bible up

to the cockpit and read. When Freeman lingered in the cockpit, I read in the gloom of the kettle. I kept out of his way unless he called me.

If you ever wondered what it would feel like to be sealed in a can, try traveling in the kettle of a military transport. Except for the netting in the cargo area and the wooden bench around the walls, everything in a kettle is bare metal. No windows. No padded seats. No carpeting. The walls are metal, as are the floor and ceiling. Even the toilet is made of metal.

Before starting my fifth trip through the Old Testament, I called up to the cockpit and asked Freeman how much farther to the broadcast station.

"I don't know," he answered.

There was no use pushing him, so I opened to Genesis.

And the hours rolled on.

We had plenty of air thanks to the transport's industrial-sized oxygen rebreather. That same unit combined enough Hs and Os to provide water for two platoons. Our food supply, on the other hand, had thinned to just about nothing.

I really did not care about survival. After months of hearing people "praise the Lord" and plow the corn, I'd decided that I would rather die in space than live on Little Man. I did, however, want to reach my own personal promised land. Even if I did not get to return to Earth, I wanted to see that broadcast station.

Amazingly, I got my wish.

The broadcast station was the last vestige of a recently defunct transportation system that once served as a superhighway across the Milky Way. Even flying at the speed of light, and no Unified Authority ships could attain that speed, it would take you one hundred thousand years to cross the Milky Way. Most of the 180 planets populated by humans were five hundred to one thousand light-years apart.

The key to getting from one planet to another was broadcasting, a technology that translated spaceships and communications into data that could be transferred instantaneously from one location to another. Some ships, mostly scientific vessels, had onboard broadcast engines that enabled their pilots to plug coordinates into a computer and "broadcast" to any location. The vast majority of space travel, however, was routed through the Broadcast Network, a system of satellites called "broadcast stations." Broadcast stations had separate discs for sending and receiving ships.

Freeman proposed a plan to try and convert a standard short-range military transport into a self-broadcaster by installing a broadcast engine. He wanted to commandeer the broadcast engine from the sending disc of the nearest broadcast satellite and attach it to the electrical system in our transport. It was a crazy idea, kind of like tying a rocket engine to an atmosphere-bound jet and flying it into space.

Assuming we could adapt the industrial-sized broadcast engine from the station to work on our ship, we could send ourselves to Earth or Mars or some other place in the heart of the Republic. Now that we had coaxed our transport two hundred thousand times farther than it was designed to fly, all we had left to do was to pull a serviceable broadcast engine out of that station, adapt it to fit on our ship, and splice it into our electrical supply.

The Broadcast Network was set up in a linear fashion. Each sending disc only sent ships to the next broadcast station down the line. The various stations did not need or have computers because their sending discs formed a dedicated conduit sending ships to a few select locations. No computers were necessary; all of the calculations were premade.

That did not bode well for Freeman and me, as it meant

we would have no way of aiming ourselves once we got the broadcast engine up and working, if we got the engine up and working. We might simply send ourselves into oblivion and never materialize again.

Dropping our speed to a mere crawl, Freeman approached the broadcast station. From the front or the back, the satellite looked immense. Both the sending disc and the receiving disc were a full mile in diameter. They were made of mirrored glass. When active, broadcast discs emitted streams of hyper-accelerated electrons that shone so brightly that a quick glimpse at them would leave you blind. The power was off now. This was the first time I had ever actually seen the front of a broadcast disc up close.

"Damn, Freeman, you actually got us here," I said.

Ray did not respond.

We went to go change into our space gear so that we could begin removing the engine from the station, and ran into a problem. Ray, the one of us with the mechanical expertise, did not fit in the atmospheric suits that came with the transport. The suits were made for general-issue military clones, men who stood just under six feet tall. Ray stood over seven feet tall and weighed approximately three hundred and fifty pounds. His torso was the basic shape and size of a wheelbarrow tipped on its nose. With his huge biceps and forearms, Freeman could not fit his arms in the sleeves. Even if he could have, his arms must have been ten inches too long to fit. His tree-trunk legs and great wide ass did not fit in the pants.

The suit did not fit me so well, either, but I managed. I stood six-foot-three, about four inches too tall. I forced my long arms into the sleeves and scrunched my back, then fastened the helmet over my head. Once I was dressed, Ray returned to the cockpit and vented the oxygen out of the kettle. With the air gone and the gravity off, he opened the six-inch-thick metal doors at the rear of the kettle. As the doors parted, an endless ocean of lights and blackness stared back at me.

Throughout my walk to the broadcast station, Freeman and I would have uninterrupted communications through the interLink—a proprietary small-area communications system developed for military use. I had a video recorder built into the visor of my helmet. From the atmosphere-enclosed comfort of the cockpit, Freeman could monitor the images captured by that recorder and guide my every move.

I hooked my tether line to a socket near the rear door of the transport and kicked off into space. Ahead of me, the dormant sending disc had the slight concave curvature of a dinner plate. If it were a dinner plate, I was smaller than the smallest fly. Its reflective glass surface seemed to stretch on forever. I drifted toward it until I was close enough to tap my finger against its surface.

My atmospheric suit was white, with lights placed on the shoulders, helmet, torso, and legs for visibility. I saw my reflection in the mirrored glass of the disc with the fabric of space as my backdrop. I reached out and touched my reflection, then used the jetpack on my suit to propel myself along its face. When I reached the top, I looked back down to where I had come from. The disc was three inches thick and a full mile in diameter. From a distance it would look sharper than a razor blade.

Ships did not actually enter sending discs. When they approached, the sending disc coated them with accelerated electrons and broadcasted them instantaneously to the next station in the Network. That was how man conquered known space, by creating a transportation and communications highway that enabled him to travel tens of thousands of light-years in an instant.

"You ever done this before?" Freeman asked. Freeman's voice

was so low that it sounded more like a rumble than a voice over the speaker in my helmet.

"Have I ever done what, free-walked in space or salvaged parts from a broadcast disc?"

"Free-walked?" Freeman asked. He knew I had never salvaged parts from a broadcast disc.

"Yeah," I said. Growing up in an orphanage—that was the term Unified Authority politicians used for the farms in which they raised military clones—we used to spend one week each year in a "summer space camp." Instead of riding horses and swimming in a lake, we did spacewalks and sham battles.

"You ever been behind the scenes on a broadcast station?" Freeman asked.

"No," I said.

I controlled the jetpack in the back of my suit using optic commands on a menu built into my helmet. This left my hands free for holding objects, using tools, and praying. Thoughts about floating forever in space ran through my head. I saw myself curled up in my suit and floating like a specimen in a jar of formaldehyde, but that was not a realistic concern. Nothing short of a laser shot would break my tether; and even if something did, I could control my flight using the jetpack.

Looking down the back of the glass, I saw the spindle that connected the sending and receiving discs like an axle between two wheels. All of the generator and broadcast equipment would be housed in that spindle. From up here, a half mile away, the hall connecting the two discs looked as narrow as a sewing needle.

"That's where you need to go," Freeman said.

"I know that," I said.

What I would have given if I could have restarted the entire Broadcast Network from this disc. Not long ago, fleets of mile-wide naval ships traveled across the galaxy using the Broadcast

Network. Then came the war. Enemies of the Unified Authority Republic took control of a self-broadcasting fleet and shut down the entire galaxy with a single shot. They destroyed the broadcast station near Mars, cutting the juice that powered the entire Broadcast Network. There would be no restarting the Network without rebuilding the Mars Station.

The Unified Authority still had the biggest and most powerful ships, but they were not self-broadcasting ships. Without the Broadcast Network, fleets that were ten thousand light years from Earth would need more than ten thousand years to travel back. Without the Broadcast Network handling transmissions, messages sent from Earth to those ships would take ten thousand years to arrive as well.

Even though they were dormant, the size of the discs made me nervous. I floated down the gap between them slowly. As I descended, I saw that the discs were one hundred feet apart. From a distance, they seemed to butt right up against each other. Dropping between them, I felt like a diver entering a massive crevice. I dropped a good thousand feet and stopped. When I glanced in the direction I had come from, it seemed like the gap between the two discs had narrowed.

As I glided toward the spindle connecting the two discs, I wondered if the tether line would reach. Just for it to reach from the top of the discs to the spindle it would need to be a half mile long. It wasn't. I was about halfway down the side of the disc when a message flashed on the visor of my helmet: "CAUTION. TETHER LIMIT REACHED."

"YOU HAVE REACHED THE END OF YOUR TETHER" would have been more accurate. Floating in space, with everything happening in slow motion and the obsidian depths wrapped around me like a blanket, things sometimes seemed the opposite of what they were. Emptiness felt smothering. Floating in a vacuum reminded me of swimming underwater.

With trepidation, I detached my tether line and watched it reel away. Had there been a loop or a stem on the back of the disc, I would have tied it on. The back of the disc was as smooth as the front.

"You there?" I asked Freeman.

"Yes," he said.

Nervous about floating untethered, I had hoped for more pleasantries. Hearing his voice, I realized he would not chat with me.

The backs of the discs were black but not reflective. Looking into the backs of the discs reminded me of staring into a shadow. Looking out the gap between them, I saw stars. I stared at the stars for a moment, then turned my attention back to the discs. It was like having a black cloth draped across my helmet. Taking a deep breath, I continued on to the spindle.

I had not appreciated the size of the tube that connected the two sides of this broadcast station when I viewed it from the edge of the sending disc, a half of a mile away. From up there, it looked short and narrow. Now that I had floated down beside it, I realized it was the size of my boot-camp barracks—two stories tall and a hundred feet long.

It only took me a moment to figure out how to enter the broadcast station. The batteries inside this station might not have had the teravolts needed to keep the discs operating, but they did have enough electricity to power the lights marking the door.

I approached. The door was sealed, of course.

"We're specked," I said.

"Speck" was the Marines' swear word of choice. During my time in the Corps, I used the word "speck" only slightly less than I used the words "I," "and," and "the." Technically, "speck" was a noun. It referred to sperm. Most military men found other creative uses for the word. If you did not like someone, you told him to "get specked." If you thought a brother Marine was in trouble, you might say that he was "specked." Almost every serviceman used the word "speck" in one form or another, but Marines seemed particularly adept at it. On a daily basis, I heard speck used to describe bad chow, stupid officers, and a bad case of the runs. You might say that we Marines were specking geniuses at coming up with new uses for that word.

"Think I should blast my way in?" I asked.

Back on the transport, Freeman saw everything I saw on his monitor. "See the red circle?" Freeman asked. Beside the door was a six-inch red circle. "That's the security panel. Press down on it."

I traveled over to the circle and pressed three fingers against it. The circle rolled over, and a laser no broader than a spaghetti noodle shot into my helmet to perform a retinal scan. I started to pull away.

"What's the problem?" Freeman asked.

"It won't recognize me," I said. "It will arm the security system."

"Most of the techs who fix these stations are clones," Freeman said.

"They're a newer model," I said.

"You think they updated the eyes?" Freeman asked.

I pressed the panel a second time and waited as the laser scanned my left eye. The door to the station opened.

"That was easy," I said. I did not need to worry about Freeman saying he told me so, that would have been too many syllables wasted.

Once inside the station, I found the master control panel. I found the switches for sealing the door and starting the gravity generator. I did not bother turning on the oxygen. Though the station did have an environmental system, I preferred my suit. I turned on the lights. "Are you getting this?" I asked.

Ray did not answer. I suppose he would have said something if he was not getting a picture.

The inside of the station looked like a warehouse. Equipment of every shape and size lined the walls. There were lockers and storage compartments. There were oxygen tanks, laser torches, jetpacks, racks of environmental suits, boxes of tools, and a credit-operated vending machine filled with snacks for the maintenance workers who would repair this station when and if it broke down. We had just about run out of food on the transport. Seeing that machine with its candy bars and potato chips nearly brought tears to my eyes.

The moment I found the broadcast engine, my luck turned sour. The engine was fifteen feet tall. It was built into the wall of the station. Because of its size and mass, there would be no way to disassemble it and carry it out piece by piece as we had planned. "We're specked," I said. "It's too big."

Freeman did not respond.

"What do we do now?" I asked.

"Cut through the wall," Freeman said.

"What about the station?" I asked.

"What about the station?" Freeman asked.

"Won't that destroy the broadcast station?" I asked.

"You see anyone who is going to complain?" Freeman asked.

I went back to the entrance, selected a laser torch, and returned. I once owned a self-broadcasting ship, a commuter craft called a Johnston Starliner. The broadcast engine on that ship looked like a crate filled with mortar shells. It had eighteen brass cylinders, each about three feet tall. The broadcast engine for the discs had the same basic design—eighteen brass cylinders shaped like bullets. In this case, each cylinder was fifteen feet tall and so specking wide that I could only reach two-thirds of the way around them.

With Freeman looking over my shoulder, I cut every cable and wire that connected the engine to the broadcast station. Before climbing under the cylinders to cut the outer shell of the satellite, I returned to the atmospheric controls and purged any remaining oxygen from inside the station. If there was any oxygen in the station when I cut through the fuselage, it could cause havoc the moment I cut a hole in the wall.

Next, I turned off the gravity. Back on Earth, those eighteen brass cylinders would weigh several tons each. With the gravity off, their weight meant nothing, but their mass still posed a problem. Moving them from the station to the transport would not be easy.

With Freeman directing me, I cut through the outer wall of the station. Once the incision was done, I braced myself against a rail and kicked one of the cylinders. The entire engine, outer wall and all, dropped out of the station as a unit.

I would have needed a crane to move the broadcast engine back on Earth. Out here in space, I conveyed it using a cargo rig—a couple of synchronized jetpacks that I attached to the outermost cylinders using canvas cords. I stood on top of the broadcast engine holding the reins in my hands and rode it like a Roman riding a war chariot.

Up to that point things had gone pretty well. After this it all went to shit.

2

I rode the engine between the discs and out to the transport. The ride went smoothly. The problems did not start until I reached the kettle.

The broadcast engine was still attached to the portion of the wall that I cut out of the station. Before I could fit the engine into the transport, I would need to cut the engine free. With the small section of outer wall attached, the engine would not fit up the ramp of the kettle.

"It's too wide to fit through the hatch," I said as I used the cargo rig's reverse thrusters to put on the brakes.

"Cut the outer wall away," Freeman said.

We did not have torches on the transport, and I had left the torch I used to extract the engine back in the broadcast station. I had to fly back to retrieve it. The trip took twenty minutes. Then, with Freeman inspecting my every move to make sure I did not damage the cylinders, I used the laser torch to cut the brackets that attached the broadcast engine to the outer wall.

I did not damage the cylinders, nor did I cut any hidden cables, but something still went wrong. We should have seen it coming. With the brackets cut away, there was nothing holding the cylinders together. It was like placing a dozen eggs on a table, then peeling away the carton holding them. With the wall and brackets gone, the only thing binding those giant cylinders together was the canvas straps from my cargo rig.

As Newton observed, "An object at rest will remain at rest until acted upon by the force of a cargo rig." Too distracted to notice that without that section of wall binding the bases of the cylinders, the canvas strap would no longer hold the various components of the broadcast engine together, I started up the cargo rig. The cylinders slipped out of the rig and floated in eighteen different directions. It looked like slow-motion footage of bowling pins struck by a ball.

Anyone else would have said, "You better go get them," or "Be careful." Sitting in the sealed atmosphere of the cockpit, Ray Freeman did not waste oxygen telling me the obvious. He sat and watched silently as I made trip after trip gathering each of the cylinders and bringing it to the transport.

Now that they had separated, I found I could move the individual cylinders using my jetpack. I would wrap my arms around the cylinder, use the rockets in my jetpack, and drift toward the transport at approximately the same speed as a ninety-year-old woman walking uphill. Once I got the cylinders into the transport, I stacked them on their sides like lumber. Freeman sealed the rear hatch as I brought in the last of them. The doors ground together slowly and sealed with a clank.

As those cylinders weighed several tons each, Freeman left the gravity off while I tried to use the internal cargo arm to stand them and arrange them. That was when we ran into the next problem.

Transports like this were meant for hauling soldiers, not cargo. The average soldier stood just under six feet tall; the cylinders were fifteen feet tall. The kettle, which had plenty of headroom for transporting Marines, had a twelve-foot clearance. Ray said that he needed to come out for a closer look. He flooded the kettle with air and came out to inspect the problem. "It's too tall," was all he said.

I looked from the tops of the cylinders to their bases. "Speck!" I said. "Can we leave them on their sides?"

Freeman shook his head. "The bottoms are insulated. Everything else is made to conduct electricity. If we left them lying there, the brass would conduct the wrong charge into the hull of the ship."

Freeman solved the problem. There were storage compartments under the floor of the kettle. Using my laser torch, Freeman cut away a thirty-foot section of floor, giving us access to the storage compartments below. The compartments were four feet deep, creating one foot of clearance between the tops of the cylinders and the roof of the ship.

With the problem solved, Freeman went back to the cockpit and purged the oxygen out of the kettle. Then I used the cargo arm to drag those massive cylinders out of the kettle horizontally, bring them in diagonally, and drop them into place vertically.

Once they were in place, Freeman sent me back to the broadcast station a third time. This time he needed insulation blankets to prevent the electricity running through the cylinders from juicing the entire ship. When I returned, I had yards of rubberized blanket. I also brought every morsel from the vending machine.

Freeman sealed the doors, pumped some O2 back in the kettle, and came to join me.

I showed him the blanket, and he nodded. "We're going to wrap this around the engine?" I asked.

"Yes."

"Won't that affect the way they conduct electricity?" I asked.

"Yes," he said.

"So is this going to work?" I asked.

He glared at me. That look might have meant, "What do you think?" or it might have meant, "Of course it won't work." Most likely Freeman's glare meant, "You knew you were committing suicide when we left Little Man."

"You hungry?" I asked.

"What do you have?" Freeman asked. I showed Freeman the stash I had stolen from the vending machine. He chose some meat sticks. I ate a candy bar.

Freeman had no trouble reassembling the various components of the broadcast engine. The design was modular. Once the cylinders were in place, he ran cables between them, then he spliced the cables into the generator that powered the shields for our transport. The operation took hours. He worked nonstop, never speaking a word.

By the time Freeman finished, there were so many cables snaking in and out around the cylinders that we could no longer walk across the kettle without tripping.

"Think the generator has enough juice for that monster?" I asked.

"There's plenty of power," Freeman said as he inspected his work.

"Should we boot it up?" I asked.

My life was coming to a close. The broadcast engines on self-broadcasting ships were attached to computers. The pilot used the computer to calculate a destination, then the engine broadcasted the ship to that exact spot. Without a computer controlling it, there was no telling what the broadcast engine might do. It might simply disintegrate us. It might send us into a star. I was reminded again that coming out to this satellite had never been anything more than a passive form of suicide. We could tell ourselves we were trying to get back into the war, but we were really just killing ourselves either way.

"You know this isn't going to work," Freeman said as he gave his work one final inspection. He turned to stare down at me, those emotionless dark eyes of his showing me neither anger nor mercy.

The top of the broadcast cylinders came closer to the roof than we expected. Thanks to the storage compartments, we had hoped for a twelve-inch clearance. Once Freeman added all the wires and cables, the clearance came closer to three inches. I could not have wedged my fist between the cylinders and the kettle ceiling.

Freeman held out his right hand and opened it for me to see what lay on his palm. The back of his hand was dark as chocolate but his palm was nearly as light as mine. In a galactic empire in which racial divisions were thoroughly eliminated, Ray and his people, the Neo-Baptist colonists of Little Man, were living anachronisms. They referred to themselves as "pure-blooded African Americans." They were, as far as I could tell, the last people in the universe that thought of themselves as "American."

The white grenade gleamed in Ray Freeman's shovel-sized hand. It was a low-yield grenade, about the size of a golf ball; but in his giant paw, it looked smaller than a Ping-Pong ball. If Freeman stretched his hand across my face, he could plug one of my ears with his little finger and the other with his thumb.

"What's that?" I asked.

"A grenade," Freeman said.

"I know what it is," I said. Having been raised in an orphanage for military clones, I threw my first grenade at the age of eight.

"What's it for?" I asked.

"If the engine doesn't work," Freeman said.

I nodded and took the grenade, doubting that I would need it. The most likely outcome of powering up the broadcast engine would be that it would not work. I would not need the grenade because the broadcast engine would explode or send a lethal current through the transport. Freeman and I would simply fry. If it did work, it would probably send us into unknown space never to materialize again.

I rolled the grenade in my hand. "Well," I said, "good luck." I turned and headed to the cockpit. I would be safe there. Correction—I would not be safe, but I would be safer. If things went wrong, there might be enough left of me to pull the pin.

The cockpit had a video screen on which I could watch Ray connect a few last cables. Giving his handiwork one final inspection, he dropped to his hands and knees and checked the insulation blankets along the base of the broadcast engine. He crawled beside each cylinder one by one, then he went to the control panel he had rigged beside the broadcast engine.

Freeman was big, but he looked like a child beside those fifteen-foot brass cylinders. Without so much as a moment's hesitation, he pressed the power button, routing the electricity from the shield generator into the broadcast engine.

The disaster started quietly. I could hear as well as see everything on the screen. The shield generator ran smoothly. A few of the cables rattled. The cylinders caught the electrical charge from the generator and amplified it. Diodes at the top of the broadcast engine glowed black, then blue, then green, then yellow, then red as the charge intensified. This did not happen quickly; more than an hour had already passed.

During all this time, Ray Freeman made no effort to communicate with me. He walked around the engine inspecting contacts and dials and diodes. He spent some time staring straight into the center of the engine, apparently looking at nothing in particular.

Neither Freeman nor I was all that knowledgeable about broadcast technology. I did not know if the next thing that happened was good or bad. I do not think that Ray expected it.

An inch-wide arc of bluish white electricity formed along the tops of the cylinders. It was as thick and solid as a rope and it danced between the tips of the cylinders. The roof of the kettle was bare metal, and some of that arc connected with it. At that exact moment, my monitor winked off, and the electrical system inside the transport shut itself down.

The entire transport went dark for less than half a second, then red emergency lights came on. The cockpit lights winked back to life, but the monitor showing the kettle stayed dark. I jumped out of my chair and started for the kettle.

I had once seen what happens when things go wrong with a broadcast engine on a self-broadcasting ship. In order to power a broadcast, you need 1 million, million volts of electricity. When things go wrong with billions of volts, they truly go wrong.

Looking out over the kettle from the cockpit door, I only needed a moment to determine that the transport was still in one piece. I climbed down the ladder to the kettle. "Freeman, what happened?" I yelled. He did not answer. "What happened?" I called.

A benevolent though considerably smaller arc danced along the points of the broadcast engine's cylinders. At first I thought there was still current running into the engine, then I saw the charred and melted stump where the shield generator had been. The last fumes of the charge had caused the explosion.

Freeman lay on the ground beside the shield generator. His face was burned. Shards of metal and plastic poked out of his skin. Rivulets of blood ran down the sweaty leather of his skin. His massive chest continued to heave with the even rhythm of his breathing. He looked bad, but he had survived. Glad to see that my friend was still alive, I pulled out that grenade and wrapped my finger around the pin.

Ray Freeman was big and strong; a few pieces of shrapnel would not kill him. The grenade I held in my right hand could do it, though. He would want that. But before I pulled the pin, I decided to make Ray comfortable.

3

Placing the grenade in a safe spot, I lifted Ray onto a bench and examined his wounds. It did not occur to me to dumb down the gravity, so I got the full brunt of his three hundred and fifty pounds as I reached around his chest and heaved him onto the bench. The tang of his burned flesh filled my nose. His clothes were moist with blood, and there was no strength in his body. His arms hung limp, and his shoulders drooped. Ray Freeman, the biggest and most dangerous man I ever met, lay totally vulnerable beside me.

I rested him on his back and placed his hands on his stomach. I cleaned his wounds. "We gave it our best," I said, looking down at him, then I picked up the grenade. It fitted neatly in my palm. It was small and white and completely lethal. Rolling the pin with my thumb, I thought about what would happen when I set the grenade off. We would die in an instant. The explosion would blow us apart. It would do more than that. It would grind us to a pulp.

I looked around the kettle, with its eerie shadows and thick metal walls. Naked girders ran the height of its walls. The grenade would not destroy the transport. Kettle walls were designed to withstand missiles. The architects who designed this bird had envisioned bombs exploding outside the fuselage, but I thought that the walls of the kettle would survive the grenade. Even with the floor cut away, there was enough insulation around the fuel supply and engine to protect them from the explosion. The cockpit had blast shields.

I looped my finger into the pin, took a deep breath, and started to pull, but I could not do it. Trying to focus my mind on pulling the pin was like grabbing a wet bar of soap. The thoughts just slipped through my grasp.

"Pull the pin," I muttered to myself. "Pull the pin." But every time I tightened my finger around the pin, I suddenly had an irresistible need to check on Freeman or run to the cockpit. It was like my brain purged the thought, and whatever thought filled the void became urgent. I would start to pull, feel a twitch, and momentarily forget what I was doing.

Programming, I realized. Part of the design process for military clones included intricate neural programming. Clones of a later make than I were programmed to see themselves as natural-born humans. They had brown hair and brown eyes, but they saw themselves as having blond hair and blue eyes. To prevent a clone uprising, Congress insisted that they be built with a gland in their heads that would secrete a deadly hormone into their blood if they learned they were clones. They called this the "death reflex."

My make of clone, the Liberators, had a different gland that released a combination of endorphins and adrenaline into our blood during combat. When things heated up, our hormone helped us think more quickly and clearly. Unfortunately, it proved addictive. Many Liberators became hooked on the hormone and required a fix of violence even after they had won their battles. They attacked prisoners, allies, fellow soldiers. It was the fear of Liberators that caused Congress to build the death reflex in later models.

As a Liberator clone, I was able to recognize my synthetic creation. As a Liberator, I knew that I was built to kill. It had never occurred to me that I had also been programmed to live. I could not force myself to pull the pin from that grenade.

"Well, that is just specking great!" I snarled, and I threw the grenade on the deck, pin and all. I stormed over to the hatch controls. They were intact. All of the transport's systems checked out in working order except the shields. Hesitating just for a moment, I reached for the button that would open the hatch. If I hit it, the rear of the kettle would split, and Freeman and I would be sucked into space. Death would come in an instant.

But I could not get myself to press the button. It was right there, big and bright red, and shaped like a mushroom, but I could not press it.

"Speck!" I shouted.

Freeman and I had an agreement to kill ourselves rather than return to Little Man. We never thought we would succeed on this mission. We came out to die. Now, thanks to my programming, I could not help but renege. I could not open the hatch or pull the pin.

I would try to fly the transport back to Little Man. What a joke. I was a lousy pilot. I could fly a bird like a Starliner, a civilian craft with simple controls that practically flew itself. This transport, however, had next to no guidance gear. Its nearsighted radar system only had a range of one hundred thousand miles, less than half the distance from the Earth to the moon.

I wasn't really sure which way to fly to get back to Little Man. With the planet more than four billion miles away, navigation by line of sight was out of the question.

I looked at the load of snacks I had brought back from the vending machine on the broadcast station. A few minutes ago, it had looked like a hoard. Now, in light of the hundreds of hours it would take to fly to that worthless colony, the food seemed insignificant.

I left Freeman unconscious in the kettle and entered the cockpit.

"Unified Authority Transport, come in. Unified Authority Transport, come in."

I looked down at the radio in complete disbelief. "This is Transport. Who is this?"

"Transport, this is the S.N.N. *Sakura.* Please hold for Governor Yamashiro."

I suppose I should have been jumping for joy or saying a prayer to that big municipality in the sky. Instead I laughed. I was four billion miles from a farming colony and untold trillions of miles from civilized space, and whoever had found me wanted me to hold so that I could speak with an old friend. The cavalry had arrived in full force.

"Colonel Harris, is that you?" the familiar old voice asked.

"Yamashiro," I said. "What the hell are you doing out here?"

"Ah, Harris, that is the question I wanted to ask you. We have been tracking you for some time, and your actions make no sense. Perhaps we can discuss your mission on my ship."

4

The War...

Freeman and I freelanced for the Unified Authority, the pangalactic evolution of the nation that had once been the United States of America. The Unified Authority explored the Milky Way, found that there was no intelligent life in the galaxy other than mankind, and colonized planets in all six of its arms.

As the exploration continued, a fleet of scientific vessels vanished while mapping out a region of the galactic eye. Fearing we had finally located bug-eyed monsters, the U.A. military went on high alert while the Senate called for the creation of a self-broadcasting fleet of battleships.

When the fleet launched, Senate Majority Leader Morgan Atkins, who had championed the project, accompanied it on its maiden voyage. The fleet broadcasted into the innermost curve of the Norma Arm and disappeared.

That was when the Liberators entered the picture. At the same time that Atkins called for his self-broadcasting armada, the Linear Committee—the executive branch of the Unified Authority government—created a superweapon of its own: a new line of military clones. Unlike later clones, which were raised in orphanages, that first batch of Liberators came out of the tube at the age of twenty. They were fast, smart, and more independent-thinking than any clones that had come before them.

To help them confront an unknown enemy, Liberators were built with a "combat reflex." When the shooting started, a gland inside the Liberators' skulls secreted a mixture of endorphins and adrenaline into their blood. It made them vicious, but it also kept them thinking clearly during the heat of battle.

Using every self-broadcasting vessel available, the Navy sent these Liberator clones to the Galactic Eye, where they soon discovered that Atkins had founded a colony. He had commissioned the self-broadcasting fleet so that he could hijack it. Morgan Atkins, one of the most powerful men in the Unified Authority, had led the first large-scale rebellion against it.

But he had not known about the Liberators. The clone invasion overran his settlement, forcing Atkins to escape into space with his fleet.

The first Atkins Evangelists appeared a few years after the battle in the Galactic Eye. They told stories about the good senator discovering a city in the center of a planet and making contact with a radiant being who threatened to eradicate mankind. According to Mogat dogma, Atkins signed a pact with his "Space Angel" in which he promised to deliver the Republic as a vassal nation in order to avert total eradication of mankind.

Atkins disciples preached independence from Earth. They called themselves the Morgan Atkins Believers. The government called them "Mogats," an abbreviation of the name MOrGan

ATkins, and dismissed them as cranks.

Over the next fifty years, however, the Atkins movement grew. The 2460 census found twenty thousand Mogats. In 2480, more than a million people identified themselves as Atkins believers. By 2510, there were over 200 million of them scattered across the 180 worlds of the Republic. They engaged in smuggling, sedition, and petty crimes. Whenever planets talked about breaking away from the Republic, Mogats were involved.

But the Mogats could never have overthrown the Unified Authority on their own.

In 2510, C.A.T.O., the Confederate Arms Treaty Organization, declared independence from the Unified Authority. The Confederate Arms included four of the six arms of the Milky Way. Only the Orion Arm, the arm in which Earth was located, and the neighboring Sagittarius Arm remained loyal. With tens of billions of citizens, the Confederate Arms provided the troops for a revolution, and the Mogats provided the fleet. The government labeled them "Separatists" and set about squashing them until the attack.

The Japanese got involved through the Confederate Arms. They had lived on a planet called Ezer Kri. When they petitioned to rename their planet Shin Nippon, the U.A. Senate branded it an act of sedition and the Mogats helped them escape.

In 2512, the Separatists took the upper hand. By defeating the Earth Fleet and destroying the Broadcast Network, they effectively shut down the Unified Authority by shutting down travel and communications between Earth and its colonies. That same day, the alliance between the Confederate Arms, the Japanese, and the Mogats collapsed. The Mogats seized control of most of the fleet. Yoshi Yamashiro had commandeered four battleships. I ended up on Little Man, not knowing how the battle royale had ended.

For months I wondered what became of Yamashiro and his four-ship fleet. Now, out of nowhere, he and one of his self-broadcasting battleships had appeared in my space. With some guidance from a flight-deck officer, I flew my transport into one of the *Sakura's* launch bays.

As the rear doors of the kettle opened, I saw Yamashiro and two of his officers waiting to greet me.

Yamashiro was a short man whose black hair was turning white. He had powerful shoulders and a wide neck. His hands were covered with calluses. The calloused hands and his quiet confidence suggested some background in martial arts.

Because he was a politician and not an officer, Yamashiro dressed in suits instead of a uniform. He seemed to own an endless supply of dark blue blazers and red neckties. The officers beside him wore the midnight blue uniform of the Shin Nippon Navy.

"May I come aboard your ship?" Yamashiro asked in a jovial tone.

"Sure," I said. "You don't have to ask."

"I would not dream of setting foot on your property without first asking permission. We spent several weeks looking for you. Do you know how we knew you were on Little Man?" Yamashiro asked as he started up the ramp.

"How did you know I was on that planet?" I asked.

"As my ship approached the planet, my radar men located the lifeless remains of a Unified Authority fighter carrier. One of them radioed me, and said, 'Someone has destroyed a fighter carrier out here.'

"I told them, 'We must have found him. Only Wayson Harris could destroy such a ship.'"

He was talking about the *Grant*. I had seen the ship blow up, but I was not the one who did it.

Yamashiro was no taller than five-six. He came up to my chest.

His skin was the color of very dark tea, and his eyes were black as ebony. He looked around the kettle with a bemused expression, smiling as he examined the broadcast engine sticking out of the cutaway floor.

"My partner is hurt," I said, pointing to where Ray Freeman lay on the bench.

"Ah, I see." Yamashiro turned to one of his men, and said, "Takahashi, call for an emergency team." Then he told me, "We have an excellent physician on board."

Takahashi went to an intercom station just outside my transport. He spoke loud enough for me to hear his voice, but he spoke in Japanese. Moments later, an emergency medical team appeared. Yamashiro and I stood and watched as the medics bent over Freeman and loaded him onto a stretcher. Before leaving, one of the medics spoke to Yamashiro.

"He says that your friend's burns are bad, but the cuts are not so bad. He has a concussion, but there has been no permanent damage."

"Can they fix him up?" I asked.

"Of course," Yamashiro said. "We have excellent medical facilities aboard this ship.

"Perhaps we should leave the team to attend to your friend," Yamashiro said. "You and I have much to discuss." With this, he pulled a pack of cigarettes from inside his jacket and lit one up. He did not offer me a smoke. We had spent some time together, so he knew I would not take one.

As we left, Yamashiro's two-officer entourage fell in behind us, one standing a pace behind him to his left and the other one a pace behind and to his right. Despite my presence, his men stayed in formation.

If he sent either of his men ahead to open a door or fetch a drink of water, the other officer would step between the governor and me. That was the point. Yamashiro was the shogun, and these officers were his samurai, always standing one step behind and flanking him on the left and right—positioned to protect.

"We have been tracking you for several weeks," Yamashiro said, as we walked. "You have proven a most interesting subject.

"At first we thought that you decided to leave the Marines and become a farmer. Then again, you must have changed your mind, or else you would not have left that planet."

"Guess I wasn't cut out for the farming life," I said.

"We became confused when you flew away in a transport. There was no place to go in such a short-range vehicle."

We went up two levels on an elevator and came out in an area filled with civilian offices. This part of the ship was brightly lit. Rows of cubicles stretched from one wall to the other. Men in white shirts and neckties worked quietly at their desks. I noticed women working in the administrative area of the ship as well.

"We soon realized you were flying to the broadcast station. There was some question about how you reached such a remote planet as Little Man in the first place. You must have traveled in a self-broadcasting ship." Yamashiro paused and waited for me to confirm what he had guessed.

"That ship broke down," I said. I neglected to mention that a suicidal pilot used it to broadcast himself into the hull of the *Grant,* the derelict fighter carrier Yamashiro's men spotted floating near Little Man.

Hearing this, Yamashiro stopped walking and cursed softly, a pained expression on his face. One of the officers walking behind us quietly laughed. As he dug into his pocket, Yamashiro said, "Takahashi said you were stranded on that planet. I told him you would not have gone to such a planet unless you had a method to leave."

"You give me more credit than I deserve," I said.

Yamashiro pulled out a money clip and stripped off five bills. "Perhaps I do. I bet Takahashi fifty dollars." He handed the money to the officer, who bowed and accepted it without a word.

"Sorry," I said.

Yamashiro started walking again.

"And when you reached the broadcast station, you behaved in a most peculiar fashion. Some of my men thought that you had discovered a way to restart the Broadcast Network or at least a way to make the station operational. We watched you remove the broadcast engine." He stopped speaking and waited for me to explain.

"We were trying to splice the broadcast engine into the transport's electrical system."

Yamashiro hissed. He dug into his pocket, pulled out another fifty dollars, and gave it to Takahashi, who absolutely beamed. Yamashiro shook his head. "That was what Takahashi believed. I thought maybe you hoped to create some sort of weapon with it." He continued walking, but now he stared at the ground instead of looking at me.

"No," I said, "I was just looking for a ticket back to Earth."

"And you tried to modify a transport so you could use it to broadcast?" Yamashiro asked. He stopped walking and turned to face me. "Harris, that would be suicide. You did not have a broadcast computer. Even if you managed to make the engine work, you could not control the broadcast. You would die."

The two officers walking behind us had been whispering back and forth. Now they stopped and listened closely.

"Yes, I knew that," I said.

"My engineers tell me that you could not fly a transport through the Broadcast Network, the electrical current would atomize the metal in its hull," Yamashiro said, sounding scandalized.

"I figured as much," I said.

"So you chose suicide over the life of a farmer?" Yamashiro looked shocked.

"That just about sums it up."

Takahashi, the officer to whom Yamashiro had just given that fifty dollars, said something in Japanese. I did not recognize the words, but I would have bet it translated to "speck" or something similar.

"Perhaps I have not overestimated you after all, Harris," said Yamashiro, a wicked smile creasing his face. He turned back toward the officer behind us. "Takahashi did not believe that a clone such as yourself would have enough initiative to consider suicide. He bet me that you and your friend would not have flown out here if you did not believe you could restart the Broadcast Network."

Takahashi sneered at me as he handed Yamashiro a wad of bills. "I bet heavily that you would rather die than live as a farmer, Harris." Yamashiro counted the bills silently, folded them, and placed them in his pocket. He made no attempt to hide his satisfaction.

"Sadly, I will not get to enjoy my winnings. Takahashi is my son-in-law. My daughter will complain to her mother that I have robbed her husband of two hundred dollars, and my wife will make me give the money back." I glanced back at Takahashi, who positively beamed.

Now that the excitement had ended, Yamashiro started walking again. I followed. The officers behind us followed in stony silence.

"How did they find us?" Freeman sat up in his hospital bed. The only time he would lie flat was when he was unconscious. At all other times, he sat up alert.

"One of Yamashiro's officers must have seen the movie," I said.

"The movie?" Freeman asked, his low, rumbling voice betraying not so much as a hint of curiosity.

"*The Battle for Little Man,*" I said. "Someone made a movie about the battle I fought on Little Man. It's a great movie, unblemished propaganda without so much as a shred of accurate information."

In the movie, a natural-born version of me takes on ten thousand Mogats nearly single-handedly and saves six Marines. In real life, we were known as the "Little Man Seven," but there was nothing heroic about our survival.

Of course, Ray Freeman did not go to movies. *The Battle for Little Man* was a big release that played in holotoriums all across the two arms that remained loyal to the Unified Authority.

Other people might have asked more about the movie. Freeman just shrugged. "Why were they looking for you?" His face had not healed. He had medical patches on his cheeks, forehead, over one eye, and on his neck. The burns left swollen areas that would become scars, but his skin had always been rough. These new scars blended into his face more naturally than the knot of scars on the back of his skull. With his dark brown skin, the back of his head resembled a mahogany burl.

"I don't know," I admitted. "The only thing Yamashiro would tell me was that he wanted to hold a summit."

"You trust him?" Freeman asked.

"What does it matter?" I asked. "We're off the transport and back in the war." Freeman was a mercenary. I was a Marine. Few things mattered more than getting back in the war.

5

When the war began, the Confederate Arms, the Mogats, and the Japanese were allies and no one quite knew who ran their navy. Yamashiro's Japanese officers, the men who renovated and commanded the ships, referred to the fleet as the "Hinode Fleet." Around the Unified Authority, we usually called it the "Separatist Fleet" because "Separatist" was a catchall phrase. Most of the senior officers called it the "Mogat Fleet," however, because they blamed all of the trouble on the Mogats.

Before the Mogats took control of the ships, or the Japanese renovated them, it was the Galactic Central Fleet, or G.C. Fleet for short. When the fleet launched, it included 200 cruisers, 200 destroyers, and 180 battleships. When it attacked Earth, it was down to 540 ships. The Mogats won that engagement, but the battle took a toll on their fleet.

Over breakfast, Yoshi Yamashiro told me that the "Hinode

Fleet" had come out of the battle against the Earth Fleet with 472 ships. To the best of his knowledge, the Confederate Arms managed to hold on to 32 battleships and 25 destroyers when the alliance collapsed.

That left the Mogats with 415 ships. He gave me an hour to discuss this intelligence with Freeman, then called for us to meet with him to discuss his plans.

"The Mogats have declared war on the Confederate Arms," Yamashiro began. "They have not yet found Shin Nippon, but I believe they plan to attack us as well."

This was not a summit. If I had to label the conclave, I would have called it a sales meeting. We sat in a small conference room with tweed-lined walls and a ten-foot table. Bright light filled the room. As the meeting began, a pretty girl in a short blue skirt that barely reached the tops of her thighs stepped into the room. She carried a tray with coffee, tea, water, and juice. I took juice. Freeman declined. Yamashiro and his posse drank coffee.

"We do not think it likely that the Mogats will attack any of the existing U.A. fleets. The Mogat fleet is too weak, and the U.A. fleets are too immobile to pose a threat," Yamashiro said.

Sitting behind Yamashiro, Takahashi and some officer whom I could not identify did their best impressions of ancient samurais. They sat perfectly still, backs erect, hands at their waists. They wore the conservatively cut uniforms of Shin Nippon officers instead of brightly colored kimonos and swords, but they bore intense expressions on their faces and their unflinching gaze took in both Freeman and me.

"We estimate that the Atkins Believers still possess over a hundred battleships. This gives them a tactical advantage over any planet in the galaxy. As we saw in the days before the attack on Earth, ground defenses are not effective against orbital attack.

"The Mogats have proven most unstable. So far, we know that they have attacked seven planets in the Orion Arm, eight planets in the Cygnus Arm, and five planets in the Perseus Arm." Yamashiro turned to Freeman. "I assume you are also familiar with Mogat tactics."

Freeman nodded.

"Are you a Marine like Harris?" Yamashiro asked.

"I freelance," Freeman said.

"Ah, so it is," Yamashiro said. The two officers behind him exchanged a quick glance. I almost expected one officer to hand a stack of bills to the other.

Yamashiro had timeless features. He might have been fifty years old, he might have been eighty. The skin on his face had dried but not wrinkled beyond the crow's-feet at the corners of his eyes.

"Has anyone tried to retaliate?" Freeman asked.

"This is a war of ghosts," Yamashiro said. "Unified Authority ships cannot retaliate unless they happen to be in orbit around a planet when the Mogat ships arrive. The Confederates cannot afford a fight. Their navy is far too small to engage the Mogat Fleet."

"Have the Mogats returned to Earth?" I asked.

"Their only interest in Earth was to cripple the Unified Authority. Once the Broadcast Network was destroyed and Earth was cut off, they turned their attention to other planets.

"From what we can tell, the Mogats attacked a few select Earth targets after defeating the Earth Fleet. I don't think they attacked Washington, DC."

Who could understand Mogat thinking? Washington, DC, was the seat of the Unified Authority government.

"Where did they attack?" I asked.

"They attacked approximately six hundred strategic targets across North America," Yamashiro said.

As a graduate of U.A. Orphanage #553, I knew what that number meant. It made perfect sense. With its fairy-tale stories about underground cities in the center of the galaxy and alien races, the Mogat system of beliefs seemed no more credible than Greek mythology. I did understand one of their tenets, however—they hated clones. To the Mogat mind, clones were demons, and Liberator clones were Satan himself. "They went after the orphanages," I said.

"The clone farms," Takahashi corrected me. His eyes bored into mine as he said this. I glared right back at him.

"It appears that the Unified Authority does not plan to rebuild the orphanages," Yamashiro said. "We have surveyed the damage from space. No work has been done."

"They may be afraid to," I said. "They lost their fleet in the war. They don't have any way to protect themselves if the Mogats return, and they may be afraid of provoking them."

"I agree," Yamashiro said. "I believe this is also the reason they have not tried to rebuild the Mars broadcast station. They are afraid of provoking another attack."

"What do you have in mind?" Freeman asked.

Takahashi looked at Freeman, and I did not like what I saw in his eyes. Maybe I imagined the whole thing, or maybe I saw something hidden in the flat expression on his face. Something about the way Takahashi smiled at Yamashiro suggested to me that he looked upon Freeman and me as expendable assets.

"Shin Nippon is prepared to form an alliance with the Unified Authority and the Confederate Arms," Yamashiro said. "None of our armies can defeat the Mogats alone. When the Mogats discover Shin Nippon, their fleets will defeat us. They will roll over us like a wave crushing a sand castle on a beach."

From his delivery, I had the feeling that the analogy of the wave and the sand castle was neither spontaneous nor original to

Yamashiro. He was rehearsing the pitch he would use to sell his idea on Earth.

"The Confederate Navy is also too small to oppose the Mogats, and their land forces are useless against an orbital attack. Only the Unified Authority has enough ships to fight the Mogats, but their ships do not have self-broadcasting capability."

"The U.A. Navy is useless," I agreed. "They're beached without the Broadcast Network."

"Exactly," Yamashiro agreed. "It is exactly so."

"If you're talking about restoring the Broadcast Network, it can't work," I said, putting down my juice and finally noticing the charts on the back wall. "We'd never be able to defend it. The Mogats would be able to shoot it down anytime they wanted."

There were several charts along the wall. One of them showed a schematic diagram of a broadcast station.

"I agree with you, Harris, we would not be able to defend the Broadcast Network even if we could repair it," Yamashiro said. "For now, I simply propose an alliance, nothing more."

"How do we play into this?" Freeman asked.

Yamashiro's expression turned to surprise. "I should have thought that was obvious. We need to send somebody to Earth to propose our alliance."

"You want us as ambassadors?" I asked, trying to suppress my sardonic smile.

"You mean you're using us as guinea pigs," Freeman said. "You want to see if we can land on Earth without getting shot."

"Yes," agreed Yamashiro. "You are perfect for the job."

6

"*Kampai*. It means, 'dry glass.'"

"Dry glass?" I asked.

"Yes, 'dry glass,'" Yamashiro said. As he generally did, Yamashiro conducted himself in a subdued fashion as we entered the officers' club. He spoke softly, wore a veiled expression, and did not look me in the eye.

We had come to celebrate the sale. Yamashiro had sold Freeman and me the concept of going to Earth. Now it was time to mark the occasion with booze.

Enlisted men are the same in every army. They like to get drunk. They drink to steel themselves before heading into combat. They drink to celebrate when they return home. On long stretches between combat missions, they drink to ward off boredom. In the unpredictable days before a campaign, they drink to calm their nerves. Had he been a Marine instead of a philosopher, René

Descartes might have said, "I drink, therefore I am." That is the empiricism of the enlisted man.

In the Unified Authority Marines, officers held to a different standard. They drank, though not as publicly as their enlisted underlings. The officers I knew might enjoy a strong libation before or after combat; but, unlike the privates and sergeants below them, they did not necessarily drink until they became drunk. Such was the culture of the Unified Authority Marines.

The officers in the Shin Nippon Navy, on the other hand, started their off-duty hours with the stated goal of getting drunk. Yamashiro, Takahashi, and six other officers led Freeman and me into the officers' club telling us that they would not take us to dinner until we were too drunk to know what we were eating.

We sat on mats beside a table that only came up to our knees. I had seen bars like this on Ezer Kri, the planet these men had once called home. This was their idea of a traditional pub. The time I entered a bar like this on Ezer Kri, the matron pretended she could not understand me unless I spoke Japanese. On that occasion, I ended up in a bar with normal waist-high tables and chairs.

Sitting around the table, all of Yamashiro's officers became equals. Hideo Takahashi sat shoulder to shoulder with Yamashiro himself, and the two men spoke freely. It no longer mattered that Yamashiro was the chief administrator of Shin Nippon or that he was Takahashi's father-in-law. Takahashi no longer played the samurai, and Yamashiro no longer played the shogun.

A pretty waitress in a silk kimono came in and placed four ceramic bottles on our table, then she handed out lacquered cups. She had long black hair combed back into an elaborate bun.

"You have women on your battleship," I said, remembering my surprise at seeing the secretary earlier that morning.

"How very observant you are," Takahashi said. "I am glad you are so alert."

"Women on a battleship, that's unusual," I said. "Don't you worry about..."

One of the officers poured cups of Sake and passed them along the table. We all took one.

"Do you know Sake?" Yamashiro asked me.

"I've heard of it," I said. "Some of the guys in my platoon tried it when we were on Ezer Kri."

"But you did not try it?" Yamashiro asked.

I shook my head.

"*Kampai!*" yelled one of the officers. Everyone tossed the Sake into their mouths and, as far as I could tell, swallowed without tasting. They threw it so fast that it practically sailed over their tongues and down their throats.

I drank the contents from my cup. It was warm.

Freeman held his cup but never drank.

The officers refilled their cups quickly and drained them with another shout of "*Kampai.*" I followed suit. Ray did not.

"I don't worry about the women on my ship, especially this one," Yamashiro said as he watched the waitress enter the room. She brought four more bottles of Sake.

Yamashiro was already on his third or fourth cup. His posture had relaxed, and he spoke less guardedly. Beaming with pride, he added, "I have had her a few times myself."

"Why isn't your friend drinking?" Takahashi asked me. English was the first language on Ezer Kri, but these officers conversed just as comfortably in Japanese. They pronounced English properly, but sometimes they strung their words together in ways that might have been influenced by speaking Japanese.

Takahashi turned to Freeman. "Don't you like Sake?"

"I don't drink," Freeman said.

Takahashi looked at me, confusion showing on his face. "How can that be?"

"I've had most of the girls in the administrative area," Yamashiro boasted. He was now on his fifth or six cup. I was still on my third, not that it would have mattered. Whether by accident or by design, Liberator clones had a nearly superhuman tolerance for alcohol. "God made us that way," I mumbled to myself. God, of course, was the government.

"*Kampai!*" Another round of Sake disappeared from the table. That pretty waitress returned every five or six minutes with more bottles. Judging by Yamashiro's responses to her, each time she returned, she became more beautiful.

"How can you not drink?" Takahashi demanded of Freeman. "Everybody must drink. You cannot live if you do not drink."

When we first entered the club, some of the officers around the table spoke in Japanese. Now they all spoke in English, and they did not seem to care if I overheard their conversations.

"If the Mogat fleet is anywhere near Earth, the clone and the black man are as good as dead."

"If the Mogats have their fleet somewhere near Earth, we're all as good as dead."

"Yeah, but they will be more dead. They're traveling in a transport."

"Dead is dead."

So we were flying into trouble. I tried to turn toward them to listen in, but...

"You know the secretary that brought the coffee to our meeting this morning? I had her, too... in that very room," Yamashiro confided in a voice both loud and proud. By this time he had downed so much Sake that his eyes seemed to roll in his head. He pulled out a cigarette and lit it. He had so much alcohol in his blood that I expected the cigarette to explode when he plugged it into his mouth.

"She was very loud," Yamashiro boasted.

"Oh," I said, trying to tune back in on the other officers.

"We won't need to get too close. The clone and the black man have already traveled four billion miles in a transport... four billion miles! Can you believe that?"

"Captain Takahashi told me they were trying to commit suicide."

"Really? I heard they were trying to restart the Broadcast Network."

"No. They were trying to commit suicide."

"Why didn't they just kill themselves on Little Man?" Across the table, Takahashi continued to interrogate Freeman. "Do you drink whiskey?" he asked.

Freeman shook his head.

"Just beer?" Takahashi asked.

"I don't drink beer."

"There is a beautiful girl in the officers' mess who will let you eat sushi off her naked body. When you finish your meal, you can have her," Yamashiro said. He closed his eyes and giggled. "She is very pretty. I have never eaten sushi so quickly in my life."

"*Kampai!*" This time Yamashiro led the charge. He opened his mouth and downed another cup of Sake. All of his officers followed.

The officers became louder and more demonstrative as they drank. By the end of the night, Yamashiro was lighting his cigarettes with the butts of the cigarettes he had just finished.

Many of the other officers smoked, too. A cloud of silver-blue smoke hung just under the ceiling. I stared into that cloud and wondered about the Jekyll-and-Hyde nature of these officers. On duty, these men were quiet, precise, in control. After hours, they drank harder than any other men I knew.

7

The last time I visited Earth, the Earth Fleet ruled the skies and the Unified Authority ran the galaxy. Since that time, the Mogats and their allies shut down the Broadcast Network. I had no idea what to expect when Freeman and I landed in Washington, DC.

During the war, I visited a planet named New Columbia a few days after a Mogat attack. When I entered Safe Harbor, the capital city of New Columbia, I found many of the buildings intact, but the society was demolished.

In the days leading up to the attack, the government had evacuated the law-abiding citizens of Safe Harbor. That left the looters, the criminals, and the military in the city when the Mogats began their attack. They orbited the planet destroying military bases, gun emplacements, and convoys.

By the time I arrived, anarchy had taken over in Safe Harbor. Rival gangs had already carved the city into territories. The only way to reintroduce civilization back into Safe Harbor would have been to fumigate the place and start from scratch.

"Think it will be like Safe Harbor?" I asked Freeman, as we carried our equipment into the transport. Freeman had been there. He'd changed the political landscape by shooting the guy whose gang controlled the Marine base. With his size and strength, Ray Freeman could tear most men limb from limb, but he was even more dangerous with a sniper rifle.

"If it is," Freeman said as he checked out the sight on his rifle, "this will be a short trip."

In his rucksack, Freeman carried a sniper rifle, two M27s with one rifle stock, a particle-beam pistol, one dozen grenades, and extra ammunition. The bag weighed forty or fifty pounds and he carried it as easily as a sack lunch. He had already strapped a combat knife to his leg. The knife had a ten-inch blade. He was a human fortress.

I'd brought an M27 and three extra clips. Ray thought like a mercenary, a lone gunman who sometimes found himself waging war against an entire army. I thought like a Marine. I preferred to travel light.

Because we had no idea what we would find on Earth or in the space that surrounded it, Yamashiro and his officers took special precautions. The broadcast generator on the S.N.N. *Sakura* needed eight minutes to generate enough electricity to power up its broadcast engine. That meant that from the time the *Sakura* arrived in Earth space to the time it could broadcast out, there would be eight minutes in which enemy ships could attack. If we accidentally broadcasted into the middle of the Mogat fleet, or if the Unified Authority somehow resurrected its Earth Fleet, the *Sakura* would need to scramble for safety. Unaccompanied battleships made easy targets when things went wrong.

The door to the launch bay opened and in walked Takahashi,

Yoshi Yamashiro's son-in-law, along with a junior officer. He came to salute us and see us off the ship.

Takahashi was a captain in the Shin Nippon Navy, but he did not command the *Sakura.* According to Yamashiro, he made a better administrator than commander. Yamashiro did not come to see us off. I wondered if he was embarrassed about the night before.

"We will broadcast in on the dark side of Earth," Takahashi said. The "dark side" was a navigational term referring to the side of Earth facing away from Mars. Historically, almost every ship heading into Earth had to come through the Broadcast Network, which orbited Mars. Now that the Mars discs were down, all of Earth was technically "dark."

"How far out are we broadcasting?" Freeman asked.

"Thirty million miles," Takahashi said. "We'll fly you within three million miles. You'll have an hour before you have to launch."

Not even the most sophisticated tracking equipment could pick up a ship from beyond thirty million miles. Tracking "anomalies" was a different story. An anomaly was the electrical field that ships generated when they broadcasted into space. Even the most basic equipment could detect an electronic disturbance such as an anomaly from a few million miles away.

On the off chance that the Mogats did have a fleet somewhere in the vicinity, the *Sakura* would broadcast well out of range. Traveling at a top speed of just under thirty million miles per hour, it would take us an hour to reach Earth, but that also meant that the broadcast engine could recharge. The *Sakura* would be able to broadcast to safety the moment our transport left the ship.

"Prepare for broadcast. Prepare for broadcast," a voice warned over loudspeakers. The message echoed across the launch bay.

Tint shields formed over portholes and windows. All of the atmospheric locks in the launch bay sealed. If you happened to glance at the "lightning" that coated ships during a broadcast, you would be blinded for life. With the tint shields up and the landing doors closed, you could not see the electricity. The broadcast itself happened in a split instant. We disappeared from the outer region of the Scutum-Crux Arm in a flash of lightning and appeared thirty million miles from Earth in that same instant.

A moment later the broadcast warning ended and the atmospheric locks opened. I knew we were back in the Sol System of the Orion Arm.

"Earth won't be like New Columbia," Freeman said as he headed up the ladder toward the cockpit. "They evacuated Safe Harbor before the Mogats attacked. The only people left on the planet were the criminals."

"They left the Army and Marines," I said, following him up the ladder.

"Yeah," Freeman grunted. This was not the transport in which Yamashiro had found us. The crew of the *Sakura* jettisoned that ill-fated ship. Yamashiro's engineers said that our broadcast engine experiment had damaged it beyond repair.

The transports on the *Sakura* were fifty years older and even less sleek than our old one. This transport had the same basic floor plan and controls. Not much had changed over the last fifty years. Military transports were still shitty little tin cans designed to take maximum abuse on short trips at slow speeds.

"Earth is different," Freeman said. "The government is still down there, not just a bunch of shell-shocked Marines." He sat in the pilot's chair and went over the controls.

We still had an hour to kill before we launched. I sat in the copilot's seat and fastened the safety harness across my chest. My thoughts wandered back to New Columbia and the gang-riddled city of Safe Harbor.

Technicians walked around the launch bay. One came and inspected the outside of our transport.

On our way out of Little Man, I'd read a Bible story in which Syria laid siege to the capital city of Israel. As the siege continued, the people starved.

One day a woman approached the king of Israel to ask for help. When the king asked what she wanted, the woman told him about an agreement she had made with another woman. They would "sodden" her son one night and then the next night they would "sodden" the other woman's boy. They did indeed sodden the first woman's son; but the next night, the other woman reneged on the deal.

When I asked Ray what "sodden" meant, he said, "stewed."

"You mean like boiled?" I asked.

He did not bother to answer.

In my mind, I imagined Washington, DC, under Syrian siege. I envisioned ruined buildings, herds of homeless people, and a city carved up by gangs.

In that Bible story, the king blamed the destruction of his city on God. "Why should I wait for God to save us?" he asked Elisha, who happened to be God's press secretary at the time. I agreed. I saw God as a metaphor for government. In my mind, the king was not really a king but just a middleman placed between God and the people. In this case, God got scared and ran away long before the Syrians arrived.

Would we find the same thing on Earth? Had the government that created me run scared when the Mogats overpowered its fleet?

"Prepare to launch." Takahashi's voice came over the radio. Yamashiro had not bothered to see us off himself. Did his absence betray a certain lack of confidence? Realistically, our chances of landing near Washington, DC, and slipping into the city undetected seemed slim.

"Ready," Freeman answered.

Red lights flashed around the launch bay. The heavy doors of the atmospheric locks slid open, revealing the curtain of space. The deck officer cut the gravity in the launch bay so that we lifted off the deck the moment Freeman touched the boosters. Freeman took us five feet up, then floated us through the doors and into space.

Had the *Sakura* maintained full speed, it would have disappeared into space before we could have seen it. Instead, it had dropped to a mere five thousand miles per hour for our launch—virtually a dead stop by space-travel standards.

We only caught a glimpse of the ship as it vanished. The ships in the Galactic Central Fleet had charcoal-colored hulls. The combination of speed and dark coloration acted as camouflage against the backdrop of space.

"Once we enter the atmosphere, they're bound to spot us," Freeman said.

Earth loomed ahead, a glowing green-and-blue sphere with polar white caps, tan-colored deserts, and swirls of cloud. We came in toward the coast of Europe, adjusted our angle parallel to the ocean below us, and flew west. A blue sky with clouds the size of city blocks stretched out before us.

"We're about two thousand miles from Washington airspace," Freeman said.

"Do you think they saw us coming?" I asked.

Freeman nodded.

"Do you think they will try to intercept us?" I asked.

"It depends on just how bad the city was hit," Freeman said.

"Yamashiro said that the Mogats only took out the clone farms and the bases," I said.

"Maybe," said Freeman. "I don't think he has spent much time around here. His officers seem nervous about running into the Mogat fleet."

We entered the atmosphere at Mach 2, though we could have flown at well over Mach 3. Before the Unified Authority fell, all atmospheric travel was limited to a maximum speed of three thousand miles per hour.

Soon Ray cut our speed to one thousand miles per hour. At that speed it took us two hours to reach Washington, DC. The Atlantic Ocean stretched out beneath us like a gray-blue carpet, but it did not seem long before we reached the end. Up ahead of us, I could see the coast. Green forests and rocky cliffs marked the edge of the sea. Clouds so effervescent they should have been steam melted into the horizon.

"Here comes our escort," I said. Up ahead, three fighters scrambled out to meet us. They left billowing contrails across the sky.

"We've got three more behind us," Freeman said. I looked at the radar screen. It showed three blips behind us and three more ahead.

"How long have they been there?" I asked.

"Within radar range?" Freeman asked. "A few seconds. They picked us up back at Iceland. They've been giving us room to maneuver."

"But they haven't tried to contact us?" I asked. That did not make sense.

Freeman shook his head.

"Maybe they're scared," I said.

Freeman responded with one of his glacial "you don't know what you are talking about" glares.

Three of the fighters formed an ellipse behind us, and the other three formed an arc just below the nose of the transport. Their contrails formed a carpet of cloud. They were clearly sent as an escort, not a guard.

"Transport pilot, this is Dulles Civil Traffic Control, please respond."

"He seems awfully polite," I observed.

"They think we are Mogats?" Freeman said. "We just came out of a GCF battleship."

"I'll bet you're right," I said. Our transport was the same make and model that the Mogats used. There were six fighters surrounding us, and they hadn't even aimed a missile in our direction. They thought we were Mogats, and they did not want to get us mad. "They're either scared or glad to see us," I said.

We were getting close to Dulles Spaceport.

"Dulles Civil, this is transport pilot," Freeman said into the radio.

"What is your destination, transport pilot?"

"We wish to land at Dulles Spaceport," Freeman said.

"You are cleared for Runway One."

"That was easy," Freeman said to me.

"I've never felt so welcomed," I agreed.

By this time we had crossed greenbelts and the bays. Flying at one thousand miles per hour, we passed from sea to city in four minutes. Freeman slowed the transport to landing speed, and we followed our fighter jet escort to the runway.

"Leave your gear in the transport," I told Freeman as we touched down and taxied into a hangar.

The Spaceport Authority would almost certainly send security to meet us. We didn't want to come off the transport with a bunch of small weapons in our hands. It would not take them long to figure out we were not Mogats, and the last thing I wanted was to give them an excuse to shoot.

8

"We've got them, sir." The sergeant paused for a moment. He was clearly uncomfortable about my hearing what he had to say next. "Sir, they can't be Mogats. One of them is a clone."

He should have been uncomfortable. The soldier was a general-issue military clone. He was programmed not to talk about clones and cloning; but he was also programmed to obey orders, and some officer had clearly ordered him to report when we stepped off our ship. The cognitive dissonance this must have caused that poor grunt.

He came with a squad of twenty soldiers. These men were regular Army, dressed in standard Army fatigues, on loan to the Dulles Spaceport Authority. They all carried M27s as a matter of course. None of them pointed their weapons at us.

The sergeant listened to a receiver concealed in his helmet. He cleared his throat. "Do you have any cargo you wish to unload?"

"No," I said.

Freeman pressed a button, and the rear of the transport shut behind us. The motor that moved those thick metal doors worked quietly, but the cogs and sprockets in the doors ground. When the doors closed, they sealed with a soft clang.

"Um, you don't have a messiah on that transport do you?" the sergeant asked. He sounded nervous.

"A what?" I asked.

"A messiah?" he repeated.

"Not so much as an angel," I said.

"Just checking," the sergeant said. "You didn't bring pamphlets or Space Bibles did you?"

"Sergeant, I have no idea what you are talking about," I said.

"Okay. Okay, just checking," the sergeant said. "Why don't you gentlemen come with us? There are people waiting to debrief you."

So much for sodden babies and an entropic society. As far as I could tell, Washington, DC, had not changed. Dulles Spaceport looked as pristine as I had ever seen it. Through the open door of the hangar, I could see atmospheric jets taking off and landing. The terminal building, a five-story box with black windows encased in white marble frames, sparkled in the sunlight.

The soldiers had parked a "covered wagon" just outside the hangar. "Covered wagon" meant an Army transport truck with a heat-shielded tarp. In a world with satellites and other orbiting spacecraft, tarps could make all the difference in hiding troop movements from prying eyes.

The soldiers, GI clones who stood just under six feet, hopped into the back of the truck without having to worry about hitting their heads on the Army green canvas tarp or the metal frame that held it in place. At six-three, I had to duck my head as I came up the three steps that led into the back of the truck. Then came Freeman, seven feet tall and hugely broad-shouldered.

There is a tendency to think of a Goliath like Freeman as slow and powerful. The stereotype did not fit in this case. Freeman was powerful all right, but he was also agile. He stepped onto the middle rung of the three-step ladder and bounded into the back of the truck. He was so tall, however, that he had to drop to his knees to scoot under the lip of that tarp. Once in, he had to crouch as he moved to an empty spot on the bench.

The clones noticed his agility, too. Some stared at him. Others simply stole sideways glances. I thought back to the first time I had laid eyes on Freeman. He had made me just as nervous as he made these boys.

Since I had never served with any of these clones, they all looked alike to me. To make matters worse, only a little sunlight penetrated the canvas tarp, leaving us pretty much in the dark. Had I served with them, I suppose I would have noted subtle differences. When I ran a platoon in the Marines, I could tell my men apart. But looking around the benches, these guys looked as identical as eggs in a carton. I wondered how the sergeant could tell his boys apart.

"You guys aren't Morgan Atkins Separatists?" the sergeant asked.

"Not likely," I said.

The sergeant had identified me as a clone when he met us outside our ship. I had the same brown hair and brown eyes as other clones. My facial features looked somewhat similar to the features on all of these boys. If you stood us beside each other, people would have thought I was their taller and more-scarred-up brother.

"Our traffic guys tracked you coming in from a Mogat ship," the sergeant said. "Your transport looks like it's Galactic Central vintage."

"It is," I said. "Not all of those ships are under Mogat control."

"No shit?" the sergeant asked.

"No shit," I agreed.

"Does that mean the Separatists are fighting among themselves?"

We rumbled up a ramp and into a covered tunnel. Looking out the back of the truck, I could see a concrete ceiling with rows of fluorescent fixtures.

"The Confederates, the Mogats, and the Japanese, it's a three-way split," I said.

"Damn," the sergeant said. "Who's winning?"

"The Mogats," I said.

"Damn," the sergeant repeated.

"What did you mean about having a messiah on our ship?" I asked.

"Oh, that? That was a Mogat thing. They dressed a transport up so that it looked like a golden chariot, then they set it down in Israel. They had some guy dressed in a white robe come out the back and say he was Jesus returning to claim the world."

We went down a ramp. The soldiers all swayed with the direction of the truck, but Freeman did not move.

"You're joking," I said.

The sergeant shook his head.

"How do you know it wasn't Jesus?" I asked.

"The guy died," the sergeant said. "He landed by some old temple in Jerusalem. They think he was hoping for Christian pilgrims, but he got Jews and Moslems instead. They stoned him to death before the police could arrive.

"Anyway, his chariot came out of a GCF ship just like yours."

The truck pulled to a stop in an underground parking area. One of the soldiers flipped the ladder out of the back of the truck, and the others started filing out.

After most of the soldiers climbed out of the truck, Freeman climbed out. He did not use the ladder to climb down. He swung his legs over the edge of the bed and hopped down. It was not much of a hop.

"And the Space Bible?" I asked. The sergeant and I were the last people out of the truck. I knew what Space Bibles were. That was the name people commonly called *Man's True Place in the Universe: The Doctrines of Morgan Atkins,* the book that the Mogats called the centerpiece of their religion. It was illegal for servicemen to read it. Frankly, the book never interested me.

"Proselyting," the sergeant practically spit the word out like a gob from his throat. "That's their latest. They come by every few weeks and chuck pamphlets and Space Bibles out of their ships. I guess they're looking for converts."

The soldiers led us into an office complex that appeared devoid of people. There seemed to be nothing wrong with the building itself, the lights and the air-conditioning worked fine. I could not tell whether it had been abandoned or evacuated, but this wing of the building was empty.

"The Mogats want to start a church on Earth?" I asked. That did not sound likely. One of the major tenets of Mogat belief was independence from Earth.

"They're not getting many converts. Sometimes they fly over cities, see; and then they start shoveling out them pamphlets and Space Bibles. I figure they've hit a few thousand people... killed most of 'em, too.

"Shit, you drop a two-pound book from a few miles up, and you got to figure you're going to deal some damage."

9

The sergeant took Freeman and me to a small office. Before we could enter that office, however, we needed to pass through "the posts."

The posts were a high-tech security device connected to a galaxywide security database. Well, it should have been a galaxywide database. With the Broadcast Network down, the database would only be Earth-wide. But even limited to a planetwide network, the posts would have no trouble identifying us.

The posts looked like plasticized pillars creating an archway. "The sprayer," the jamb to the left, emitted a short blast of oil, water, and air in the form of a fine mist. The jamb on the right, "the receiver," vacuumed in that mist along with any dandruff, hair, flecks of skin, and other debris that the blast dislodged. Computers inside the receiver analyzed the DNA inside the hairs and other debris and spit out the person's identity.

You could not fool the posts. You could wash your clothes,

shave your head, and scrub every inch of your body with pumice, and it would make no difference. You could pour buckets of dandruff from one or one thousand other people over your head, and the posts would sort it out. The sprayer would always find some eyelash or scale of skin that belonged to you. The receiver would analyze every molecule and identify the ones that were yours.

According to my Marine Corps record, I had been killed in action. In truth, I swapped identities with a dead Marine, making me absent without leave.

Like any other criminal on the lam, I dreaded passing between the posts.

Freeman and I passed through the security check and entered a small office in which the only furniture was a desk and chairs. The sergeant followed us in and sat on the desk. I selected a chair. Freeman preferred to stand near the door and stare out at the other soldiers who stood guard just beyond the posts.

Bringing us into this waiting room may have seemed like a wasted effort, but I knew why we came. Somebody wanted to identify us. Once they knew our names and read our files, they would send us along.

There were no lights in the office. The only light came from the hall. We waited for nearly an hour in that dark room, then the sergeant received a message on his radio. We might have been cleared; but for all I knew, he might have been told to place me in the nearest brig.

"Time to deliver you both," the sergeant said, and he led us out to the hall. He and his men marched us into a much larger room. It was an auditorium with a well-shaped gallery that could easily hold two hundred people. The sergeant had Freeman and me sit on two chairs placed on the stage at the bottom of the room. Beside our chairs was a podium with a carving of an eagle carrying arrows. The eagle was the emblem of the Linear Committee—the executive branch of the U.A. government.

Freeman and I sat silently as men and women entered the auditorium and filled the gallery. I recognized most of these people, and many of them seemed to recognize me. The group included high-ranking officers such as Admiral Alden Brocius of the Central Cygnus Fleet and General Alexander Smith of the Air Force, who had been head of the Joint Chiefs of Staff when the Separatists attacked Earth. Both of them had been closely allied with the late Admiral Bryce Klyber, the officer who'd had me created and overseen much of my career. In all, approximately fifty people came in to observe or interrogate Freeman and me.

"They don't know what to do with us," Freeman said in that low, rumbling voice. He did not whisper, but his voice was so low and filled with bass that I felt what he had to say more than heard it.

"If they thought we were Mogat, they don't anymore," I said, trying to decide what information those posts might have given about us.

William Grace, a member of the Linear Committee at the outset of the war, approached the stage. He stopped to examine Freeman and me, then stepped behind the podium.

"Men and women of the security council, good afternoon," Grace said. "For the record, on this, the third day of October, 2512, we are convening an emergency meeting of the Unified Authority Security Council.

"Will the visitors please rise."

Freeman and I got to our feet.

"Please identify yourselves," Grace asked.

"Raymond Freeman," Freeman said.

Grace looked down into his podium. I supposed he had a computer readout built into it. He took a moment to examine

Freeman's record. Then he looked back at Freeman and considered him for several seconds. I had the feeling he was studying the bandages on Freeman's face and neck. "Are you injured, Mr. Freeman?"

"We had an accident," Freeman said.

"Do you require medical assistance?"

"No," Freeman said, his voice low and distant.

"I see that you are a freelance contractor who has worked with the U.A. military on several occasions. Is this correct?" Grace had to have read that from an official dossier.

Freeman nodded.

"According to this record, you have provided valuable services to the U.A. Navy in the past."

Freeman said nothing. What was there to say? Grace moved on to me.

"And you?" Grace asked. "Please identify yourself."

"Colonel Wayson Harris," I said.

By the reaction my name elicited, you would have thought that I had identified myself as George Washington. Individual conversations flared up around the gallery. A few people shouted questions down at me. William Grace picked up a gavel and banged it on the top of his podium until the room quieted down.

"Colonel Harris," Grace echoed my name back to me. He stared into his chest-high podium. "My records show that you were raised in Unified Authority Orphanage #553. Is this correct?"

"U.A.O. #553. That is correct, sir," I said.

"According to one of your former commanding officers, you are aware of your nature," Grace stated.

"If you are asking whether or not I know that I am a military clone, I *am* aware that I am a clone," I said.

"And you are a Liberator-class clone. Is that correct? You are, as far as you know, the last of your kind?"

Grace knew I was a Liberator. Hell, they'd once announced it on the floor of the House of Representatives. Once he established that I was a Liberator, he could probably have me hauled away and executed. I had the feeling of being played like a toy. At any moment, the smile would disappear, and he would bare teeth as sharp as daggers.

"Yes, sir," I said, a sinking feeling beginning in my stomach. Had Grace already been a senator when Congress banned Liberator clones from Earth and the entire Orion Arm? He looked old enough.

"Are you the same Wayson Harris who survived the battle on Little Man?" Grace asked. "Are you one of the Little Man Seven?"

"Yes, sir," I said.

"And you testified about that battle before the House of Representatives?" More and more this was sounding like a military tribunal.

"Yes, sir," I said. The rapidity of Grace's questions left me nervous.

"You were reported as killed in action at Ravenwood Outpost," Grace stated.

"That is correct, sir," I said.

"But you were not killed there?" Grace asked.

Apparently not, I thought. What I said was, "No, sir."

"According to your military record, you were promoted to the rank of colonel in the Unified Authority Marines by Admiral Che Huang. Is that correct?"

"That is correct, sir," I said. A massive headache brewed in the back of my skull.

The entire room broke out in loud applause. I turned toward the gallery and saw that every man and woman had risen to their feet. The only person remaining in his seat was Freeman. He managed to camouflage his confusion much better than I did. He sat looking straight ahead toward William Grace, his hands by his side.

"Welcome home, Colonel Harris. It is a distinct pleasure to welcome back a war hero like your."

"I'm afraid I am confused, sir," I said. He could not hear me over the applause, so I waited a moment for the gallery to quiet down then repeated myself. "I don't understand, sir."

"Not expecting a hero's welcome?" Grace asked.

"I'm not sure I deserve one," I said.

Grace laughed. "We know more about you than you might think. After the Mogats defeated the Earth Fleet, we found a video record among the late Admiral Huang's possessions. The record included conversations you had with Huang about infiltrating the Mogat Fleet."

"I didn't know he kept a record of that," I said.

"For his memoirs," Grace explained. "Huang saw himself as a man of destiny."

"I see," I said.

"We also have received another account of your actions on the enemy ship. We know, for instance, that you were captured while transmitting Mogat battle plans to Huang."

That was not entirely accurate. While I had managed to infiltrate the enemy flagship, my life as a spy did not last long. The Mogats caught me trying to sneak off of one of their battleships after planting a listening device on the bridge.

"How did you get onto their ship?" somebody called from the gallery.

"Excellent question," Grace said. "How did you manage that?"

Again the room rang with applause.

I decided it might be prudent to leave some of the gorier details out. "Everybody knew that the Mogats were going to attack New Columbia," I said. "I flew into Safe Harbor after the planetary authority evacuated the city. When the Mogats arrived, I located one of their commando teams and stowed away aboard their transport." It sounded so simple and benevolent when I phrased it that way. I did not mention that I snapped a man's neck and stole his uniform.

More applause. This time the applause was longer and louder than before.

I'd used the term "Mogat" in a less-than-accurate fashion. The majority of the sailors I ran into had come from the member planets of the Confederate Arms Treaty Organizations. The top officers and engineers were all Japanese from Ezer Kri. If I wanted to help establish an alliance between Earth, the Confederates, and the Japanese, however, I needed to downplay the roles that the Japanese and the Confederates had taken in the war. And we did need that alliance.

With their four hundred self-broadcasting ships, the Mogats would win the war rather easily if they fought us individually. If we formed an alliance, we might stand a chance, though I could not see how.

"As I understand it, you warned Admiral Huang that the Mogats planned to attack New Tuscany," Grace said. "That was how he was able to rout their fleet."

"I believe that is correct," I said.

"Why have you returned to Earth, Colonel Harris?" Grace asked. William Grace, they called him "Wild Bill" Grace in the media, was a short, chubby man. He may have been five-foot-three, or maybe even shorter. He weighed a good three hundred pounds. He was bald from his forehead to his crown, with a bushy ring of gray hair running between his ears. He smiled genially, but something in his eyes suggested strength and suspicion.

"Yoshi Yamashiro, the governor of Shin Nippon, sent me," I said. "He wants to form an alliance with the Unified Authority and the Confederate Arms."

"Are you working for the Japanese?" Grace asked. The applause had vanished. The auditorium became as quiet as an operating room. Grace's smile evaporated as he waited for me to answer.

"No, sir. Yamashiro found us stranded in space. He rescued us and brought us here, and he asked me to deliver the message that he wanted to make an alliance," I said.

Several silent moments passed. It was the loudest sort of silence, with Grace glaring at me and curious onlookers watching to see what Freeman and I would do next.

"What does Governor Yamashiro have in mind?" Grace asked.

"The Mogats declared war on C.A.T.O. and the Japanese," I said. C.A.T.O. was the Confederate Arms Treaty Organization.

"We were aware of their split," Grace said.

That surprised me. Without the Broadcast Network, Earth should have been completely cut off. The beginnings of the Mogat-Confederate Arms War might have started near Earth space, but there should have been no way for Unified Authority Intelligence to track the progress of the war.

Then something that I should have noted from the start occurred to me. Admiral Brocius of the Central Cygnus Fleet was sitting in the gallery. He should have been marooned sixty thousand light-years away with the ships of his fleet. How could he have come for this meeting?

"The Mogats have the upper hand. They control more than four hundred ships."

I supposed that Brocius might have been on Earth when the Mogats attacked Earth; but with the Republic on high alert and a mobile enemy, he would most likely have stayed with his fleet.

"The Japanese escaped with four battleships. Is that correct, Colonel?" Grace asked.

"Yes, sir, four ships," I said.

Maybe Yamashiro had set us up. Maybe he knew what kind of reception awaited him on Earth. But why go to all of the trouble of finding me only to throw me to the wolves?

It wasn't only Admiral Brocius. As I looked into the gallery, I started noticing other officers. Having served under Brocius, I spotted him before I saw the others; but they were there. I saw a commander whom I remembered from my days with the Scutum-Crux Fleet.

I did not have time for associating names, faces, and fleet locations. How did they know that I broadcasted the information about New Tuscany to Admiral Huang? Arrogant and antisynthetic, Huang would never have admitted that I gave him the information.

"How did you know the Japanese had four ships, sir?" I asked Grace. It did not make sense. The Mogats, the Japanese, and the Confederate Arms would all have that information, but how could they know it on Earth?

"We know a great deal about the battle between the Atkins Believers and the Confederate Arms," Grace said. "The Unified Authority is not as stranded as you might think, Colonel Harris."

10

When strangers flew an enemy ship into a city that was recently attacked, the government appointed organizations to watch over them. Whether it was Central Intelligence, or Republic Security, or Naval Intelligence, some agency had the job of watching us discreetly, and they did a fine job of it, too. Freeman and I knew someone was watching us, but we did not feel like prisoners.

When that first meeting ended, a government driver picked us up. He did not come in one of those long limousines that are so often used for VIPs, nor did he come in a troop carrier. He drove a sensible black sedan. As we stepped into the car, the driver introduced himself simply as, "The guy they pay for taking you wherever you want to go," then drove us to the Washington Navy barracks, where we each had rooms in temporary housing meant for visiting officers.

By standards of a luxury hotel, our quarters had a certain spartan quality about them. By military standards, they were the Taj Mahal. Our rooms included a single bed, a three-by-three closet in which I found a freshly pressed uniform for a colonel in the Unified Authority Marines, a dresser, and a bathroom. Having grown up in a military orphanage and graduated to the Marines, I found these accommodations the utmost in comfort. Anything bigger would have left me feeling out of place. The agency in charge of us did not post guards outside our doors, though they probably had people watching us from nearby buildings. The base commander gave Freeman and me our own electronic identity cards for use as keys to get in and out of the facilities. By all appearances, we could come and go as we pleased. My room must have been wired for sound and video, but I did not bother to check. Having nothing to hide, I had no reason to look for surveillance devices. They could watch me to their hearts' content, I didn't mind.

Freeman undoubtedly did check his room for microphones and cameras. He left nothing to chance.

He and I ate a very quiet dinner that first evening in the officers' mess, then returned to our rooms. The next morning, we met at 0700 and had breakfast.

"It's like they never had a war," I told Freeman as I ate my eggs and bacon.

He neither answered nor nodded. Freeman must have believed they were watching us. Fiercely independent, he did not tolerate intrusions as calmly as I.

At 0900, our unnamed driver showed up at the barracks and took us into town. He drove the same black sedan or possibly a reasonable facsimile. I did not know or care. Freeman, I suspected, both knew and cared. I was a Marine. He was a mercenary.

The more I saw of Washington, DC, the more confused I became. It was not the city under siege that I had imagined. The streets showed no telltale signs of battle. I saw no burned buildings on vacant lots. More importantly, Washington, DC, society still seemed intact. Men in suits and women in dresses walked the sidewalks looking as if they had important meetings to attend. Traffic flowed smoothly. When we passed through a residential area, I saw young children playing on the streets.

Freeman took all these sights in as well as he sat silently beside me. He did not lean forward or turn his head to stare out the car window. He never tipped his hand by showing interest in anything around him. Even so, few details ever slipped past him.

I had noticed something about Ray that morning. He seemed liked a caged animal, coiled tight and ready to lash out or escape. I could not read him as we drove through DC.

In the distance, I saw the Capitol, a twenty-story building topped off with a three-hundred-foot marble dome. It was the largest building on the face of the earth, with twenty-four thousand miles of corridors. We did not drive to the Capitol, however. Nor did the driver pull into the Pentagon, a monolithic cube that, despite the geometric significance of its name, had only four sides.

Instead, our driver took us into the heart of Washington, DC, where the real deals were crafted. Skyscrapers filled with law offices and banking operations lined the road. Our driver passed the ostentatious thirty- and forty-story structures, then pulled into a five-story affair. Civilian guards met us as we entered the underground garage. They directed us down five floors. We left the sedan in a dimly lit level on which there were no other cars. As we approached the elevator into the building, armed soldiers asked us for our identification. We showed them our cards, and the driver gave them his orders.

I expected an armed security man to follow us into the elevator, but the building security system had something far more dangerous. As our driver held his orders under a scanner which automatically chose our floor, I noted the vent opening in the chrome bezel along the ceiling. I had seen an elevator ventilation duct like that before. Should an intruder be caught in this car, deadly gas would pour out of that opening.

Four security men with holsters and pistols met us when the elevator doors slid open. They accompanied a young woman who identified herself as William Grace's secretary. "Mr. Freeman, Colonel Harris, if you would please follow me," she said.

Our driver left us in her custody. "This is as far as I go," he said. The man did not even attempt to hide his government identity at this point. He wore his shades indoors like every spook I had ever known. He did not button his black suit coat, but rather allowed it to swing open, showing just a hint of his holster and pistol. He caught a glimpse of me eyeing the pistol and smiled. The guy thought of himself as a big specking deal.

The halls were dark and decorated in a timeless style. Dark wood panels lined the walls. Brass-and-crystal light fixtures hung from the ceiling. When the men of the Roman Senate plunged their knives into Julius Caesar, I am convinced they did it in a room with brass fixtures and cherrywood-paneled walls.

The secretary led Freeman and me into a large conference room, and I froze in midstride. "Wild Bill" Grace and Gordon Hughes stood to greet me. Grace, the senior member of the Linear Committee, I had expected to see. Hughes, the Chairman of the Confederate Arms Treaty Organization, I had not.

Hughes had once been the speaker in the U.A. House of Representatives. He abandoned the Republic at the beginning of the war and became the most powerful politician in the Confederate Arms. Now he and Grace stood, casually chatting like old friends.

Grace and Hughes came to the door to shake hands with Freeman and me. They seemed entirely at ease with each other, as if the war had never taken place.

"Colonel Harris, this is a distinct pleasure," Hughes said, reaching out to shake my hand. He and I had met once before, shortly after the battle on Little Man. Back then, as a Marine, I had been summoned to testify about the battle in Congress. On that occasion, I had entered the chambers as a heroic survivor of a battle and left in derision. As we shook hands, I think Hughes sensed both my anger and my confusion.

"You're surprised to see me here," Hughes said.

"Hell, yes," I said.

That response earned a knowing laugh from both politicians. "Quite understandable," Hughes said.

"We have a lot to discuss," Grace, clearly the man presiding, said in a businesslike tone. "Perhaps we should get started."

It was a small meeting—ten people sitting around a conference table discussing the future of the galaxy. Gordon Hughes came with a female secretary and two plainclothes men. William Grace brought General Smith from the U.A. Air Force and two aides. The only other people in the room were Freeman and me and a couple of guards.

"I might as well begin by explaining what you are doing here," Grace said, looking over at Hughes. He turned toward Freeman and me. "Colonel Harris, the Mogat attack on the Mars broadcast discs shut down the Broadcast Network, but that does not mean it shut down all pangalactic travel."

"The scientific fleet," I said, suddenly realizing the obvious. The Unified Authority built its first fleet of self-broadcasting scientific ships decades before it began work on the Broadcast Network. I felt embarrassed for not figuring that out sooner.

"The scientific fleet," Grace agreed. "We have nearly two thousand self-broadcasting ships on Earth and in the field. They may not be combat-ready, but they are able to travel.

"You are not the only one who forgot about our civilian fleet.

From what we can tell, the Mogats seem to have entirely forgotten about our civil ships as well."

"We certainly overlooked them," Gordon Hughes added.

"Using our exploration ships, we have been able to locate all eighteen of our Navy fleets. Sending supplies out is not as convenient as it used to be, but we have managed to reestablish supply lines."

I felt like an adult man learning addition for the first time in front of people who had mastered quantum notations. I should have remembered the scientific fleet. Here I had thought that the Mogats left Earth isolated and helpless when in reality galactic communications could still be achieved.

"Gordon, here, was the one who told us what you did to help fight the Mogats," Grace added. "Once we discovered your identity, the chairman told us all about your exploits on that Mogat ship."

"Yoshi isn't the only one who realizes that we need an alliance," Hughes said. "The Mogats launched an attack on us within hours of the invasion." He meant the invasion of Earth.

Judging by the way Gordon Hughes and William Grace spoke, Confederate Arms' participation in the attack on the Earth Fleet was still a sensitive topic. Grace referred to the enemy fleet as the "Mogat Fleet," avoiding any mention of Confederate Arms involvement. For his part, Hughes seemed just as anxious to pretend the Mogats had launched the attacks on their own. Hughes and Grace acted like old friends, just a couple of businessmen planning their next big merger.

"We sent an ambassador to Earth to ask if we could sign an accord with the Unified Authority ending our hostilities," Hughes said. He smiled. "That's not quite as dramatic as sending back a war hero bearing an olive branch and a flag of truce, but Yoshi and I had the same goal in mind."

11

Yamashiro and his four-boat Shin Nippon Navy gave Freeman and me one week to enter Washington, DC, locate whoever was in charge—if anyone was in charge, and propose an alliance. At the end of one week, he would fly past Earth and scan for our signal. If he received the wrong signal, or there was no signal at all, he would fly past and never return. He did not offer to search for us. We were not from his clan.

As it turned out, we didn't need a week to pass on Yamashiro's invitation. Had he returned within twenty-four hours of dropping us off, we would have had more than enough time. By lunch that next day, both William Grace, chief member of the Linear Committee, and Gordon Hughes, chairman of C.A.T.O., had already agreed to meet with Yamashiro.

"Next week?" Grace asked, when I explained that I would not be able to signal the *Sakura* right away.

Hughes politely expressed his disappointment. “That’s Yoshi,” he said. “He’s always so darn cautious.”

I did not mind waiting. I had a good idea how I wanted to use those few free days.

At one point during their conversation, William Grace asked me if I had any questions about the alliance between the Confederate Arms and the Unified Authority. I could not pass on the opportunity. “What about war criminals?” I asked.

“Criminals?” Grace asked. “What do you mean by ‘war criminals’?”

Gordon Hughes sat silent, curious to hear what Grace might say.

“The Confederate Arms sent terrorists into Unified Authority territory to attack civilian targets,” I said. “What about William ‘The Butcher’ Patel? What about…”

“Ah, William Patel,” Grace said, a smile coming to his face. “If I am not mistaken, you were in Safe Harbor when he set off a bomb.”

“It wasn’t just a bomb. He destroyed an entire city block,” I said.

“Those were desperate times,” Grace said. “We were at war, Harris. I don’t suppose we shall ever invite Patel to the Capitol for tea; but in light of our new arrangement with the Confederate Arms, I think that a pardon is in order.”

“I see,” I said. “What about Tom Halverson? Are you going to pardon him for sinking the entire Earth Fleet?” Halverson was a U.A. admiral who had defected to the Confederate Arms. He’d led and commanded the fleet that attacked Earth.

Grace and Hughes huddled together and spoke in whispers. “I suppose we will extend full amnesty to Tom,” Grace said. “We can’t very well arrest the man commanding our combined fleet.”

“Commanding the fleet?” I felt staggered.

“Certainly,” Grace said. “Halverson is the commander of the Confederate Arms Navy. Chairman Hughes has made it very clear that he will not trust anyone but Halverson to command his self-broadcasting fleet."

Freeman distanced himself more and more as the meeting continued. He let me do all of the speaking. When the politicians asked us questions, he sat mute. He did not ask questions himself. Freeman's face remained as implacable as ever, but something in his posture showed a certain restlessness on his part.

We broke for lunch. Freeman and I ate downstairs in a cafeteria with our driver and some guards, while the politicians and officers ate upstairs. Freeman only said one thing during the entire meal. He mumbled, "I'm going to walk," as he ate his sandwich. He said the words so quietly that no one else in the room could possibly have heard him.

Freeman did not want to leave his life in Grace's hands, and maybe he had the right idea. Now that we had delivered Yamashiro's message, neither William Grace nor Gordon Hughes showed interest in Freeman or me. We returned to the same conference room and sat ignored as all of the big shots discussed the benefits of adding Shin Nippon's four battleships to their navy.

As the conversation shot back and forth, I noticed Freeman sneak a furtive glance at the door. He climbed out of his chair. The conversation froze, and everyone turned to look at him. Having delivered our message, we might not have mattered to anyone, but when a seven-foot giant stands, people instinctively stop to watch him. It was an instinct of self-preservation, I suppose.

Looking profoundly nervous, a guard approached Freeman, his hand on the grip of his pistol. Freeman spoke quietly, his rumbling voice so hard to hear from a distance. He said, "I need to go to the restroom."

Grace nodded to the guards, and said, "Perhaps you could show Mr. Freeman the way."

Freeman left with the guard. As they left, I already knew that I would not see Ray Freeman again for some time to come.

The meeting broke up a few minutes after that. "Wild Bill" Grace shook my hand and left with his entourage. Gordon Hughes repeated that it was a pleasure to meet me and left with his entourage. My driver came to the room and suggested that we wait for Freeman. I told him, "That might take a while."

"Is he sick or something?" the driver asked.

"No," I said.

I had a pretty good idea about what was next on the agenda for me. In the next day or two, the Marines would recall me to active duty. As far as "Wild Bill" and his U.A. generals were concerned, they owned me. I was a clone, created by the state. They had just as much right to recall me as they would to recommission a tank or an old battleship.

A few minutes passed, and the driver looked at me, and said, "Should we go check on your friend?"

"Sure," I said. "Where shall we look?"

"He went to the can," the driver said.

I laughed. "You think so?"

"No?" the driver asked.

"He isn't there," I said.

With catlike speed, the man jumped to his feet and sprinted from the room. He knew that he did not have to worry about me, I was military. I would be here when he got back. I had no place to go.

I sat at the table and waited. About three minutes later the driver returned, an angry look on his face. He pulled off his shades and placed them on the table, then walked over to me. He stood over me like an interrogation officer. The man was Intelligence, and he wanted me to know it. Gone was the pretense that he was just a chauffeur. "Okay, smart guy, so where did your pal go?"

"How should I know that?" I asked. "You've seen him. You think he asked me for permission?"

The driver thought about this for a moment, then said, "No, I guess not."

"You've had us under surveillance," I said. "Where do you think he went?"

"Who says we had you under surveillance?" the driver asked, holding the door for me to leave.

"Don't be an ass," I said. "You're from Intelligence, right?"

"Let's just say that I'll have some buddies looking for your friend," the driver said, sounding downright cocky. We headed down the hall. The armed guards were gone, replaced by men in business suits. A man in a black suit—probably another agent—held the elevator for us.

"You better call them off," I said.

"You think we're scared of Freeman?" the driver asked. He sounded a bit too confident, like a dog with its hackles up even though it is not sure of itself.

"If you're smart, Freeman scares you. What happened to the guy who walked him to the bathroom?" I asked.

"We found him on the stairs." The elevator doors closed behind us.

"Dead?" I asked.

"Unconscious," the driver said. "He's got a concussion and a broken wrist."

"So Ray took it easy on the guy," I said. "Let's see, he was unarmed, and he took out an armed agent. Now you have an agent with a concussion, and Freeman has a gun.

"Yes, I'd be scared of Freeman if I were you."

"We'll find him." The driver stretched out the word "we'll" so that it sounded like "Weeee'll find him." It sounded too comfortable. "He's a seven-foot black man, how hard can he be to locate?"

I could not help but laugh. The man did not have Freeman's

measure. The military police would not have taken Freeman so lightly; but these cocky Intelligence types, they thought they had the world under control.

"So are you with Central Intelligence?" I asked.

"Naval Intelligence," the driver said.

The elevator doors opened to the cool cement of the parking garage. Freeman might have been down here, or at least passed by. The dim lighting would have appealed to him. He would have had no trouble taking out guards and hot-wiring a car.

"You should have a file on Freeman," I said.

"We do."

"I suggest you read it," I said.

"You think so?"

At that point I realized this guy was an idiot and saw no reason to keep talking. "Take me back to the base," I said in a voice that did not hide my boredom. I took a seat in the back of the car and we drove out to the street.

"What makes you think I haven't read his file?" the driver asked.

A pewter sky hung over the city. The air outside was humid and cool, but the clouds did not break.

I looked out my window, speaking almost as if talking to myself. "If you'd read the file, you wouldn't go after him. He's a freelance contractor, but he works exclusively for the Unified Authority. He's not going to the Mogats. He doesn't like them. The only thing you are going to accomplish by sending agents after Freeman is losing men."

"Yeah? You think he's a pretty tough guy?"

"You have the files," I said.

"Okay, hotshot, fifty bucks says that we'll have Freeman back in his room by supper."

"Fifty dollars?" I thought about the bets that Yamashiro made with his son-in-law. "That's a scared man's bet."

"You want to bet a hundred? Let's bet a hundred," the driver said.

I did not actually have any money, and I said so.

"Now who sounds nervous," the driver said. "Tell you what... I think you're good for it. I'll spot you the money. If I win, you can owe me the fifty."

"So spot me a hundred," I said.

"Fine. We'll make it a hundred. You can owe me the hundred on credit. I may not have checked your friend's file, but I've checked yours, pal. You got a lot of back pay coming."

"Done," I said.

We did not talk after that. He drove me to the base without saying another word. I felt no compulsion to break the silence.

As we pulled up to the barracks, the driver finally spoke. "Call me if you need to go somewhere. Go out on your own, and you'll be in just as deep shit as your friend." Then he pursed his lips into a sneer, and said, "On second thought, go out on your own, if you like. Believe me, rounding you boys up is not much of a problem."

As I entered the barracks, it occurred to me that I was just about back in uniform. Maybe I should have run with Freeman. That said, there was something strangely comfortable about returning to the service. Maybe I was still euphoric about escaping farming, Neo-Baptists, and Little Man; but maybe it was because the Unified Authority Marine Corps was the only place where I fitted in.

Entering my room, I spotted a package that someone had left on my bed. The note on the outside of the package said it was from Admiral Alden Brocius. Inside the package I found general-issue essentials—a leather toiletry kit with the emblem of the Unified Authority Marines embossed on it, and a pair of shades—glasses designed for viewing the mediaLink.

Before the Mogats iced the Broadcast Network, the mediaLink had been the communications system that kept the galaxy connected. You used it to send messages, talk with people, hold conferences, etc. The mediaLink also carried news and programming. Each of the six arms of the galaxy had its own news networks and shows, but you could access them all through the mediaLink. You could use shades to access libraries of books, listen to music, and watch movies. The best part was that almost anywhere man traveled in the galaxy, mediaLink service was available for instantaneous access—all through the miracle of the Broadcast Network.

When the Separatists destroyed the Mars broadcast discs, I assumed the mediaLink system went with it. Trapped on Little Man, I never stopped to realize that most planets had their own media and their own local-area mediaLink networks. They might not be able to access the galaxywide network, but that did not mean they would abandon communications and programming on a local basis.

I did not miss the movies or the music. You could keep the mail, I didn't have anyone to write to. What I missed was keeping up with current events. I missed the news.

I sat on the edge of my bed staring at those shades, amazed at my excitement over such a simple thing. Finally, I slipped on the glasses. Little lasers projected interactive images onto the retinal tissue in my eyes. Using ocular commands, I sorted through menus until I found an all-news channel, then I lay back against my headboard and watched.

The events of the day could not have been more mundane. With galactic communications shut down, I would only find local news. From what I could tell, life on Earth had not changed much since the Broadcast Network went down. The news analysts I saw never mentioned the war. They talked the economy to death. There was a lot of talk about sports and weather. No one so much as hinted that a top secret alliance between the Unified Authority and its former enemies might be in the making. No one mentioned Shin Nippon or even the Confederate Arms.

I watched the news for three hours, then went to the mess for dinner. When I returned to my room, I sat on my bed and slipped on the shades. Sometime after midnight, I fell asleep.

12

A warning tone sounded from the communications console beside my bed, waking me out of a restless sleep. For a moment I did not remember where I was as I fumbled around in the dark. My mouth felt dry. Finally I found the switch.

"Colonel Harris?" The voice had a familiar stodgy quality.

With my windows tinted against the sunlight and cool air pouring in through the vents, it felt like midnight in my room. The blood rushed to my head as I sat up, and I felt slightly dizzy but mostly alert.

"This is Harris," I said.

"Colonel, please hold for Admiral Brocius," the woman said in an officious manner.

"Colonel Harris, how are you this morning?" Brocius sounded unusually chipper for an admiral. "I believe you served briefly under my command some years back."

Vice Admiral Alden Brocius commanded the Central Cygnus Fleet. I almost saluted when he identified himself, just out of reflex, even though he wouldn't have seen me since our connection was only audio. That latent salute might have been programming in my Liberator nervous system, but it probably had more to do with my upbringing in the orphanage. As lowly clones in a military clone farm, we learned to salute by the age of three.

"Colonel, I was wondering if you would join me for breakfast this morning," Brocius said.

"Thank you, sir," I said. I had not been recalled to active duty, so I did not technically need to call him sir. My recall was just a formality, however. Considering who had extended the breakfast invitation, I expected to be recalled to active duty by the time I finished my eggs.

"Do you want to meet in the officers' mess?" I asked.

"That won't be necessary," Brocius said. "I know a little place near Annapolis that might be just right."

It took me two minutes to run a razor over my stubble and sterile-light my teeth. I did not worry about brushing my hair. As a veteran of the military orphanage system, I considered a crew cut the height of fashion—and I was always in fashion. The only fresh clothes I had was a colonel's uniform. I dressed and left.

A limousine idled outside the door of the barracks. As I approached, a driver in a petty officer's uniform climbed out of the car, opened a door at the back of the car, then saluted. I returned the salute and climbed into the car.

"Glad you could make it," Admiral Brocius said, as I slid onto the seat.

"I'm not familiar with the protocol. Am I supposed to salute the chauffeur before entering the limousine?" I asked.

"You should if you are on active duty," Brocius said. "But you are not on active duty yet."

"I get the feeling I may be recalled," I said.

"Would you like to return to active duty?" Brocius asked.

"I hadn't thought about it," I said. That was a lie. I had also tried to convince myself that I did not want to be recalled, but I knew it was a lie as well. I was designed for military use. I had recently chosen suicide over a quiet peaceful life on a farming planet.

"I asked around. If you came back, you might not be able to reenter as a colonel," Brocius said, pretending I had told him that I could not wait to reup. "That was never official, you know. Admiral Huang sort of muscled that last promotion of yours through for security purposes.

"We might be able to preserve your officer status."

"I'm happy as a civilian, sir," I said. I did not want to make this too easy for him.

Brocius ignored this comment. "How do you see the war going?" He asked this with a relaxed but interested air. He sounded like a man asking a salesman for advice about cars. "What do we need to win this war?"

The first time I had seen Alden Brocius, he had black hair, brown eyes, and the typical officer's disdain for enlisted men and clones. He was tall and slender back then. That was four years ago.

Over the last four years he had put on a few pounds and grown a beard. The hair on his head and in his beard had turned gray. He looked like a man struggling to hold on to his fifties. The wrinkles around the corners of his eyes blended into his cheeks. He looked tired.

"What can we do to win this one, Harris?" he repeated.

"The Mogats won't engage in a surface war, they're not that dumb, so you're going to need a self-broadcasting fleet if you want to engage them," I said. No brilliant observations there, but I did not have anything brilliant to add on the spur of the moment.

"Do you think we have time to build another self-broadcasting fleet?" Brocius asked.

"That depends how long it would take to build it," I said. Then, realizing just what an asinine statement I had just made, I added, "I've been out of the loop, sir. I only know what you and the Japanese have told me.

"From what I hear, time might be short. I don't see the Mogats waiting around forever. I mean three years..."

"Three years?" Brocius asked.

"We built the Galactic Central Fleet in three years," I said.

"Ah, yes we did. But we had the Network up and running back then. Without the Network, we can't send unfinished ships between dry docks. We'll have to start and complete each ship in the same facility.

"We're not looking at three years this time, we're looking at ten if we get lucky. Maybe twelve if things don't fall into place."

We drove out of town and through a wooded countryside. Finally, we ended up in a residential area. To me, the mansions along the street looked as big as hotels. They had manicured lawns and acre-long driveways. We pulled up to a three-story home with a redbrick façade and brown tile roof.

"Nice place," I said. "Your home?"

"Not very often," Brocius said. "My home is the fleet. I guess that makes this more my vacation house. When I'm in town on business, I generally stay in the barracks. It's much more convenient."

The car stopped in front of a redbrick walkway that led to the door. Our chauffeur came around and opened the admiral's door. Not sure if I should wait for the man to open mine as well, I let myself out.

"The place has been in the family for generations. I make it out here two, maybe three times a year," Brocius said, still continuing the same conversation.

We went inside. Whoever had decorated Admiral Brocius's home could not decide whether to go modern or antique. The entry had bright lights and shiny smooth walls made out of a modern stone-and-glass hybrid. The builders had made curved corners and pleated the walls. The look was chic, I suppose. Beyond the entryway, the glass/stone material gave way to cherrywood walls, leather furniture, and lots of bookcases. The house had a musty feeling.

We entered a parlor decorated with antique brass instruments. The room had a telescope on a large hutch and a compass the size of a coffee table in the center of the floor. Brocius had an ancient map of some Earth ocean framed on the wall.

We moved on to Brocius's private study. In this room he had an antique rolltop desk. A painting of an old-time sailing ship cutting through a stormy sea hung on the wall. In one corner of the room stood a cutaway model of an early orbital space station. Like the rooms we entered before it, the office had carpets in the center of the floor with a wide hardwood border.

"What do you think?" Brocius asked.

"It's comfortable," I said. In truth, I found the furnishings so dull and dark that they made me sleepy.

"I'll tell you a secret," Brocius said. "I hate this room. As an admiral, I'm obligated to have at least one room like that in my house. We're all supposed to love the sea. We're supposed to be fascinated by the history of navigation. That's our public image. We have to decorate our houses to look like monuments to naval history."

"Bryce Klyber had a room like this in his house, too. I think he actually liked his." Bryce Klyber, my mentor, had been the highest-ranking officer in the U.A. Navy until his untimely death. I was sure that he did have a room like this one in his house, and I was just as sure that he often retired there to meditate.

Brocius led me upstairs. The staircase ended in an enormous parlor. When he turned on the lights, I saw mirrored walls, old-fashioned neon signs, and bulbs that blinked on and off. He had two rows of antique slot machines, the oldest of which took coins instead of credits. Some even had mechanical wheels with symbols instead of computer screens.

In one corner of the room was a twenty-foot display that looked like a track for horse racing. It had six tin horses on a mural that depicted a straightaway. There was a betting counter beside the game with six stools. It was impressive.

"What do you think?" Brocius asked.

"I like it," I said. It beat the hell out of the naval museum downstairs.

"It all works. Even the horse-racing game," Brocius said.

That was not an invitation to come back and play. He probably held enormous parties for his fellow alumni from Annapolis—officers, natural-borns. Clones and enlisted men need not apply.

"Some of these machines are over five hundred years old," Brocius said. He pointed to three pinball machines against a far wall. "Those machines are American twentieth century."

They looked shiny and new, with flashing lights hidden behind gaudy glass marquees. There was a kind of practical whimsy about these old toys. Many of them captured the way their ancient owners envisioned the future—all chrome and flashing lights. The people who designed them had it all wrong, of course, but I liked the look of the future as they saw it.

We had "Budge" pinball machines in the game room at our orphanage, holographic machines that let you use a predesigned course or create your own table. Everything from the ball to the bumpers looked solid and real, but it was all laser projection. One of Brocius's pinball tables had a volcano made of plastic and winking lights to simulate lava. With Budge machines, you could have an erupting volcano that spat molten lava, or, if you wanted to play like the ancients, a holographic version of a toy volcano made of plastic and lights.

Growing up, I never saw anyone select antique-looking elements. We all wanted volcanoes and roller coasters that looked real, and monsters that breathed air and spat fire. If ever I got my hands on one of those machines again, I decided I would go with all antique elements.

"This room is a gambling man's dream," I said. "You must be quite a player."

"You've got me all wrong, Harris. I don't gamble, I win," Brocius said.

"The gamblers are the people who put money in my machines. Once in a while they walk off with more than they brought, usually they leave empty-handed. Me, I always walk away with more than I started with. I'm the house." He leaned toward me as if to confide a secret. "I get better odds."

He shut off the lights and led me back down the stairs, back to his stodgy museum of maritime history.

We ate in a large dining room on a hardwood table that could have served twenty people. A petty officer in a dress uniform served us our meal. The man looked so serious as he handed us our plates, you would have thought Brocius had threatened him with a court-martial.

"Did you know that the Mogats routed one of the fleets in the Perseus Arm?" Brocius asked. This was the first time he'd spoken since we sat at the table. It was one hell of a conversation starter, especially as I had been laboring under the impression that the Mogat ships could not stand up to the modern U.A. Navy.

"One of our fleets?" I echoed, lamely.

"Fortunately for us, they only sent a few ships. Our ships didn't put up much of a fight.

"Some Outer Perseus ships overtook five Mogat ships as they broadcasted in an area they were patrolling. That's it, just five ships. Good thing. If there had been more of them, we might have lost the whole damned fleet.

"The Outer Perseus Fleet is Adam Porter's outfit, mind you. Porter served on one of my ships a couple of years before he got his star. He's no atom-splitter, that one. He never had much of a mind for strategy."

"You called it a rout. How bad was it?" I asked.

Our waiter returned with eggs Benedict, hash browns, toast, and wedges of cantaloupe. He placed the plates with the eggs Benedict in front of us, then placed the rest of the food in the center. He poured us coffee and orange juice. I half expected him to put down his tray and start reciting poetry, he was taking so long. I wanted to know what happened, and Brocius did not seem willing to speak with anyone else in the room.

Finally, the petty officer left the room.

"Porter went after them with a fighter carrier, five battleships, ten frigates..."

"Beat by five Mogat ships?" I asked. That sounded bad.

"Porter's fleet has the oldest ships in the galaxy," Brocius said. I briefly considered reminding Brocius that the ships in the Mogat fleet were older than our oldest active ships but decided against it.

"We're talking about the Perseus Arm, Harris. Nothing much happens out there. Before the war broke out, Congress wanted to shut the Outer Perseus Fleet down."

"What kind of ships did the Mogats bring to the fight?" I asked.

"Five battleships," Brocius said. "We've built our strategy around the idea that ship-per-ship we can beat the Mogats any time. Now we have to rethink that. By the time they were done, Porter lost a fighter carrier and three battleships. The Mogats didn't even bother with his frigates."

"What did they lose?" I asked.

"We don't know how much damage Porter did to the ships that got away, but he only sank one of their battleships." Brocius took a long drink of coffee, but his eyes remained fixed on me.

I cut a triangle from my eggs Benedict. This was not the kind of breakfast I normally ate. I preferred my eggs scrambled and my bacon straight instead of with hollandaise sauce. The muffin on the bottom of this stack was still crunchy. This was too rich a breakfast for my taste, but I did not say so. I cut more, watched the yolk spill out across my plate, then took another bite of the slimy thing.

"Like it?" Brocius asked.

"It's good," I chose to be politic. "Earth-grown?"

"That's all you can get with the Broadcast Network down," he said. "Do you have any idea how much it would cost to ship in eggs and bread from the territories?"

I should have figured that.

"Porter is still in command of the fleet for now, but his career is specked. There's no room in the U.A. Navy for officers who let their fleet get chased by five ships," Brocius said.

"So the Mogats sank a few of his ships... then what? They wouldn't just let him leave," I said.

"That is precisely what they did," Brocius said. More than anything else, he sounded disgusted.

"Why the speck would they do that?" I asked. It didn't make sense. Having defeated an enemy with superior numbers, why let him flee and regroup? I thought about this for a few seconds. "Have there been any other engagements?"

"No," Brocius said.

"Before they merged with the Confederate Arms and Halverson took over, the Mogats never seemed very bright," I said.

"Did you know Halverson's been promoted to fleet admiral?

Our fleet admiral?" Brocius asked, obvious distaste dripping from his voice.

Admiral Tom Halverson, who led the attack on the Earth Fleet, joined the Confederate Arms while they were allied with the Atkins Believers. He left the Unified Authority as a rear admiral, received a few additional stars, and emerged as the head of the combined Mogat-Confederate Arms Navy. The notion that Halverson could return and take command of our fleet clawed at my stomach.

Brocius went after his eggs Benedict in a methodical fashion, cutting the open-faced sandwich into six bites, then downing three of those bites in a minute-long feast. He chewed each piece mechanically, washed it down with a sip of orange juice, and then speared the next bite with his fork.

"I'll ask it again, Harris, what do we need? How do we stack the deck? What do we need to do to give ourselves house odds?"

"They're hard to read," I said. "I always knew that the Mogats were not military-minded, but allowing a fleet to escape is strange, even by their standards."

I thought about what I'd said and changed my mind. "They almost act surprised when they win. I mean, when they beat the Earth Fleet and shut down the Network, the planet was theirs. They should have landed troops and taken DC.

"Now you tell me that they had a fleet at their mercy and let it escape. It's almost like they want to convert us, not beat us."

"Did you hear that they tried to land a messiah in Israel?" Brocius asked.

"Yes, I heard about the Space Bibles, too."

"I agree with you, it does sound like they're out to convert us," Brocius said.

"We need one of their ships with its navigational computer in one piece. That is how we can find them," I said.

"We can send a salvage team to the battleship Porter sank," Brocius suggested.

"No, we need a boat in working condition."

Brocius began his eggs Benedict–eating ritual again. He cut a sandwich into six pieces and speared the first piece. "Capture a battleship? That would be a trick."

"We have people who could do it," I said. "Can you get me to the outer Scutum-Crux Fleet?" I asked.

"Why Scutum-Crux?" Brocius asked.

"Because the *Kamehameha* is in that fleet," I answered.

13

In the entire Unified Authority Navy, there was only one Expansion-class fighter carrier active in any of its fleets—the *Kamehameha*. All of the other carriers were of the more modern Perseus-class variety. They were five thousand one hundred feet wide and carried eleven thousand troops—fourteen battalions of Marines just spoiling for a fight. The *Kamehameha* measured half that size and carried a mere one thousand combat men, but they were special. They were Navy SEALs; and more than that, they were Adam Boyd clones. The *Kamehameha* might have been undersized and obsolete, but with that complement of Boyd clones, it could win a war.

Larger than any battleship and smaller than other fighter carriers, the *Kamehameha* traveled with the rest of the Scutum-Crux Fleet as well hidden as a shark among dolphins. From the cabin of the self-broadcasting explorer ship, I watched the whole fleet and remembered my days as a Marine. I spent almost two years on the *Kamehameha,* back when it carried Marines. I reported in as a corporal and transferred out as a lieutenant.

On the charts and simulations, you always see ships laid out in a flat formation—even when the charts are three-dimensional. Coming in this time, I was struck by the way the fleet had grouped. The fighter carriers were in the center of a three-dimensional diamond with layers of destroyers and battleships surrounding them from above, from below, and from every side. A trio of battleships led the formation.

All of the ships had the same beige hull and light gray underbelly. Lights on the outsides of these ships illuminated their numbers and bows. The Unified Authority Navy placed little stock on stealth when it came to its fleets. The Scutum-Crux Fleet thundered across its corner of the galaxy with all the subtlety of a herd of elephants crossing the plains.

As we circled around the back of the fleet, I watched the blue-white flames that flared from the ships' engines. "We've been cleared for approach, Colonel," my pilot told me. My pilot was a natural-born lieutenant who seemed to resent playing chauffeur for a clone.

Brocius cut me orders, too, but they were purposely vague. They identified me as being on Central Cygnus Fleet business and told people to cooperate with me and nothing more. Brocius's orders gave me enough leeway to land myself in the brig for life. They gave Brocius enough wiggle room to say I had acted on my own.

Rereading these orders I realized how easily I allowed myself to be swept by the tides. I did not need to carry Yamashiro's olive branch to Earth just because he found me in space. I did not need to partner up with Brocius or rejoin the Marines just because I returned to Earth. I just seemed to let the tide of events sweep me along. I had not officially rejoined the Marines, but here I was, with the Scutum-Crux Fleet, preparing to leave on an unofficial mission. I was wearing a Marine's uniform, talking like a Marine, and acting like a Marine. Even worse, much as I tried to fool myself otherwise, I knew I was exactly where I wanted to be.

I was built for war, and was pretty sure that I was programmed to be incapable of fighting for anyone other than the Unified Authority. When I really tried, I was capable of passive resistance—living with farmers instead of fighting with the Marines, trying to adapt a transport for broadcast instead of putting a pistol to my head, but in the end, I was in the warrior class, and this was my republic.

My mind wandered as I sat alone. I was the only passenger in a cabin designed to hold two hundred scientists. The explorer was the size of an atmosphere-bound commercial jetliner—too big to fit in the *Kamehameha's* launch bay. We had to fly within a mile of the fighter carrier and match her speed. From where I sat, it looked like both ships had come to a stop.

The *Kamehameha* sent out a ten-man skiff to meet us. The skiff "mated" with the explorer, sealing its temporary air lock over our hatch like a tick attaching itself to a dog. The intricate process took several minutes. Once the air lock was ready, and the gangway was set, I crossed over and rode the skiff to the *Kamehameha*.

The welcoming crew that met me in the launch bay included the ship's captain and several high-ranking officers. They did not know why I had come. They only knew that I had orders from Earth.

As the hatch opened, and I stepped out to the deck, I saw recognition on a few of their faces. Some of these men had served on this ship four years ago when I returned with six other survivors from the battle on Little Man.

I saluted the captain, and he returned my salute. I was still dressed in the colonel's uniform I had worn to breakfast at Brocius's house. Technically I was impersonating an officer, but the uniform was the only clothing I had at the moment.

"Requesting permission to come aboard," I said as I stood at attention.

"Welcome aboard," the captain said.

"Thank you, sir," I said. "May I present my orders to the captain?" I remained at attention, chest out, shoulders back. High-ranking officers noticed when you did or did not show them the proper respect.

"At ease, Colonel," the captain said.

I spread my feet fifteen inches apart. I clasped my hands behind my back. I released the air in my chest.

"Let's see your orders, Colonel," the captain said.

I handed him the sheet. He read it. "You wish to meet with my SEALs..." he said. "I don't suppose you are able to tell me what you might discuss with them?"

I said nothing and looked straight ahead.

"I didn't think so," the captain said.

"Ensign, conduct Colonel Harris down to the barracks. See that he meets Illych."

I saluted. The captain saluted. His salute seemed more formal than it had a few moments earlier.

The ensign led me out of the launch bay and down the corridor. I studied the walls, the ceiling, the lights. Everything looked familiar. With the exception of the orphanage, I had spent more time on this ship than anyplace else in the universe.

Back when I served on the *Kamehameha,* they'd called the lowest deck "Marine Camp." On that level we had our own barracks, gymnasiums, and training grounds. Marine clones caught on other decks of the ship were apt to receive rude treatment by sailors, officers and clones alike, who considered them nothing more than cargo.

During my day, Marine Camp was home to two thousand sea

soldiers. Walking these halls during business hours, you would see men in fatigues drilling or jogging, or rushing to the firing range. Eighty percent of them were general-issue clones—five-foot-ten and stocky, with a full head of brown hair, brown eyes, and a light complexion.

Now the deck belonged to Navy SEALs. Some men wore fatigues, and some wore jumpsuits. They were short, maybe five-five. The few that did not shave their heads had stubbly light hair. They all had dark skin, and fingers that came to sharp points.

They trained differently, too. In battle, Marines marched up the street and shot everything that got in their way. SEALs specialized in stealth and infiltration. I'd seen their work. They could sneak up behind you, slit your throat, and slip away into the night before you gurgled your last breath.

From what I could see, there were no officers among them. Men sauntered up and down halls in small groups. They talked quietly. Everyone had the same face, the same tan, the same brantoo on his forearm—a map of the six arms of the galaxy with banners above and below. The banner above said "NAVY SEALS." The banner below said "THE FINAL SOLUTION." The banners and each of the arms of the Milky Way were branded into their forearms, then dye was injected into the wound to add color. Brand the pattern and color the skin, and you end up with an embossed tattoo. I have never felt the need to get a brantoo, though having one is considered a mark of machismo.

I could not get over the feeling of déjà vu as we walked the halls. Oh, the layout had been changed a bit, and the clones did not look like the clones with whom I served, but I still recognized the rec room and mess hall. When we passed by the door to my former barracks, I wanted to stop and peer in. Finally, the ensign delivered me to a small briefing room.

The SEAL who came to the door and saluted us wore a star and three red stripes on his arms. That made him a master chief petty officer. He had gone as far as he could go in the noncommissioned ranks. In the world of cloned SEALs, this man was the ultimate authority.

"Colonel Harris, this is Illych. He pretty much runs things down here," the ensign said.

This was the first time I had seen a Boyd clone so close without fighting him. I had not realized exactly how ugly they would be. He had a small mouth and almost no lips. A thick ridge of bone ran along the tops of his eye sockets. That ridge would offer protection in hand-to-hand combat. I knew from experience that it made them hell with a head butt.

I stood ten inches taller than Illych. Looking down and trying to hide my nervousness, I returned his salute. I had seen Boyd clones in action. They killed without hesitation.

"Illych," I said, using the bored voice that officers use when addressing enlisted men.

"Colonel," Illych said.

"Ensign, perhaps Mr. Illych and I could have a word," I said.

The ensign saluted, turned, and left us. During my tour as an active Marine, I had two actions in which I fought clones of Illych's make. Luck played a large part in my survival. No one and nothing I have ever seen scared me quite so much as Boyd clones.

Illych seemed to recognize me. I thought I saw tension in his face. The intense look in his eyes reminded me of a pit bull guarding its den, but a slight grin played on his lips. He had a mysterious Cheshire Cat smile that was too big to disregard and too small to label as insubordination.

I tried to ignore that smirk as we sat to discuss my orders, but I kept coming back to it. "Is there something on your mind, Chief?" I asked.

"You're a Liberator clone," Illych said.

Feeling a little nervous, I said, “Nothing gets past you Boyd clones,” hoping to put Illych in his place. To the contrary, however, his grin only broadened.

“You know, Colonel, Admiral Huang always referred to us as ‘Special Operations clones.’ We were never called Adam Boyd clones. There was a clone from our outfit who went by the name Adam Boyd, but the official term was ‘Special Operations clone.’

“Interesting thing about Adam Boyd, Colonel. He was killed in a tough-man competition on an Earth island called Oahu. That was our original base of operations.

“Have you ever been to the Hawaiian islands?” Illych asked.

I could feel the muscles in my stomach tensing. My sphincter had probably shrunk to the size of a pin. We were getting far afield, but this had to be resolved. “As a matter of fact, I have.”

“So you’ve been to Hawaii, sir. May I ask, is that where you got that scar over your eye?”

I had a half-inch-thick scar over my left eye. It made a bald stripe across my eyebrow. “That is correct,” I said.

“A swimming accident?” Illych asked.

“Not swimming,” I said.

“Rock-climbing accident?” Illych asked.

“Not exactly. I was at a place called Sad Sam’s Palace,” I said.

“I’ve heard of the place,” Illych said. “Don’t they hold tough-man competitions there on Friday nights?”

“Yes, they do. As it turns out, I was there on a Friday night. I went to watch the fights, but I got suckered into entering.”

The petty officer sat still and silent for several seconds, that strange grin unchanged as he studied me. I could not tell what went through his mind. For all I knew, he had been in the audience watching as I beat his brother clone to death. Time passed as we sat and regarded each other, neither of us wanting to be the one to end the silence.

I pulled out the orders Admiral Brocius had given me and slid them across the table. They glided across the slick surface, coming to a stop in front of Illych. Without saying a word, he picked them up and read them to himself. Then he looked up, that grin still in place, and said, "Got anything exciting in mind, sir?"

14

Space is not black. Looking into a night sky or staring out the portholes of some large starship, it's easy to think that outer space is black. It's not black. It's clear. It is so wide and immense and open that it seems to crowd around you, but only because the human mind cannot comprehend the length of a single light-year, let alone a hundred thousand light-years.

An enemy ship could easily hide in the vastness of space. With their charcoal-colored hulls, Mogat ships could slip into an empty pocket of space and vanish.

I took a team of SEALs with me to view the battlefield where the Mogats had made short work of the Outer Perseus Fleet.

Inside the explorer, an unarmed vessel, the SEALs had a good reason to feel nervous. Designed for scientific expeditions, the explorer's top speed was under ten million miles per hour. Its broadcast engine needed a full twenty minutes to recharge between broadcasts. Mogat battleships and cruisers had a top speed of thirty million miles per hour. They could charge their broadcast engines in eight minutes. If the Mogats spotted us, they could outrun and outshoot us. If it came to a battle, we might as well have been flying in a coffin.

Considering the number of ships Admiral Porter lost, his battle with the Mogats took place on a relatively condensed field. A swarm of dead fighters floated in a tight formation around our ship. Looking from the deck of a battleship or a fighter carrier, the dead fighters might have looked like the carcasses of insects caught in an old spiderweb. Looking through the window of a small explorer with no armor and no shields, the broken ships looked ominous. Our explorer might have been five times the size of those fighters. They did not look so small from where I now sat.

Bigger wrecks loomed in the distance. No lights showed through their portholes, and their observation decks were dark. We passed within a couple hundred feet of a U.A. fighter carrier. I could see its fatal wounds. Ten-foot-wide holes dotted the front section of its bow. The big ship hung motionless.

"They're like ghosts," Illych said as he fastened his armor. He looked tense as he checked and rechecked his gear.

Maybe it was SEAL culture or maybe it was in their programming, but Adam Boyds behaved differently than Marines before combat. General-issue clones hid their nerves behind crude jokes and loud boasting as they waited for the doors to open on a mission. Clones who were too scared to bluff became sullen and sometimes despondent. These guys carried on quiet conversations. They talked about sports or plans for the next time they took leave. Did they feel nervous at all? I wondered. Fighting in open space would take them out of their element.

Marines wore armor in all combat situations. SEALs did not. They had armor for deep-space operations, but I doubt they found much use for it. While I practically jumped into my armor, they moved more tentatively. They fastened their armor on one piece at a time. Watching them, I was reminded of a swimmer climbing into cold water. I wondered if their helmets made them claustrophobic.

Working in armor did not make me nervous, but the derelict fighters floating around our ship gave me a shiver. The explorer pushed through this graveyard at a slow drift, giving us a good look at each broken craft as we slid by. Around us, everything was silence, stillness, and death.

The old sailors who traveled Earth's seas were said to have loved the ocean. The great captains said they were married to the sea or called the sea their mistress. Modern sailors held no such fantasies about outer space. Space did not love or hate, it simply killed anything it touched.

"Pardon me, sir, but what are we looking for out here?" one of the Boyd clones asked. So far, the Boyd clones kept to themselves mostly. It took a moment before I realized that someone had asked me a question.

The man who had approached me had scars around his mouth and nose. Several white lines streaked his lips and faded into his chin. All of the Boyds bore scars. They were inevitable when you did not wear armor in battle.

"Sir," the clone repeated, "what are we looking for on the Mogat ship?" If this SEAL was scared, he hid it well. I would have described him as "on edge," but not scared.

"I want their broadcast computer for openers," I said. "If we can figure out where their ships have been, we might be able to drop in on the Mogats' home base."

The Boyd nodded. I did not need to elaborate about what treasures that computer might hold. If the boys back in Naval Intelligence could tap into its databanks, assuming the databanks had survived the battle, we might find enough information to win the war.

Functioning battleships give off virtual beacons that identify their name and fleet. According to Admiral Porter's report, a derelict Mogat battleship lay somewhere in this mess; but the ship's computers had all gone dark. We could not locate the beacon, so we had to fly past every wreck and identify it by sight.

"Colonel Harris," a voice called over the intercom.

"Have you got something?" I asked.

"We found their ship," the pilot said.

"I'm on my way," I said. I turned to Illych. "You want to come up?"

He nodded.

The explorer had three distinct compartments—a cockpit, a cabin for passengers, and a cargo area/engine room. The SEALs had moved to the cargo hold waiting to deploy, leaving the cabin empty.

One of the chief uses of this particular ship was space cartography. It had an all-glass cockpit. Looking at the view from the cockpit felt like floating in space. The only light in the pilot's area came from the low glow of the instrumentation.

"It's that one over there," the pilot said, pointing at a huge wreck. The explorer moved very slowly past the wreckage of a Tomcat, nudging the crumpled fuselage out of its way.

Off to the right, I saw the target. At first it looked more like a shadow than a battleship. It was a black hole in the middle of a field of stars. Then I recognized the shape—the bulbous bow and the wide-diamond hull. I did not actually see the ship. I saw the shape of its silhouette against a backdrop of stars.

Illych asked, "How do we get in?"

"That's your problem," the pilot said. "My job is to bring you here. I've done my part."

"We look for an open door," I said.

Illych nodded. As he turned to leave the cockpit, he said, "I thought you would say something along those lines."

We went back to the cargo hold and put on our helmets. The SEALs wore armor made specifically for them. My armor was green. Their armor had smart camouflage. As they maneuvered, sensors in their helmets would read the color and lighting in the environment, changing the color of their suits. There were limitations, the armor could only match basic coloration. It offered camouflage, not invisibility.

We stepped onto the cargo elevator at the very back of the ship. It lifted us into an air lock in the roof, where we boarded a ten-man space sled. There were only seven of us, and the SEALs were small. It might have held twelve of them.

"Are you ready, Colonel?" the pilot asked over the interLink connection in my helmet.

"Open the lock," I said.

The metal dome that covered the air lock peeled back slowly to reveal the stars behind it. I hit the release button to retract the sleeves that clamped our sled in place. With a small burst of air, the sled dislodged from the explorer and lifted into open space.

Normally we would attach jetpacks to our armor before traversing open space. We did not on this occasion. Once we entered the derelict battleship, we would likely enter unstable areas with radiation and chemical contamination. Who could predict what we would find on that ship? We could not risk wearing jetpacks.

We had half a mile to traverse between the explorer and the battleship. As we covered the silent distance, some of the Boyd clones played their search beams along the hull of the derelict ship. The hull looked smooth and untouched from what I could see. Their lights cast yard-wide circles that bleached the ship's armor gray. The circles of light stretched and deformed as they played over the various portholes, gun emplacements, and hatches.

"It doesn't look like there are any open doors on the top side, sir," Illych's voice came over the interLink.

"Not that I can see," I agreed. "Not that I can see." I sighed. These things never came easy.

Something else was missing. Not only did I not see any breaks in the hull, I did not see scorch marks. That part of the battleship looked pristine, as if it had never been hit. We flew over the top of the diamond-shaped hull. Because of the curve of its fuselage, the battleship's bulky wings seemed to dissolve into space.

We flew over the bridge. On a ship like this, the bridge more closely resembled government offices than the wheelhouses of the old seafaring ships. There was no wheel. The navigation was handled by a set of computers. Touring the bridge of any capital ship, you would find six large computer stations. One station handled navigation, another facilitated internal and external communications, another monitored radar and tracking, and another managed the weapons systems. Gone were the days when marksmanship mattered in ship-to-ship combat.

Gone, too, were the days when specialized technicians sat around the engine monitoring its performance. Modern ships had a set of computers that constantly checked every flange and dial.

The final computer sat in the command station. That computer lifted information from the other five and organized it. On working ships, you would find groups of sailors clustered around each of these stations. Looking into the viewport of this wreck as we flew by, I saw nothing but darkness.

We dropped down the front edge of the ship. In space, of course, down is a relative thing. With no gravity determining what was up and what was down, I set my bearings by focusing on the battleship. We had just flown across its top side, and now we dropped down to examine its underbelly.

"What happened here?" Illych asked.

An enormous gash ran half the length of the ship. It almost looked as if some giant had grabbed the battleship by its wings, stabbed a knife into its underside, then slashed it across its belly.

"Shit. Someone specked them over bad," I said.

"Yes, sir," Illych said. Illych's voice had an offended tone to it. It took me a moment to decipher what might have bothered him. As I thought about it, I realized I had never heard Illych swear. None of the Special Operations clones did. They might slip up behind you and slit your throat, but they would not use bad language. Admirable… very specking admirable.

As we dropped under the battleship, its keel extended over us like a pitch-black sky. The breach across it looked like a gigantic crater. Four of the SEALs played their lights across it exposing a forty-foot-wide gash through which a careful pilot might successfully fly a small ship. From the look of things, the outer shell around these wounds had simply melted away. Bubbles, some popped and some whole, pocked the blackened edges of the gash.

As we flew toward the opening, one of the SEALs shined his light directly into it, illuminating the ship's skeletal girders. The light uncovered torn wires and something that I first thought might be a ladder and later realized was the aluminum framing between the ceiling of one deck and the floor of the next. The gash through the hull extended up three decks of the ship.

So this is what it's like when you die out in space, I thought to myself. "There's our open door," was what I said. I steered the sled into the gash.

Sitting in an enclosed spaceship, you develop misconceptions about how things work in space. In a ship, you get the feeling that you can simply cut the gas and coast to a stop. I always envisioned pilots stepping on the brakes to stop their ships the way I would in a car. When we studied space combat in boot camp, we trained in smaller vehicles than this sled; but those vehicles had armor plating to shield their works. I never appreciated everything that went into changing direction and coming to a stop.

On this sled, with its wide-open design, I saw how twenty different booster engines worked in concert to change our speed and direction as we flew. Before I could come to a stop, engines had to provide counterthrust to stop my forward momentum. A set of thrusters on the bottom of the sled fired forward. As we rose into that gash, several engines burst on and off as I fine-tuned the ascent to avoid jagged edges and debris.

"Stop!" one of the SEALs shouted.

The sled did not stop on a dime, but it stopped quickly enough. "You're not going to believe this, but I'm picking up security sensors," the SEAL said.

"Active sensors?" Illych asked.

"That's what I'm reading," the SEAL responded. "They're ancient, and I mean ancient... electronic motion-tracking sensors."

"This ship is fifty years old," Illych reminded the other SEAL.

At first I thought their reconnaissance armor contained technology that my combat armor lacked. All six SEALs stood huddled together staring straight up like bird-watchers trying to spot some rare species. Then I saw that they each held some sort of remote in their hands.

"Think we can jam it?" Illych asked.

"No problem," that first SEAL replied. He held up the remote, something the size of a deck of cards with a row of buttons across it. He pressed one of the buttons. The button lit up red.

"Nice spotting," Illych said. He turned to me. "You won't have one of these stealth kits, sir." He held up his remote for me to see. "Stay with me. As long as you are with one of us, the sensors won't detect you."

I nodded. "Is it safe to enter?" I asked.

"Yes, sir, Colonel," that first SEAL said. "If you have one of these stealth kits, you can skip rope, pass gas, and cook cheeseburgers all at the same time, and the sensors won't spot you."

I restarted the sled. Rising through the wreckage, we passed two decks and stopped on the third. We rode past hallways so dark that they seemed to digest the SEALs' spotlight beams. I did not have a spotlight. I had to rely on the night-for-day lens built into the visor of my helmet. In that blue-white version of the world that the night-for-day lens showed me, I saw flat black spaces instead of corridors. Night-for-day vision let you see in the dark, but it took away your depth perception.

Whatever Porter and his fleet had fired at the battleship took out every system. I saw no signs of working electricity. The artificial gravity was out. The life support was down.

"You seen anybody?" one of the SEALs asked all of us over an open interLink frequency. "I expected dead sailors floating around."

"Think they evacuated the ship?" Illych asked me.

"Don't count on it," I said. "Anybody in this area would have gotten flushed out." I had seen big ships explode. Once something pierces the hull, the pressure of the ship's atmosphere flushes bodies, furniture, and other debris out of the gap until the pressure equalizes.

"So you think we'll find bodies?" Illych asked.

"Sure we will, over a thousand of them if this battleship had a full crew. You and your boys aren't squeamish?" I asked. I knew they were not, but I could hardly pass as a credible officer if I did not take a cheap shot every now and then.

After landing the sled on the first solid stretch of floor I found, I told the SEALs to divide up.

"What did you have in mind, sir?" Illych asked.

I sent five of the SEALs to the bridge to examine the navigation computer and whatever charts they could find. There was no need to tell them what to do if they found live enemies. These clones had tactics hardwired into their brains. They knew what to do in these situations as instinctively as they knew what to do in a latrine.

"Why don't you come with me to the engineering section?" I asked Illych. The smart display in my visor read the SEALs' virtual dog tags, allowing me to tell them apart. I'd had enough trouble telling them apart before they put on their identical armor.

Illych saluted and followed.

Before leaving the *Kamehameha,* we preloaded the general deck map of a GCF battleship into our helmet computers. The maps were based on fifty-year-old information, but they proved reliable. I had no doubt that the other team would find the navigation computer in the bridge on the top deck by following the map. Whether or not they could remove the data storage from the navigation computer was a different issue. For that matter, I did not know how I would remove the data storage unit from the broadcast computer in the engineering section.

What we saw on this trip was almost as important as what we stole. We had video-recording devices in our helmets. Anything we saw would be stored on a chip. I wanted to explore as much of the ship as possible so that I could create a video record to show Yoshi Yamashiro and his engineers. The Japanese renovated these old ships when they partnered with the Mogats.

I suspected that something had changed since the Separatist alliance fell apart. When the Mogat Fleet attacked Earth, Unified Authority ships had more than enough firepower to sink its ships one-on-one. Now a handful of Mogat ships had routed the Outer Perseus Fleet. What changed?

"What's in engineering?" Illych asked me as we pulled our way across the deck. With no gravity to hold us down, it was easier to float than walk. We sprang from bulkheads and pulled ourselves along walls.

"The broadcast engine, for openers," I said.

In truth, I think I had already started to piece some things together. I was a Marine, not a sailor; but I had seen some big space battles. I had a good idea of what happened to ships in those battles, and I had never seen a gash like the one on the belly of this ship.

Illych must have noticed it, too. "Do you have any idea what could have cut through a ship like that?" he asked as he peered down the well of the gash and into space.

"It had to be a laser," I said. "Did you see the damage on the outside of the ship? The plating around the edges melted. Particle beams blow things apart; lasers cook their way through."

"But this?" he asked. "It must have been some kind of new laser."

"From what Admiral Brocius told me, the Outer Perseus Fleet doesn't have anything new, just hand-me-downs," I replied. "If you had some miracle laser, would you waste it out here?"

Illych said nothing. He might have nodded in agreement, but that gesture would have been lost inside his helmet. Trying to communicate by nodding or shaking your head was a rookie mistake made by people who had not acclimated to armor. When it came to combat armor, Illych came across as a rookie.

We headed down a corridor. Through the night-for-day lens in my visor, I saw the hallway ahead of us in blue-white and black. It was as smooth and as featureless as a sheath for a sword. The walls, ceiling, and floor were entirely untouched. There had probably been people in this area of the ship when the laser breached the hull. There may once have been bodies, chairs, and equipment around the hall, but all of that would have been flushed out along with the oxygen. The corridor ahead of us was chillingly immaculate.

"If they just had a run-of-the-mill laser, how did they make that hole?" Illych asked.

"Simple," I said. "Someone on board this ship must have shut down the shields."

15

Illych and I floated through the ship like superheroes flying through an abandoned city, stomachs down flying parallel to the floor. We passed hatches, some opened and some closed. Nowhere did we see any signs of life.

"Why would somebody lower the shields?" Illych asked. "That would be suicide."

"I'm only guessing here," I said. "I think one of their officers committed suicide and took the ship with him. This would not be the first time the Mogats sent a crew on a kamikaze mission."

When they attacked the Earth Fleet, the Mogats destroyed the Unified Authority's most powerful ship by broadcasting a cruiser into it. That was classified information. Illych could not have known about it.

"You believe that the entire crew of this ship willingly committed suicide?" Illych asked. He sounded skeptical. "That would have been hundreds of men."

"You wouldn't need a kamikaze crew," I said, "just one man. Once the guy controlling the shields turns off the power, it doesn't matter what the rest of the crew believes."

"But they were winning the battle when this ship went down. They could have had the whole damned fleet on a platter."

"Yeah," I said, wondering why the Mogats would purposely lose a battle. A saboteur, maybe. But that did not fit. U.A. Intelligence had not penetrated the Mogat military. For some reason the Mogats had apparently sacrificed the ship and the battle.

We came to a companionway that ran between decks. Peering through a window, I looked into the shaft. "There might be air in here," I said. Air in the shaft would present a hazard. The pressure from that air would send everything flying out at us the moment we cracked the hatch.

"May I have a try, sir?" Illych asked. I had already come to like working with Adam Boyd clones, these synthetic men created specifically for special operations. They moved carefully and deliberately. They observed their environment and took sure steps.

I pushed away from the hatch.

Illych replaced his particle-beam pistol in his belt and pulled out a tiny laser torch. It was a tool, not a weapon, though you could certainly use it to burn through an enemy in a pinch. Illych aimed his laser at the hatch and bored a pinprick hole. First the red dot appeared, then the beam intensified. The material of the door bubbled and melted away. Had there been oxygen in the stairwell, it would have leaked through the hole. Nothing happened.

"Looks like it's safe, sir," Illych said.

"Can you remove the hatch?" I asked.

"Yes, sir," Illych said. He slowly traced across the hinges. A minute later, he gave the hatch a tug, and it drifted out of our way.

Kicking off the walls, we dropped down the open companionway to a lower deck. Haphazard webs of icy black beads shimmered inside the shaft. With a light push, I shattered my way through them, not wanting to see what awaited me on the other side. The webs were frozen blood. Below me, looking more like deformed marble statues than human beings, were the bodies of three dead sailors. I passed over them and entered the vast cavern of the engine room.

Normal battleships needed huge generators to power their shields and weapons systems. Self-broadcasting ships required twice the generator capacity of their general-issue counterparts to power their broadcast engines. The engine room we now entered on this ship was twice the size of a basketball gym.

"Colonel, we may have a problem," Illych said, interrupting my thoughts.

"What is it, Illych?" I asked.

"I just got a call from the guys on the bridge. One of their stealth kits failed."

"Did the sensors spot them?" I asked.

"Yes, sir," Illych said. "Whether or not someone was watching is another question. They say they switched to a different kit quickly."

"I better radio the pilot and have him keep an eye out for visitors," I said. I did so, then went back to exploring the engine room.

The dead men inside the engine room were not dressed in pressure suits or space gear. When the laser sheared through the hull and the vacuum of space replaced their pressurized atmosphere, the blood pressure in their bodies burst through their skins. Blood vessels, veins, eyes, and skin all popped like balloons. The basic shapes of the men sprawled along the floor looked human enough, but it looked like someone had tried to peel their faces from their heads.

Large flaps of skin and tissue hung open from their heads and hands—the only fully exposed parts of their bodies. They wore jumpsuits with long sleeves. They wore boots. Who knew what I might find under their heavy clothes.

Without oxygen to cause soaking, the beads of their blood had penetrated their uniforms like water pouring through a sieve. The face of the man below me floated off his skull, his nose and mouth frozen but still recognizable. His burst eyes remained in their sockets looking like crushed white grapes. His lipless mouth grinned up at me.

During my days as a Marine, I'd seen worse. So, apparently, had Master Chief Petty Officer Emerson Illych. He quietly surveyed the area.

The engine room itself lay in ruins. Some of the equipment must have exploded before the air ran out. I saw scorch marks on the walls, and a few of the bodies bore signs of incineration. Looking around the room, I saw overturned desks and smashed computers. There was not so much as a working console in the entire vast cavern. Even the emergency lights in this morgue were dead.

Across the floor from me was a dormant broadcast engine of enormous proportions. Each of the brass cylinders stood thirty feet high. They were shaped like bullets but were the size of missiles.

"What happened in here?" I asked.

"Colonel, back here," Illych called.

He headed toward the back of the engine room. As I followed, I saw an odd flickering glow that shone on the walls and furniture. I almost missed the subtle light changes surveying the room through my night-for-day lens. Switching to my standard, tactical lens, I saw the blue-white glow of an electrical arc. It looked as if someone might have been using a spot welder around the corner.

"What do you think of this?" Illych asked me. "How do you think it survived when everything else got blown up?"

Peering slowly around the corner, my pistol drawn, I saw a second broadcast engine. It did not have the thirty-foot-high brass cylinders of the battleship's main broadcast engine. It was smaller and tucked away at the back of the ship. The eighteen cylinders in this engine were about eight feet tall and connected together by a web of cables as thick as my arms. Across the top of the cylinders, jagged lines of electricity danced from joint to joint.

"That's not possible," I said. It did not make sense that something as delicate and power-consuming as a broadcast engine could be up and running when every other system had failed. Also, when it came to broadcast equipment, I had never heard of any ship carrying spares.

I started toward the engine for a closer look, but Illych pulled me back. "I wouldn't do that," he said. "There may be a shield around it."

I inched slightly closer but did not see the telltale glimmer of an electrical field. Had I had more time, I might have fired a particle beam at the floor beside the engine, but I did not get that chance.

"Colonel, they're coming!" the pilot sounded frantic.

"Mogats?" I asked.

"Who the speck cares," the pilot said. "I've got to get out of here!"

"Where are they?" I asked.

"They just broadcasted in. I picked up the anomaly."

"I'm going to need a couple of minutes..."

The pilot interrupted me. "I don't have minutes! I don't have seconds!"

"Everybody back to the sled!" I called over an open frequency so that all of the SEALs would hear me. I pushed off against a railing and bounded back toward the companionway.

"Colonel, what is it?" Illych asked, sounding impossibly calm.

"Mogats," I said. I had already flown half the distance back to the stairs.

"In the ship?" Illych asked. These Special Operations clones were small, but they had muscles like steel cables. He kicked off a wall hard enough to catch up to me.

"Outside," I said. "The pilot picked them up on radar."

"What's happening out there?" I asked the pilot.

"Two ships coming in quick," the pilot said. "I can't wait for you. I need…"

"You can't outrun them," I said. "Find someplace to hide and play dead."

"I've got to get out of here," he screamed.

"You can't…" But the connection was already broken.

I tried hailing the explorer twice more, but knew I would not get through.

"Shit," I said.

"Sir?" Illych asked.

"We just lost our specking ride," I said.

On our way to the engine room, Illych and I passed a room with a broad window looking out into space. I headed toward the room and told Illych to tell his SEALs to join us. There was no reason to head for the space sled anymore; our explorer was gone.

"Regroup on my mark," Illych told his men over an open band. His men responded without comment.

I went to the glass wall and stared out, not knowing what I hoped to find. In the back of my mind, I guess I expected to see the smoldering wreckage of the explorer. It was nowhere to be found, of course. In the seconds that I spoke with the pilot, he might have flown ten thousand miles.

"Do you see anything out there, sir?" Illych asked.

I did. Just for a moment I saw a black shadow that got between our ship and the stars. It moved quickly, and I lost track of it, but it was out there. I imagined that ship, big and unstoppable, knocking the carcasses of dead fighters out of the way with its shields.

"How the speck can they know that we're here?" I asked.

I voiced the question out loud, but it was mostly directed at me. The signal from the security sensors should not have traveled faster than the speed of light. Could it even have traveled 100 million miles in the few moments we had been on board the ship? Yet the Mogat ships had broadcast in. Broadcasted in! That meant that they had come from a long way away. They would have had to have been close to receive the signal, but they should not have needed to broadcast in if they were close enough to receive it. How far could they go and still hear their burglar alarm?

My mind flashed on the working broadcast engine we'd seen in the engineering section. "There is no way that broadcast engine could have survived. The room is a disaster," I said out loud, even though I was only thinking to myself.

The other SEALs entered the room.

"The Mogats shot down our ride," I said in frustration. "They shot down our specking ride." I was swearing more than usual, possibly because the damned Boyd clones were so specking calm about the whole thing.

Illych—I knew it was him because my visor displayed his virtual dog tag—walked past me. "We've got company," he said, staring out the viewport.

I turned and looked. Two Mogat transports floated in our direction, their naked steel hulls appearing flat gray in the darkness. I had a particle-beam pistol. We all had particle-beam pistols. That was the general-issue weapon for combat in nonatmosphere situations.

Each of the approaching transports could carry a complement of a hundred Mogat commandos. The way I saw it, we had two options. Our best bet was to hide. Using those stealth kits, we could move undetected by their sensors. The only other option was to attack the Mogats as they stepped off their transports. It would be seven of us against two hundred of them. That gave them the house odds, as Admiral Brocius would have put it.

The SEALs came up with a better option.

"I always heard that you Liberator clones were lucky," a SEAL named Simmons said.

"What do you mean?" I asked.

"Listen to this," he patched me into the frequency he was listening to over the interLink. *Okay, so we break up into eight groups. The sensors only picked them up for a second. They were in the bridge but that...*

"You tapped the Mogats' communications?" I asked.

"All of their equipment is stuff they stole from us," Simmons said. "I just did a frequency scan and there they were."

16

You cannot change clothes in unpressurized space. If you do, the pressure of your body will cause you to explode. You will end up like the sailors in the engine room, lying dead beneath the frozen splashes of their blood.

As a military clone and a Marine, I only knew one way to engage the enemy—head-on. I knew how to make an enemy die in space. I did not think in terms of vanishing into his ranks. My objective might require me to snipe a guard or infiltrate a building; but in the end, my area of expertise was combat. The SEALs thought in terms of special operations.

Illych had one of his SEALs give me his stealth kit. He teamed that man up with another SEAL and sent them out. He sent his other three SEALs out on their own. They scattered around the ship. The two-man team headed for the bow. One of the lone SEALs returned to the engine room. Another went to the top deck.

The last man went midship. When the time came, they would lead the Mogats on a wild-goose chase. They would do it one at a time, jamming and unjamming the security sensors in such a way that there only appeared to be one intruder on the ship. I had no doubt about the SEALs' ability to pull off this trick.

Using Illych's stealth kit to neutralize the motion sensors, he and I stole to a corridor that reached all the way across the ship. The corridor ran along the lowest deck. When the laser had hit the belly of this battleship, it carved out huge sections of the floor and walls.

I listened to the Mogats blunder through their maneuvers as we went. One of their teams had a sergeant barking out orders which, from the sound of things, no one understood. The more he screamed, the more confused his men became. Soon he could barely breathe because he had screamed all of the oxygen out of his lungs. I imagined that the inside of his visor was covered in spit. I enjoyed listening to the man.

The Mogats' other teams operated more efficiently.

The old battleship was two-thirds of a mile wide and just under a half a mile long from bow to stern. We did not tire flying through the corridor; hell, our feet never even touched the deck. At midship, we reached a fifty-foot stretch of corridor below which the entire hull had been sheared away during the battle. All that was left of it was the right-hand wall and ceiling—everything else was wreckage and stars. Seen through the night-for-day lens in my visor, space looked flat and black with a swirl of blue-white specks.

You cannot swim in space. Launch in the wrong direction in open space, and there is no course correction without some sort of rocket. When we reached the break in the corridor, we stopped. The hall ahead of us had a slight bend to it. If I launched ahead and missed the curve, I would fly into space without a prayer of turning myself around. I would fly in a straight line at a constant speed until I ran into a planet or a black hole, or maybe a meteor shower.

I locked the fingers of my right hand unnecessarily tight around the grip of my pistol. I let the fingers of my left hand drag along the edge of the wall to feel around for emergency handholds should I need one. Then I pushed off the wall and over through the missing section of corridor. I drifted slowly, focusing my attention on the floor ahead.

Illych followed.

I heard: *Delta Team, check the lower-deck main corridor.*

Got it.

That placed one of the Mogat teams on the same deck as Illych and I, probably no less than two walls away. If they came into our hall before we reached the other side of the gap, we would have no place to hide and little chance of defending ourselves.

It didn't happen that way. The Mogats preferred the safety of corridors with all four walls intact. From listening to their communications, I could tell that the Mogat commandos did not believe anyone had trespassed onto the ship. They thought the alarm was proof of a malfunctioning sensor.

You see anything? a Mogat commander asked one of his group leaders.

Nothing.

All clear here, another volunteered.

I'm thinking malfunction, Captain.

We caught an enemy ship prowling around outside, the captain pointed out.

Maybe he bumped the wreck. Would that set it off?

Don't be stupid, the captain said. *He would have been killed if he crashed into a battleship.*

Maybe he barely bumped it.

Shut up, Anson, the captain said. *You think you can shake a battleship by nudging it with a little ship like that?*

I changed frequencies to speak to Illych. "We'd better show them some bait before they lose interest."

Illych radioed the order.

Captain, I've got 'em! I've got 'em, some idiot Mogat radioed a moment later.

Illych led the way as we continued across the ship. The camouflage device in his helmet turned his armor the same pale gray color as the walls. Through the night-for-day lens in my visor, both he and the walls looked nearly white. Because of the poor depth perception the lens gave me, he was all but invisible.

"Do you have any idea how much of the ship is wired for motion?" I asked.

"Every inch of it from what I can tell," Illych said.

"Good thing your boy looked for sensor fields," I said.

Illych did not respond. I suppose that kind of precaution came as second nature when you worked in SpecOps.

Near the front of the ship, we crossed a major corridor that ran from one wing of the ship to the other. This hall was so wide you could drive two tanks side by side across it. Illych traveled along the ceiling. I hung low, an inch above the floor. We saw no signs of damage. Here the ship looked dormant, not derelict. I saw no debris, though I did see dead sailors when I peered into the hatches.

"How did they get into the launch bay?" I asked. "There shouldn't be any power in the doors."

"Maybe the atmospheric locks were open," Illych suggested.

"Illych," I said, "your ship is under attack, and you're going to send out unarmed transports?"

"Maybe the locks opened when the battleship blew up," Illych suggested.

"Yeah, sure, and all Mogat ships carry pint-sized broadcast engines along as a spare." I tried to sound sarcastic, but I had trouble whispering in a sardonic tone. "When the Mogats sacrificed this ship, they had something up their sleeves."

We moved ahead. I continued to listen to the Mogats, leaving Illych to figure out our course.

"Stop," I hissed, just in time.

We lost them again, one of the Mogats said. *No, wait, there they are. They're near the engine room.*

These guys are fast.

Get down there, the captain bellowed. *Don't let them anywhere near that broadcast engine.*

"You hear that," Illych radioed over an open frequency for the rest of us to hear. "Stay away from the engine room. Lead them back to midship."

Up ahead, a squad of soldiers crossed the hall. They had not adjusted to the lack of gravity and tried to move along the floor as if in a ship with gravity and an atmosphere. We slid gracefully above the deck; they waddled and bounced with every step.

There were eight men, all carrying lasers in one hand and searchlights in the other. Had they shined their lights in our direction, they could easily have spotted us; but not one of them even paused to make certain the path was clear before crossing. They simply cut across the hall and continued walking in their square formation without looking back. Had I wanted to, I could have ambushed the lot of them just for sport.

"Pathetic," Illych said. "Didn't anyone ever teach them to look both ways before crossing? We should have picked them off, just on principle. What do these Mogats teach their boys in basic, knitting?"

He turned toward me. "I cannot believe they are winning this war!"

Illych yelled this so loud that I jumped and half expected the Mogats to hear him. The Mogats would not hear him, I reminded myself, not wearing combat helmets in nonatmospheric conditions. I had been whispering, but I wore combat armor so often that I sometimes forgot it was on. He seldom worked in his armor.

"Are you always this chatty on stealth missions?" I asked.

"Is that a rhetorical question, sir?" Illych asked. Now that the action had begun, I sensed a mildly giddy tone in his voice and wondered if the Special Operations clones had some form of combat reflex.

Illych and I remained perfectly still as we waited to make sure that the Mogats did not have a fire team bringing up the rear. They did not, so we turned down the hall and headed in the direction from which they had come.

This part of the ship had significant internal damage. We passed shattered bulkheads and an occasional corpse. Thanks to their torches, we spotted the next squad of Mogats the moment they entered the area. They passed without looking as we dodged into the first open hatch.

"They're like robots," I said. "They didn't even shine a light into the room."

"They know the room is empty," Illych said. "Their motion sensors aren't picking anything up, so they know that no one is down here."

"Because you're jamming the sensors," I said.

"But they don't know I'm jamming their sensors. All they know is that their alarm system says the coast is clear."

When I considered that point, that their alarm system told them the coast was clear, I realized that the Mogats had made an easy mistake. I did not like to admit it, but I might have made the same mistake, though I would have remained more alert. I filed the lesson away as we started down that hall again.

Looking down the various arteries that we passed, I spotted

distant lights as the Mogat squads and fire teams made their way through the ship.

"They're getting too close," I said to Illych.

"I'll take care of it," Illych said. He contacted the team in the bridge and had them set off some sensors. Moments later, the Mogats turned and headed toward the bow of the ship.

"It's all too easy," I said. "They're idiots."

By this time we had nearly reached the main launch bay. Crossing that last empty stretch of corridor, we peered in. Two transports sat on the launch-bay deck. Lights shone in the nearest transport's cockpit. Using a telescopic lens, I could see the shape of a pilot's head though the glass. I pointed him out to Illych.

"I see him," Illych said.

Three guards stood talking at the base of the transport. I could easily have killed them, but our plans would have failed if I had. In order for our plan to work, we needed the guards to give the all clear.

"You do know how to fly one of these birds?" I asked.

"Fly a transport? Colonel, I picked that up in basic," Illych assured me.

"This one is fifty years old," I said.

"No problem."

"But what do you do once you touch down on their ship?" I asked.

"I catch a ride to their base," Illych said.

"They may have to broadcast there. Then what? You won't be able to tell us where you are."

"This is recon," Illych said. "Never underestimate the value of having a trained saboteur in your enemy's base."

I had to admire him. The clone had nerve.

The launch bay gaped into space, as depressurized as the rest of the ship. The locks and blast doors might have been blasted open as the Outer Perseus Fleet sank this ship, but my guess was that the same person that lowered the shields opened the locks.

Why did the Mogats care about a wrecked ship? How had they known we were here? Why had they gone to all of the trouble of installing a second broadcast engine and protecting it during the attack? The same questions flashed again and again in my mind.

Those thoughts running through my head, I hid beside the door and aimed my pistol at the men guarding the nearest transport. I could have picked them off so easily. I could have hit the first two Mogats and finished the job so quickly that the third man would not have had time to notice his two buddies explode before he died as well.

But that was not the plan.

"Do you know how to use this?" Illych asked, showing me the handy little remote he had used to jam the motion sensors.

I pulled out my remote. It was the size of a deck of cards. Light emitted from one of those buttons. "As long as this light is on, the sensors are off," I said, pointing at the lit button.

"Close enough," Illych said.

"Then I'm good," I said. "Good luck, Illych."

"Thank you, sir," Illych said. He crouched in the hatch and waited until the guards looked the other way, then he entered the landing area and sprang up the side of the wall, reaching the forty-foot ceiling in mere seconds.

The rear of the nearest kettle sat wide open—an easy target. With their obsolete design, the guards' helmets offered limited peripheral vision. Their helmets were what Unified Authority Marines had worn fifty years ago. I knelt in the shadows and watched as Illych glided along the ceiling, then dropped onto the roof of the transport.

"How does it look from there?" he asked.

"Free for the taking," I said.

I stood and took a deep breath. I could feel the soothing warmth of the adrenaline and endorphins mixture filtering into my veins. I was out of practice. I should never have had a combat reflex watching somebody else in action. Now, after all that time I spent living among the farmers, the reflex started prematurely.

"My turn to play fox," I called out over the interLink, warning the SEALs to lie low. I pressed the lit button on my stealth kit, shutting off the jamming device. The sensors discovered me instantly. Inside the launch bay, all three guards drew their guns. Though they did not see me, alarms inside their helmets told them I was just outside the hatch.

They're inside the launch bay! the Mogat captain shouted.

Just outside it! a guard called back.

We got 'em!

The guards came tromping toward me, firing blind in my direction. Silver-red lasers streaked past me and seared the wall of the corridor. I pushed hard against a bulkhead and launched myself full speed down the hall. Laser fire followed me, striking walls and floors moments behind me.

Under normal circumstances, I would not have worried about three untrained idiots shooting lasers in my direction. Judging by the spread of their shots, they would not hit me unless they were aiming at somebody else. But this was different. Under normal circumstances I could fire back. This time I could only run away.

I continued just ahead of them, feeling no panic. The combat hormone flowed through me, keeping my mind keen. I pushed off walls, turning right and left down whatever small arteries looked clear. I found a ladder shaft leading between two decks and shot up to the next deck. The Mogats came ambling after me, leaving their transports completely unguarded. Once I reached the top of the ladder, I had to slow down to keep from losing them.

I turned one corner, then the next. Moving at this speed with little depth perception, I slid past several junctions too fast to change direction. Lasers struck the walls above and below me. The Mogats were closing in.

Nearing the end of a corridor, I managed to push off a wall and bounce into a long foyer. It was an ugly, abrupt change in direction that I made by kicking off one wall and slamming headfirst into another, before rolling sideways into the entryway. The maneuver sent a shock down my shoulders and back.

"Illych, report," I said.

"I'm in," Illych said.

"You have the pilot?"

"Sure."

When I peered out the hatch, I saw the Mogats ducking for cover at the other end of the corridor. One of them shone a light in my direction, pointing it above my head. It was comical. These boys were so poorly trained. The commando stuck his head way out to get a good look, then fired blindly down the hall, missing me by several yards.

"You took out the pilot?" I asked.

"Done," Illych said.

The idiot fired again. This time he was less than three feet off. For the first time, I started to worry about them spotting me.

"Have you traded clothes?" I asked. The plan was for Illych to kill the transport pilot, then change places with him. Illych would dress the pilot in his Special Operations armor and dress himself in the pilot's flight gear. He would do so in the pressurized cockpit, the only place on the entire battleship in which we could now control the environment.

"It's not a very good fit. Their pilot had a few inches on me. I'm not sure which looks worse, him crammed into my armor or me in his flight gear."

"Worry about that later," I said. The guards were back to

missing me by five or six feet, all aiming at the same blank spot on the wall.

"I'm under fire here. How soon can you get the body out?"

"It's out, sir," Illych said, as casually as if he were talking about the weather.

He'd killed the pilot, stolen his clothes, and prepared the body to use as a decoy in a minute at most. I was impressed but did not feel like saying so. "Nice of you to let me know," I said, looking for something to complain about.

"I just placed him a moment ago, sir," Illych said.

"Who gets to play fox next?" I asked.

"Ready," one of the SEALs reported.

I pressed the button on the jamming device. Now I had to stay out of sight and hope the Mogats were every bit as dumb as they acted. Somewhere below me, one of the SEALs shut off his stealth kit and entered the corridor behind the Mogats.

I've got your man, the Mogat captain radioed. *He's headed for the launch bay.*

Springing to the ceiling, where they would be slightly less likely to spot me, I watched the Mogats leave. All the Mogats knew was that I had somehow vanished from their tracking devices. They did not know how to respond. Anyone with an ounce of sense would have known that I had jammed their security system. These idiots simply crawled out from behind their cover, shrugged their shoulders, and started back to their post, apparently convinced that I had found a passage between decks.

Illych was right. These guys should not have been winning the war.

I found an open duct and crawled into the ventilation system. There I waited as Illych and his team carried out their plan. Illych, wearing space gear belonging to the recently deceased Mogat pilot, would crawl back into the cockpit of the Mogat transport.

Another SEAL would lead the Mogats to the body of the pilot and initiate a firefight. Though he had orders not to, the SEAL would probably kill a few of the Mogats for the fun of it.

Once the firefight got hot enough, our boy would offer them their pilot dressed in SEAL armor as a target. He would hold the dead pilot up for them to shoot. If they did not blast the decoy in the head, our SEAL would do it himself. All the proprietary technology in SEAL armor was located in the helmet. The SEALs would not allow a working helmet to fall into enemy hands.

As soon as the Mogats managed to kill their already-dead pilot, our SEAL would push the corpse out into the open and slip away unnoticed by all.

These tactics would not have worked had we been fighting a veteran army, but this was the Mogats. With their security sensors jammed, the Mogats would happily assume they had killed the lone intruder on their ship. Even if they continued looking for us, we could listen in on their conversations and avoid them. Sooner or later they would decide they had won the battle and leave.

Once the Mogats left, the only thing I would have to deal with was that I was stranded on a dead battleship in a deep-space graveyard with no way of contacting Earth.

In the same situation, Illych would have said, "No problem."

17

"Well, they're gone," I said.

We stood on the bridge of the derelict battleship watching the Mogat transports rendezvous with their battleship. Two destroyers loomed in the background like guardian angels. Hundreds of twisted wrecks floated about the scene.

"Do you think they'll be back, Colonel?" one of the SEALs asked.

"Sooner or later. We should be long gone by then," I said.

"Do you think Illych will be okay?" the SEAL asked.

"You know him better than I do, but I think he can take care of himself." I believed that. Master Chief Petty Officer Emerson Illych had proven himself in my book. Now that he was on one of the Mogat battleships, he would lose himself among the crew. What could he do once he reached their base? He seemed resourceful. All of these Boyd clones seemed resourceful.

"What now, sir?" one of the SEALs asked.

I told them about the broadcast engine and sent them out to find any other systems that might be online. I did not think they would find anything, but their helmets would record everything they saw. They might stumble across something without knowing it.

In the meantime, I remained on the bridge. I removed data chips from the navigation computer and searched for maps, charts, and anything else that looked valuable. I found nothing. The bridge had been stripped clean. No surprise.

The strange thing was, as long as the Mogats did not return, we could have lived on that ship for days. There was plenty of food in the galley, though I suppose we would have needed a pressurized and oxygenated chamber in which to eat it. Since our suits had rebreathers that recycled our oxygen, breathing was the least of our concerns. Things might get uncomfortable if anyone needed to take a shit; but I figured these boys could hold it together as long as they had to.

Ten hours passed before the *Kamehameha* sent a ship out to search for us. Wheels turned slowly in the Unified Authority Navy.

Upon returning to the barracks in Washington, DC, I went to my room and took a long, hot shower. I shaved. I tint-shaded the windows of my quarters, making the room as dark as night, stripped down to my underwear, and climbed into bed. I was tired, but sleep did not come easily. Those same questions echoed again and again in my brain. Why were the Mogats watching a derelict ship? What secrets did it hold? How far away were they when we entered, and how had they heard the alarms? What about that second broadcast engine? Nothing made sense.

Less than an hour after I climbed on my rack, I received a call on the communications console. A car had come to take me to meet Admiral Brocius at Navy headquarters. Considering where

I had been and what I had found, I expected a lengthy debriefing.

"So where is your friend hiding?" an angry voice demanded as I climbed into the car. It was that same guy from Naval Intelligence, but no longer dressed disguised as a chauffeur. He wore the dress uniform of a lieutenant commander—two and a half stripes on his shoulder boards and a star.

"Oh, it's you," I said as the car pulled away. "Couldn't find Freeman?"

"I'm not joking around, Harris," he snapped.

"Don't you owe me a hundred bucks?" I asked.

"I'm going to give you one last chance to tell us where he is, Harris. After that, I'm hauling you in for a court-martial."

"Does that mean I've been officially recalled to service?" I asked. Looking through the car window, I watched monuments and marble buildings shoot by as we weaved our way through traffic. We had already entered downtown DC.

"You're not on active duty yet," the driver said.

"Then you can't court-martial me," I said.

"Get specked," the driver said.

"And you owe me a hundred dollars."

"Why the speck would I give you anything, Harris? You're a specking deserter."

"Did Brocius send you, or are you just here for conversation?" I asked.

The driver did not speak again for several minutes. By the time he did, we were entering the main gate at HQ. This time, sounding more contrite, he said, "Look, Harris, if you know where Freeman is hiding, you might as well tell us. It's only a matter of time until we find him. Help me out here, and maybe you'll save us all some trouble."

"Do you have my money?" I asked.

Still twisted around so he could look at me, the guy stretched out his right leg and dug his wallet out of his pocket. He opened it and fished through a wad of money. "Here," he said, sneering as I took the bills from him.

"Thanks," I said, glad to have some money in my pocket for the first time in months. "Let me know if you want to go double or nothing."

"So?" the driver asked.

I looked at him, purposely donning a confused expression.

"Where is Freeman?"

"How should I know?" I asked.

"I hear you had quite an adventure," Brocius said, as an aide let me into his office. A file with my name across the top sat on his desk. He picked it up. Flipping between the pages he said, "Entered enemy-held territory without clearance... boarded an enemy ship..."

"A wreck," I pointed out. "It was the battleship that we sank. As I understand the aeronautical law, that made it common property."

Brocius looked up from his report as I spoke, then looked back down giving no sign that he heard me. "Unauthorized reconnaissance operation... engaged the enemy... Your unauthorized side trip cost us a valuable self-broadcasting ship. It cost your pilot his life.

"Oh, here's my favorite. You impersonated an officer. You led a team of SEALs to believe that you were a colonel in the U.A. Marine Corps."

"You said you were going to recall me," I pointed out.

"Not to the rank of colonel." Brocius almost yelled this.

"I never told anyone I was a colonel."

"You went in a colonel's uniform!" Now he was yelling.

"I didn't have any choice. That was the only uniform I had," I said. "Hell, except for the clothes I arrived in, those were the only clothes I had.

"Admiral, if you wanted me to go to the *Kamehameha* dressed like a civilian, you should have said something." He had me dead to rights, but I had to say something.

"So you misled six highly trained Navy SEALs into believing they were on an authorized mission with a colonel in the Marine Corps. One of those men is still missing in action," Brocius said, lowering his voice.

He closed the report and stared at me, his face unreadable. "Admiral Brallier is calling for your head." I did not know the name, but I assumed he was the commander of the Outer Scutum-Crux Fleet.

"Sorry, sir," I said. But I wasn't sorry. That was my first taste of combat in months. I had done what I was made to do, engage the enemy. I had felt the hormone in my blood, and it felt good. Even as I stood and apologized, I already had started plans for my next big excursion.

"Did you really send one of those SEALs back with the Mogats?"

"Yes, sir, assuming they didn't catch him."

Brocius shook his head. "Damn it, Harris, I don't know whether to shake your hand or shoot you."

"Semper fi," I said.

"You're not officially back in the Corps," Brocius said. "As far as the Marines are concerned, you are still absent without leave or killed in action. Either one will land you in the brig."

"I suppose," I said. More than ever, I wished I was back on active duty.

"Do yourself a favor. Help us catch your friend, Freeman, and maybe I can get HQ to overlook your little adventure.

"Any idea where we can find him?" Brocius asked.

"Can't say," I said.

"Can't say or won't say, Harris?" Brocius asked. When I did not answer, he mumbled, "I suspected as much."

"When are you contacting Yamashiro?" he asked.

"Not for a few more days," I said.

"How do you plan on doing it?"

I did not answer. Brocius must have known I would not tell him.

"Have your labs downloaded the video record from our helmets?" I asked.

"They are working on it at this moment, Harris. What exactly will they find?"

I told the admiral everything. He listened quietly from the start. When I got to the broadcast engine, he pulled out a pad and began to scribble notes. "A working broadcast engine," he grunted. "Sounds as if Warren Atkins has found some new technology to stack the cards in their favor." Warren, Morgan Atkins's son, presumably ran all Mogat operations.

"When Yamashiro comes, we'll want to show those records to his engineers," I said. "Maybe they can figure it all out." I did not tell Brocius what I really thought. I doubted that the Mogats had come up with any of this on their own. Someone with a good grasp of strategy and technology had helped them.

Here is how I contacted Yoshi Yamashiro. On the appointed night, I went to Dulles Spaceport, boarded the transport, and sent out a kind of signal known as a virtual beacon. All very-low-tech mundane stuff. Sending a virtual beacon was the military equivalent of passing notes in school.

The beacon contained three words: "red light, go."

Let the clowns in Intelligence try to decipher the message. In this case, the medium was the message. Yamashiro and I agreed that it would not matter what message the beacon carried. What mattered was that I sent out the beacon at all. When the communications officer on the *Sakura* located a beacon on that frequency, no matter what it said, he would tell Yamashiro to send an envoy to Washington, DC.

18

I did not hear about Yamashiro landing in Washington, DC, until four days after he arrived. Gordon Hughes, "Wild Bill" Grace, and an honor guard met his transport as it landed. What an entrance for a man who until recently was considered an enemy of the republic. Soldiers with flags, an honor guard with guns, and the two most powerful men in the galaxy all waited for Yamashiro at the bottom of the ramp as he stepped out of the transport.

A few months earlier those same soldiers and weapons would have stood in a firing squad had Yamashiro shown his face. Apparently returning to the scene of the crime with four self-broadcasting battleships covered up a multitude of sins in the political game of "What have you done for me lately?"

That was a ceremony to which I received no invitation. Lowly sergeants did not, as a rule, attend diplomatic functions. Whether

Brocius or somebody else made the decision, I was recalled to active service as a master gunnery sergeant. That meant that my men would likely call me "Master Guns." I hated that nickname. A few smart-asses might call me "Master Blaster."

Fortunes of war.

When I asked Admiral Brocius about the rank, he gazed at me and asked in a voice drenched with boredom, "Not high enough for you?" He spoke with the sort of menacing civility that officers often pull when they wish to put enlisted men in their place. Every admiral I had ever met could use that voice; I suppose they learned it at the academy.

"Last time I checked, I was a colonel. That's one hell of a demotion," I said.

"Welcome back," Brocius said with a grin that dared me to challenge him. Then, as a consolation, he said, "Look, Harris, there are no other clone officers in the..."

"What about the Little Man Seven?" I asked. I did not normally interrupt admirals in midsentence, but six other clones who survived the battle on Little Man had been bootstrapped. I cared about them. They came from my platoon.

"Yes, I thought you might ask that, so I hedged my bets. Dealer's odds, right, Harris?" Brocius pulled a sheet of paper from his drawer and scanned it.

"Four of your pals died when the Mogat Fleet attacked Earth. Three of them were on the *Doctrinaire.* One was on a frigate called the *McDermott.*

"One of your pals died during routine exercises in the Norma Arm.

"Now here's the interesting one. Lieutenant Vincent Lee was assigned to the *Grant.* The Scutum-Crux Fleet sent that carrier to investigate reports of squatters on Little Man. The *Grant* set out just before the Mogats downed the Broadcast Network. Fleet

Command originally presumed that the ship was trapped in space, but we have never been able to locate her.

"No one knows what became of the *Grant.*"

I knew what became of Vince Lee and the *Grant,* but I knew better than to offer that information.

"The truth be told, Harris, it doesn't matter what rank we give you. Every officer around you is going to know that you are the one calling the shots when it comes to you and your platoon.

"What I need is for you to keep doing what you have been doing. You got a man into Mogat space. Now I want you to find some way for us to get a whole platoon there. You got me, Harris? I want to turn this whole war around so that the chips start to fall in our favor."

In truth, I didn't mind being bucked down to sergeant. I actually felt more comfortable around enlisted men than officers. As a boy growing up in U.A. Orphanage #553, my highest aspiration in life had been to make sergeant.

I offered token resistance, then accepted my new life among the conscripts. I remained on the Navy base outside Washington, DC, until further orders arrived, my career entering a two-week period of almost-cryogenic stasis. I had no duties and no assignments.

I spent a lot of time lying around and watching current events on my mediaLink shades. Time wasted. Without the Broadcast Network, the only galactic information the analysts could find came stripped down, prepackaged, and fully spun from the government. The general population had no idea about the attack on the Outer Perseus Fleet. The only events the public heard about were ones that occurred on Earth.

Most political news came in the form of feel-good stories about the Unified Authority restoring its natural glory. "Troop readiness is at an all-time high," "Wild Bill" Grace said in a State of the Republic address. Members of the Linear Committee met with key senators to discuss opening several new orphanages. Construction could start any day, but it never did. A new shipyard was under construction orbiting Earth. The global stock exchange rebounded nicely after a lackluster week. The Seattle Mariners, the oldest and winningest sports organization in the galaxy, looked like a shoo-in to win its fifth straight Galactic Series. There was no news from space and no hint that Washington, DC, was in contact with the fleets of its former enemies.

I switched off the mediaLink shades that had come with my room and pulled out a disposable pair I'd purchased with my hundred-dollar winnings. The disposables came with a temporary account that I set up under the name Arlind Marsten—an alias I used during my two years away from the Marines. This would not stop Naval Intelligence or any other organization from tapping into my calls, but it might lull them into thinking I was trying to get around them. Using an optical command, I punched in the code that I wanted to call.

"Hello?" the voice asked cautiously. It was the voice of a little girl.

"How is life on the lam?" I asked.

"Who is this?" the girl asked.

The voice was young and innocent, but the inflections were incongruent. They made her sound indifferent.

"Cut the shit," I said. Then I added, "All of the Intelligence agencies have computerized receivers that see right through voice masking."

"Did they recall you yet?" Freeman asked. He continued to use the voice mask, making him sound like an eight-year-old girl. Try as I might, I could not envision the seven-foot hulking giant on the other end of that voice.

"Yeah. I'm a sergeant. How's that for a demotion? They haven't told me where I'm going to be stationed."

Freeman did not respond. A moment later, he asked, "Has Yamashiro shown up yet?"

"Yeah, he arrived a couple of days ago. I only heard about it this afternoon. I don't know how the negotiations are going. I wasn't invited."

"You expected an invitation?" the little girl's voice asked.

"Did you hear about the Outer Perseus Fleet?" I asked. Freeman said no, so I told him what Brocius had told me, then followed by telling him about my visit to the Mogat ship. I told him every last high-security detail, including the part about the working broadcast engine.

Freeman listened carefully, then changed the subject. "The Mogats have a base near Washington. It's an old brownstone mansion in Chevy Chase."

"What kind of a base?" I asked.

"I can't tell," Freeman said, as the technology in his microphone turned his low, rumbling voice into a high burbly voice. "I haven't figured out how to get inside it."

"Do you think the good guys know about it?" I asked.

"No. I set up a surveillance site in the woods across the street. The Feds never go by."

"They could be watching by satellite," I said.

"Yeah," Freeman said, which meant he did not take the idea seriously.

I almost called Freeman by name but stopped myself for the sake of those listening. That would have come across as too cavalier. Whether or not the Intelligence boys had already tapped into this mediaLink account, they had almost certainly bugged my room. This call was as much about feeding information to Navy Intelligence as it was about trading information with Freeman.

The difference was, Freeman knew what we were up to.

"Remember the limo driver who brought us to the base?" I asked.

"The Navy spook in the civilian suit?" Freeman asked.

"That's the one. He's looking for you, and he's pressuring me. Now that I'm back on active duty..."

"Don't sweat it," Freeman said. "I'll handle the situation." That comment would have sounded a lot more menacing had it not been for Freeman's little-girl voice.

The next morning, a new operative came dressed as a chauffeur to drive me into town. My old driver, he said, was taking personal leave.

Message delivered.

19

"Harris, you have a most unstable career. When you came to Ezer Kri, you were a corporal. In the movie they portrayed you as a lieutenant. When we found you in space, you were a colonel. Now you are a sergeant," Yoshi Yamashiro said, with an uncharacteristic smile. He had yet to light up a cigarette, so he had already bucked tradition, but he wore his usual dark suit and red necktie. He shook his head sadly as he repeated, "A most unstable career."

I smiled, and said, "When I first met you, you were the governor of Ezer Kri, a loyal colony of the Unified Authority. The next time I saw you, you had allied with the Atkins Believers. Now you are the governor of an independent planet hoping to sign a treaty with the Unified Authority." I shook my head. "You have a very checkered career."

Yamashiro smiled and laughed softly. His teeth looked very white against the teak color of his skin.

We met in a conference room with a large screen. Admiral Brocius and I sat on one side of the table. Yoshi Yamashiro sat with an officer and two civilians on the other. The civilians belonged to the Shin Nippon Corps of Engineers. The officer was Captain Hideo Takahashi, Yamashiro's son-in-law, aide, and full-time shadow.

From what I could tell, the Shin Nippon military only had one branch, a Navy. It could have a second, possibly larger, branch if it militarized its corps of engineers.

The current meeting did not go off without the usual Shin Nippon touches. Yamashiro sat directly at the table with his entourage spread in a protective fan behind him. Yamashiro was still the shogun. Engineers or officers, the men behind him were still his samurai.

"Did you find anything of value in the computer parts Harris brought back from that ship?" Brocius asked. I could tell that he already knew the answer.

"Sadly, the data storage unit was empty," Yamashiro said.

"Too bad," Brocius said.

"I find it strange that the storage was empty and not destroyed," Yamashiro said.

"What do you mean?" Brocius asked.

"How did a ship with an unused navigation computer find its way out of their docks?" Yamashiro asked.

"Who says it was unused?" Brocius asked.

"Then perhaps they erased the data from the unit during battle," Yamashiro said. "Maybe that is why the ship was destroyed, the crew was so busy erasing information from the computer that they forgot to defend the ship."

"Don't be ridiculous," Brocius said.

"Ah, so I see. Maybe the crew had time to purge their navigation computer while a massive laser cut through their bow," Yamashiro suggested.

"No one worries about computer maintenance during battle," Brocius said.

"I agree," Yamashiro said.

Brocius thought about this but said nothing. He was a career officer; politicians and diplomats infuriated him. He wanted to finish the meeting and leave as soon as he could. "As I understand it, you wanted to question Sergeant Harris about the video record?"

"My engineers have some questions," Yamashiro said with a gesture somewhere between a nod of the head and a bow. He looked over and spoke quietly to one of the engineers in Japanese. The man took a remote from the table. He sat down, pressed a few buttons, and the lights went out.

On a wall screen, our approach to the derelict battleship played out in slow motion. Judging by the angle, this segment had to have come from my helmet. I was in the front of the sled and was ten inches taller than everyone else. The record had been edited so that it never showed the Boyd clones.

"Sergeant, were you able to see this damage up close?" the engineer asked. "You flew your vehicle through this breach in the hull?"

"Sure," I said. "That should be in the record. We entered the ship through that breach."

"Ah." He grunted the word, affecting great surprise. "That was not in the record we received."

Brocius fidgeted. "We edited the record slightly for security purposes."

"We flew our craft through that breach. It was a ten-man sled... a very small craft."

"But the hole was big enough for you to fly through?" the engineer asked.

Yamashiro's engineers traded a few excited words. "I know you are not an engineer," Yamashiro's second engineer prefaced, "but could you tell if this damage was made by a single shot?"

"One swipe," I said with absolute surety.

The feed on the screen froze displaying a straight-in view of the gash. I could see up three decks. I stood up and walked to the screen. The scene it displayed was dark except for the spotlights that the Special Operations clones used. "Can you make the picture brighter?" I asked.

Using gamma controls, the engineer bleached the picture on the screen. I studied the screen and realized that the unnatural lighting made details even harder to find. "Oh yes, this was a single shot," I said.

"Do you want to know what I really think?" I asked. "I think that someone on the bridge lowered the shields."

Admiral Brocius laughed. "Someone lowered the shields in a battle situation? That's absurd."

"Permission to speak freely, sir?" I asked.

"Go ahead, Sergeant," Brocius said. His reference to my rank was meant to remind me of the limitations to my latitude.

"I think they meant to leave that battleship behind," I said.

"You think they purposely sacrificed a battleship? Why would they do something like that?" Brocius asked.

"I must agree with Harris's appraisal," Yamashiro said. "When lasers hit ships with shields, they create small areas of damage as the shields fail. This ship should have several scorched areas along its hull from attacks penetrating its shields. Instead, there is this one large hole."

"The *Doctrinaire* had lasers that would hit one side of a ship and shoot right out the other, shields or no shields," Brocius argued.

"Maybe that was a particle-beam weapon prepared especially for the *Doctrinaire,*" Yamashiro said. When you made a mistake, Yamashiro never came right out and told you you were wrong. Instead, he would say, "Maybe this..." then give the correct information without challenging the speaker.

In this case, he could well have told Brocius that he was making an ass of himself. The *Doctrinaire* was an ubership that the Navy had hoped would win the war. It had one-of-a-kind shields and weapons designed to sink entire fleets.

"Is your navy testing ships with the same experimental particle-beam weapons as the *Doctrinaire* in the Perseus Arm?" Yamashiro asked.

The room went silent. "Not likely," Brocius admitted, clearly glad to back away from the discussion.

"This damage was done by a laser," one of the engineers said. "As you can see along the edges of the gash, the armored plating has melted from heat."

Brocius focused on the screen and did not speak. I could tell that he was a man who hated to be proven wrong; it must have felt too much like losing.

One of the engineers asked Yamashiro a question in Japanese. Once Yamashiro nodded approval, the man walked over to the screen. He turned to Admiral Brocius. "Admiral, the nature of the particle beam is that it strikes a fixed target and disrupts it. Maybe it is more like a shotgun than a knife.

"This breach is long and relatively straight. The laser that did this cut through the hull like a knife."

"I am quite aware of the differences between a laser beam and a particle beam," Brocius said. "You still haven't answered the bigger question. Why would the Mogats scuttle a perfectly good battleship?"

Brocius paused for a moment to think. Revelation showed in his expression when he spoke again. "Better than good. You're telling me that the only reason we managed to sink it was that they dropped their shields, right? That would mean that we don't have any weapons that can get through their shields."

"I saw the topside of that ship," I said. "It was unmarked. Either that ship spent the entire battle floating over Porter's head, or its shields blocked everything Porter fired."

After this, the room went silent again. Finally, Brocius broke the silence with an officious question. "Is there anything else?"

"Yes," said one of the engineers. "From what we can tell of the record, there were two broadcast engines on that battleship. There was a small engine still working. Is that correct?"

"That is what I saw," I said.

"Ah, very curious," the engineer said.

"Maybe the large one broke down a long time ago," Brocius said. "Maybe that ship had always operated with a spare."

"Maybe so," Yamashiro agreed. He sat nodding, a solemn expression on his face. "We need more information. My engineers have told me that judging by its size, this smaller engine would not be able to generate enough of a field to broadcast a full-sized battleship."

"Interesting theory. Is there anything else?" Brocius asked. When no one said anything, he left the room.

Several questions hung in the air.

"If we can't wear down their shields, our ships won't stand a chance," I said quietly. "Did they have anything like this when you were on their side?"

Now that Brocius had left the room, Yamashiro finally produced a pack of cigarettes. He lit one. I could tell he had wanted that smoke all meeting long. "Harris, we never saw the Mogats produce any sort of military technology. They are a population of converts.

"From what we saw, they lacked the resources to manufacture this smaller broadcast engine. In my experience, there are few engineers or soldiers among them."

"They do have Amos Crowley," I said. Crowley was a highly

decorated general who had defected to the Atkins Believers.

"Yes, but maybe General Crowley is involved in land strategies more than naval." In non-Yamashiro terms, this translated to, *He's with the Army, asshole.* Yamashiro took a deep drag and held it in his lungs. A fine curl of smoke escaped his lips.

"So where did the Mogats get the shields?" I asked. "Why couldn't we hurt their ships?"

"In my opinion, they must have a new ally," Yamashiro said.

"A renegade from the Confederate Arms?" I asked. "Maybe they have an ally in the Perseus Arm."

"Maybe not a Confederate planet," Yamashiro said. "If any of the Confederate planets had such technology, we would have used it when we attacked Earth."

"Whoever it is, they have to be in the Perseus Arm. The Mogats had to have had their fleet somewhere nearby to know we had boarded their ship," I said.

"Maybe not," Yamashiro said.

"Maybe not?" I asked.

"My engineers and I have spent a great deal of time discussing possible uses for this second broadcast engine. We all agree that the Mogats protected that engine even as they sacrificed their ship."

"What did you come up with?" I asked.

"This is just a theory," Yamashiro said. "Some of my men believe that they are using that ship as a broadcast station. If they place enough stations around the galaxy, they can create a network," Yamashiro said.

I thought about that. "But they don't need a broadcast network. They have a self-broadcasting fleet." After a moment's more consideration, I said, "You said that engine was too small to send a big ship."

"Perhaps they do not want the network for transportation. Maybe they will use their network for communications. The engine you saw was running continuously, just like the engines in a network. It could send and receive signals anywhere in the galaxy."

"The Mogats," I said, shaking my head. "Who can understand those lousy speckers?"

20

EARTHDATE: NOVEMBER 9, A.D. 2512
LOCATION: OPEN SPACE
GALACTIC POSITION: CENTRAL CYGNUS ARM

"Is that a Bible?" Colonel Grayson's face was full of mirth as he asked this. He looked about ready to burst into uncontrollable laughter.

"Yes, sir, it is," I said. I had just stowed my two rucksacks in the locker and started back to my seat.

"You afraid of broadcasting, son?" the colonel asked.

I knew a bit about Grayson. He was a recent promotion. Until this year, he'd commanded a boot camp. When the Mogats destroyed the orphanages, the Unified Authority Marine Corps ran out of recruits, and the boot camps closed. Men like Grayson, who'd spent their careers bullying clones, had to move to the field.

Grayson was an older man, probably in his late forties. Some of the stubble along the freshly shaved sides of his head had turned white.

"Do you always travel with a Bible?" he asked.

"No, sir," I said. "I just brought..."

"The way I always heard it, you clones don't believe in God. That right, son? You're that Liberator clone. You're the clone that knows he's a clone."

I knew what was happening. This was my comeuppance. Grayson probably knew my background better than I knew his. Grayson knew that I had once held the rank of colonel, and he wanted to make sure I knew my place. I was no longer an officer, and I had never been a natural-born. Boot-camp officers. You can take them out of the camps but you can't take the camps out of them. *So what if you were once a colonel,* Grayson was telling me. *I still have clusters on my shoulder boards.*

"I can't speak for all Liberators..."

"Sure you can, boy. You're all that's left of them." There was a gleam in the colonel's brown eyes. He enjoyed this shit, but he would not take it much further. On some level he had to know that I had Admiral Brocius watching my back. Unless he wanted to spend the rest of his career commanding an abandoned boot camp, Grayson would know when to quit.

"You planning on reading that Bible or just holding on to it?" Grayson asked.

"Reading it, sir."

"You must be a fast reader, son. We'll be parked on the *Obama* in another five minutes." He gave up on bullying and asked an interested question. "When was the last time you took a transfer?"

"It's been a few years," I said.

"Yeah? I'll bet it took a few hours for you to reach your post last time you had a transfer. Am I right, Sergeant?"

"Days, sir. My last transfer was to a ship patrolling the outer edge of the Scutum-Crux Arm." That was not exactly my last transfer, but I did not think Grayson was looking for specifics.

"That was the old Marine Corps, son. This here is the new

Marines. We don't have a Broadcast Network anymore, so we deliver you right to your new assignment."

"Thank you, sir," I said. I didn't mind the "sirs" and salutes. I could put up with officers and egos.

Colonel Grayson started to leave, then turned back to look at me. "Do you really read the Bible, son?" he asked. "I don't suppose you could tell me the name of King David's son?"

"Who do you mean, Solomon or Absalom?" I asked. There were more, but those were the only two I could name offhand.

"Who is Absalom?" the colonel asked.

"He was one of David's sons. He rebelled against David and tried to take over the kingdom."

The colonel turned and walked into the passenger cabin. "Son of a bitch," he muttered to himself. "Had a son who tried to take over the kingdom... son of a bitch."

I took my seat. A few minutes later we flew out of Earth's atmosphere. In the old days we would have spent up to five hours flying to the Mars broadcast station, depending on where Earth and Mars were in their orbits, and many more hours flying from the last broadcast station to the fleet. Transferring in a self-broadcasting ship took mere seconds. We cleared Earth's atmosphere and tint shields formed over our portholes. An instant later, we were approaching the Central Cygnus Fleet.

As I returned to my locker to stow my Bible and grab my sack, Colonel Grayson came up to me again. "So do you believe in God, son?" he asked.

"I'm a true believer," I confessed. If God was a metaphor for government, then my enlistment in the Marines made me some kind of cleric. During my days as a colonel, I might have qualified as a high priest.

"You know what, Harris? You're nothing like I expected," Grayson said. "Admiral Brocius called me in the other day and told me to let you do whatever you wanted with your platoon. What do you want to do with it?"

"I haven't reviewed my men," I said.

"They're good men. I run a tight operation."

"Yes, sir," I said, knowing full well that Marine colonels have little to do with the readiness of platoons. There were too many layers between the colonels and their grunts.

"Sounds like you and Admiral Brocius are great pals," Grayson continued. "Having an admiral watching your back, now that's a pretty good trick for a sergeant in the Marines." His expression became more serious, and the old smile vanished. "You just remember, Liberator or plain old government-issue grunt, war hero or fresh recruit, it's all the same under my command. And you are most definitely under my command, Master Gunnery Sergeant Wayson Harris. Screw with me, and I will bury you deep before your admiral can help you. Do you read me, Marine?"

"Yes, sir," I said. It was a warning, and a fair one.

We traded salutes, and Colonel Grayson left the ship. I grabbed my gear and followed.

My orders placed me in charge of a platoon on the U.A.N. *Obama*, one of twelve fighter carriers in the Central Cygnus Fleet. The *Obama* was home to two hundred platoons. In all, over eleven thousand Marines lived on the ship. My platoon would stand out.

When Admiral Brocius gave me command of the platoon, he told me to "make things happen." He gave me the license and the equipment to do just that. Of the two hundred platoons on this ship, my platoon would be the only one to which the admiral had assigned a self-broadcasting scientific explorer. The bird we transferred in on was to remain behind for my use.

No one met me as I entered the *Obama*. No surprise. During

the old days, when the Broadcast Network let you talk to anybody almost anywhere in the populated parts of the galaxy, subordinates or commanders met you as you entered new posts. Now, without the Broadcast Network, transfers went unheralded.

Not that I needed an escort. Having served on two fighter carriers, I had no trouble finding my way around the *Obama.* I located the barracks, then found the unit that housed my platoon.

A sergeant approached me as I entered. "Can I help you?" he asked politely. Though we were both sergeants, I outranked the guy. He was a staff sergeant, an entry-level sergeant. I was a master gunnery sergeant, one rung from the top of the only ladder that enlisted men could climb.

"You can help me find my rack," I said. I introduced myself.

"So you're running the show?" the sergeant asked. He introduced himself as Sergeant Ross Evans, and said, "You know, we had a captain running the show before you."

"From an officer to an enlisted man," I observed. "That must mean you're in for some action."

"I like the sound of that," Sergeant Evans said.

"Round up the men," I said. Yes, I was already issuing orders. I did not come to make friends. Besides, Evans was a standard government-issue military clone. He was built to take orders.

I went to the back of the unit and found my space. I stowed my gear, kicked my rack a few times to make sure it was solid, then set off to review my platoon. What I saw gave me hope.

Marine platoons are divided into squads. Evans was one of my three squad leaders. Staff Sergeant Dave Sutherland and Sergeant Kelly Thomer ran the other two.

Every squad has three fire teams. Every fire team has four men—a team leader, a rifleman, a grenadier, and an automatic rifleman. The fire teams and squad leaders make up thirty-nine of the forty-two men you typically find in a platoon.

I quickly learned that Evans and Sutherland were by-the-book leaders who tolerated no nonsense in their squads. They made them run double time in drills. Either one of their squads would have made a good backbone for any platoon.

As the lowest-ranking squad leader, Thomer inherited the problem cases. Evans's squad ran the obstacle course in four minutes flat. Sutherland's boys did it in 4:20. All but one of Thomer's boys ran the course in 4:10, but that last one shuffled in at 5:12. That was the first time I laid eyes on Mark Philips, the Marine Corps' oldest E1.

An E1 was a buck private. That was the rank they assigned you the first day at boot camp. When you graduated from camp, the Corps automatically promoted you to private first class or E2. Philips, however, who looked to be in his forties, still held the rank of plain old private. When I checked his records, I saw that he'd once worked his way up as far as lance corporal—an E3, but now he was back down to E1.

I watched the rest of Thomer's group dash across open ground. They flashed across rope bridges and other obstacles. Philips brought up the rear, trotting at a comfortable pace and not looking the slightest bit winded. He had no trouble climbing rope lines hand over hand. Monkey bars did not faze him. He simply felt no need to push himself.

"Who the hell is that?" I asked Sutherland as I watched Philips stroll to the end of the course.

"That's Private Philips," Sutherland said. "He's the platoon asshole."

"That's why God invented transfers," I said.

Sutherland smiled and nodded his agreement.

"Why don't you send Thomer by my office," I told Evans.

He smiled and left without a word.

* * *

"You might want to check his records before you transfer him," Thomer said.

"We don't need a slacker," I said. "Not in my platoon."

"If we're going to see some action, Philips might be exactly what we need," Thomer suggested.

"I've got his file," I said.

"Have you read it?" Thomer asked.

"Not yet," I said, feeling a shudder when I realized how much Thomer sounded like me talking about Ray Freeman to that Naval Intelligence officer. "Tell you what. You bring Philips here at 1500 hours. That will give me a chance to go over his record."

"Thank you, Master Sergeant," Thomer said. Enlisted men addressed master sergeants as "Master Sergeant." Simply calling us "sergeant," a name generally used for sergeants and staff sergeants, did not pay sufficient respect to the rank.

I had twenty minutes to read the Philips file. I only needed five.

Thomer and Philips showed up at my desk precisely on time. Thomer reported in his charley service uniform. Philips came in a government issue tank top and boxer shorts.

Philips and Thomer and every other member of the platoon, for that matter, looked approximately alike. They were all standard government-issue military clones. They all had brown hair, shaved along the sides of their heads, and brown eyes. Philips, however, stood out. Because he wore a tank top, I could see the scars on his arms and chest. He'd been shot twice in the right arm and once in the right shoulder. The scars were closely grouped as if the bullets had been fired in a single burst. It was the kind of wound you got in combat.

"I watched you run the obstacle course this afternoon," I said to Philips.

He gave me a lopsided smile and said nothing.

"I've read your record. You are a forty-six-year-old buck

private. So far as I know, you are the only forty-six-year-old buck private in the seven-hundred-year history of the Marines."

"The folks at the orphanage always said I would make something out of myself," Philips said, his face bursting with pride.

"According to your file, you recently pissed on a sergeant while he was asleep in his rack," I said.

Philips shrugged. "It was too far to walk to the latrine."

"You glued a major's grenades to his armor?" I asked.

"They never proved it was me," Philips complained.

"Was it you?" I asked.

Philips shrugged his shoulders. "Maybe."

"Are you hoping for a court-martial, Private?"

"Sergeant Harris," Thomer interrupted.

"Yes, Sergeant?"

"Have you reviewed Philips's combat record?"

"Are you trying to protect him?" I asked.

"I'm just making sure you've seen his record."

"As a matter of fact, I have." Philips had been in four major battles in the early part of the Separatist War. He'd been involved in several smaller actions before the war, too. He'd received and probably lost more medals than the three next-most-decorated men in the platoon. "Yes, Sergeant Thomer, Philips has a good combat record. That does not mean I want to babysit a burnout."

"You talking about drumming me out?" Philips asked.

"That just about sums it up," I said.

"Sergeant, you see, I horse around some, and I don't take well to authority, but I love the Corps. My problem is, I came to fight. I get real fidgety when I have to sit around on a ship."

"Are you saying you want to stay?" I asked.

"That's what I'm saying," Philips agreed.

"Maybe we can take care of some of that excess energy,

Private," I said. "I hate to lose a man with combat experience.

"But about pissing on that other sergeant... If I so much as see your pecker, Marine, I will cut it off. You read me, Marine?"

"I do," Philips said.

"Now if you will excuse us, Philips, I would like to speak with Sergeant Thomer for a moment."

Philips looked from me to Thomer, then back to me. Neither Thomer nor I spoke as he left.

"I understand you and Philips are buddies," I said, once Philips was away.

"He's a good Marine," Thomer said defensively.

"And you believe he can perform in combat?" I asked.

"I'd stake my life on it," Thomer said.

"You just did," I said. "That will be all."

Over the next two weeks I tested my platoon. I took the men to the firing range and liked what I saw, particularly from Philips. Because of my Liberator genes, I could shoot better than any man I have ever known. I set unchallenged records in the orphanage and boot camp. No one ever outscored me on a firing range, until the first time I took my new platoon to the firing range. Shooting at targets three hundred yards away, I had a hit rate of 96 percent that day. Philips's rate was 97 percent.

I did not know how well he had shot right away. As we left the firing range, I stopped to look at the board that listed our scores. I had known that Philips did well; but until I saw the score by his name, I had not realized that he outshot me. I stood there puzzled, trying to figure out why the highest number on the board was not next to my name.

"Still want to transfer him out?" Thomer asked as he walked past me.

At the moment, the answer was, "Yes. Absolutely." No one had ever outscored me.

"He's a good shot," I conceded. I told myself that my marksmanship had deteriorated during the time I spent playing farmer. Had I taken the time to warm up, I would have easily outshot Private Philips. I normally scored a perfect 100 percent at three hundred yards.

Philips did well in hand-to-hand. I did not fight him, mostly because I did not want to take a chance of breaking his neck. He partnered up with the three men from his fire team and subdued each of them quickly.

Evans and Sutherland generally asked me if I wanted to go hit the noncom bar with them when we turned in for the night. I always said, "No." I liked working with them, but I did not like them. They were too damned by-the-book for my taste. Also, I had a mission that I wanted to plan out.

One night, though, Evans and Sutherland brought Thomer along with them. "Hey, Master Sergeant, the whole platoon is headed out to the canteen," Thomer said. "You want to come along?"

I smiled and closed down my computer. "I'm feeling a little parched," I said. I got up and followed the men out of the barracks.

When we got to the bar, the place was chaotic. Five hundred, maybe even six hundred, Marines had crammed into a bar meant for no more than three hundred men at a time. The crowd was so loud that you had to shout to be heard, and everybody wanted to be heard. The din smothered the room and gave it life.

"We're over there," Evans yelled, pointing toward a corner of the room that was particularly crowded. My entire platoon had crammed in there, and it looked like men from a couple of other platoons had come to join them.

"Can I get you a beer?" Thomer asked.

"Thanks," I said. "I'll pick up the next round." He nodded but probably did not hear me.

As I approached the table, I heard a harmonica. Somebody was playing an old folk tune. The music was fast and lively, like a square dance only faster. Peering through the crowd, I saw Philips wearing that same mangy tank top he had worn to my office. He had slung fatigues over his shoulders, but he didn't bother fastening the buttons.

Philips worked that harmonica like a master. His head swayed one way then the other as his harmonica sawed back and forth across his lips. His face was bright red, and a vein ticked across his forehead. He had his right foot up on a bench and tapped his heel with the rhythm. The music whirled and spun. A few of the Marines clapped their hands with the beat.

When he finished his song, Philips tucked the harmonica in his pocket and smiled at me. The crowd thinned once people realized that Philips would not play another song.

"Hello, Master Sarge," Philips said, mixing Marine slang and derogatory Army lingo.

"Philips," I said.

Some of the other men greeted me. I shook a couple of hands. Enlisted men do not salute sergeants.

Thomer handed me a beer. He handed Philips a beer, too.

"You play a mean harmonica," I said.

"Shit, no. I do okay for self-taught, I guess," Philips said.

"He plays guitar, too," Thomer said.

"I know a song or two," Philips corrected. "That ain't the same thing as playing."

"How about you, Thomer. What are you good at?" I asked.

Thomer shrugged.

"He's the one who keeps this platoon running," Philips said.

Thomer glared at Philips.

"What about them?" I asked, pointing the top of my beer bottle at Evans and Sutherland. They were at the other end of the table, too far away to hear.

"Them?" Philips asked. "They do okay."

"They run the show," Thomer said. "At least they used to, before you came."

"Like I said, they do okay," Philips said. "Nobody likes them much. I guess they like each other plenty."

Thomer, who had started to take a swig of beer, laughed and spat beer back in his bottle.

"You were asking me about the time I pissed on a sergeant. Well, I thought it was Sutherland," Philips confessed. "I wish it had been the son of a bitch."

"You have a problem with Sutherland?" I asked.

"He's all right, I suppose," Philips said. "I like him the way a dog likes a fire hydrant. The good thing about Sutherland is that he can sleep through anything. If that had been Sutherland, I'd still be a corporal right now."

"He pissed on Sergeant Edmonds instead," Thomer said. He smiled, took another quick drink of beer, then added, "Edmonds is a light sleeper."

"Son of a bitch," Philips muttered. I did not know if he had just called Edmonds a son of a bitch or if he was referring to Thomer. "The bastard woke right up and started screaming. Probably thought he was being attacked by an albino boa constrictor."

"He told me he thought it was a macaroni noodle," Thomer mumbled.

"Are we going to see some action soon?" Sergeant Sutherland asked as he came to join us.

"Any day now," I said. "I just need to clear it with Colonel Grayson."

"You going to get me some Mogats to shoot?" Philips asked.

"That's the general idea," I said.

Given the mission that I had in mind, I would have traded half my platoon for an Adam Boyd clone, but Navy SEALs seldom ran with Marines.

"You want to what?" Colonel Grayson asked. "You must be specking with me, son. You can't take a Cygnus Central platoon into the Perseus Arm. They have their own damn fleet and their own damn Marines. You do realize that Outer Perseus is halfway across the galaxy? Think about it, son. Think, why don't you?"

"Colonel, Admiral Brocius has charged me to engage the enemy any way that I can."

"So engage them in your own damned arm of the galaxy!" Grayson roared. He tried to look angry but a rogue grin played on his lips. I got the feeling that he liked the idea of poaching in another part of the galaxy. "What do you expect to get out of this raid?"

"The war," I answered. "The whole specking war."

21

"I heard the last pilot you took out here got fried," our pilot said as we glided into the space graveyard on our way to the Mogat battleship.

Looking out from the cockpit of the explorer, I saw no sign of that last ship. It had simply vanished into the debris, pilot and all. We might nudge it out of our path and not notice.

"We'll be more careful this time," I said.

"How is that?" the pilot asked.

"Last time we didn't know the Mogats were watching for visitors. This time we do."

"I hope you don't expect me to wait around for you," the pilot said.

"Yes, I expect you to wait till we tell you to leave. Waiting wasn't what killed our last pilot. He got killed running away. If he'd just sat still and blended in with the scenery…" I let the sentence hang.

In order for my plan to work, we needed the Mogats to know we had trespassed onto their property, and to think they had scared us away. The best way to do that was to give them a show.

As we approached the battleship, the pilot scanned for booby traps and burglar alarms. Once we boarded the derelict, we would use the stealth kits I had requisitioned from naval headquarters. Until then, we would need to rely on the explorer's sensors. Fortunately, this was a scientific ship. It had sensors that could pick up all kinds of fields. The coast seemed clear, but there was one kind of signal the vessel would not detect—a signal transmitted by a broadcast engine.

As we opened the cargo hatch and started to unpack, the pilot hailed me over the interLink. "I'm not waiting around," he warned. "Listen, Sergeant. Command said nothing about babysitting a bunch of clones on a suicide mission. If I get a whiff of a Mogat ship, I am going to leave."

"They won't find you if you hide, sir," I said. "They will find you if you run."

"Then maybe I should leave now," the pilot said.

"We're still on your ship, sir," I pointed out.

"I mean once you are off."

"Are you talking about abandoning us?" I asked. "Don't you think someone will ask questions when you show up short forty-two men?"

"No, I don't. Not if they are clones."

They had a term for officers who were prejudiced against clones—"antisynthetic." In my experience, most officers were antisynthetic to some extent, but things were changing. There used to be six hundred clone factories/orphanages pumping out over one million clones every year. Now that the Mogats had destroyed the orphanages, clones were no longer the inexhaustible resource they had once been. Once the military complex ran out of its current supply of clones, the government would have to start sending natural-borns to the front. After years of relying on clones to do their fighting, few natural-borns would willingly fight or die.

"You strand us out here, sir," I growled, "and you'd better pray the Mogats find you before I do."

"Are you threatening me, Sergeant?" the pilot asked.

"Yes, sir," I said.

"You have just officially crossed over the..."

"Maybe we should take this up with Admiral Brocius," I said. "He's the one who assigned you to this platoon."

"Admiral Brocius?" the pilot asked.

As a lieutenant, the pilot outranked me. But rank and authority did not always mean the same thing in the Marines. A veteran sergeant is at the top of the arc as enlisted men go. He may not make as much money as the lowest-paid officer, and he may sleep on a mean rack in dingy barracks, but an experienced sergeant merits more respect than a lieutenant who is still wet behind the ears.

A master gunnery sergeant is a veteran and a man who knows his way around the Corps. Let a lieutenant and a master sergeant go head-to-head, and the sergeant may take a token vacation in the brig; but unless that lieutenant has some good answers, his career will be specked for good.

That said, I'm not sure which rattled the lieutenant more, my bringing up Admiral Brocius or my threatening his life. Either way, the good lieutenant decided to park his bird and leave the meter running.

He sidled the explorer right below the sunken Mogat battleship and brought it to a stop. Then it was our turn. We exited the ship in groups of ten, each of us shepherding crates and equipment toward that huge hole in the bottom of the Mogat ship. Nearly a month had passed since I came here with the SEALs. The memories were still fresh in my mind.

The first team on the spot fastened hooks onto the hull and started building a long scaffold that would stretch all the way across the breach. The next crew brought more scaffolding. By the time the third group arrived, enough of the scaffolding had been set to create a staging area. We were preparing to put on quite a show.

Our show props included scaffolds, a complete laser welding rig, crates for storing samples of the ship's armor plating, and several changes of clothes. We unloaded our props and built the scaffolds in double time. Even though my threats had made our pilot more agreeable, we could tell he was spooked and unreliable.

"That's the last of the cargo," I told the pilot, as three of my men ferried over a set of crates on a sled. "Go hide your ship in the debris." He could not leave yet, but he could park a safe distance away and watch if the Mogats came and massacred us.

The lieutenant did not say anything. The explorer's engines started, and the ship drifted away, but the pilot did not say a word. We continued building.

First we attached base rods to the bottom of the battleship using a bonding glue that worked better than welding in the coldness of space. Once the rods were in place, we erected the rest of the scaffold using pins and sockets. The work went slowly.

It took us two hours to set up the scaffolding along the battered bottom side of that battleship. That is a long time to spend undefended in enemy space, but we needed it to make our show believable. We had to convince the Mogats that we were naval engineers, come to study the damage to this battleship. As things worked out, we did run one test on the armor plating.

Once the scaffolding was fastened in place, I had two of my men remove a plate from the hull. The plate was a flat square about eight feet along its edges. Had there been gravity, it would have weighed a couple of hundred pounds. In a gravity situation, its bulk would have crushed the thin rods of the scaffolding.

One of my men shoved the plate into space. As it slowly glided away, I drew my particle-beam pistol and fired. The plate absorbed the bright green beam. I thought I saw it quiver slightly, but I might have imagined that. My beam was too small to destroy it, but I wanted to test the integrity of the plating.

In truth, I did not need to test the plating. Looking straight up, I had plenty of evidence about what happens when laser cannons hit an unshielded hull. Rows of plates melt into slag, leaving foot-long stalactites in their wake.

"The stage is in place, Master Sergeant," Sergeant Evans reported.

The "stage" was impressive. The scaffolding crisscrossed the breach on the bottom of the hull like stitches closing a knife wound. From a distance it might look like stitches. Some of the men built a launch area. If we had been engineers instead of jarheads, we could have spacewalked out to examine the shield antennae.

We spent the next hour removing entire rows of armor plates, some battered and some untouched. We rigged test stations and communications arrays. This was all for show, just a set decoration for the Mogats to shoot at. Once they arrived, our setup scaffolding would prove absolutely indefensible and clearly the work of engineers who had no concept of battle tactics.

"You know what, Sutherland, you'd make a good engineer," I said as I traversed the scaffold.

"Thank you," he said.

"That was an insult," I said.

"Then go speck yourself," Sutherland said.

Taking one last look up and down the length of our work, I asked Sutherland if he had everything he would need for the mission. He held up his satchel. "I'm good for a day," he said. That was an exaggeration. In the discomfort of space, he would not be able to eat or shit. Our armor did have a hydration wire to protect us from the dry air our rebreathers produced, and our undergarments included a vacuum tube and bottle for urine. If everything went according to plan, however, Sutherland might not have much of a stay on that wretched battleship.

The stealth kits I had requisitioned for this mission were not the sleek three-inch remotes used by the SEALs. Central Cygnus Fleet did not carry those. Our general-issue kits were ten inches long and shaped like the bottom half of a combat boot. Our stealth kit had meters for measuring sensor fields. They even had a handy-dandy little device that left virtual beacons so you could mark your trail.

When I was in boot camp, I used to like cunning, space-saving devices that combined knives, cooking utensils, and communications equipment in one convenient handle. After a battle or two, I learned to despise them. I wanted my gun to shoot, my knife to stab, and everything else to perform the task God meant it to do. I did not like fishing through handles to find the right blade. The only exception was my combat helmet. God went above and beyond the call of duty when he created Marine combat armor. I loved each and every lens in my visor, and I liked the way my helmet protected my head, too.

My helmet had lenses that let me see in the dark, scan areas for heat, and zoom in on objects. It also had a sonar device that did double duty measuring distances and locating hollow areas. The lenses in my visor also contained a chip that recorded everything I saw and an interLink terminal that let me communicate with everybody or anybody in my platoon. In my religion, with the government as God, combat armor was divine.

Using the oversized stealth device to jam the Mogats' security sensors, Sutherland made his way to the engine room. There he would set up camp and wait. I watched him pull his way into the belly of that battleship, an insignificant speck moving through layers of metal, plastic, and wiring that really did look like a wound.

"Lieutenant, are you there?" I hailed the explorer.

"Sergeant?" The pilot tried to control his voice, but I heard desperation in it. "Are you finished?"

"We're dividing up now. Most of the platoon is ready to leave whenever you are, sir," I said.

"What about the rest?" the pilot asked.

"You get to leave us here," I said. "That's the good news. The bad news is that you are going to miss the big show." I added, "Come back in five hours. We'll need you to pick up whatever is left."

The explorer lit up and drifted in our direction. Old as it was, the little ship had a bright, sleek look. If this had been a transport, it would have been bulky and bulged around its center. Civilian-designed vessels like this explorer had style. The explorer had a brightly colored fuselage, dramatic hull lighting, and an all-glass cockpit that bulged like a bubble. It would never hold up under fire, but it was not meant for war.

The explorer pulled right up to the scaffold at a speed so slow you would have thought someone was pushing it.

"Master Sergeant, are you sure you don't need more hands?" one of my men asked. "I wouldn't mind staying back."

"I can stay," another Marine volunteered.

"Better to have too many men than too few," a third man offered.

"You have your orders," I said, barely acknowledging the offer. Master gunnery sergeants do not thank people often. Soldiers can be as polite as they want; Marine sergeants do not say "please" or "thank you" to their men.

The dome at the rear of the explorer opened. When we'd

arrived a few hours earlier, we had four sled-loads of men and equipment. Now thirty-one men would return. Watching the last load of men disappear into the explorer ship, it occurred to me that this was not a Marine operation. It was a bloody SEAL op being run by an overly ambitious Marine.

"You going to be okay out here?" the pilot asked over the interLink. It was a hollow inquiry. He did not ask this until he had sealed up his ship and started away.

I wanted to ask if he was offering to stay, but I played it politic. "We're good, sir," I said. "See you in five hours."

22

The first time out, we fooled the Mogats with a cat-and-mouse chase and a single body. We didn't need luck that time, the SEALs were more skilled at playing that kind of game than my Marines.

I stood on that scaffold with the torn section of hull above me and the vastness of space as a backdrop. I watched the explorer pick its way out of the space graveyard, nudging the ruins of fighter craft out of its way. Ten men had stayed behind with me. Some of the men waited beside me on the scaffold. We watched the explorer, none of us saying a word. It was a small ship, and it soon vanished out of sight. A moment later, I saw the flash of a distant anomaly and knew that the ship had broadcasted.

Watching the anomaly fade, I realized that the silence in my helmet had a profoundly sobering effect on me.

Marines generally chatter over an open interLink. This time they stood silent and still. I wanted to tell them that everything would work out. I wanted to tell them that they would be back on the *Obama* in a few hours and they would get to rest in their own racks.

Okay, ladies. Switch on those Stealth kits, we have work to do," I said. "The first man I catch slacking gets a particle-beam enema." For the average Marine clone, hearing a sergeant growl offered more comfort than a glass of mother's milk.

Last time out, I rode up the gash in a sled. This time we kicked off the scaffolding and leaped up three floors. We did not take spotlights or laser torches. We took satchels with clothing, oversized stealth kits, and particle-beam pistols.

Our props for this delicate performance included empty suits of soft-shelled armor. The combat armor used by Marines was not bulletproof, but it was rigid. Engineers, firemen, and other noncombat personnel wore flexible armor. It was not as pliable as cloth, but it was a lot softer than the metal-resin alloy used in our armor.

"You boys ready for the cadaver roundup?" I asked. We split up in groups and searched the ship.

The next task on the agenda was morbid but necessary. We went scouting for bodies.

When the U.A. sank this boat, the bodies in the open areas were flushed into space. We would need to scour closed rooms and compartments now. I started my search in a latrine on the third deck, just behind the birthing area.

The entire ship would have been pitch-black had I not used the night-for-day lens, but the latrine seemed particularly dark. Maybe it was the small size of the room and the way the stalls reached out like fingers. The darkness just seemed to close in around me. There was something eerie about the empty latrine. It reminded me of walking across the barracks late at night. Stainless-steel urinals hung from the walls, the sinks were pristine, and the floor was clean, but no one moved. I went to look in the toilet stalls.

I found the first of my corpses wedged into a stall. The man hovered an inch or two above the seat. When the lasers struck the ship, he had probably just finished his business. His pants were up and sealed. His neck was broken. Depending on his luck, that might have killed him. Otherwise, he might have suffocated, or died as his own blood pressure caused his body to explode, or frozen to death. Death in space came in many flavors, all of them fast.

The man's blood hung frozen just above the floor like an icy web of beads. Walking in on the scene, you might have thought he'd vomited up glass.

I unpacked the top half of a soft-shell suit and used it like a net to scoop up the blood. The brittle strands snapped and shattered into beads inside the armor.

Then I pulled the dead sailor out of the stall and dressed him, and his blood, in the armor. The man's body was frozen as stiff as stone in the absolute chill of space. Had I hit him against the wall with enough force, he might have shattered into tiny pieces like a pane of glass. As I tried to force him into the suit, flaps of his skin kept snapping like crackers between my fingers, and I eventually had to break his arms off and shove them into the sleeves of the armor separated from his torso. Once I finished dressing the sailor, I sealed his armor. It pressurized, read his body temperature, and heated itself automatically. It would take this boy a long time to thaw.

"How is it going out there?" I called out over the interLink.

"I feel like a ghoul," one of my men responded.

"Are you eating them or dressing them, Marine?" I asked.

"Dressing them."

"Ghouls don't dress bodies, they eat them," I said.

"Then I feel like a specking grave robber," the Marine returned.

"You're not fleecing them, are you?" I asked.

That Marine did not answer.

"They're so frigging stiff," another Marine commented. "I keep snapping off this guy's fingers."

"I had to break my guy's arms off," another Marine said.

"This seems kind of disrespectful," another Marine added.

"They're not going to fool anybody. No one is going to believe that these stiffs are alive." It was the one who said he felt like a ghoul. "Maybe we could paint them white and sell them as marble statues."

"The Mogats won't be watching for flexibility," I said.

I checked my first puppet. Some of the skin from his face had thawed, but his face was no longer attached to his skull. I had broken his legs and arms at the joints so that they would fold in the right places. I shook his helmet and saw liquid blood.

I found two more bodies in the halls beyond the birthing area and dressed them. It was unpleasant work.

"Okay, report. How many puppets do we have?" I called over the interLink.

"I have four ready," one team called in.

"We have five and a half stiffies," Private Philips, always the joker, reported. He had partnered up with Sergeant Thomer. I would not have trusted him on this mission without Thomer looking after him.

"Thomer, what does he mean by a half?" I asked.

"Don't ask," said Thomer.

"I'm asking," I said.

"Philips thought it would be funny to kick one of the sti... puppets while I was loading him in his armor. He went flying backward and snapped in half."

"He was an officer," Philips explained in his own defense.

"Just shove the legs into some pants and seal him up," I said.

"That might be a problem," Thomer said. "His ass hit a bulkhead and shattered." I heard the other men laughing over the interLink.

"We have nine," the last team radioed in.

"Ass kiss," one of the men muttered. I was pretty sure it was Philips.

"We need this puppet show to happen just the way we discussed. Any questions?" I asked.

"How many Mogats do we get to off?" Private Philips asked.

"Our puppets are supposed to be Navy engineers," I said. "We have to keep this simple."

"Ten of them?" Philips asked.

"None if we can help it," I said.

"Philips is right. We have to kill some of them," another Marine complained.

"Not one," I said.

"Ahhh, c'mon, Master Sergeant, how about just one?" Philips pled.

"Well, yeah, maybe one," I said. "But open your speck receptacle one more time, Philips, and I'll load you in a puppet suit," I growled. "Any more smart questions, assholes?"

No one said anything. I liked their attitude.

23

Before a battle, Marines do not have time for ghosts. After a battle and a few drinks, Marines have time for just about anything.

Traveling around the deck of this demolished ship, I became consumed by the feeling of walking among ghosts. Perhaps it was the shadowy blue-white world that my night-for-day lens showed me. Maybe the way we abused the bodies of these dead Mogat sailors got to me. A few of my Marines tried to hide their nerves behind gallows humor, but we all felt it. The Mogats had died a fast but gruesome death. They were the enemy, but Corps honor seldom made room for abusing the dead, friend or foe.

I felt closed in. I felt trapped. The combat hormone had not yet kicked in to my system, but the anxiety of battle was there. I had entered the Liberator version of no-man's-land.

I dropped down to the scaffold below the ship. I had been in and out of the gash in the hull four times now, and each time the trip left me with a different impression. The first time I came up, I thought that the breach looked like a gaping wound in a human body. The next time I thought it looked like a tear through a building. The third time my mind stayed more focused on the job, and I thought about the air flushing out of the ship, washing thousands of bodies out with it. This time, I felt like I was falling through an open grave.

Once I landed on the scaffolding, I switched from night-for-day to my standard tactical view lens. We had lamps set up along the scaffold. I would have seen everything more clearly with night-for-day vision; but feeling morose as I did, I wanted a moment to myself in which I could see color and depth. There are areas of color in space, but you do not see them often or clearly. Seeing the charcoal-colored hull and the silver pipes of scaffolding did not improve my spirits.

I came down to examine the nine puppets we had placed along the scaffold. I tried to think of them as puppets, not bodies, and especially not corpses. Their faces were buried behind faceplates. I did not need to look into the colorless tissue flowers that filled their eye sockets. For all intents and purposes, the soft-shells on the scaffold could have been empty. Except they were not empty, and I knew it.

Sergeant Evans and two other men posed the puppets so that they would look like engineers cowering during an attack. They placed five of the puppets in a kneeling position behind the welding rig. One of the puppets had thawed enough for Evans to bend his body. He seemed to peer over the top of the rig. One puppet sat near the far side of the scaffold. Three more hung from wires—puppet strings. Once our audience arrived, we would effect their escape by pulling them back into the ship.

Maybe I felt jinxed by the ship, but I did not think we could make our puppet show believable. It was one thing for a squad of SEALs to put on a magic act in which they fooled the Mogats into shooting their own pilot. The SEALs specialized in reconnaissance, not combat. Our show would be more ambitious and the men less skilled. I trusted my men. I worked them hard and knew they would not fold in battle, but the clones were made for storming buildings and routing enemies. Finesse was not in their DNA.

"How does the stage look, Sergeant?" Evans called to me on the interLink. He and Corporal Kasdan stood three decks above me, holding the puppet wires.

"I think they'll buy it," I said.

"You know this is crazy?" Evans said. Once the Mogats arrived, he and Kasdan would reel in their puppets and disappear into the ship.

"Is everyone in place?" I called over an open frequency.

When all of my men answered, I launched myself from the scaffold and back into the ship. On my way up, I switched off my stealth kit. The sensors spotted me that instant and the show began. Philips, the man from my platoon in whom I had the least confidence, met me as I reached the third deck. With one arm around a railing, he hooked me and tugged me toward an open corridor.

"Think they know we're here?" Philips asked.

"I'd bet on it," I said. "It might take them a minute to scramble their battleship in our direction, but they know about us."

Thomer joined us as we entered a corridor. I don't think the sensors knew or cared that there were three of us. They recorded our movement. Wherever they were, the Mogats knew someone was mucking around the ship.

With the sensors reading our movements, Philips, Thomer, and I traveled a route we thought engineers might take. We meandered through corridors as if studying the wiring. We took detours past system junctions. The one thing we made sure we did not do was move in the direction of the engine room. If the Mogats knew that we knew about the secondary broadcast engine, they might abandon it.

Other Marines joined us as we floated through the halls. Soon nine of us met. Only Evans and Kasdan stayed in place. We wanted to give the impression that a body of men had entered the ship through the bridge, then separated to examine its arteries. The men used their stealth kits as they joined us, then switched them off. Some of my men headed for the bridge. Others went to examine the shield generator, which was in the front of the ship but three decks below the bridge. Now, with three simultaneous alarms, I hoped the Mogats would become nervous.

Once I was alone, I switched on my stealth kit. Once again invisible to the sensors, I headed for the launch bay. For the rest of the mission, I would hide in the launch bay and wait. Everything hinged on one point—they could not know I was there.

The landing area was huge, dark and empty. It was so vast that I could not see all the way across it with my night-for-day lens. With the doors of its atmospheric locks wide open, one side of the bay opened out to space. As I looked for a good place to hide, I stumbled across an emergency elevator. The opening to the elevator was fifteen feet tall and twice as far across. Fire engines and bomb disposal carts rode in that lift. Peering into the gap in the door, I saw that the shaft ran the entire height of the ship.

I pried the doors apart and left them wide open. I doubted if anyone would notice the open doorway. The lift was dead. The ship was dead. Who would care about an elevator shaft? Besides, according to the Mogats' sensors, no one had entered the launch bay.

Before stepping into the shaft, I looked down to make sure it did not open into space. Below me, the shaft yawned like a giant gullet. I did not see a bottom, but I did not see stars below me, either. The car itself was about ten feet above me, the bulky metal reinforcements beneath its floor forming a roof over my head. I sprung up to the roof, then pushed off it to drop down the length of the shaft.

The emergency shaft ended in a storage room on the bottom deck. In this room I found a few dead men and a trove of battered equipment. Parts of the floor had been shorn away in the fighting. Judging by the amount of destruction around me, I decided that I could not have been far from the gash in the hull. The holes must have occurred at the end of the fight after the hull had been pierced and the atmosphere had equalized; otherwise, the men and equipment would have been flushed out with the air.

Bright flashes of lightning sent a momentary glare through the holes in the deck. I saw the blinding light shine and looked away. That light could only have been the anomaly of a Mogat ship broadcasting into the area. If I looked into it, I would be blinded. Even looking in the opposite direction with tint shields blocking my visor, I still registered the flashes. When the lightning stopped, I peered out a hole and saw the black silhouettes of two Mogat ships against the fading brightness of their anomalies. A moment later I saw a transport leave one of the ships and head in our direction.

Unified Authority armored transport ships have heavy shields and no guns. The Mogats might have claimed this transport fifty years earlier, but it was still of a bulky, slow, and unarmed Unified Authority design. As the transport approached us, it slowed to a crawl. The doors at the rear of the kettle slid open and out flew five Mogats in unwieldy deep-space armor that the Unified Authority Navy had abandoned decades earlier.

"Evans, reel them in!" I shouted over the interLink. From my vantage point, I could not see the puppets rise as Evans and Kasdan reeled them up into the battleship. I did see the Mogats fire their lasers into scaffolding. I could see a small section of scaffold. I had enough of a view to see it blow apart in a flash. In the midst of the debris, the seven puppets we left on the scaffold must have flown off in every direction. Very satisfying.

One of the puppets coasted into my field of vision. As I watched, a Mogat commando fired at it. The laser cut through the soft armor, causing a small explosion in the oxygen-pressurized suit. The puppet exploded, spraying out body parts and blood.

"They bought it," I called over an open frequency. "Now let's give these specks a good show."

The deep-space commandos rocketed toward the break in the hull. They would fly into the ship on their own while their transport parked in the launch bay above me.

"Evans, get out of there," I barked over the interLink.

"I saw them coming up the well," Evans said.

"Are you clear of them?" I asked.

"All clear," Evans answered.

I had just started to tell everyone that Evans was safe and the first act of the show was over when the anomalies started flashing. Ships began broadcasting in by the dozen. Just looking away from the glare was not enough. I had to bury my visor in the crook of my arm. The walls around the storage hold flashed so brightly I would have sworn someone was flash-welding steel an inch away from my face.

"Oh, shit," I whispered to myself, knowing full well that every last man on my team would hear me. The problem was, I could not change the frequency with my eyes closed; and with all of that lightning going out there, I turned away, covered my face, closed my eyes, and still saw bleaching.

"What's going on?" nine of my men asked me at the same time. Philips, the tenth, said, "That doesn't sound so good."

24

Even looking away and covering my eyes, I could feel the intensity of the anomalies outside. They came at a rapid staccato, like thousands of blinding-white arc bulbs popping on and off at an impossibly fast speed.

"I think the whole specking Mogat Navy is out there," I said over the open frequency.

"How many ships?" one man asked.

"I can't look out to count, they just keep coming."

I knew it would not be the entire Mogat Fleet. Broadcasting four hundred ships into a tight lane of space is a complicated matter. You would need to stage the broadcasts so that the ships came in far enough apart. Broadcasting ships do not need to bump each other to cause damage; the electricity from their anomalies is enough to cause havoc. Besides, it would have taken hours for the Mogats to broadcast their entire four-hundred-ship navy into our space. The lightning storm ended a mere five minutes after it began.

When the flashes stopped, I turned back toward the break in the deck for a look. From this narrow window, I counted thirteen ships milling about. Had I had a more panoramic view, I suspected I might have spotted fifty. The Mogats probably had another hundred on reserve in case the battle turned nasty. Despite their recently nonaggressive stance, the Morgan Atkins Believers were spoiling for a fight over this little acre.

The Mogats could field as many battleships as they wanted; it wouldn't affect us in here so long as their ships cleared out before our ride returned. Our pilot had struck me as a guy with a strong sense of self-preservation. He would broadcast in far away and find a safe zone from which to scan the area before flying into a potentially hazardous situation. The mission still seemed on track, but then things took an unexpected turn.

A formation of transports drifted into view.

"Bad news, puppeteers, your audience just got larger," I said.

"How bad?" someone asked.

"Three more transports," I said. If each transport carried a full load, we would have a grand total of nearly four hundred Mogats trolling the halls. This old battleship was starting to feel crowded.

"Speck me with a three-legged dog," Private Philips grumbled. "This show of yours was already standing room only." As always, he called on a platoon-wide band. Philips enjoyed an audience.

I heard a few Marines laughing. I wanted the platoon to be serious, but I needed them calm. Philips was a joker, but he was also the old man of the platoon. Even if he was a private, some of my men looked to him for leadership.

"Listen up, Leathernecks," I said. That was us. We were "grunts." We were "jarheads." We were "Leathernecks." Marines get shitty-sounding names and shitty-sounding jobs and take pride in them. "Things are getting tight in here, but the show goes on exactly as planned."

"How the speck are you going to sneak on their specking transport with three hundred specking Mogats milling around the specking launch bay? Not meaning any disrespect, Master Sarge, but you're specked," Philips said.

"Can it, Philips," I said.

I agreed with Philips. After taking another look at my stealth kit to make absolutely sure it was engaged, I leaped to the top of the elevator shaft for another look. As I flew higher, light from the Mogat transports illuminated the walls around me. Had one of the Mogats glanced into the elevator shaft at that moment, he would have seen me. I would have made a dandy target, alone in an empty shaft with only a pistol.

I found a handhold and stopped myself just below the light. Inching slowly along the wall, I got to the door and peered out.

Somehow, the Mogats had wedged four transports side by side onto the deck. The ships' landing lights shone down, illuminating the entire bay. I turned off my night-for-day lens and viewed the scene through the tactical lens in my visor. Even with the lights, there was a distinct lack of color—dozens of men in dark armor climbing out of bare metal kettles and lining up in front of the white walls of the launch bay.

Using optical controls for the interLink, I started scanning frequencies to find the band the Mogats used, but the signal got buried under the chatter from my men. "Keep it down," I said. "From here on, I do the talking and you listen unless there is an emergency. Do you read me?"

We would have a hard time outmaneuvering these boys unless we could eavesdrop on their conversations.

Mogat interLink technology included a narrow and obsolete

band of frequencies. The Unified Authority armed forces had abandoned those bands years ago.

I found their chatter, but their signals overlapped each other. When I was here with the SEALs, the Mogats sent two transports, and we had no problem listening in on them. This time, with four transports and four hundred men, the messages seemed to scramble themselves. It would have taken a cryptography computer to untangle who said what and which statement responded to which question. From what I could tell, however, they were confusing themselves as well with this chatter.

Apparently no more impressed with the chaos than I was, a group of Mogat platoon leaders weighed into their mob. The platoon leaders wore magnetic-gravitation boots that anchored their feet to the ground. Thanks to their gravity boots, they could stand firm as they sorted through the cluster and found the men from their various platoons. Every so often they would spot a man out of place and grab him by the arm or the neck. The sergeants would yank these unfortunate conscripts and sling them. In a weightless situation, a man with gravity in his shoes can throw other men as if they had no more substance than a wet towel.

I switched to a frequency my platoon would hear. "Get ready, they're sending teams out."

"How do they look?" asked Evans, probably the most serious man under my command.

"You've never seen anything like this. They're about as organized as a pond full of ducks," I said.

"What does that mean?"

"It means that these boys can't tell their boots from their helmets," I said.

The Mogats from the first transport had long since filed out into the ship. Two of my men, Evans and Kasdan, tracked their movements, while other members of my team led them on a wild-goose chase that would end somewhere near midship.

The teams from the secondary transports started filing out. Listening to my men, I heard them abandoning routes and altering plans as additional Mogats poured out. Maneuvering like ghosts around a ship with four hundred Mogats crowding the corridors would present a challenge.

I took reports every two minutes.

"This would be a whole lot easier if you could get them to stay in one place," Private Adams signaled me after nearly two hundred Mogats converged by sick bay, a single hatch away from where he and PFC Nielsen lay hidden. They had planned to enter the vent system; but when the dozens of Mogats flooded the area, they hid in a room without any vents.

"They're closing in on us," Nielsen called. Military clones seldom panicked, but they were prone to confusion when they did not receive close supervision while under fire.

"Does anybody have a puppet ready?" I called over the open frequency. "Nielsen and Adams are boxed in."

"I've got a stiffy for you," Philips said.

"A stiffy?" I asked.

"Where do you want it?" Philips asked.

"They're in second-deck sick bay," I said.

I called to Adams. "Hang tight. I'm sending Philips in your direction."

"Think you can hurry?" Adams asked. "It's looking crowded next door."

A moment later I radioed Philips. "Where are you?"

"Master Sarge, there are a lot of Mogats down there," Philips said.

"You in place?" I asked.

"Yes, sir, Master Sergeant, right over their heads."

"Think you can lead them on a chase and still get away?"

"No problem. I left old Wallace with his head sticking out of a vent two blocks away."

"Who's Wallace?"

"The stiffy you wanted. I posed him two blocks away."

"Adams, Nielsen, prepare to bolt." I radioed, still not sure how much to trust Philips.

"Just give the word," Adams said.

"Philips, you're on," I said.

I imagined the scene in my head. The ventilation shafts were four feet wide and four feet tall. Without gravity pulling you down, you could easily fly through them without ever touching the aluminum-alloy walls. Philips would turn off his kit and scramble to the vent where he left his puppet poking out. The Mogats would chase him. If he lived up to his battle record, Philips would pass the puppet and turn on his stealth kit. Knowing his recklessness, he would fire a shot at the Mogats before clearing out, but he could still get away.

"Adams, what's happening?" I asked.

"Sick bay is clear," Adams said.

"Get the hell out," I shouted.

A moment later they signaled to say they had entered the vents.

"See you on the other side, Wallace," Philips muttered. "Here they come. Can I hit a Mogat when they come, Master Sarge? It would make me feel a whole lot better about sacrificing old Wallace."

"Get serious," I said.

"I am serious," Philips said. A second later he said, "That one's for Wallace. Sorry about that, Master Sarge. I accidentally hit one of them Mogats."

I remembered the time we spent drilling and Philips outscoring me on the firing range. "Accidentally my ass," I said. "Get out of there, Philips."

"Uhh! Poor Wallace," Philips groaned.

"What happened?" I asked.

"They just shot his head off," Philips said. "You should have seen it, Master Sarge. Wallace's head just about burst like a damned water bomb. His legs are still in the vent but the rest of him went flying across the room."

"Philips, get out of there!" I yelled.

"I'm leaving... I'm leaving," Philips grumbled. "See you around, Wallace."

"Sergeant, may I just take a moment to point out that Private Philips is a lunatic and a danger to this mission," Evans chimed in.

"He just saved two men from your squad," Thomer said.

Evans did not answer.

I chanced another look across the launch bay. A few guards congregated near the entrance to the corridor. The closest ship, no more than twenty feet from the elevator shaft in which I was hiding, sat entirely unguarded.

Adams and Nielsen might have nearly gotten themselves caught, but they had also drawn off most of the Mogats milling around the landing deck.

"Start the final act, I'm going in," I said over the platoon-wide band.

If everything worked right, all of my men would converge in the corridor near the bridge, where Evans and Kasdan had built a barricade. Hidden in the bridge, Evans and Sutherland would track the Mogats' movements while the rest of my men put on that last act, hiding behind the barricade and staging a losing gunfight. As the Mogats shot their puppets, my men would hopefully escape into the vent system.

At this point I no longer had time to worry about how the show went over. I had a trick of my own to perform. I needed to slip into one of the transports.

Before leaving the lift shaft, I pushed off the walls and went up as high as I could for one last look around the flight deck. The Mogats had left their landing lights on, flooding the bay with bright illumination. Across the way, fifteen guards clustered around a ship on the far side of the deck.

I felt the combat hormone enter my circulatory system. I felt the warmth and the calm. My breathing slowed. The wing of the nearest transport was no more than a few feet from me. I took a deep breath, held it, and exhaled. I took another breath, held it, and launched myself at the landing gear of the nearest transport.

With the landing gear between me and the guards, I could not see them. I could not listen to them because of all of the chatter on the Mogat frequencies. The Mogats' commandos were excited. They were closing in on the enemy.

"Evans, report," I called as I peered around the landing gear. The guards were still in place, still clustered together uselessly by the entrance. Idiots.

"All according to plan," Evans said. "They've nailed all but three of our puppets."

"And our guys?" I asked.

"Everybody but Philips is out of there."

That was according to plan. We couldn't make the puppets aim and shoot, so we had to do it for them. Philips had volunteered for the job. He liked the idea of shooting at Mogats.

"Okay, I'm almost on board. I want you boys to go dark and stay dark the moment I'm in place. You got that?"

"Got it," Evans said.

"And that goes double for Philips," I said.

By this time the hormone had saturated my blood. My muscles tingled the way they might tingle after a perfect workout. My skin had a pleasant sting that reminded me of stepping into a hot shower on a cold night. I took a quick glance around the transport's landing gear. If the guards had been looking for me, they would have spotted me; but they were too busy talking among themselves.

Pulling myself quickly along the outside of the transport, I rounded a corner and had to grab anything I could find to stop my momentum. Floating inside the kettle, all by himself, was a lone guard.

I managed to hook my foot on a pole before I flew into view. Then I backed out and headed for the next transport.

Maybe the Mogats had assigned a man to stay on each ship or maybe the guy simply did not like a crowd. I should have known something was wrong. Fifteen men guarding four ships—had I stopped to do the math I would have noticed the uneven number.

I pulled myself back off the transport and glanced around the edge of the kettle. Those fifteen useless Mogat guards all faced away from me. Why should they stay alert? Their security systems told them that the only enemies on the ship were a quarter mile away, surrounded by hundreds of commandos.

I looked at the guards and wondered what they were doing. They must have been chatting. You can't play cards in zero gravity. You can't smoke or drink in a space suit.

After one last perfunctory glance, I launched myself toward the next transport. It was a tense moment. I had to cross an eighty-foot open area in which I would be completely visible. If someone happened to notice me, I would be an easy target. But my stealth kit jammed their sensors and the guards never looked in my direction. I jetted across the open area at what might well have been fifty miles per hour and caught hold of one of the shield antennae on the next transport seconds later.

From the outside, transports looked bulky and bloated. The kettle, the soldier- and cargo-carrying part of the ship, was a dome with a twelve-foot roof. The core of the ship was a narrow spine with stubby wings. The spine ran across the top of the kettle. From the side, transports reminded me of a severely pregnant dragonfly.

I pulled my way around the next transport. When I came to the opening at the back, I looked around the door and saw three men floating inside. Given the opportunity, I would have pulled my particle beam and shot all three of them. I did not have that option.

"Philips?" I called on the interLink.

"Master Sarge, you on their transport yet? It's getting a bit hot up here," Philips said, sounding more bored than anything else.

"I'm in trouble here. You have any puppets left?"

"Sure, Sergeant. I've still got a stiffy for you." The rest of the platoon heard this. I heard them giggling over the interLink.

"Grab your stiff... your puppet, and get down here," I ordered. "Thomer, watch his back."

"I'm already on it," Thomer said. Thomer protected Philips, not that the guy needed much in the way of protection.

Less than ten seconds passed before Evans came on line, and said, "They're sending in a scout to check out the barricade."

"Are you dark?" I asked. Dark meant that he had engaged his stealth kit and hidden himself.

"I'm in a vent. I can see them from here. They're examining the bodies."

"Are they fooled?" I asked.

"You sick bastard," Sutherland yelled.

"What is it?" I asked.

"There's a Mogat playing with one of the bodies. He's posing it like a doll."

"Someone's playing with my stiffy?" Philips asked.

"Where are you, Philips?" I asked.

"Right outside your hangar. You ready to roll?"

That was the thing about Philips—you never knew whether you should court-martial him or give him a medal. He could fight better than any Marine in my platoon. In his own way, Philips was a specking battlefield genius.

I looked around the ship just in time to see the bright green flash of a particle beam. Philips fired three times and hit three guards. The rest scattered and ran for cover.

"I don't know what's happening on your side of the boat, but this side just emptied in a hurry," Evans called down from the bridge.

"I'll bet. They're all headed this way," I said.

The Mogats in the transport flew out, their pistols drawn. Across the launch bay, the twelve remaining guards fired at the doorway.

"You okay out there, Philips?" I asked as I glided into the empty kettle.

"It's like kicking an anthill," Philips said. "My oh my, do those little buggies come after you." A moment later, "Oh, they got my stiffy in the leg. Guess I better hide."

Once inside the transport, I opened a cargo hatch and hid. The compartment was dark, small, and empty. I pulled my pistol and kept my finger on the trigger. In my mind, I imagined myself as a scorpion hiding under a leaf, waiting to sting anything that disturbed it.

I could not see what was happening around me. If somebody happened to open this compartment, they would spot me one moment and die the next.

"Okay, I'm in," I called over the interLink.

"I hope this works," Evans said.

"Watch your back, Master Sergeant," Sutherland said.

"I miss my stiffies," said Philips.

25

My time in the compartment was not quite as bad as being buried alive. Everything around me was dark and still, but I could move my arms around my sides. The compartment was so shallow that moving my arms across my chest took serious squirming.

Even after they boarded the transport and the kettle doors closed, the Mogats continued communicating over their obsolete interLink band. I listened in to some of their chatter—one hundred soldiers babbling on in two dozen different conversations. One guy bragged endlessly about the three "bargers" he bagged. "Bargers" must have been Mogat slang for U.A. sailors.

I did not hear a shred of valuable information eavesdropping on these lowlifes. When the pilot restored the atmosphere inside the kettle, the men took off their helmets and the interLink went silent.

The shell of the transport vibrated as the thrusters lifted it off the launch bay deck. I did not hear the engines so much as feel them. The metal beneath my back trembled so hard that its spasms shook me inside my armor.

"Evans, can you hear me?" I called over the interLink.

"Did you make it out?" Sergeant Evans asked.

"I'm on the transport," I said.

"Are you hidden?" he asked.

"I'm in a crawl space under the floor," I said. "What's the situation over there?"

"Three of their transports are out. The Mogats on that last one must not be in any rush to get home. They're taking a stroll around the ship."

"And our guys?" I asked.

The shell of the transport began to spasm again. I heard the thrusters working. They whispered through the hull. The transport made an eerie creaking sound.

"We're all in the vents."

"Stay hidden," I said.

"Aye, aye," Evans responded.

He was a good and reliable Marine. He was a bore.

The landing gear clanked as it struck the deck and its struts whined under the weight of the transport. We had landed on a Mogat battleship. The men in the kettle would file off the ship as fast as they could. Pilots usually took their time shutting down systems. I was deaf and blind down in the crawl space, so I would allot him plenty of time to leave the ship before opening the hatch above me. I remained motionless, lying on my back, alone in the dark.

I went over the layout of the derelict battleship in my mind. The layout of this ship would be identical. I remembered the path I took to get to the launch bay. I could not hide in an emergency elevator or pass through the vents this time. I would have to blend in.

"You there, Master Sergeant?" It was Evans on the interLink.

"What is it?"

"The last transport just flew out."

"Did they leave sentries?" I asked.

"The ship is clear," he said.

"How long till the explorer comes back?" I asked. I should have known that, but I had lost track of time.

"Should be another hour," Evans said.

"Okay, Evans, keep an eye out for my signal." That was the point of the entire exercise. If Yamashiro was right, and the Mogats had built themselves a communications superhighway, I would be able to send messages back to Evans no matter where the ship went.

Hiding in that small compartment went more smoothly than getting myself out, thanks to the zero-gravity conditions inside the derelict battleship. When I entered, I'd floated into place. Now, in gravity, I had to drag my own weight. The process would have been easier and quieter in soft-shell armor. I could barely move my limbs in the tight space, and that formerly weightless door now weighed over a hundred pounds.

If I ran into a guard or a maintenance worker, I could easily kill him; but I had learned from experience that the Mogats kept count of their crewmen. They were a religious people and they kept careful tabs on all of the sheep in the herd.

The kettle was dark and the rear doors were closed when I emerged from the compartment. I knew I was alone. At that moment I realized the stupid mistake I had made. My only access to the interLink was built into my helmet, but I could not walk around this Mogat ship wearing the combat armor of a Unified Authority Marine. I would need the Link, though; so even if I left my armor hidden on the transport, I had no choice about taking my helmet. I considered hiding in the transport until I was sure we had broadcasted into Mogat space, then trying to slip out; but down here in this compartment, I would not know when we broadcasted into Mogat space.

"Master Sergeant?" It was Evans.

"What is it?"

"You're reading me?"

Dumb question, I thought. "Sure, I'm reading you."

"Then your plan worked," Evans said, sounding excited.

"We've already broadcasted?" I asked.

"The last Mogat ships just broadcasted out."

"Thanks for the update," I said, trying to sound calm.

"Nice going," Evans said.

In the early days of the war, I received promotions for doing a lot less than this. Locating the Mogat home world could be the key to the war. With any luck, I would find their galactic coordinates and take an informal inventory of their military strength. Wars were won and lost on that kind of information.

But I did not have time to celebrate just yet. I still had to get out of the transport and on to the Mogat home world unnoticed. I had to gather information. I had to transmit the information back to Earth. I had to survive.

26

The kettle was dark and the hatch was sealed when I emerged from my lair. No one remained on board, not even the pilot. Sitting on the floor with my legs dangling into the crawl space, I removed my armor and stripped down to my tank top and skivvies. I'd brought a change of clothes for the occasion—a pair of unmarked fatigues that I borrowed from a mechanic on board the *Obama.* My costume might fool people around the battleship, but I needed a Mogat uniform. I also needed a box for my helmet. I left most of my armor buried at the very back of the crawl space under the floor.

Taking one last look through the night-for-day lens in my helmet, I located the controls for the rear hatch and opened the kettle. As the thick metal doors slowly rolled apart, revealing a bustling launch bay, I stowed my helmet in the latrine. Armor that had helped me slip past a dozen guards deserved better than a stay in a Mogat shitting booth, but I had no choice.

Teams of mechanics stood around the opened engine compartment of a nearby transport. A pack of commandos entertained several onlookers telling stories about how they had routed "those U.A. bargers," using their guns as props as they spoke.

None of this could have happened without Philips. If I survived this, I planned to petition for him to be restored to the rank of corporal. I thought I could talk Brocius into approving the request, but I had no idea how to keep Philips from getting himself busted back down to private without retiring him or throwing him in the brig.

Before I could do anything for Philips, there was the little matter of surviving the trip. I thought, just for a moment, of Samson captured and put on display in a Philistine temple. Samson asked God to give him the strength to destroy that temple, committing suicide in the act. Me, I had no desire to go down with these particular Philistines. I would pull a fast exit before I sent in the coordinates. The Unified Authority made a vengeful god indeed.

"You. What are you doing there?" An engineer walking by the base of the transport saw me standing in the darkened kettle.

"Tertiary system back up," I said, trying to come up with a lie no one would investigate. "The pilot asked me to have a look at it."

"No, shit," the man said. I pretended to laugh because the man looked so specking pleased with his pun.

"I wish," I said. "There's a mountain of it. Where are the septic removal kits?"

The man grimaced and pointed to a row of doors.

"I know it's in the supplies, but which door?" I asked. "I mostly just mop and polish."

"Third door. Have fun," he said.

"You ever clean up a crapper that overflowed in zero gravity?" I asked. "That's not my idea of fun."

The guy grunted a laugh and walked away. If he asked any of the commandos about the toilet, my goose was fried; but I doubted he would.

The storage room turned out to be a gold mine. The septic removal kit came in a twenty-four-inch tin cylinder that could easily hold my helmet. I also found a laundry cart filled with grimy janitorial crew smocks. A guy in a dirty smock carrying a "septic cylinder"—there is no better camouflage.

So I stepped into janitorial rags. The cloth smelled bad and felt wet against my skin. The pile I stole it from was headed for a washing. So much the better. I took a septic kit and headed back to the transport. Locked in the booth-sized latrine, I emptied out the kit—a large cylinder for waste and chemicals for cleaning. I flushed the chemicals down the crapper. Then I loaded my helmet into the cylinder and sealed it. In a real tertiary situation, I would compress the refuse and discharge it into the cylinder. For good measure, I fished some slime from the septic system and smeared it around the top of the cylinder. Both my hand and that cylinder reeked fiercely. When I left the transport, I felt confident that no one would bother me. I looked bad, smelled worse, and had a big slimy septic cylinder in my hands. No one would approach me unless he had a good reason.

By the time I came down the ramp, the last of the Mogat commandos had already left the launch bay. They would go back to their barracks. They would shower and change. Their commanders would give them the remainder of the day to rest as a reward for winning the skirmish. They deserved it. They'd taught Philips's stiffies a thing or two. They would go off to whatever served as a bar on the ship, get drunk, and tell ever-more-exaggerated stories about the deadly firefight they had won.

As for me, I needed information. I needed to know where I was and if I was near the Mogat home base. Knowing how to find the

Mogats would be valuable enough. That information alone could turn the tide of the war, if we could reach them. The galaxy was one hundred thousand light-years across. The Unified Authority had eighteen fleets; but without the Broadcast Network, they could only patrol one-one-thousandth of 1 percent of galaxy.

The Mogats, with their self-broadcasting fleet, could go anywhere. Their base could be a single light-year from Earth in any direction, and without some facility to broadcast its ships, the U.A. Navy would never reach it.

On the plus side, I thought that I might have an ally nearby. True, nearly a month had passed since the SEALs and I distracted the Mogats while Illych boarded their transport, but I thought I might find him somewhere lurking around their base. The problem was that I had no idea how to contact him.

Leaving the launch bay I entered a main corridor of the ship. A group of sailors loitered near the door doing, as far as I could tell, absolutely nothing. They might have been off duty, but they were still in uniform and standing in one of the most highly trafficked areas of any ship. It did not surprise me to see that the Mogats ran a relaxed ship. They were, after all, civilians in sailor uniforms. In a real navy, men go to rec rooms and canteens during their off-duty hours. If they are tired they remain in their barracks.

The dawdling oafs paid little attention to me as I walked by. They showed no signs of suspicion. One man sneered at me. He probably resented my dragging a septic cylinder down his clean corridor. On the most part, the only interest I elicited in the men I passed was interest in seeing me leave.

After two excursions on a derelict battleship, I had no trouble finding my way around. I went up three levels and headed toward the bow of the ship. This would take me into an observation deck below the bridge. Once there, I would scout the space around us for stations, ships, and planets. If I did not find anything, I would need to go to the bridge. That might be a problem; I'd stand out like a leper carrying a septic cylinder onto the bridge.

I made my way down the main corridor. People steered clear of me and generally ignored me until I stepped onto an elevator. The door opened and there stood a lieutenant. "Where do you think you are going?"

"Fifth deck, sir," I said.

"Not with that shit can," he said. "Take the cargo lift."

I saluted with my refuse-stained hand. He did not return the salute.

When I found the cargo lift, I decided I liked it better than the elevator. I had the car to myself, for openers; no stuffy lieutenants. The car was an open platform. The only light in the shaft came from floodlights in the ceiling, but I did not need creature comforts.

The lift let me off in a dark service corridor. I did not know how Mogat sailors spent their time, but ship maintenance could not have ranked high on their priority list. A row of work carts lined the wall, ending by a pile of empty pallets.

I thought that I might have a use for this empty corridor. I needed a place to hide my helmet. The area was not secure enough to test the old interLink, but I did take the opportunity to stash the cylinder with my helmet, cylinder can and all, on the floor between the carts and the pallets. Then I went to explore.

I found my way out of that service corridor and meandered in the general direction of the observation deck. It was essentially a rec room. Off-duty sailors came here to drink and talk. I worried that a man in janitor clothes would stand out; but now that I had ditched the smelly cylinder, no one paid attention to me.

The Mogats ran the rec room like a nightclub. It had chrome-and-glass furniture, dim lighting, a bar made of some kind of obsidian glass. Men lounged about, some drinking, some smoking, some doing both. I could not tell if the mix included officers and enlisted men. In a navy as informal as this one, officers and enlisted men might share the same bar.

"Hey, Mr. Clean, you here to work or to gawk?" a sailor shouted in my direction. "Move it, fellah. You're stinking up the air."

I nodded and moved out of his way. Under other circumstances, I might have broken his neck.

The observation wall was twenty feet tall and forty feet wide, like a giant movie screen that showed nothing but outer space. Today's panorama displayed at least fifty other ships, three out-of-use dry-dock facilities, and a distant planet that I did not recognize. The planet had a uniform gray-brown surface. Whatever sun had once shone on this planet had long since expired. I had gone to war on a planet like it before. The gas on that planet would strip you to the bone if it got through your space gear.

I needed more information, and I knew I could not get it as a janitor. I wanted to explore the bridge and I especially wanted to get down to that planet. In the meantime, I would not complain about a sandwich. Between the puppet show and the ride to this ship, a lot of time had passed since my last meal.

27

"Evans, where are you now?" I asked.

"I'm on a Perseus Fleet frigate," Evans said. "We're about six million miles from the wreck."

"And the signal is coming through?" I asked.

"We're talking," Evans pointed out.

"Did everyone make it back?" I asked.

"The entire platoon is present and accounted for, except you."

"I need you to get a message to the *Kamehameha*. Ask them if they have any suggestions about how I might be able to locate a SEAL."

"You mean the Special Ops guys?" Evans asked.

"One of their men is behind enemy lines," I said.

"I thought the whole thing about the SEALs was that they never left anyone behind," Evans said.

"It wasn't like that," I said. "It was more like they sent him ahead."

Though I had the boiler room to myself, I saw no reason to push my luck. I told Evans that I would call back as soon as I could.

If the Mogats had their entire fleet around here, Illych could have been on any of those ships. If the Mogats had a base on that dead planet, I suspected I would find him in their base. He would go wherever he could do the most damage.

A month had passed since he landed on Mogat territory. Alone and cut off from his platoon, Illych might think he had no real hope of ever getting home. A guy like him would want to go out making the biggest bang he could. He might already have made his mark.

Still dressed in my janitor's smock, I entered the officers' laundry and stole a lieutenant's uniform that fitted reasonably well. I found a gym and showered, then visited the mess hall. The place was nearly empty, but the Mogats had a twenty-four-hour self-service counter. I slid my tray along a stainless steel counter and scooped up a helping of some sort of casserole, three slices of bread, a cube of Jell-O, and a salad.

The chow the Mogats fed their men tasted bad, really bad. They ate hard bread that crumbled to dust in my fingers. The chicken-and-cheese dish looked nice until I dug into it with my fork. Under its yellow and white surface, the entire dish was gray. The stuff that passed as meat was more likely chicken-flavored gluten. The salad might have been made out of the same stuff as the chicken. It did not contain genuine vegetables. Looking around the mess hall, I noted that the other men in the facility ate with no enthusiasm.

If I hoped to learn anything of value, I would not hear it in the mess hall. The men gossiped about various officers and little else. One sailor spoke endlessly about going down to the planet to visit his family. The more I listened to him, the more I believed that the Mogats had settled the rancid planet near which we had moored.

The bad food told me something, too. When news analysts spoke about the Morgan Atkins Believers on the mediaLink, they described them as the human equivalent of a swarm of locusts. Before the war, Mogat colonies did not mix with society at large. They sent missionaries into communities, but they generally remained in their own private districts. Whatever food and goods they produced, they sold among themselves. Now I thought I knew why. Who would buy shit like this? And where did they get it? Not from that planet.

If the Mogats really lived on the cinder ash of a planet below us, eking out enough food to feed an army would take a miracle. I ate what I could of my meal and threw the rest away, knowing its substances would be recycled and served at that same counter in some other form within the week.

Now that I was unofficially a Mogat lieutenant, I could move around the ship more easily. I entered an equipment depot and told the man at the desk to find me an empty box. He disappeared through the door and returned a few minutes later with a two-foot cube that looked just a shade too big for transporting my helmet.

"It's bigger than I wanted," I growled, though I was actually quite pleased. Officers never accept the first offer no matter how good.

"Better big than small," the man said.

"Do you have any padding for this box?"

He took the box and disappeared through the door again.

No more than a minute later, he handed the box back to me. Along the bottom he had spread a few inches of packing gel.

"Good enough," I said and left.

The variety of faces on the ship left me feeling off-balance. On a Unified Authority ship, the man at the supply desk would have been a clone. Clones performed all of the menial work. They worked in crews, each clone's neural programming struggling to convince him that he was the only natural-born sailor in the entire Navy who mopped decks or lugged cargo.

I took my box back to the service hall. After making sure no one was around, I removed my helmet from the septic cylinder and placed it in the box, pushing it deep into the packing gel. Then I sealed the box and labeled it, "HQ Urgent."

I returned to the launch bay and found the officer directing traffic. "When is the next ride down?" I asked.

"I've got one leaving within the hour," the man said.

"Do you have space for one more?" I asked.

"No problem," he said. "Two if you want to bring a friend along."

"Just this," I said, holding up my box.

"Want me to pack that for you?" he asked.

"I think I'd better keep this one with me," I said. "Thanks, though."

The man cast a wary glance at the word "Urgent," but knew better than to ask about it.

I expected to travel down in the absolute discomfort of a military transport. With their bare benches and steel walls, kettles had a torture-chamber charm about them.

As it turned out, the next ride was a Johnston R-56 Starliner, a commuter plane. I found a seat and watched the other passengers to see if they would have space gear.

The planet below would have a toxic atmosphere. If it was anything like Hubble, the burned-out planet on which I fought my first real battle as a Marine, the planet would have toxic oily gas instead of air. That oil dissolved flesh and soft plastics. Seven other passengers showed up for the flight down to the planet. None of them had space gear.

When the deck officer called us to board, I followed the other passengers onto the Starliner. All of them wore regular uniforms with not so much as an oxygen tube.

My box did not fit in the compartment above my seat. Fortunately, the flight was almost empty. No one complained when I placed my box on the empty seat beside my own.

I was glad to relax and ride a comfortable commuter down to the planet instead of a transport. In a windowless kettle, I could only sit and count the minutes until the heavy metal doors at the rear slid open. From my seat on the Starliner, I could start scouting the moment we left the battleship.

The launch-bay officer walked through the ship. He went to the cockpit and spoke to the pilot. Then he came back down the aisle and counted passengers. Then he left.

"Prepare for takeoff," the pilot radioed back to us. A moment later we taxied to the front of the launch bay. The atmospheric locks closed behind us. I heard the thrusters flare and we lifted off the deck.

As we left the ship, I began counting ships. Once more showing their military incompetence, they had allowed their navy to park in disarray. One battleship was so hemmed in by the smaller ships around it that I doubted its crew could fire its engines without blasting two destroyers behind it. I saw clusters of ships in every direction, all with bulbous bows and charcoal-colored hulls. The stars were thick in this part of the galaxy, and the silhouettes of the ships stood out like crows flying through a clear noon sky. I did not have time to make a full count; but from what I saw, it seemed entirely possible that the Mogats had their entire four-hundred-ship armada circling the planet.

I spotted dozens of ships by checking for shadow shapes against the stars. There were ships floating beneath us. I saw them very clearly against the murky atmosphere of the planet.

I thought about that battle on Hubble. The Mogats had dug in long before the Unified Authority arrived with its overwhelming force. We sent a hundred thousand Marines down for that invasion. We had tanks and Harriers and gunships, and they had snake shafts—hidden trenches that were twenty feet deep and even farther across. No one knew what snake shafts were used for, but we found out on Hubble. The shafts gathered corrosive gas. Once our forces were in the middle of their trap, the Mogats blew the tops off their snake shafts. Marines and equipment fell in alike. Those shafts became shallow graves.

It took only three minutes to reach the atmosphere of the planet. We entered into the atmosphere at a sharp angle, then leveled out a few miles up. Beneath us, stretched out like an ancient leather scroll, the Mogat planet looked devoid of life. The surface was dark. I saw no sign of water, just a black-and-brown landscape with ash for dirt and obsidian mountains. The rockets on the Starliner ignited small explosions in the oily air outside. I saw no clouds or light in the sky, just a smoggy haze as thick as smoke and even less breathable.

So this is their "promised land," I thought. By serving their false god they had condemned themselves to this.

We flew across that dead planet for three hours. According to the 2508 census, over 200 million people identified themselves as members of the Morgan Atkins Movement—a sizable population. You might be able to hide 200 million people on a settled planet like Earth, but not a planet like this. They would have needed an enormous environmental dome of some sort.

The Starliner had a top atmospheric speed of Mach 3, which meant we had probably covered nine thousand miles when the plane slowed and began its descent. Searching the horizon ahead, I saw more plains and yet another obsidian mountain range. There was nothing else to see. I expected a giant dome or the glow of lights against the horizon. Nothing.

We were no more than a few hundred yards above the mountain peaks when I finally spotted our target. Instead of a dome, we flew to an isolated mountain. We dropped lower and lower as we crossed the plains that separated the peak from the others. Craning my neck so that I could see ahead, I spotted a row of blinking lights marking some sort of tunnel. A moment later we entered.

Someone had cut a doorway into the face of the mountain. The opening was so large you could fit a navy cruiser through it. I saw the rows of synchronized lights that winked on and off along each of the walls. Looking out one side of the Starliner, then the other, I estimated that this entrance was half a mile wide and at least a quarter mile in height.

I felt a slight tremor as the pilot killed the Starliner's engines. We had not yet landed. In fact, staring down as far as I could, I saw no sign of a landing area. I did see an occasional flash of light, and I saw other ships rising straight out of the darkness. They just seemed to levitate straight into the air.

Having extensive experience flying a Starliner, I had a working knowledge about the thruster rockets Starliners used for vertical lifts. They were made for use in zero- and low-gravity situations. They were far too weak to hold the ship in place for an extended period. Starting to panic, I listened for the thrusters and did not hear them. I would have noticed if the pilot had landed the ship. Looking out the window, I saw that something was conveying us downward slowly, but I did not know what.

"Still not used to the gravity chute, Lieutenant?"

When I turned around, I saw the pilot staring down at me. I shook my head.

"I don't think I will ever get used to it," the pilot confessed. "It still scares me." He patted me on the shoulder and walked away.

A "gravity chute"? I had never heard the term before and had no idea how such a thing could work. All I knew was that we were dropping miles below the surface of the planet, and here the pilot stood gabbing with me instead of sitting by the controls. Something else occurred to me, too. Had I been in a better temper, I might have joked that my chance of survival had just gone down the chute.

28

When Morgan Atkins, the majority leader of the Senate, hijacked the self-broadcasting fleet and vanished, he must have already had thousands of followers. He had hundreds of millions of followers when the war broke out. But nothing explained what I saw when we reached the bottom of the gravity chute.

The man-made subterranean plateau on which his people lived stretched farther than I could see. To have said it was sparsely populated would have been an act of criminal understatement. The ground below us was an endless plain with an occasional building. But the main feature here was not the occasional building, it was the endless plain. Had I viewed the cavern from space, I might have been able to see all the way across it; then again, it might have stretched beyond the curvature of the planet. Below us, streets as straight as rulers formed a perfect grid. The only buildings I saw were stubby cubes spaced two or three miles apart.

The Starliner's engines kicked on as we dropped out of the gravity chute. I looked out the top of the window for a last glance at the chute and saw something unexpected. Instead of the rock roof of a subterranean cavern, I saw an expansive night sky. It was as if I could see straight through miles of rock and right into that polluted sky above the surface of the planet.

I wanted to stare, I wanted to gape, I wanted to ask a million questions; but I had already drawn too much attention to myself. I forced myself to look away from the window and act casual about the impossibilities outside.

Just before we landed, I saw a military transport rising straight up from the spaceport below us. That ship easily had one hundred times the mass of the streamlined Starliner, which was dagger-shaped and aerodynamic. That transport, with its bloated kettle, was anything but aerodynamic. It looked like something made to fall, not fly. It relied on powerful rockets to maneuver in gravity. It rose from the ground through the hard effort of a dozen booster rockets, then it reached the bottom of the gravity chute. The rockets switched off, and the transport rose as smoothly and effortlessly as an air bubble in water—thousands of tons of steel, rising straight up through the chute.

Unlike the transport, which had skids instead of wheels, our Starliner came to a rolling stop along the runway. The engines slowed, and we taxied forward toward a terminal. As we rolled ahead, I studied the cube-shaped buildings in the distance. If I had the distances and proportions correct in my head, those buildings stood approximately four stories tall. I saw no windows on their rose gray facades.

The Starliner pulled up to a terminal, if you could call it that. It was a ten-foot arch with people waiting under it. A moment after we came to a stop, the pilot walked into the cabin and opened the hatch. My seat was one row back from the hatch. A cool breeze blew in around me.

"Welcome home, boys," the pilot said to the cabin in general. There were nine passengers on the flight including me. We all wore Navy uniforms.

I pretended to fidget with my box while the first passengers stepped out of the Starliner. I did not want to lead the way off the plane. Not knowing the lay of the land or the protocol, it would be too easy for me to expose myself by making some obvious mistake.

As I stepped into the fresh air of the deep underground cavern, I saw three children running to meet one of the other passengers. A woman in a blue dress followed, coming up to the man and kissing him on the mouth. I tried to tell myself that women and children were not a problem. The Mogats had started the war. They attacked civilian sites. In order to win, we would need to do the same. My arguments fell on deaf ears.

I thought of the times in the Bible when God directed His generals to annihilate entire populations of enemies. In His new guise as the Unified Authority, He had not become any more forgiving. The Mogats won that first round on Hubble with their snake shafts, but we settled the score in that battle. Lord did we ever settle that score.

I followed the other passengers across the empty landing field and out to the street. The guy with the family headed in one direction, his children buzzing around him and his wife like bees in a flower bed. The man had his arm around her waist.

"How long are you down for, Lieutenant?" the pilot asked me.

"I'm not sure," I said.

"R and R?" he asked.

He was trying to be friendly. Even if I had been a real Mogat lieutenant, I would not have wanted to chat. I could have pretended, but I preferred to play things as close to real as possible. I did what I would have done on Earth if I didn't feel like talking. "Yeah," I grunted. "R and R." I hoped I sounded like somebody who wanted to be left alone making a halfhearted attempt to sound friendly.

"Well, have a nice stay," the pilot said. Message received.

I looked up one side of the street, then down the other. The nearest buildings were at least a mile away in every direction. From here, they looked exactly alike. They were made of the same dull plastic material, and they all appeared to be approximately fifty feet tall and shaped like cubes. Resolutely uniform.

During the battle on Hubble, the Mogats lived in a large underground cavern; but it was nothing like this. The cavern on Hubble was rough-hewn. When we sent probes down, we saw no cube-shaped buildings and no gridwork of streets. They had oxygen and strings of lightbulbs powered by portable generators. I wondered if they could ever have made something like this on Hubble, had they been given enough time. On that occasion, we gave them no time.

As I thought about Hubble, a small shudder ran the length of my spine. I lost friends on Hubble. I witnessed a massacre. The planet made me feel desolate when we landed. By the time we left, I had no feeling at all.

The ground around me on this planet was flat, with no notable features. The sheer uniformity of this city left me disoriented. The computers in my helmet could have created a virtual map to mark my path as I explored, but I could not go walking around a Mogat city wearing the combat helmet of a Unified Authority Marine.

In fact, I could not afford to do anything suspicious. If this was the Mogat promised land, there would be a sizable population. As I looked around, I saw only a scattering of people walking the streets; but I might have arrived during their night or perhaps a time of prayer. I knew so little about Mogat beliefs. Maybe they had prayer hours like Moslems, a time when every man spread his mat and prayed. The Starliner might have let us off in an unpopulated district. Perhaps we would take a train into a larger city.

I needed someplace to hide and access the interLink, but I saw no alleys, just scattered buildings with endless open space between them. I saw no signs to indicate one street from the next. No vehicles moved along the streets. They were broad and clean and entirely unused. I had the feeling I could sleep in the middle of any road without worrying about ever being hit by a car.

All of the other passengers had left, and I did not want to call attention to myself by loitering. Since the pilot went right, I headed left. I simply grabbed my box by its handle and started walking toward the closest building in that direction.

Cubes play optical illusions on your eyes. From the air, all of the buildings looked four stories tall. From the street, the nearest building looked smaller and closer, maybe a mile away. It was a cube in an open space. It could have been ten miles away and forty stories tall. If I had my helmet on, I could have measured the distance to the building and the height of the walls. I ached for my armor.

It took me about twenty minutes to reach that building. As I got closer, I realized that its blank façade gave no clues about what the Mogats used it for. It could have been a movie holotorium or a penitentiary or a home for wayward violinists. It might have been abandoned. From what I could see, it had no windows. The only feature I saw was an open doorway in the front. It reached almost all the way to the roof.

This cannot possibly be the Mogat home world, I thought. I had traveled a mile or two and seen no homes, no vehicles, and barely any people. If there were really 200 million Mogats, and this was their planet, I should have seen crowds.

When I reached the first building, I put down my box, peered in through the doorway, and found myself alone. I strolled in through the tall doorway and paused. The building was hollow, a four-story empty cube. Its gray façade had a strange rose-colored tint. It was made out of some smooth, cool material that looked like a merging of plastic and marble.

Thinking that I might have come to an abandoned structure, I turned and stared back down the street. Something else caught my eye. This planet did not have a sun, but there was enough ambient light to create the illusion of daylight. Looking back into the sky, I recognized the layer of phosphorous gas that must have provided the light for the internal world. I assumed it was phosphorous gas, and I assumed they could charge the ions in that gas to simulate an entire day-night cycle.

I wondered about the Mogats. They had no concept of how to run a military or maintain battleships, but I had never seen such technological miracles as I found here.

Back in the direction I came from, the Starliner took off from the spaceport with the customary rolling start of an atmospheric craft. It zipped over the ground at a shallow angle, hung a wide, looping curve, then decelerated as it spiraled back toward the opening of the gravity chute. Just as it reached the chute, the Starliner came to a dead stop. It did not drop. Caught in the mysterious updraft, it hovered higher until it disappeared from sight. At that same moment, a military transport dropped out of the chute. Its thruster rockets ignited, and it hovered toward the ground.

I did not understand what technology governed this planet. I did not believe that the Unified Authority Corps of Engineers could hollow a planet, and I knew they had nothing resembling a gravity chute. Maybe Atkins and his followers had more luck converting scientists than they did converting soldiers. On the other hand, I had heard that Atkins's Space Bible told wild stories about an underground city and aliens with light emanating from their being. Well, they certainly had an underground city. I would need to keep my eyes peeled for radiant beings.

I turned and entered that hollow building. As I entered, I

realized that I could see through the inside of its walls. They'd built the structure using some kind of translucent material. From the outside it looked like a mixture of marble and plastic. From the inside it seemed more like tinted glass.

Inside the building I found nothing but a gigantic foyer. There was no furniture, no signs, nothing but a waist-high wall with a rail around it in the center of the floor. Feeling discouraged, I examined that wall and realized that I was peering over the edge of a terrace. Below me, I saw a crowded city block. The drop from this rail was a good hundred feet, but it was not the drop that interested me.

Below the building, a thriving sea of humanity bustled along, completely unaware of me. It was like staring into a paved and urbanized ant colony. I saw businessmen and women and soldiers in uniforms. I saw a street and cars.

Up here I was alone and ignored; but one hundred feet below me, an entire society existed. Though I barely believed what I saw, I needed to report it. Looking out at the street through the walls around me, I saw no one nearby. I crouched down behind the waist-high wall, opened the box, and took out my helmet. After one last unnecessary look around to make sure no one would see me, I lowered the helmet over my head and tried the interLink.

"Evans, are you there?"

"Sergeant, are you on?" Sutherland asked.

"Yeah," I said, still feeling a dreamy kind of unreality. "I'm on."

"Where are you?" Sutherland asked.

"I think I'm on the Mogat home world. I'm going to send you some visuals." I stood up, checked again to make sure the coast was clear, then headed out the door.

"What the hell?" Sutherland asked.

"This is what their buildings look like," I said.

"They're made of glass?"

"Not from the outside," I said. The street was still empty. I stepped out and turned toward the building so that Sutherland could see. From the outside, the building was opaque.

"That's some magic trick," Sutherland said.

"I'll show you a better one," I said. I went back in the building and looked over the rail. All of Mogat humanity walked below me.

I was transmitting all of this to Sutherland so that he could see exactly what I saw. More importantly, his helmet recorded the transmission. He could send the images up the chain until they landed on Admiral Brocius's desk.

"Are you getting this?" I asked.

"Are you shitting me?" Sutherland asked. "Have you been down there?"

"No," I said. "I just got here. Look, I need to get going before someone comes by. Do you know if Evans contacted the *Kamehameha?*"

"The question about how to find a SEAL? Yeah, he got through. They told him to do a little sabotage. You're supposed to blow up a couple of buildings, then travel six hundred yards at a 110-degree angle from front and center. Do that enough times, and they claim their boy will find you.

"And by the way, they say they want their SEAL brought back to them in one piece and unharmed."

"Do they?" I asked.

"Yeah. They also say that if you don't bring him back in the same condition you got him in..."

"That I might as well stay here?" I interrupted.

"No, that you will wish you never made it off Ravenwood alive."

Ravenwood Outpost was a testing ground for SEALs. The Outer Scutum-Crux Fleet Command sent Marines to defend a small outpost on that planet. Then they sent SEALs to infiltrate the outpost and kill the men guarding it. I was the only Marine who'd ever made it out alive.

29

The first time I entered the building, I did not notice that the rear wall was opaque. As I removed my helmet, I saw it. After stowing my helmet back in the box, I went for a closer look and quickly realized that this great hollow shell of a building was little more than an elevator station. The entire back wall of the building was taken up by a bank of thirty-six lifts.

I did not like stepping into an enemy elevator. As the door shut behind me, I remembered the days I spent locked in the brig of a Mogat battleship. I knew nothing would happen here. The Mogats could not know that I had landed on their planet and, as far as I could tell, nobody saw me enter the elevator; but I felt a claustrophobic shiver when the doors shut behind me.

The lift had no controls. The doors opened and closed automatically when the car dropped to the next floor. A lighted display beside the door showed that there were six more subterranean levels. Thinking about the sheer size of the place as I stepped off the elevator, I felt like I was lost at sea.

Every step I took seemed to take me farther from ever returning home, assuming I had a home. I had broadcasted into an unknown quadrant of space on a Mogat battleship, dropped miles beneath the surface of a seemingly uninhabitable planet, and descended one level deeper into that planet on an elevator.

Each new step was another move deeper into a heart of darkness. That may sound overly dramatic, but when I looked up to see the terrace from which I had viewed the city block, I saw nothing but sky. Once again I could see through everything above me as if it had not been there. All I saw was that dark and hazy sky with its phosphorous-induced simulated sunlight.

The floor to which I had just descended sprawled in every direction. The terrain was as uniform as the landscape on the floor above. Like the floor above, it had its own horizon.

This layer of the Mogat planet qualified as a city. While the sky appeared to be several miles up, I knew it was an illusion. I had just seen that stretch of street from an elevator no more than a hundred feet up from the spot where I stood. Like me, the architects who designed the buildings around this amazing place knew the limitations. Four-story and five-story buildings, grouped like trees in a forest, dominated the landscape. The only buildings that actually reached the sky were these tall narrow pillars spaced several miles apart. When I looked back at the elevator from which I had come, I realized the pillars were elevator shafts.

Now that I had stepped out in the lower level, I found it far from crowded, but busy nonetheless. A steady flow of people walked past me as I looked across the skyline and tried to find my bearings. Men, the majority of whom wore military uniforms, walked into buildings so nondescript that they would have fitted in on any Marine base in the galaxy. Scanning the crowd, I saw people of every description—tall men, short men, fat men, men with blond hair and others with red hair. What I did not see was clones.

As a group of men walked past me, one stopped to give me a second glance and said something to his friends as they walked away. His pals did not give me a second glance as they continued down the street, but the first guy turned back for one more look. I decided to head in the opposite direction, turning at the next corner to disappear from view. As I passed the façade of a long, two-story building, a man in a Mogat Navy uniform stepped out. He seemed to watch me for a moment, then smiled to himself and shook his head. Perhaps he had mistaken me for a friend. Maybe I had made some mistake with my officer's uniform. In the moment that the man seemed to think he recognized me, I thought I saw fear in his expression.

Walking alone in enemy territory made me paranoid. Atkins Believers considered clones evil. In their pantheon of wrong and right, Liberator clones were the kith and kin of Satan himself. Fortunately, after those first few encounters, no one else seemed to take notice of me.

I found a train station and entered. Apparently it did not cost money to ride the trains. I saw no booths or machines for taking money. Just inside the station, I found a large map, which I stopped to study.

The Mogats had laid their world out in sectors. In one corner of that map, I saw a diagram showing all of the sectors on the planet. It included industrial, residential, and government districts. I saw no financial sector. I was in their military sector, one of the smaller portions of the metropolis.

In the center of everything was a compound marked only as the "Morgan Atkins Society." I had no idea what that might be, but I suspected it was religious.

So the Mogats had grouped their entire military complex

into one concentrated area. From a tactical standpoint, that was idiotic. By grouping their military, they had presented the Unified Authority a perfect target. If we could reach this planet, we could neutralize their entire military complex with one shot. Maybe they knew that. Their subterranean location would protect them from an orbital attack.

The map offered a street-by-street detail of the military sector. I located several munitions depots within striking distance of where I stood. I thought about the chicanery I hoped to accomplish and started to formulate a plan.

I also picked up a shadow while I was at the train station.

30

He was an old man. He might have been in his eighties, he might have been in his nineties. That old fellow might have lived on Earth when man first attempted instantaneous travel, for all I knew. After a certain point, the ravages of age do no more damage. This ancient fellow had long since left that point behind. His white hair was as fine as cotton filaments. The hint of pink on his wrinkled white skin was the only color in his face, and his stiffly hunched shoulders rode high on his neck.

He made no effort to hide his curiosity about me but walked right up to me and stared into my face. His dark eyes did not flinch under their bushy white eyebrows, and his thin lips seemed to curl over his gums as he stared up at me. He squinted, and then put on old-fashioned glasses with half-inch-thick lenses that made his eyes look too large for his face.

It did not occur to me at the moment, but I should have realized that an old Mogat like that might well know my face. Well, he would not know me, but he would know my kind. Fifty years earlier, a battalion of Liberators invaded the Mogat stronghold and ended the Galactic Central War. But, as I say, that had not yet occurred to me as the old man gaped at me.

"Can I help you?" I asked.

"You." His voice was as dry as a reed in December. "You, what is your name?" he demanded.

I did not want to alarm the old fellow, so I humored him. "Klein," I said. A large portion of the Mogat population went by a single name. Klein was a Mogat I met shortly after joining the Marines. He tried to kill me twice. The first time he lost a hand. His second attempt ended with his execution.

"Klein," the man repeated. His lips worked the name a few more times, but only whistling breath came out of his mouth. Then he shook his head and walked away.

I thought he was gone and breathed a sigh of relief. Five minutes later the old man returned with a solider—a tall, muscular-looking gent. The soldier wore the jade green fatigues of the Mogat Army. He had a sidearm. He might well have been with the military police.

Withered old prick, I thought to myself as I saw the old man and his companion heading toward the train platform. They were about two hundred feet away. The soldier clearly wanted to run after me, but the old man now clung on to him for support. As the soldier studied me, our eyes met. Even from this distance, I did not like what I saw.

At that moment, a cool wind blew across my neck and a train rocketed into the station. The train was long, low, and squat—about thirty feet wide and ten feet tall, traveling on a cushion of magnetic levitation.

I chanced a quick look back and saw the soldier running in my direction. The old man stood watching the scene, still pointing at me. It was at that moment that I finally woke up to the possibility that the old man might well have fought in the Galactic Central War. Suddenly I realized that he might not have mistaken me for someone else. With that momentary epiphany, I jumped onto the train, not caring where it took me. Had I realized where the train was headed, I would never have boarded. It took me to Military Administration—the Mogat Pentagon.

Looking through the train window, I could see the soldier sprinting after me. *Come and get it, big boy,* I thought to myself, knowing that the best outcome for me would be for the soldier to catch me before he reported sighting a Liberator. Right now it was just the soldier, the old man, and me. I would not feel bad about killing the soldier or the old man if I had to.

The soldier scrambled past pedestrians and leaped up onto the platform. I lost sight of him from there, but he certainly boarded the train before it pulled out of the station.

Each car in the train could carry a hundred passengers, but mine was almost empty. There were only about ten or maybe twelve other passengers. I stood on one end of the car. The soldier entered from the opposite side. He stood staring at me for a moment as he caught his breath. Even if the old man had recognized me as a Liberator, why should the soldier believe such a thing? We had supposedly gone extinct decades ago. I was even more of a fossil than the old geezer who spotted me.

Deciding to take the straightforward approach, I walked right up to that soldier, and asked, "What was with that old man?"

The soldier was a big man. He stood an inch or two taller than me. He probably stood six-five, and he might have outweighed me by forty pounds. He had bristly red hair cropped well above his ears.

"He came up to me in the station looking upset about something," I continued, still hoping to defuse the situation.

The soldier glared at me and nodded. "He thinks you're a clone."

"A clone?" I asked.

"A Liberator clone," the soldier said.

"A Liberator clone?" I asked, trying to sound as if I had just heard a joke. "I've been called a lot of things, but this is the first time anyone has accused me of being a Liberator."

"You and I are going to step off the train at the next station," the soldier said. He sounded angry. The insignia on his sleeves must have identified him as military police of some sort. He did not hesitate to order me off the train. If I read his bars correctly, he was a sergeant. I was disguised as a lieutenant. He should not have been speaking to me this way. Only an MP would act so rashly.

"I'm late for a..."

Up to this point, we spoke to each other in polite tones. None of the other passengers should have heard us. "Get off at the next stop," he growled. He punctuated the command by resting his hand on his pistol.

"If I miss this meeting, it will be your ass," I said.

As the train started to slow, a young couple stood up to leave. The woman had her arm around the young man's bicep. They looked like they were in love. The man, a sailor in uniform, saw me, and did a double take. Then he saw the soldier with his hand on his pistol grip. He scurried out of the car the moment the doors opened, pulling the woman behind him.

"What's the rush?" she asked.

"Hurry!" he snapped.

By the time we stepped onto the platform, the young lovers were halfway down the stairs to the street. I stood in front with the MP inches behind me and to my left. "That old man was wrong," I said, without looking back.

I could see the MP's reflection in the train window. He still had that angry expression. His hand was still on the pistol in his belt. I was unarmed.

"They showed us video feeds from the invasion when I was in school. The Liberators in those records looked just like you," the MP said.

I did not respond. With those words, he had sealed his fate.

By this time the sailor and his girlfriend had completely disappeared and the train had continued down the track. The MP shoved me from behind. Up ahead, I saw a doorway. It might have led to a security station or maintenance closet.

I felt something poking into my back and knew that the man had pulled his gun. "This way," the MP barked. The man was big and tough. He held the gun steady, but he held it too close. He stood too close.

"Move," he said.

"You don't need the pistol," I said.

"I'm tired of telling you to move," he said.

I looked around the platform. We were alone. I could see people walking along the sidewalks outside the station, but there was a fence around the platform. The pedestrians could not see us clearly.

"For the last time, clone, move."

The MP shoved me a second time. I spun on my right heel, sweeping the barrel of the pistol away from me with my right hand and slamming the edge of my left hand into the man's neck. The strike to his neck stunned him and stopped his breathing. I kept my hand on his neck to control him as I slammed my knee into his groin, knocking the wind and fight out him. Then I slid my hand from his neck to his shoulder and guided him down to the ground. Low and out of sight, I snapped the man's neck. It was an easy kill. It happened so fast that my combat reflex did not kick in.

I would have liked to have borrowed his gun. I even toyed with the idea of switching uniforms, but ended up playing the game safe. I rolled the MP into the magnetic slot through which the trains ran, gun and all. The electricity flowing through that track would not hurt the body but with any luck, the next train would smash him and run over the leftovers before more commuters arrived. Whatever was left behind would not be worth the cost of the autopsy.

31

Somewhere not too far from the train station, somebody set off a bomb. The reverberation of the explosion rushed through the buildings like a flood. Several columns of black smoke rose high into the air. The percussion was powerful, but the black color of the smoke and narrowness of the plumes suggested very little damage had been done.

All around me, men in green, blue, and tan officers' uniforms ran out of the various buildings and headed toward the explosion. Women in uniforms joined the queue. They formed a steady stream of humanity that funneled down the streetlike tributaries gathering into a river. I followed. As we got closer to the blast site, the crowd grew thicker. By the time I turned a corner and saw ground zero, I stood in a crowd of thousands.

No one paid any attention to me. All they cared about was the bombing. So the Morgan Atkins Believers had a terrorist among them, and I had a pretty good idea who that terrorist might be.

The smoke came from a row of cars that now lay on their sides with flames bursting out of the chassis. Because the air inside the cavernous settlement had a pleasant chill, I could feel the heat from the burning cars two hundred feet away.

"That's every day this week," a man complained. He shook his head. "I'd love to catch them myself… specking murderers."

"Every day this month," another officer corrected.

"Not again," a man said to no one in particular.

"Can't they catch the bastards?" asked a woman who stood behind me.

Up ahead, a team of emergency techs sprayed foam on the smoldering automobiles to douse the flames. The techs wore yellow soft-shelled armor. They had red foam tanks on their backs. A blast that topples cars should damage buildings as well. This one did not. As the smoke cleared, I saw that the buildings around the explosion looked untouched. Perhaps the terrorist wanted to assassinate the drivers.

I did not look for long. I squared myself to the center of the explosion, then turned and walked away. Threading my way through the crowd, I formed a compass in my head and set a heading for 110 degrees. I headed west, southwest, pushing my way through a growing tide of people.

I found Illych standing in the middle of a crowd, craning his neck with all the other people to get a look at what had happened. He was shorter than the men around him, shorter than some of the women, too. He wore the uniform of a Mogat Marine. He wore leather gloves that hid his sharp-ended fingers, but nothing hid that ugly ridge of bone that ran above his eyes. The ridge gave him a caveman forehead.

"I hope they catch that bastard and wring his nuts," I said as I approached Illych.

"Yes, sir. Security has really gone to pot around here."

"*Gone to pot*," I thought. *Not* "*specked beyond repair*," *or* "*for shit*." The man had just left a bomb that blew up cars and presumably drivers, but heaven help us if he swore.

Illych looked at me, and the smile of recognition crossed his lips. "Clever disguise, sir. Coming to a Mogat planet masquerading as a Liberator carrying a big suspicious box. I would never have thought of that one."

"Shall we get back to work, Sergeant," I said. He had a sergeant's uniform.

"Yes, sir, Lieutenant," Illych said. "The sooner we get you under wraps, the better."

"Get me under wraps?" I asked. "I'm not the terrorist here."

"I knew you would come," he added as we walked away. "I knew you would come."

"What made you think a stupid thing like that?" I asked.

"You had to come. It's in your programming."

I shook my head. "No. That's SEAL programming." We were walking past hundreds of people, and no one noticed us. Anyone within earshot could hear what we said, but that did not matter. No one looked in our direction. We were just a Navy lieutenant and a Marine sergeant comparing notes about this latest terrorist attack.

Behind us, the emergency team had doused the cars, and a truck came to carry the wreckage away. The show had ended. The rest of the crowd would soon head back to work.

"How many more of you are there?" Illych asked.

"Just me. I came alone."

Illych looked at me and nodded. "This is a switch," he said. "Now you're in the Navy, and I'm the grunt Marine."

"Is there anyplace we can talk?" I asked.

"Sure," Illych said. "I'll show you my new digs."

"What happened?" A man in an army uniform came jogging toward us.

"Another bomb," Illych said.

"Did they get anything?"

"Couple of cars." Illych laughed. "I don't know why those bastards bother." There was a bitter edge to his voice.

"Damn. I hope they get that guy," the man said.

"Yeah, don't we all," Illych agreed.

"Why cars?" I asked, as the army man walked past us to gawk at the latest terrorist attack.

"Harris, I attached the bomb to the building behind the cars. You cannot hurt these buildings.

"Remember when you said that the Mogats lowered the shields on that battleship? They have the same thing going on down here. Bombs and mines don't hurt these buildings. I've tried particle beams. I've tried grenades. I've tried rockets. The buildings have some kind of shield on their outer walls. Nothing gets through."

Illych led me several miles across the military sector. We left the admin area far behind, entering a neighborhood of warehouses and motor pools. He gave me a running commentary as if he had lived in the city all his life. He knew which motor pool had the latest equipment and which ones had lazy mechanics.

"How do you know all of this?" I asked.

"Word gets around" is all he would say.

The phosphorus layer in the sky was turning dark by the time we reached Illych's "digs." He'd found himself a small armory with enough weapons to wage a tribal war. He had rifles, rocket launchers, Jeeps, and a particle-beam cannon.

"How in the world did you secure these premises?" I asked, trying to talk Marine-colonel talk.

"I killed the former occupants," he said.

"No one comes looking for them?" I asked.

"An MP came by. I told him that the guys never showed for work."

"And that was it? The Marines never followed up?"

"Harris, as far as the Marines are concerned, the old guys went AWOL and everything else is running right. I work the desk. If someone wants to requisition a Jeep or a tractor, I give them the paperwork and issue the equipment." He handed me the inventory chart. Over the weeks that he had been here, Illych received shipments of uniforms, machine parts, and munitions. He logged everything.

"Very thorough," I said. "You expecting an inspection?"

"Luck favors the prepared, sir," Illych said.

"Lose the 'sir,'" I said. "They busted me back down to master sergeant."

"How does it feel to be back among the ranks of the enlisted?" Illych asked.

"I like it," I said. "I always felt embarrassed when people saluted me."

Changing the subject, I said, "You know, you nearly got me arrested. They're going crazy looking for terrorists around here. Some old man spotted me for a Liberator and sent an MP after me."

"You lost him?" Illych asked.

"Killed him," I said. "I left him on the train tracks. He's probably been atomized by now."

"These people are obsessed with Liberators," Illych said with a wry smile. "They think there's a Liberator terrorist running wild on the planet. Whenever anything bad happens, they always think there's a Liberator behind it."

I wonder what they would think if they knew about Adam Boyd clones, I thought to myself. I did not share that thought. Instead, I asked, "You got any chow?"

"Yeah, but it's all Mogat chow," Illych said. Anyone else would have called it "shit," but Illych talked like a Boy Scout, a homicidal Boy Scout. "Do you want carbonized soup, carbonized casserole, or carbonized stew?"

"Does one taste better than the others?" I asked, remembering the meal I had on their battleship.

"Not really. They all taste the same."

"I'll take whatever you've got," I said.

Illych handed me an MRE and a knife. The label said "BEEF CASSEROLE." I peeled back the tin with the knife and tried a bite. It tasted disgusting.

Illych drank a tin labeled "CHICKEN SOUP." It looked more like split pea soup.

"So how are we going to get out of here?" Illych asked.

"Funny you should ask," I said as I opened my box and pulled out the helmet. "I think our best bet is to arrange for a ride home."

I never understood the finer mechanics of broadcast technology. Something about broadcast engines allowed them to generate a superaccelerated electrical field. They could not only translate and send matter, they could also translate certain wavelengths. Sending engines attracted frequencies from millions of miles away. Receiving engines broadcast those frequencies over millions of miles with next to no latency.

Radio and even laser communications would have had clunky delays just communicating from the earth to the moon. Without broadcast accelerations, conversations between Earth and Mars moved at the pace of a world championship chess game. One person said something or asked a question, then waited. The other person finally heard the statement or question, answered, then waited. Through the miracle of broadcast engines, I could speak with Marines on the other side of the galaxy as if we were standing side by side.

I put on my helmet, knowing I would reach Marines from my platoon using the interLink connection. "Evans, you there?"

"Hey, Master Sarge." It was Private Philips. I recognized his slow, languid tones even before I saw the identification.

"Evans left you to monitor the Link?" I asked.

"Nah. Thomer was supposed to be watching for you, but he had to run to the shitter. I volunteered to watch for him."

I liked Philips. Strangely enough, I respected him, but I could not send him on the errand I had in mind. Philips rubbed authority the wrong way, and the errand I wanted would involve a lot of authority.

"Can you get Evans for me?" I asked.

"Not a problem," Philips said. "Master Sarge, are you really in the Mogat Motherland?"

"I'm on a Mogat-held planet," I said.

Philips laughed but said nothing. A moment later, I heard him say, "Hey, Evans, Harris wants to talk to you."

"You better not be playing with me, Philips, or you'll be cleaning latrines for the rest of your..."

"I'm not playing with you."

"Better not be," Evans muttered. I heard a noise that sounded like Philips taking off his helmet.

"What are you doing?"

"Harris wants to talk to you, Evans," Philips repeated. "I'll use my own helmet."

Smart, I thought. Knowing Philips's disregard for authority, he might spit in the helmet before handing it over.

"Master Sergeant?"

"Evans," I said.

"Did you find the SEAL?"

"Standing right next to me. Thank you for putting in the call to the *Kamehameha.*"

"I can't believe you found the bastard," Evans said. "I mean, I can't believe it worked."

"Evans, I need to make some arrangements before we can get back to the *Obama.*"

"How can I help?" Evans asked.

"Glad you asked," I said. "I'm going to need to talk to somebody a bit higher in the chain of command."

"You want me to contact Faggert?" He meant Captain James Taggert. I had a cold moment in which I wondered what Evans called me behind my back.

"This might be a bit big for him," I said.

"Colonel Grayson?" Evans asked.

"Over his head, too," I said.

"Who did you have in mind?" Evans asked.

"We can start with Admiral Brocius, but we're going to need to talk to Admiral Brallier and Admiral Porter by the time we're done."

32

Admiral Samuel S. Brallier, commander of the Outer Scutum-Crux Fleet, insisted that his SEALs take charge of the operation once I explained what I had in mind. I had no problem with that. Surprisingly enough, neither did Admiral Brocius. Brallier had more experience with this type of mission than we did.

It would take time to plan out all of the logistics for the operation, so I got to spend the next several days hidden away in the back of Illych's private armory with the corpses of the people who used to run the joint. Illych played the front man, receiving shipments, signing out equipment, and keeping the books. I had the feeling he enjoyed himself.

When no one was around, I went "shopping." That meant that I walked around the warehouse opening crates and looking for useful information. I quickly learned that the Mogats had not developed any new weapons. The only gear I found was fifty-year-old U.A. equipment and inventory that the Confederate Arms provided during their brief alliance with the Mogats.

In the back of the warehouse I found crates of bric-a-brac that the Mogats had all but discarded. On one shelf I found a crate of old military Bibles. This surprised me. The Mogats must not have known what the crate contained. Their culture had no room for Earth religions. They believed in self-determination and independence from Earth. They also had their own holy writ—*Man's True Place in the Universe: The Doctrines of Morgan Atkins*. As we called it back home, the "Space Bible."

The Bibles I found were small enough to fit in your pocket, with green leather covers and tissue-paper pages. This particular Bible included the entire New Testament and selected readings from the Old Testament.

I did not like the New Testament; it confused me. My theory that God was a metaphor for government worked well with the Old Testament. When God directed the Israelites to massacre enemies, pay taxes, and build temples, their civilization worked. No matter how hard I tried to wrestle with the god of the New Testament, I could never understand him. In my experience, no self-respecting government would forgive those who trespassed against it.

When Illych saw me reading a Bible, he asked about it. "What book is that?" he asked. He might have thought I was reading a Space Bible. We were enlisted men, and only officers were allowed to read that book.

"The Bible," I said.

"You're not supposed to read the Space Bible," Illych said.

"Not the Space Bible, the Christian Bible," I said.

"You read the Bible? You can't possibly believe that stuff."

"Sure I do," I said, and I told him my theory about how God was really just the government. He listened quietly then said,

"If God is the government, would that make clones his chosen people?"

"That is precisely how I see it," I said.

"I like that," Illych said. He was my first convert. I felt like quite the evangelist.

Admiral Brocius checked in every few days to update me on different events. Yamashiro signed an alliance with the Unified Authority and the Confederate Arms. He sent engineers to the remote Golan Dry Docks facility, the most advanced aerotechnology program in Unified Authority space. I had always imagined that the people in the dry docks were marooned after Mogats-Confederate Arm forces destroyed the Broadcast Network; but, in fact, maintaining the dry docks had been a top priority. Explorer ships bearing food and medical supplies had visited the dry docks within twenty-four hours of the battle.

Brocius updated me on the Naval Intelligence hunt for Ray Freeman. "It's like the man is a damned ghost," Brocius said once.

"He'll turn himself in when he's ready, sir," I said.

"Do you know where he is?"

I did not answer. We had been through this before.

"He assaulted an Intelligence officer," Brocius said. "I could have you arrested for aiding and abetting."

"Why don't you send some men out to arrest me?" I asked.

"You're on your way home," Brocius said. I could hear mirth in his voice. "We can arrest you once you're back."

Changing the subject, I asked, "What about the House of Representatives?"

"What about it?" Brocius asked.

"With the alliance..."

He interrupted me. "The Confederate Arms is an ally, not a member. Hughes says his planets have no interest in rejoining the union. We have a military alliance, and not a very strong one at that."

As the chairman of the Confederate Arms Treaty Organization, Hughes would know, I thought to myself. "What about Yamashiro?" I asked.

"What about him?" Brocius asked.

"Is he just an ally?" I asked.

"We've offered to take him back. So has Hughes. Nobody knows where his base planet is located. If he's based in Orion or Sagittarius, I suppose he'll sign with us.

"Something you should know. We had another scrape with the Mogat Navy this week. This time it was in the Orion Arm."

"Mogats in the Orion Arm?" I asked.

"The inner curve of the Orion Arm, yes. You want to guess how it went?"

"There were three or four of them," I guessed.

"Six, this time," Brocius corrected me.

"And we destroyed one of their ships?"

"Right you are. Five of their ships went completely undamaged. The one that we managed to hit, we damn near sliced in half.

"The other Mogats ran away," Brocius said.

"Is the wreck near any place of value?"

"Olympus Kri," Brocius said.

"That's Gordon Hughes's home planet," I said.

"Yes, that occurred to us, as well."

With just a few minutes to go before we left the armory, I could not find Illych anywhere. I checked the different supply rooms. I checked our on-site living quarters. Finally, I found him out by the Jeeps. I arrived in time to see him placing bombs inside the various cars. He used card-deck-sized bombs, which he placed under the chassis of trucks and Jeeps. One bomb should have been enough to demolish the entire depot. Illych said he had already placed fifty, and he must have had another thirty ready to go in a box.

"That's a lot of bombs," I said.

"It should get the job done." He was on his back lying under a Jeep. He placed a bomb near a fuel tank.

"What if something goes wrong?" I asked.

"Goes wrong?" Illych parroted.

"Oh, I don't know. There are all kinds of things that could go wrong. What if the Mogats don't send our battleship out to the Perseus Arm?"

"What about it?" Illych said. He stopped working and looked up at me from beneath the chassis.

"We'll end up right back here," I said.

"We'll come back somewhere," Illych said. "We won't come back here. I'm blowing up the place."

"But if you don't blow the place up, we could come back," I said.

"That wouldn't be a good idea," Illych said. "They already suspect us."

"Who suspects us?" I asked.

"Army Intelligence. They sent a couple of guys to investigate this morning."

"I didn't know about that," I said.

"I didn't want to worry you," Illych said. He finished placing the bomb and crawled out from under the Jeep. "I took care of it."

"So we're okay?"

"For now," Illych said.

He wasn't telling me something. "You killed them?" Considering Illych's homicidal leanings, it seemed like a safe bet.

"They're in that Jeep. With any luck, whoever investigates the explosion will mistake them for us and say that we accidentally blew ourselves up."

"You don't honestly believe that will happen."

"No," Illych agreed, "but we should be safe on a Mogat

battleship. It won't matter." He carried a stack of three bombs and wired them to the electric eye that guarded the front door.

"You ready to leave, sir?" he asked.

"I'm a master sergeant," I said. "We're the same rank."

By this time Illych had done just about everything he could to disguise me. He requisitioned green dye for my eyes. He shaved my head and bleached my eyebrows. He tried to stain my skin; but my cheeks and forehead burned instead of tanning. I thought I looked like a bald Liberator clone with olivine eye stain, bleached eyebrows, and bad skin.

"They've probably got the building under surveillance," Illych said, as we climbed into our truck.

"Is that a problem?" I asked.

"Yes and no," Illych said. "They'll outnumber us; that's a problem. If they get a good look at us, they might radio a warning. That might make it hard for us to make our flight.

"On the other hand, I'm guessing that we're better armed than they are." As I opened my door, I saw the stash of weapons Illych had placed behind the seat. We had rocket launchers, laser pistols, automatic rifles, and grenades. He'd also thrown a copy of the Bible back there. I made a trade, stowing the box with my helmet behind my seat and taking a grenade and a laser pistol for the ride.

I ducked low in the cab as we rolled out. Illych, still wearing his sergeant's uniform, hit a button closing the gate behind us and, incidentally, arming all of the bombs he had placed in the motor pool.

The Mogats placed their training grounds and armories on the second level of the military district. Who knew what they had on the third, fourth, and fifth. The sixth level was an enormous freeway that not only laced together the entire military sector, it reached under the other sectors as well.

Illych knew the way to the ramp that led down to the sixth level. He had never driven there before, but he had memorized the route. It took us past a couple of buildings he had tried to blow up. He pointed them out as we went by.

"There must be a broadcast engine working somewhere on this planet," I said.

"You think they're planning on broadcasting the planet?" Illych asked. He could not stop himself from laughing at his own droll joke.

"I think they have some kind of newfangled shield on this planet that they broadcast out to their ships," I said.

Illych's grin disappeared. "So the same shield that protected those ships is protecting the buildings? How do people get in and out? Wouldn't a shield stop them?"

"You're thinking about technologies we understand," I said. "When we use shields, they're like walls in front of our ships, right? Their shield technology could be totally different. It's only a guess, but it's my best guess."

I saw the ramp up ahead. It was a half mile wide, big enough to accommodate a formation of tanks. We bounced as we went over the incline and started our way down. The ramp headed down at a shallow angle. We drove for more than a mile before reaching the bottom deck.

A black cavern with pockets of orange-pink lights spread out in every direction. It was a dark world in which tan, green, and blue cars—the colors of the military branches—scurried like rodents. In the bad light, the green and blue cars looked black.

Other vehicles passed us at incredible speeds. We traveled at 150 miles per hour, and I had the feeling that some vehicles more than doubled us. "These guys drive like maniacs," I said to Illych.

"We don't have to go very far," he said.

Illych had done a good job memorizing his route. He found

the next ramp and drove up to the top level, taking us right to the spaceport. We parked along an empty street. I waited outside the Jeep while Illych changed out of his Marine sergeant's uniform and into his Navy pilot's duds. Since I still had the uniform I stole on my way down, I was already a lieutenant.

We drove to the port and presented orders Illych had drawn up back at the supply depot. We had no trouble getting in. Hacking into the Mogats' computer system, Illych had already booked us on a military transport. The transport would drop us off on the battleship Illych had flown in from the Perseus Arm—very likely the battleship I'd flown in on as well. We built our escape around the idea that this particular ship received the alarm signal from the derelict in the Perseus Arm. If we were right, the ship would take us back into Unified Authority territory very shortly.

If everything went according to plan, I hoped to see this planet again very soon.

33

Even with my bald head, bleached eyebrows, and temporarily green eyes, I did not want to socialize. We traveled in the kettle of a transport, a lucky break. In a Starliner, people would have been able to get a better look at me.

Illych and I sat apart so that if the Mogats caught one of us, the other might still escape. He sat toward the front of the kettle, not far from the stairs that led to the cockpit. I sat in the shadows toward the back.

A Mogat officer came and sat beside me.

"Good Lord, Lieutenant, what happened to your face?" he asked.

"I got burned, sir," I said. He was a lieutenant commander.

"What happened?" he repeated.

"You know the bomber? I was just outside an admin building he attacked. The explosion burned off my hair and did this to my skin," I said. It sounded good for spur of the moment.

"Lord," the lieutenant commander said. "Did you hear the good news?"

"What news?" I asked.

"You're going to love this. It turns out there were two bombers, and it looks like they blew themselves up. They were hiding out in a supply depot."

"Great to hear," I said.

The hatch of the kettle ground shut and the only light inside was red emergency light. The flight went quickly. We hovered horizontally for a minute, then entered the gravity chute. My stomach dropped below my feet. The chatty lieutenant commander sitting beside me started to moan, then brought out a plastic bag and vomited into it. The ammonia smell coming from that little bag nearly made me retch.

The lieutenant commander looked up at me and apologized. "Late breakfast," he said. When we left the chute, and our flight pattern normalized, he excused himself and deposited his prize package down the toilet. Probably embarrassed about having coughed up his meal, he found another place to sit.

Up to this point, our plan gave the Mogats nothing to worry about. To them, this day began like any other day. We arrived on a routine shuttle flight to the fleet.

Illych and I deplaned with the other passengers. No one paid any attention to us at all as we crossed the launch bay and went our separate ways.

34

The alarms started before the announcements. First we heard the alarms sounding general quarters. This meant that every man on the ship—sailor and commando—had to report for duty.

Then came the announcement: "All commando teams, report to launch bay. All commando teams, report to launch bay."

A second announcement followed on the heels of the first: "Prepare for broadcast. All hands, prepare for broadcast."

Amber lights flashed in the halls. Men scrambled to their posts. In a moment, our ship would enter a battle zone.

I stood in the open hatch. Men ran past me without a second glance. No one noticed the bald, bleach-haired, green-eyed Liberator. They ignored me, and I ignored them; it was a reciprocal relationship that would come to a rapid end. I needed commando armor. The only way I could get it was to take it.

An entire platoon of commandos darted past me. They all

wore the armor I needed, but they ran with the herd. I needed a straggler. And here he came, right on time. The man was nearly my height. The boy looked to be in his midtwenties, the same age as me but still just a boy. His black hair hung past his ears. He held his helmet like a bowl of water. He seemed distracted. He did not pay attention as he walked.

We were near a latrine. I approached him. I was about to shove him in the open door of the latrine. There I would…

"Jason."

The boy turned. "Oh, hey, Frank. Any idea where we're headed?"

"Perseus Arm."

"Not again," the boy whined.

I had no choice. I kept walking and headed into the latrine and watched as my armor on the hoof walked away.

Standing in the door of the latrine, I watched as sailor after sailor trotted past me. I saw no more commandos. I was going to miss my specking transport. I was going to sit out the mission I had specking planned. Then I saw him.

He was the last of the commandos, maybe a sergeant bringing up the rear. As he rumbled past the door of the latrine, I made my move. I grabbed his shoulder armor and swung him into the latrine using his own momentum to force him around the corner and face-first into the wall. He spun so quickly that his feet nearly left the ground. I hoped the shock would cause him to drop his pistol. It didn't.

I must have picked a fight with the wrong man. The guy kept his wits about him. I expected him to reach for his pistol, leaving himself open for a dozen different deadly attacks. Instead, he took a lethal swing at me with his helmet. The plasticized metal was light but hard, and that old helmet design had lots of corners. He landed a glancing blow with the helmet that bounced off my shoulder and across my face.

Had the guy been wearing normal clothes, I could have hit him in the sternum and knocked the air out of his lungs. Of course, if he'd been wearing normal clothes, I would not have needed to kill him. In a normal fight I might have broken his arm or his leg, but his armor protected his elbows and knees against hyperextension. It also protected him from groin and kidney shots.

At least the guy was too tough to yell for help. Small miracles.

I grabbed the hand with the laser pistol and pushed my weight against it as I spun into his body, coming in too close for him to shoot me. By this time, my combat reflex was in full flow. I felt strong. Still pinning down the arm with the pistol, I twisted my shoulders and flung the man toward a bathroom stall with a poorly executed flip. My move did not lift the guy off the ground, but it had enough force behind it to make him stumble backwards into a stall.

He tripped over the toilet and dropped both his helmet and gun as he caught himself against the wall. I slammed my fist into his face. Blood splattered everywhere. I smashed the cartilage in his nose, and he grunted softly. He must have known he was in trouble as he started waving his hands wildly, but I pinned my knee into his chest and caught him between the wall and the toilet.

Realizing that he would not win the fight, he started to call out. I cut into his throat with the blade of my hand. Blood and spit flew from his mouth. I had no time for sympathy. My third punch shattered both the front and back of his skull.

My fist shattered the bones around his right eye socket. The force of the punch smashed the back of his head against the lip of the stainless-steel toilet. When I pulled the guy up to hit him again, I saw blood in his hair and realized that his skull had caved in. Men have survived with a shattered skull, and a live man has the potential to set alarms. I snapped the man's neck.

I did not need to hide the dead commando very carefully. Sailors do not visit the latrine during general quarters. The ship was on full alert. Its laser cannons were lit and its rockets ready to fire. Any sailor worth his salt, even a Mogat sailor, would piss down his leg before leaving his station during general quarters.

I did not have so much as a second to waste. Using toilet paper to wipe blood off the armor as I went, I stripped the commando and put on his combat suit. The blood turned into droplets on the waxy surface of the armor. I did not have time to clean it well. I cleaned what I could and dressed in under a minute. During the mass hysteria of general quarters, I did not think anyone would examine me closely.

After placing the dead commando on the toilet seat, I closed the stall. I put on his helmet and holstered his laser pistol, then ran to the launch bay as quickly as I could. Small beads of blood trickled down my right arm as I ran. There might have been blood on my chest plates, as well, but I could do nothing about it.

Sailors ran in and out of hatches around me as I raced down the corridor. I noticed no other commandos. A bad sign. Wondering if I had missed my boat, I skidded through the launch-bay door and leaped between the doors at the rear of the kettle as they slowly closed.

"You took your sweet time, Belcher," somebody said over the interLink in my helmet. "Good thing Smith wasn't watching."

"Yeah," I said in a voice that sounded a lot like a cough. I knew I wasn't fooling anyone with that voice.

"I saved you a seat. Over here." My new friend Corporal Alberts stood and waved his hands, so I pressed my way through the crowd and joined him.

"You okay?" the commando asked as we sat on the bench running along the wall.

"Yeah, just winded," I said.

"You don't..."

"Listen carefully." I placed my laser across my lap so that it pointed at Alberts's ribs. "This can go either way for you. Take off your helmet and place it on your lap until we reach the drop zone."

Alberts did not move.

"Now!" I yelled, and I made a show of tightening my finger around the trigger.

He reached up and removed his helmet. Now I could see his mouth and face. He could not make a sneaky little frequency change and warn some other commando using the interLink.

Alberts had fine blond hair cut to stubble. He had brown eyes. I saw anger in his eyes. Like Belcher, apparently the man I killed in the latrine, the guy had some fight in him.

With the doors closed and the emergency bulbs casting their shadowy red light, no one would notice my finger on the trigger. The other commandos were loud.

I reached up with one hand and removed my helmet so that I could whisper to Alberts. "Welcome to Unified Authority Airlines," I said. I wanted to provoke him into making a move. He was as good as dead already. I wanted him to give me a reason so that I would not need to babysit him. He obliged.

Alberts made a grab at my laser, and I fired it into the side of his ribs. The wound cauterized, but that did not stop part of his armor from bubbling as it melted into his chest.

By the look of things, there was a complement of a hundred commandos in the kettle—a full, standing-room-only flight. No one seemed to care about the flash from my laser. They did not notice Alberts's hands drop or the way he slumped to the ground before I pulled him back on the bench. The shadowy environment of the kettle had worked in my favor. In a moment, however, somebody was bound to notice the smoke rising out of Alberts's collar as the highly flammable environmental suit inside his armor continued to burn.

I propped Alberts against the wall and placed his laser pistol on the seat beside him. Then, I rose to my feet and stepped away from the scene without looking back. The kettle was filled to capacity—men sitting on every inch of bench, men standing under all the harnesses on the floor. I took a second to place my helmet back over my head, then weaved my way through the crowd and headed toward the ladder that led to the cockpit.

"Hey... hey, this guy is dead!" somebody yelled just as I reached the top.

Looking back, I saw the commandos crowding into the corner of the kettle where Alberts still sat huddled against the wall. I heard one man shouting for a medical kit. I saw somebody pull a flashlight and shine it on the late corporal's face. Then I opened the door and stepped into the cockpit. The pilot, a.k.a. Master Chief Petty Officer Emerson Illych, pulled his pistol and watched carefully as I removed my helmet.

"I see you already killed one," Illych said, nodding to the monitor beside his flight controls. On the screen, men gathered around the dead commando.

"You're one to talk," I said. Illych's dead copilot lay on the floor, his back sprawled around the pedals. "Besides, I made it look like a suicide."

We were already deep in the graveyard, so to speak. We were back in the battleground where the five Mogat ships had stood down the Outer Perseus Fleet. I saw dead fighters floating around us, more closely packed together than the debris in an asteroid belt. We inched ahead, maybe only ten miles an hour. We should have gone faster. With its shields and armor, the transport could have shunted these broken Tomcats out of its way like dried leaves. Instead, we waded through.

"You see anything?" I asked.

"Oh yeah," Illych said. "Take a close look when we approach that fighter."

We glided toward a fighter. It had a gray hull with an oblong nose. The area around its cockpit was entirely melted and the glass was smoke-stained and crumpled. One of the fighter's wings was sheared off. Wires hung from the amputation.

On the remaining wing, clinging and blending in like a chameleon on a leaf, lay a SEAL. I spotted him because his shape did not blend in with the contour of the wing to which he clung. The color of his armor matched the fighter perfectly. As we passed that fighter, I spotted two more SEALs clinging to the fuselage.

"How long can they stay out there?" I asked Illych.

He thought for a moment. "I've gone twelve hours. It wasn't comfortable."

"Twelve hours in open space?" I had always heard that you would go insane after two hours. There's not much you can do in space, just cling to an object like a drowning man holding a raft. No pleasant thoughts would pass through your brain as you sat there with only your armor separating you and an infinite expanse of death. "That must have been one hell of an important mission."

"It was for training. You don't get your brantoo until you clear a twelve-hour spacewalk."

"Do all SEALs go through that?" I asked. Before the Navy switched to Adam Boyd clones, only natural-born volunteers could became SEALs.

"We did," Illych said. He never talked about the days of natural-born SEALs.

We were coming up on the derelict battleship. I saw it ahead. We approached it from a side that had not been damaged in battle. From this angle, the battleship looked ready to fight.

"You'd better lock the door," Illych said as he pulled off a pair of headphones.

"The door?" I asked.

"Your buddies in the kettle don't believe the kid you killed committed suicide. They're on their way up looking for a killer"

"Have you blocked out external communications?" I asked. The transport had an interLink override that could block passengers from communicating with outside sources.

The door rattled.

"I cut their communications the moment we left," Illych said. The man had ice in his veins.

The door rattled again. This time someone started pounding on it.

"This will quiet them," Illych said. He reached across the controls and flipped the switch that controlled the gravity generator.

"Let's hope no one was taking a shit," I said.

By the annoyed look Illych shot me, I could tell that he did not approve of my language.

Pounding on a door in zero gravity takes some thinking. Hit the door hard and you will fly in the other direction. Try to shake the door without finding some way to anchor yourself, and you end up shaking yourself instead of the door.

"You'd better do something," Illych said. "They're going to pull their lasers next." The door to the cockpit was made with a laser-dampening clay-and-metal alloy. It would hold for a minute or two of laser abuse.

"How long before we land?" I asked.

"Almost there," Illych said, still as cool as ever.

I looked through the windshield. We were just outside the launch bay. The door was wide open. The atmospheric locks were disabled. We drifted in and hovered for a moment as Illych rotated the ship.

"Motherbird, we have landed. Repeat, Motherbird, transport one has landed. The coast appears to be clear," Illych called in.

Outside the cockpit, a dozen laser beams pecked away at our door.

"I believe they're calling your name," Illych said.

"Thanks, pal," I said.

"Harris, I have a present for you." I looked back and saw him holding out his right hand in a fist, palm up. When he spread his fingers, I saw he was holding a grenade.

"Won't that damage the transport?" I asked as I took the grenade.

"Not a chance," Illych said. "It's a dud."

"A dud? Why do I want a dud?"

"Those boys are in zero gravity," Illych said. "Chasing a grenade should keep them busy."

A distraction, I thought. *It would work on me.* "Can you crank up the lights in the cabin? Let's let them see it coming."

Illych switched off the emergency bulbs and turned on the cargo lights. The kettle would not be bright by any means, but the commandos would see what I tossed to them.

"Are you going to share in the fun?" I asked Illych as I went to the hatch.

"Sorry, sport, I have to sit this one out. As the only qualified pilot on this mission, I'm indispensable."

"Indispensable my ass," I said, knowing that he was right. I put on my helmet. In another moment, having sealed armor would be the deciding factor on who lived and who died.

I opened the door just a crack. In the moment before the storm of lasers speared the door and wall, I saw men floating under the metallic cathedral ceiling. I bowled the grenade underhanded and resealed the door as the first lasers struck around me. Then I waited for the grenade to have its effect.

When I opened the door again, nobody fired at me. The commandos were hiding as best they could and waiting for the grenade to explode.

Had the grenade been real, it would have juiced every last one of them. It would not have destroyed the transport, but it would have done damage. The dud, however, just tumbled harmlessly through the air, causing absolute chaos. The Mogat commandos pushed off each other and collided into one another in their general panic.

The cockpit opened to a three-foot-wide catwalk which led to the ten-foot ladder from the floor of the kettle. Seeing my grenade, everyone had scattered down. When I peered over the ledge of the catwalk, I saw men hiding under benches and men floating pell-mell across the cabin.

"Illych, drop them," I called over the interLink. He restarted the gravity generator, and the commandos who had been floating dropped to the deck. Then I opened fire.

My job was to distract the commandos. In this case, death was a perfectly acceptable form of distraction. I saw a man hiding behind a girder and fired, hitting him in the arm. He dropped into a crouching position. My next shot hit the top of his helmet.

No one seemed to know what happened, so I targeted another Mogat as he ran to help my first victim. I waited until he bent over with his back to me, then aimed at the knot in his armor that housed his rebreather. He collapsed onto the first guy. It would have looked comical, like one dead guy had tripped over the other, but the rebreather exploded, and flames danced out of the hole.

I had visions of building a pile of dead Mogats.

Another commando looked up in my direction and fired at me before seeing where I hid. His laser seared into the wall about five feet to my left. My shot hit him square in the visor. He fell near the metal doors at the rear of the kettle. So much for my pile.

It felt good to be back in combat. I felt the hormone surging through my blood, but I knew I could stop when the battle was over. Early Liberator clones had crawled out of the tube battle-ready. Most of them got hooked on violence because they never knew anything else. I was raised in an orphanage and steeped in military protocol. Self-control was less of an issue.

At least twenty commandos fired back at me. I ducked low. I had the high-ground advantage. They could hit the catwalk, but they could not hit me. Some guy bucking for a medal leaped toward the front of the kettle. He probably wanted to shoot up from under the catwalk. He might have even planned to shoot through it. I hit him as he jumped, and he fell facedown on the deck.

"Grab a handhold," Illych called over the interLink.

As I wedged myself into a corner, Illych cut the gravity. A commando immediately launched himself in the air. I shot him, and his dead body slammed headfirst into the roof.

It wasn't the gravity that Illych was warning me about. On the other side of the kettle, the heavy metal doors started to slide apart. As their seal broke, the pressure of our oxygenated atmosphere swept unprepared commandos against the rear of the transport like leaves in a hurricane.

It took approximately three seconds for the pressure to right itself. During that time, at least a third of the Mogat commandos were sucked up and flung against the rear of the kettle. I have no idea how many survived the experience.

Then the SEALs stormed up the ramp. Five Navy SEALs, dressed in the same antiquated armor as Mogat commandos, charged up the ramp firing lasers. They charged into the cargo-loading area, killing everyone they saw, then found cover and dug in. More SEALs waited outside the transport doors. The entire shooting match took less than a minute.

"The transport is secure," I called out over an open frequency.

"That was easy," Illych responded. "Now for the hard part."

35

"Motherbird, this is Away Team."

"Did you find anything?" the Mogat communications officer asked.

"The ship's clean," Illych said.

"Clean?" the officer asked.

"Not a clone to be found," Illych said.

"I'll put you through to the captain."

A moment later a voice asked, "What is the situation, Away Team?"

"The ship is clean, sir," Illych said. In the movies, soldiers always push it when they make these calls. They say puns or play with words, giving their enemies clues that go unnoticed. Illych, a SEAL instead of a Hollywood actor, did not play that game. We had an unarmed transport, they had a heavily armed battleship with seemingly impregnable shields. Illych stuck to the script.

"Have you searched the ship?"

"Yes, sir, every deck. I've been monitoring the security sensors. They picked up our guys, but that's it."

"Somebody set off the alarms," the Mogat officer said.

"They must have cleared out before we got here." Illych was a great liar. His voice showed not so much as a note of emotion. His eyes remained on the monitor. Sometimes dishonest people stare too long into your eyes thinking it will prove they are telling the truth. Illych stared just enough.

"Very well. Make one more sweep of the ship and see if our visitors left anything behind, then come on back."

"Aye, aye, sir," Illych said. He waited for the captain to sign off before turning back to us. "We're in."

The SEALs had 121 men on that derelict battleship, but they only used fifteen to capture the transport. The SEALs adjusted to their environment. Having as many men as possible might win battles on an open field; but in the confines of a crowded transport, too many men meant impaired mobility.

We took no prisoners as we captured the transport. From the commandos to the copilot, we made sure that everybody died. The dirty part of reconnaissance work is that it leaves no room for mercy.

After clearing out the bodies, we crammed 116 SEALs into the kettle. The five we could not fit had to wait on the derelict. They got a better deal than the men hiding among the wrecked fighters outside. There are no injuries in a space battle. If anything breaches your armor, you die. It does not matter whether an enemy laser pierces your heart or your foot. If your armor depressurizes, you may freeze or suffocate or burst; but you will certainly die.

We packed the transport so tightly that three of the SEALs had to ride in the cockpit along with Illych and me. We wasted no floor space. Not in the kettle. Not in the cockpit.

As they had before, the SEALs headed into battle in silence. In the cockpit, we stood pressed together, watching the five who could not come with us salute as our transport lifted from the deck.

Illych broke the silence. "Think we can pull this off, Harris?"

"Against these stiffs?" I asked. "What could go wrong?" Even as I said this, I regretted it. It had the ring of other famous last words.

"You're joking, right?" Illych asked. We both knew we were flying a load of 116 men into a ship with a two-thousand-man crew, not counting commandos.

"Yeah, I'm joking," I said. That was a lie. Had Illych asked me earlier, I would have said it was not possible to take an entire transport without losing a man. Sometimes it seemed like the Mogats were sleepwalking.

Illych and I never took our gazes from the scene outside the cockpit during the return flight. Between the SEALs and the Marines, we had two thousand men hiding in the wreckage around us. They waited to pounce like camouflaging insects.

Things look smaller in death than they do in life, even battleships. Looking at the derelict battleship with its darkened windows, I did not appreciate its size. The ships of the old Galactic Central Fleet had diamond-shaped hulls with rounded bows. Like all U.A. ships, they were wider than they were long.

Coming around the stern of this live battleship, I saw that we were smaller than the tips of its wings. Our transport was meant to hold one hundred men, one man for every twenty on that ship. We were a flea creeping up on a big dog. If we got in, we might draw blood.

"We're coming in for a landing," I called back over the interLink. We had to watch what we said now that we were wearing Mogat armor. The interLink equipment in the old combat armor had limited frequencies. We used a frequency we had never heard the Mogats use, but we had no way of knowing if they listened in on us.

We floated into the launch bay and hovered over the deck as the first of the atmospheric locks sealed behind us. In this fifty-year-old ship, the locks did not have the transparent electrostatic shields you saw on modern ones. The doors were enormous metal blast shields. We flew forward twenty yards, and a second gate closed behind us. Now we were inside the ship's atmosphere. Illych used the thrusters to guide us down, but he cut them a bit soon, and we landed hard.

"Nice landing," I said. "Now that you are dispensable again, are you going to join the fun?" Having flown the transport back, Illych was no longer any more important than anyone else to the mission.

"That's why I came," he said, and he had that same giddiness that I heard the first time I saw him in combat. He pulled out his laser pistol and held it up for me to see. "You know, I'd give up a week's pay to use a particle beam instead of a laser on this one."

"They have lasers, so we use lasers," I said. "We need to blend in."

"Yeah, yeah, yeah, I know," Illych said.

"Well, good luck, Illych," I said.

"Good luck, Harris."

I left the cockpit and practically slid down the ladder. We stood silent, staring at the rear hatch as the big metal doors slid open. The bright lights of the launch bay shone in from the top, pouring a wedge of glare across the floor.

We had our orders. We would divide up. Fifteen men would remain in the transport, hiding wherever they could and killing any unlucky maintenance men who happened to see them. Another forty men would head to the engine room to shut down the shields. Illych went with that group.

That left sixty-three men to head for the bridge. I went with that squad. We would "clear the bridge" quickly, a polite way of saying we would kill every officer and seal the hatch. If we moved quickly enough and targeted the helm and communications, we could prevent the ship from fleeing the scene or putting out a distress signal.

Having flown return flights with Mogat commandos, I knew that they generally removed their helmets before stepping off their transport. We kept them on. The SEALs were all clones of the Adam Boyd variety. They all looked alike. They were short, bald, and marked with the distinctive bony ridge across their brows. Had we removed our helmets, I would have been the only non-Adam Boyd face in the crowd, and the Mogats knew my kind.

In a world with no clones, a transport loaded with one hundred identical men would raise suspicion. So might a hundred commandos pouring out of a transport wearing their helmets. We had no other options. We rushed off the transport and walked quickly across the deck of the launch bay. One sailor stopped to watch us. He waved in our direction. Not knowing what else to do, I waved back but kept with the pack.

"Everything okay?" a crewman asked as we hustled past.

No one answered. He stood and watched us, but did nothing. Then we were out the door and down the hall.

We marched toward the central corridor of the ship. The smaller squad broke off and headed toward the engine room at the back of the ship. My squad turned toward the front. We knew in advance that the elevators were too small to hold sixty-three men; so we divided up and took separate paths. By the time I reached the last bank of elevators, there were only six men with me.

We moved through the hall in absolute silence. We did not draw our guns. We did not remove our helmets. Some of the crew stopped and stared at us, but no one approached us. Their ship was in enemy territory, and they were on alert. The brass had wisely not withdrawn the call to general quarters, so the entire crew was engaged.

The seven of us took the elevator at the front of the ship. I did not like traveling in an elevator. It was a bottleneck. Once the doors sealed, we would be helpless prisoners until they reopened. We waited for our elevator, watching sailors running past. Two sailors came to wait with us. We did not speak with them. If they headed to the bridge, we would kill them in a few minutes. We were a hundred men capturing a ship with over two thousand able-bodied crewmen. We would have no time for prisoners.

I stepped into the elevator and stared straight ahead when the door opened. The SEALs crowded around me, leaving an unreasonable amount of room for the two sailors. They congregated on the other side of the car, quietly whispering to each other. Two floors up, they left us without so much as a sideward glance. We continued to the top deck.

I decided to risk a communication. "Illych, you in place?"

"We're just waiting for the signal. What's taking so long?"

"We had farther to go," I said. I was not in charge. This was a SEAL operation, with regular Navy and Marine support.

Leaving the elevator, I led my little band to the main corridor. When I looked back over my shoulder, I saw the rest of the team catching up with us. They pushed through the halls quickly. Sailors stepped out of their way.

"Launch Bay Squad, are you in position?" the SEAL commanding the mission asked.

"Locked and loaded."

"Blue Team, are you in position?" Blue Team was the one sent to capture the engine room and shut down the shields.

"In position."

"Gold Team, everyone in position?"

This time I answered, too. "In position."

The six SEALs and I led the way into the bridge. We stepped through the hatch, drew our laser pistols, and began firing. I dropped to one knee and targeted the two sentries standing guard across the deck. I hit the first man before he could even reach for his pistol and the second man as his fingers closed around its grip. The men wore no armor, so my laser cut through them like a javelin. Their blouses caught fire around the wounds. When they fell, I saw the burns on the wall. The laser had shot right through them.

More SEALs jammed in through the door.

The bridge looked more like an office than the control room of a ship. It had computer stations instead of steering wheels. Navigators plotted its course on a computer screen. Beside that station, three men slumped dead in their seats. In the next station, the communications officers lay dead as well. They had been our primary targets as we entered the bridge.

A door on the far side of the bridge opened. The man in the doorway reacted quickly. He swung back into his room, sealing the doors behind him. Alarms went off. Amber and blood-colored lights flashed everywhere.

"Engine room report?" the mission leader called over the interLink.

"We have control. The weapons are down. The shields should be down any minute," Illych said.

"Step it up. They know we're on board," the mission leader said.

"What happened up there?" Illych asked.

"We got spotted. The situation is under control. Now get the shields down. If we don't see the cavalry soon, we're in for a beating."

"You okay, Harris?" Illych asked on a band that the mission leader would not hear.

One of the SEALs used a torch to short-circuit the door to the room off the bridge. He pulled his pistol and stepped in. I saw the red glow of the laser flash across the walls as the SEAL fired two shots into the man at point-blank range.

"We're pinned down! We're pinned down!" The call came from the squad guarding the launch bay.

"What is your status?" the mission leader asked.

"We are trapped in the transport."

"Do you have control of the target area?"

No answer.

"Launch Bay Squad, do you have control of the target area?"

"Grenade! Grenade!" was the last we heard from the squad in the launch bay.

Then someone in the corridor tried to open the hatch and enter the bridge. He had cracked the door less than an inch when one of the SEALs fired through and ended the problem.

"Seal the hatch!" our team yelled. That seemed like a good idea.

"It's going to get hot up here," I told Illych. I was not complaining.

"Wait a moment. Just a… Okay, the shields are down," the Blue Team leader called in.

"We've lost Launch Bay Squad. Gold Team, break into squads. Gold 1, hold the bridge. Gold 2, retake the launch bay." I was in Gold 2, the emergency squad. We were the ones who would catch the shit face-first.

Now that's a specker, I thought. *Why didn't we just leave more men to hold the launch bay in the first place?*

There were forty of us in Gold 2, almost twice as many men as in Gold 1, with good reason. All Gold 1 had to do was hold on to the bridge. The forty of us would have to run the gauntlet. We were going to have to go back down the elevators, if we made it that far. Before we worried about the elevators, we needed to fight our way out of the bridge. And if we failed… At that moment, two thousand men were floating in space outside the ship. They were armed, and they had combat gear, but they would be sitting ducks in a shoot-out with men on a ship. Hell, until we got the launch-bay door open, those men out there were doing little more than waiting to die.

“Harris, are you Gold 1 or Gold 2?” Illych called over.

“Two,” I said.

“You’re in for a fight.”

“Against these stiffs?” I asked, purposely echoing my famous last words from the cockpit. “They didn’t give us any trouble when we took the bridge.”

“I think they’ve figured out what we’re doing,” Illych said. “They’re all over the halls out there. Good thing they have to come to us. Man, I would hate to be the one squeezing through a narrow hatch to get in.”

“Thanks,” I said, knowing that in order to retake the launch bay, Gold 2 would run through the corridor and hatches.

“Oh, you guys will make it through, no problem,” Illych said. “I meant I would hate to be a Mogat squeezing through those halls.”

“Gold 2, stage.”

At the order to stage ourselves, we drew our guns and approached the hatch. SEALs from Gold 1 opened the door for us. Two Gold 2 men leaped through the door firing lasers, hoping to clear a path for the rest of us. The Mogats shot them with so many lasers that they seemed to dissolve into the air. The door slid shut, cutting through the bloody puddle.

36

We had to get down to the launch bay quickly. Looking at the viewport at the front of the bridge, I could see squads of SEALs and Marines heading for the ship like a swarm of locusts. They were armed and trained, but they could not defend themselves unless we opened the launch-bay locks and cleared a path for them.

"Gold 2, prepare!" the mission leader yelled.

A Gold 1 SEAL tripped the door mechanism, and the panels slid open. With the panels just inches apart, another SEAL ran toward the door, somersaulted past the opening, and tossed a grenade into the hall. The guy at the controls closed the panels the moment the grenade cleared.

There they go using the old dud grenade trick, I thought to myself. It was impressive the first time.

But nobody made a move for the door, and a moment later an explosion rocked the deck.

"Move it! Move it! Move it!"

The hatch slid open. A cloud of smoke rolled in. Another group of SEALs dashed into the smoke, firing blindly. Even with heat-vision technology in their visors, they would not see anything through the smoke. The heat and fire would cloud their vision.

I was in the second wave to leave. We did not fire our lasers. Had we fired, we would have been more likely to hit one of ours than theirs. We ran into the thick white smoke. If we'd had to breathe that smoke, we might have suffocated, but we had rebreathers.

The floor was red and slick with blood. Looking down to get my balance, I saw armor boots with legs still sticking out of them. The blood looked like a bouillabaisse made with bits of armor instead of fish. The grenade tore holes in the walls.

The silver-red beam of a laser flashed past my head. I dropped to one knee, turned in the direction it had come from, and fired. I could not see the person who fired at me. He had probably not seen me, either. I did not have time to check for the kill. As I stood up to continue my charge, a SEAL slammed into my back. I felt another jolt. No doubt someone had run into him.

One of the SEALs in my group had taken a shot in the thigh as he ran through the hall. Three-quarters of the thigh had disintegrated, leaving a strap of inner thigh that looked like cooked meat. The man vacillated. When he could stand the pain, he rolled onto his stomach and shot at the Mogats. When the pain became too much, he rolled onto his side and wrapped his arms around his legs. He was in that position when a laser struck him in the back and killed him. Even in death, he never released his pistol.

Gold 2 lost four men just fighting its way out of the bridge. I did not even bother counting how many men the Mogats lost. There were dead men and body parts all along the corridor. That grenade had blown some of their men right through walls. Some had been blown into walls that did not give. Bloody starbursts outlined the spots where their bodies struck.

At one moment it did not look like we could possibly clear the hall; and then in the next, we were through that gauntlet. A few Mogats halfheartedly fired at us from behind. They had other problems. A Gold 1 sharpshooter was picking them off from the door of the bridge.

We ran into limited resistance as we made our way across the deck. There might be a man hiding behind a hatch here or a couple of men hiding around a corner there. They were sailors—unused to this kind of combat and completely unorganized. They tried to shoot us from the front instead of letting us pass and hitting us off from the back. We almost always got off the first shot.

"There are elevators down the corridor to the left," one of the men called over the interLink.

Head for the first bank of elevators—a dumb idea, I thought. A few of the men ahead of me turned left, but I did not follow. My orders were to get to the launch bay, not run with a suicide squad.

Turn around! Turn around! I heard a few moments later.

Oh Lord! Oh damn! The SEALs did not use bad language, even in death.

"What are the losses, Gold 2?" the mission leader called.

"At least five so far."

"Harris, how are you doing up there?" Illych called.

I spotted two Mogats ducking behind a corner a hundred feet ahead and took a skidding right around the next corner to avoid them. I caught the sailor up the hall unawares and shot him as he reached for his pistol. Only after I dropped the guy did I realize he had only been waiting for a lift.

"Not too badly," I said. Adrenaline and endorphins now flowed through my veins in intoxicating levels. Had they been alcohol, it might have been a big enough dose to kill me.

37

I heard a constant stream of reports from the rest of Gold 2, Gold 1, and Blue Team. If anyone remained alive from Launch Bay Squad, they had gone silent.

Gold 1 and Blue Team were dug in or pinned down, depending on how you wanted to look at the situation. Blue Team had enough men to defend the engine room for now, but no men to spare. Gold 1 had all but welded the hatch to the bridge shut. They disabled it.

As I dragged the dead sailor into the elevator, I heard a report from some other members of Gold 2. They had found a stairwell that led to Deck 3. What they would find when they reached the bottom of the stairs was any man's guess, but it would not be pretty.

The Mogats must have known we wanted to secure the launch bay. We might have taken the bridge and engineering, but we did not have a prayer of capturing the ship with a mere hundred men.

We would need reinforcements, and there was only one place the cavalry would land—launch bay. The Mogats might or might not have figured out about the men we had floating around their ship, but they certainly knew how to stop us from receiving reinforcements.

Remembering the battle my platoon had fought on that derelict battleship, I rode the lift down to the lowest deck. The doors to the elevator opened to a darkened corridor in which no one walked. I felt like a mouse scurrying through a maze. I followed the mainline corridor to the back of the ship and realized I had gone too far. The vault I needed would be almost directly under the launch bay.

As I ran down another hall, I heard, "Hey!"

His shot flew over my shoulder and burrowed into a wall as I spun, dropped to one knee, and fired. I hit the first man. The second jumped back into the open hatch. I could not afford for him to radio for help, so I followed.

I opened the door and entered a mechanics workshop. Across the room, the Mogat fired a wild shot that came far too close, then hid behind a workbench. I aimed at the barrel of solvent behind him. It exploded into a pillar of fire that shot up to the ceiling and rained down in a cascade of flames. I heard the man screaming as I left.

Two decks above me, the twenty-three remaining members of Gold 2 had fought their way out of the stairwell and reached the launch-bay hatch. And there they stopped. They had the same problem that the Mogats had retaking the bridge and engine room. To get into the launch bay, they would need to funnel through a narrow hatch, no more than three at a time.

I found the door marked "Emergency Storage" at the end of the corridor. It was not even locked.

Inside the dimly lit storage area, three mobile firefighting units sat side by side. These were not the big, thirty-foot fire trucks you saw in cities. These were compact three-man units that looked like small tanks. They were ten feet long, small enough to fit on the emergency lift… powerful, but designed for emergency situations, not gunfights.

I lit one of the mobiles up and drove it onto the lift. I had hidden in a shaft just like it as Philips had used his "stiffies" to lead the Mogats away. On that occasion, in that wrecked battleship, I had been content to wait and hide. This time, I planned to fight.

"Gold 2, report?" the mission leader asked.

"We're pinned down outside the launch bay."

"Can you break in?"

"Negative, mission leader. They have shooters on every side of us."

"How long can you hold out?" I called over the interLink.

"Harris?" the mission leader asked.

"Reporting."

"Where are you?" asked Gold 2 Leader.

"I'm on my way up," I said. "I'll have the doors open in another minute."

They kept talking, but I did not have time to listen. The elevator doors opened. The launch bay spread out before me, with its gray walls and ceiling and its bright lights. I saw men crouched behind barricades pointing lasers at the hatch. They paid no attention as the elevator opened across the deck. It might not have mattered if they did.

I put the mobile firefighting unit in gear. It rumbled forward slowly on its own as I jumped out to the deck. Then I grabbed three grenades, pulled their pins, and tossed them. I ran for cover. The grenades exploded in rapid succession. The rumble of the first grenade did not have time to settle before the next grenade blew.

The damage those grenades made… I was a hundred feet away, hidden behind a ten-ton mobile fire unit, and I still felt the deck rumble under my armored boots. As I looked around the rear of the firefighter, I saw that the force of the grenades had tipped a forklift on its side.

White smoke as thick as a gauze hung in the air. I ran into the smoke, my laser ready; but there was no one left to shoot. As I passed through, I saw dead men and body parts. An inch-deep stream of blood ran down the drainage grooves in the floor. The first grenade had probably killed them all, leaving the second and third to pulverize the walls. The grenades had blown huge dents in the walls, and the shrapnel had chipped and gashed everything in sight.

"Get ready to run," I called to the men on the other side of the hatch.

"Hurry," one of them responded.

I opened the door. Diving through a cross fire of lasers, the thirteen remaining members of Gold 2 dived into the launch bay, and I sealed the doors.

"How did you get in here?" Gold 2 leader asked as he caught his breath.

"I came in through the back door," I said, pointing to the elevator.

"What's going on down there?" the mission leader called.

"We're in."

"Can you get the bay doors open?"

"We already have."

Two SEALs hunched over the console that controlled the atmospheric locks. It only took them a moment to open the outer door of the locks.

The first group of three hundred men passed through the locks. These were the engineers, navigators, and mechanics borrowed from other battleships. They would be little use in capturing this ship, but we could not risk losing them on a spacewalk. Among these swabbies would be a few civilian pilots with experience flying self-broadcasting explorers.

Outside the ship, Marines and SEALs rushed the novices into the launch bay, making certain that no straggler fell behind. The next seven hundred men to arrive were the SEALs and Marines—including the men from my platoon. They were the expendable ones.

38

"SEALs leader, this is Colonel Aldus Grayson, do you read me?" I knew Grayson. He was the pontificating bastard who had ridden on the explorer with me when I transferred out to the *Obama*. He was the kind of officer who wants people to know he is in command even when he can't tell his dick from his compass. His voice cut through all frequencies on the interLink. Chances were that the Mogats heard him as clearly as we did.

"Yes, sir," the mission leader said.

"I'm taking command of this shindig. Can you brief me on the situation?"

I could brief him on the situation. We had small groups of men in the bridge and a second small group of men in the engine room. They were holding on for dear life, while the perfectly capable man who had led us this far wasted time updating the windbag of an officer who wanted to seize control.

"We have twenty-three men holding the bridge and thirty men holding the engine room, sir," the mission leader said.

"Opposition?" Grayson asked.

"Several hundred Mogats outside each position, sir." The good news was that the Mogats needed the engine room and bridge as much as we did. They were not about to throw grenades into either area.

"How long can you hold out, son?" Grayson asked. I did not like the sound of that question. Officers ask questions like that when they only care about their own skin. A former bootcamp operator, Grayson had probably never seen combat in his career.

"They're trying to cut through the doors with welding torches, sir," the mission leader answered. "We need assistance."

"I see," Colonel Grayson said. As an officer, he had blundered into a situation way beyond his abilities.

"This is Blue Team Leader."

"Yes, son?" Grayson asked.

"They've almost cut through the hatch down here."

"I see," Grayson said. He showed no signs of life. He was a chess player contemplating his next move with all the time in the world.

I could no longer handle watching this pompous inactivity. "Evans, Sutherland, Thomer, round 'em up. We're breaking out of here," I said on the Marine frequency reserved for my platoon.

"Glad to," Evans said.

Only a minute later, my platoon started lining up in front of the hatch. I took my place at the front of the platoon. We would toss a grenade to clear the corridor, then come out shooting. I asked one of the SEALs to work the hatch.

"You, by the bulkhead. Where do you think you're going, son?" came over the open frequency that could be heard by Marine and Mogat alike.

"Sir," I shouted like a kid in boot camp speaking to a drill sergeant, "the sergeant and his platoon are simply lining up, sir." Then, in a quieter tone, I added, "You are broadcasting over an open frequency, sir. The Mogats can hear you."

"I don't give a rat's ass who can hear me, son," Grayson yelled. "You can't open that launch-bay door, there might be a thousand Mogats waiting to—"

He never finished the sentence. "Did anybody see who fired that shot?" I asked as I replaced my pistol in its holster.

"Wish I did," Philips grumbled.

"Must be a sniper in here," Evans said.

No one else responded.

"Mission leader, this is Master Gunnery Sergeant Wayson Harris from Platoon 103." I called on a proprietary frequency that our men would hear but the Mogats would not.

"Where's Grayson?" the mission leader asked.

"We had a problem with a sniper. It appears you are back in command, sir. Requesting permission to retake the ship."

"Permission granted, sea soldier."

"Let's give them a housewarming gift," I said. The SEAL opened the hatch partway and I tossed my grenade through. He sealed the hatch for the explosion, then opened it wide. Philips, Thomer, and I were the first ones out, followed by the rest of the platoon.

Despite the grenade, we entered into a cross fire. A corridor ran parallel to the launch bay, and another corridor led straight to it. Teams of Mogat commandos had set up barricades on either side of the door and up the hall straight ahead. The grenade sent the Mogats running around corners, but it did not kill many of them.

A Mogat peeked around a corner and fired at Philips.

"Kiss my pecker!" Philips shouted when the laser glanced his shoulder, burning through his armor. He spun and fired.

The hatch opened behind us, and hundreds of SEALs poured out. Lasers came from every direction. They had more men and cover, but we dug in quickly.

A Mogat laser struck the man standing to my right. Served him right, the fool was standing erect in a gunfight. Anyone who wanted to survive would crouch or kneel—at least, anyone but Philips and Thomer. Leading the way, the armor covering his shoulder still bubbling, Philips ran straight up the floor, jumped over the barricade, and caught a knot of Mogats flat-footed. He'd shot the first three before Thomer caught up to help.

The Mogats fell back.

"Illych, you hanging in down there?" I called to Illych.

"Nice to hear from you," he said. "Can't talk now. We've got company coming."

We needed Marines more than SEALs for this fight. This was not recon work; this was a battle. We needed bodies to secure the area.

We poured down the hall like floodwaters from a broken dam. Twenty or more Mogats tried to make a stand by the first bank of elevators. One of Evans's fire teams pinned them down while another team found a parallel corridor and flanked them. They killed every last one of them without taking a single casualty.

"You still with me?" I called to Illych. I found a stairwell and led my own mix of SEALs and Marines toward the engine room.

"Harris, they're like ants. You squish 'em, and they just keep coming. I've cooked more than thirty so far."

"How is the rest of the team?" I asked as I leaped a flight of stairs, caught my balance, and started down the hall.

"We're down to three," Illych said. I heard no fear in his voice. "Make that two."

"I can see you," I said. Actually, I saw the entrance to the engine room. Someone had cut the doors out of the hatch, which was now just a hole in the wall. A flood of Mogat commandos dressed in fatigues tried to rush that hole, then backed off.

"Time we pecker-slapped these boys, Master Sarge!" Philips shouted. He had the heart of a poet. Philips, Thomer, and a few dozen men came into the hall from one side as my group attacked from the other.

"It's getting crowded in here," Illych called.

We opened fire, and the Mogats turned on us. It looked like stalemate for a moment. We had cover and position, but they had three men for every man in our group. The stalemate ended quickly, though. With the Mogats packed so close together, we hit them with every shot.

They did not give up easily, though, and we lost men. One lucky bastard hit Sutherland as he and his squad ducked for cover.

"Keep them pinned," a SEAL leader radioed me over the interLink.

"Lay down fire," I shouted to my men. We hid behind corners and in hatches. Lasers burned into walls, the floor, and the ceiling. Had the hatch not presented a bottleneck, the Mogats would have escaped into the engine room. Because it did, Illych managed to pick off the Mogats who tried.

In the meantime, more SEALs and Marines poured into the hall. We had cut off the Mogats' escape routes, then we pinned them down. Soon we closed in on them. That ended the battle.

"Illych?" I asked.

"Blue Team, reporting." Illych and another SEAL emerged from the engine room. When we'd arrived, Blue Team had forty men. Only two survived.

The battle for control of the bridge went much more smoothly. The Mogats never managed to cut through the thick bulkheads surrounding the bridge.

We captured the bridge, the engine room, the launch bay, and more. Realizing that they had lost the battle, two hundred Mogat sailors fell back into a cargo hold to make a last stand. When they refused to surrender, the SEALs welded the cargo-hold hatch and carried them home as prisoners of war.

39

"Colonel Grayson died a hero, sir," I said, looking Admiral Brocius straight in the eye. "One of the bravest officers I have ever known." Now that I had killed the late Colonel Grayson, it only seemed fitting that I should elevate the son of a bitch to hero status. Semper fi, Marine.

"A hero to the last, I'm sure," Brocius growled. Whether he admitted it or not, he knew the score. Grayson had died in a sealed room surrounded by over a thousand men. Someone from our side shot him, and I fit the profile.

"I always hate it when natural-borns die in battle," Brocius said. "Reports, letters to relatives, all that hero bullshit. Any idea who shot him?"

"No, sir," I said.

"Did you shoot him?" Brocius asked.

"Certainly not, sir," I said.

"Harris, you came back with a specking Mogat battleship. You come back with another prize like that, and you can shoot 'Wild Bill' for all I care." "Wild Bill" Grace was the most powerful man in Unified Authority government.

"I do not want to shoot anyone but the enemy, sir," I said.

"Whoever that enemy might be," Illych muttered under his breath. He knew me too well.

This was a private briefing. Illych and I stood at attention. Admiral Brocius and Admiral Brallier sat behind a table reviewing us. Brocius would give me a one-on-one briefing when he got the chance. I would learn a lot more without a competing admiral in the room. Brallier would do the same with Illych.

"Harris, I've reviewed the records from the battle," Brallier said. "I must say, I'm impressed."

I stood at attention, staring straight ahead, but I could see the satisfaction on Brocius's face. His man had stolen the show. Illych might have been the first man on the Mogat planet and one of the last men holding the engine room, but nothing upstaged my launch-bay pyrotechnics.

"You bucking to become an officer again?" Brocius asked.

"No, sir. The sergeant is not looking for a promotion, sir," I said. Later I would ask him about promoting Philips, but this was neither the time nor the place.

"How about you, Illych?" Admiral Brallier asked. "Do you think you deserve some bars for this?"

"No, sir," Illych answered.

We both knew the same thing—becoming an officer meant living with natural-borns and dabbling in their petty politics. We preferred field work to command.

"I see," said Brallier, sounding a little like the late Colonel Grayson.

The interview went on for an entire hour. Both admirals

wasted time beating us down to make sure we did not put in for promotions. As we left the office, our caps tucked under our left arms and our minds swollen with frustration, Illych said, "Colonel, can I buy you a drink?"

"I'm a sergeant," I said.

"A master gunnery sergeant... yes, I know," Illych said. "You were a colonel when I met you, you did nothing to get demoted, and thinking of you as a colonel makes me feel better about the boys with bars and clusters.

"So, can I buy you a drink, Colonel?"

"How do you feel about doubling up?" I asked.

"Doubling up?"

We were in the administrative offices of the Golan Dry Docks. The polished plastic floor showed our reflection as cleanly as any mirror. The white walls gleamed under the bright fluorescent lights. The halls ran as far as the eye could see. Men in pressed uniforms and men in business suits, natural-borns all, walked the floor.

At the end of the hall was a sight that seemed incongruous in these polished premises. Thirty-six men in Marine tans stood loitering near an elevator. Everyone around them moved silently and efficiently. The boys joked in loud voices and laughed like drunks.

"I promised to take my boys out. You mind drinking with a bunch of Leatherneck clones?"

"Can I bring my SEALs?"

"We'll drink with them if they'll drink with us," I said.

Illych gave me a rare smile. "I'll get them."

"Did you have to invite them SEALs?" Philips asked as he watched Illych and his SEALs enter the bar. "Those boys give me the willies." Philips sat on a stool with his back to the bar. He held his beer in his right hand and leaned back on his left elbow.

"They should scare you," I said. "Those 'boys' are death dressed in a Navy uniform."

The bar was big and dim with brass lamps and lots of mirrors. Along the walls were models of the many different spacecrafts designed in this facility. Behind the bar, three bartenders in white shirts and red vests sorted through shelves of odd-shaped bottles.

This was a businessman's bar. People came here to talk, not to drink. Soft music rolled from the speakers.

"Do they make you nervous?" Philips asked.

"Not especially. Not as much as you do," I lied.

In truth, Philips would be more dangerous than the SEALs in most battlefield situations. He had absolutely no fear of dying. He could shoot as well as any man I knew, and he did not hesitate when it came to pulling the trigger. With his temperament, Philips would have washed out of recon training, but he knew how to carry himself on the battlefield.

"Shit, Master Sarge, you're embarrassing me," Philips said as he downed the rest of his beer. He immediately turned around and asked the bartender for another one.

I'd known men who preferred hard drinks or insisted on Earth-brewed beers. Not Philips. The man held no pretensions. He wanted his drinks cheap and fast and plentiful.

Thomer came to join us just as Illych and his company arrived.

"Are we still invited?" Illych asked as he strolled up.

There was something I noticed about Illych and his strain of clone—they all had an inferiority complex. They seemed to think that no one could like them.

When I first met them, the SEALs' quiet mannerisms impressed me as independence. Later I amended that and thought they were introverts. Now I realized that they considered themselves somehow beneath the rest of society, even other clones.

"It's an open bar," Philips said, waving his beer to show the mostly empty tavern. "Pull up a seat."

"I'm Kelly Thomer. Most folks just call me Thomer," Thomer said, reaching out to shake Illych's hand.

"Emerson Illych," Illych said.

Thomer broke the ice with his easy style. The SEALs fell in around us, trying to start up conversations, then letting the Marines do most of the talking. Just watching them I knew these boys had demons that vexed them. When they stood on friendly soil, the Boyd clones reminded me of lonely children. If any of my Marines paid for another drink that night, I would have been surprised. The SEALs gladly caught the tabs and offered to buy more.

"You the one that went off to that Mogat planet?" Philips asked Illych.

"Illych, this is Philips," I said.

Illych listened to me and nodded, then turned to Philips. "Mogatopolis."

"Mogatopolis?" I asked. "Official name?"

"That's what we're calling it," Illych said.

"You couldn't come up with anything better than Mogatopolis?" Philips asked.

"Can you come up with something better?" Illych asked.

Philips thought for a moment. "You could call it Planetary Home of Morgan."

"That's better?" Illych asked.

"Planet HomeMo for short," Philips said.

"You've got to be kidding," Illych said. There it was again, the revulsion to vulgarity. The revulsion had to have been programmed into his brain, just like vulgarity was tattooed onto Philips's supposedly nonexistent soul.

"It beats the hell out of Mogatopolis," Philips said. He knocked down another beer and excused himself to go "siphon the pond."

I laughed when Philips said that, but Illych did not even smile. He stood in silence as Philips walked to the bathroom.

"Don't be so hard on him," I said.

"He's a clown," Illych said. He changed the subject. "Did you look around that battleship?"

"Which one, the wreck or the one we flew back?" I asked.

"Both?"

"Sure. Are we talking about anything in particular?" I asked.

"The engine rooms are completely different," Illych said.

"The one we brought home only has one broadcast engine. Did you notice that?"

"I didn't look," I admitted.

"Did you know that we've had run-ins with the Mogats in all six arms now?" Illych asked. "They've lost a ship in every fight. They've lost four in the Orion Arm."

"They lost a lot more than that around Earth," I said.

"No," Illych said, "I mean over the last three weeks." Illych drank gin, not beer. He took long, slow sips that lasted for seconds. Watching him closely, I had the feeling he was not very interested in his drink.

"Do you know who Yoshi Yamashiro is?" I asked.

"The governor of Shin Nippon," Illych said.

I had not expected him to know Yamashiro. "He thinks they are purposely scuttling those ships to set up a communications network."

"Did I miss anything?" Philips asked as he rejoined us.

"We were just talking about Mogat battleships," I said. I could tell by the way Illych tightened up that he did not want to continue the conversation in front of Philips. They were polar opposites, those two. Illych was quiet, thoughtful, and very calculated. Philips let his whims make his decisions. Illych spoke in a hushed voice and never swore. Philips swore and could not manage a whisper. That they should not trust each other seemed inevitable.

I decided to show Illych what he would never have guessed about Private Mark Philips. "Philips, you were on both Mogat ships."

"Both ships? You mean the sucker we sank and the one we stole?"

I nodded. "Did you see any differences between them?"

"You mean besides the forty-foot laser gash on the bottom of the dead one?"

"Yeah, besides that," I said.

"Not outside of the engine room," Philips said. "But the engine rooms were completely different." He went on to describe the two broadcast engines and the special shielding around the working engine on the derelict ship.

Illych listened to this and nodded, looking impressed. "I noticed the same things. Do you have any theories about the differences?"

"Any theories? I'm just a specking grunt. Us specking grunts don't come up with theories, we just pull the damned triggers and shoot our damned guns."

All admiration evaporated from Illych's expression.

40

I was not drunk or hungover after seven glasses of beer, but I needed some sleep. Less than thirty hours ago, I had woken up on a rack in a Mogatopolis armory.

We stayed in a dry-docks dormitory. Most of the Marines had to share their apartments, but I had one to myself. The last time I had stayed here, I'd had a much larger apartment. Of course, the last time I stayed at the Golan Dry Docks, three men tried to beat me to death. When that failed, they tossed a grenade in my room.

My apartment was ten feet wide and ten feet deep with a ten-foot ceiling. It was a perfect cube. My bed was six and a half feet long and three feet wide. There was a closet on one side of the bed and a closet-sized bathroom on the other. I liked the room. It had absolutely no luxuries, but it made me feel secure.

As I settled onto my bed, I saw the flashing light on the wall console warning me that I had a message waiting. I went to the console and punched in my code. The message was from Brocius asking me to call him. I punched in the return code.

"There you are," Brocius said, as his face appeared on the screen.

"I went out for a drink with my platoon," I said.

"And you're still sober?"

"More or less," I said.

"Glad to hear it, we have things to discuss," he said. "Come to my quarters."

"Yes, sir," I said.

"And don't worry about the uniform, Harris, this meeting is off the record."

When you spend time with high-ranking officers, you quickly learn that there is a difference between being "at ease" and relaxed. When an officer gives the order, "At ease," you spread your legs and relax your shoulders, but remain alert and erect. You remain that way until the officer says, "Dismissed," at which time you walk away alert and erect until you are out of sight.

Brocius told me not to worry about my uniform, but that did not mean he wouldn't notice if I came dressed like a civilian. Above all else, officers want you to show them respect, even when they try to act like your friend. I changed back into my Charlie Service uniform and reported to the admiral's suite.

Brocius, still wearing the same uniform he had worn to my debriefing five hours earlier, came to the door. "Good of you to come, Sergeant," he said. He stepped away to allow me in.

The couch in Brocius's suite would not have fitted in my quarters. He had a full-sized bar, a living room, and a pool table. The suite probably came with a bartender, too, but Brocius would have excused the man before discussing sensitive matters. As he led me into the area, I spotted Yoshi Yamashiro sitting on the sofa.

"Hello, Harris," Yamashiro said as he stood. He wore his traditional dark blue blazer and red necktie. Between the middle finger and forefinger of his left hand, Yamashiro held his traditional half-smoked cigarette.

We shook hands.

"Admiral Brocius has told me about your latest adventures. Perhaps we might have saved you some trouble had we allowed you to commit suicide on your transport ship." On his ship, Yamashiro showed a strong preference for hot Sake, but he seemed comfortable with the whiskey he now held.

"Suicide?" Brocius asked. "I don't believe I heard about that."

"Harris and his friend tried to adapt the broadcast engine from a broadcast station for use on a transport," Yamashiro said.

"On a transport? That would never work. You would not have had enough power," Brocius said.

"Ah." Yamashiro nodded. "Maybe even if you generated enough power, the metal hull of a transport would not be well suited for the electrical discharge." It was a cultural thing. What he meant was, *There's more than enough power, asshole, but you would blow up your ship.*

"Really?" Brocius asked. "I have long wondered why our engineers have never retrofitted transports for broadcast. Now I guess I know." He pointed to the furniture. "Have a seat. Harris, I know you're probably well lubed after a night with the boys, but can I fix you a drink?"

Yamashiro's whiskey on the rocks looked good, but I decided to play it politic. "No thank you, sir," I said. Had it just been Yamashiro and I, I would have been on my third drink by this time.

We took our seats.

"I'm betting that Admiral Brallier is giving his boys a briefing as we speak. I apologize for not getting to you sooner, Harris. You deserve to be in the loop."

"Thank you, sir," I said.

"We've compared the video record you took on the derelict to what we've found on the captured ship. Any guesses on the differences between the two ships?"

"The second broadcast engine," I said.

"You're halfway there, Harris," Brocius said. "They changed the entire engine room. They also changed the shields."

"The ship you brought back has changed very little since my engineers renovated it two years ago," Yamashiro said. "The broadcast engine is untouched."

"From what we can tell, the Mogats placed components for two additional shield systems on the battleship Porter sank. One of the shields came with its own generator. It was designed to protect the secondary broadcast engine. As you probably noticed, both the shield and the broadcast engine are still running.

"The Mogats stripped out the ship's original shield system and replaced it with something new.

"Whatever they have, it's powerful. Porter hit that battleship with lasers, particle beams, and torpedoes before it went down. We've gone over that battle from every angle. Until the fatal shot, nothing came close to penetrating its shields."

Brocius sat silently for a moment. He sipped his Scotch and considered what to say next. Finally, he placed his drink on an end table, and said, "You know what our engineers are saying? They think the damn shields eat energy. No kidding. They absorb energy out of lasers and particle beams and use it to recharge their batteries. Hell, they think that shield can even strip the kinetic energy out of explosions.

"Of course, that's all conjecture. We won't know anything until we see one of the shields on this ship up and running."

"What about the shields on the battleship—"

"The one you captured?" Brocius interrupted. "We found the

shield system but not the shield generator."

"Maybe they used the generator from the original shield system," I suggested.

"We do not think that is the case," Yamashiro said. He finished his whiskey and went to the bar to fix another.

"While we were dissecting their ship, we found a signal receiver hooked into the weapons systems. This is all theory, of course, but it looks like the Mogats are broadcasting the shields as some kind of signal to their ships. The problem is, the only way to test that theory is to fly the ship into Mogat territory," Brocius said. "I suppose we could take the ship back to where we found it."

"Maybe not just there," Yamashiro called from behind the bar. "My engineers estimate that there will be a hundred-million-mile radius in which you can receive that signal.

"You remember when I told you that I thought the Mogats wanted to create a broadcast network? I thought they would use it for communications. After seeing this shield system, I have changed my mind. Now I believe they are using their network to broadcast their shield signal." He filled his tumbler four fingers full and rejoined us.

"What happens if we shut the signal down?" I asked.

"The Mogats have disabled the original shields on their ships," Yamashiro said, a wicked smile on his lips. He took a deep drag from his cigarette, then blew the smoke out through his nostrils. "If they lose their shield signal, they will be completely unprotected. I would enjoy seeing that battle."

"I heard the Mogats lost four ships in the Orion Arm," I said. "What if they are using those ships as broadcast stations for their shield signal?"

"They probably are. Fortunately, they don't seem interested in placing a station near Earth."

I thought about my last conversation with Freeman and

realized that they already had a broadcast station in place.

Brocius had a tall Scotch which he would likely nurse all night. He seldom touched it. When he did pick it up, he swirled the ice around the glass and took short sips.

"You remember Ray Freeman?" I asked.

"Of course," Brocius said. I did not even bother looking for a nod from Yamashiro. He would remember Freeman vividly.

"He found a Mogat base," I said.

"On Earth? Impossible," Brocius said. "We would have known about it. Where did he say it was located, somewhere near Antarctica?"

"Washington, DC, sir," I said.

"And you believe him?" Brocius asked.

"Freeman? If he says it is there, it's there."

Yamashiro listened without offering any information. He lit a new cigarette and enjoyed the smoke. I got the feeling that he agreed with me about trusting Freeman.

"So you think the Mogats have a secret base on Earth, somewhere near Washington, DC?" Brocius said. "Rubbish. That's just pure... fantasy."

"After the Galactic Central War, we went forty years without seeing a single Mogat ship," I said. "The battle in Outer Perseus was our first sighting in months. Now, over the last two weeks, they're all over the place. Each engagement ends the same way—they lose one ship and run away."

"It does seem like they are ramping up." Brocius forgot himself and took a long pull of his Scotch.

"If they have a working base on Earth, they may be ready to attack," Yamashiro said.

"Admiral Brallier wants to send his SEALs out to disband their network. He wants to send them out in demolition teams to blow up the Mogat wrecks," Brocius said.

"I'm not sure that would work, sir," I said.

"I know," Brocius agreed. "Waste of time. We might be able to blow up the ships, but with those shields, we can't touch the broadcast gear. It's a specking nightmare. It's like having a damned tumor and not being able to cut it out."

"Our only choice is to strike first," I said.

"Take out their shields at the source?" Brocius asked. "It does seem like the only alternative, assuming we are not too late." He thought for a moment, "Assuming Freeman is right about that base, and we're not too late."

Clearly shaken by the news that the Mogats had landed on Earth, Brocius drained the Scotch I had expected him to hold all night. "I'm glad we talked," he said, and he stood, signaling both Yamashiro and me that our meeting had ended. As we rose to our feet, Brocius added, "You know what frustrates the hell out of me? It's the feeling like we've won every damned battle, but we're still losing the war."

Admiral Brocius paused to think about what he had just said. "Listen to me. I'm swearing like a specking Marine."

PART II

EXTREMISM... NO VICE

41

We had breakfast in a cafeteria meant for dry-dock employees. They fed us whatever we wanted. I grabbed a tray and ordered a four-egg scramble, five strips of bacon, a double order of potatoes, two slices of toast, and two cups of orange juice. The food felt heavy on my tray.

That chow tasted good. A Marine could get spoiled. A few of my men even ate their eggs without smothering them in ketchup.

We ate breakfast early, at 0600, and had the place to ourselves. Rows of tables stood empty on either side of us. I had hoped to see the SEALs this morning, but they might have already left.

"Hey, Master Sarge, when are we going back to the ship?" Philips asked.

Only Philips called me "Master Sarge." Soldiers may call their sergeants "Sarge," but in the Marine Corps, the term "Sarge" is demeaning, not that it bothered me... much. I had not yet accustomed myself to the name, "Master Sergeant," because I did not think of myself as a master gunnery sergeant. Back when I had the rank of colonel, I never thought of myself as an officer. The only rank I ever felt entirely confident about was private first class, and I got promoted out of that after three months.

"We're not going back to the *Obama,*" I said. "We're headed Earth-side, boys."

They greeted my announcement with a moment of hushed awe. The thirty-six remaining men in my platoon all knew what that meant. It meant war.

"We're not going back for our gear?" one of the men asked.

"It's already been crated and shipped to Fort Houston." I sat down, and they moved in around me.

"You wouldn't happen to know the next stop after Fort Houston?" Evans called from across the table.

"I could make an educated guess," I said.

"Strap on your bayonets, we're headed to Mogatopolis," Philips said to the Marine sitting beside him. He surprised me by not referring to it as "Planet HomeMo."

"We're still a few men shy of a platoon," Thomer pointed out. He was a cautious one.

"I'm not sure what they're going to do about that," I said. "Now that the orphanages are gone, reinforcements are harder to come by. Maybe someone will shift some companies around."

"Think they'll break us up?" Thomer asked.

"No. They don't break up teams that produce. Not if they can help it."

Thomer nodded. He was skinnier than the other clones. He ate light and preferred jogging to lifting weights. He left the tough talking to the other Marines, but he held his own in combat.

I picked up a strip of bacon and ate it followed by two forkloads of eggs. "The brass has a bigger problem than a few empty slots," I said. "They have to figure out some way to land enough men to make a stand. And they have to do it without the Broadcast Network."

"How many men will they need?" Evans asked.

"This is off the top of my head, but I'm guessing we'll need one hundred thousand or maybe two hundred thousand fully equipped troops just to get our boot in the door.

"The 2510 census said there were 200 million Mogats. If they have 200 million people on that planet, we're going to need a couple million men along with tanks and gunships to support them."

Evans whistled. "Two million men?" he asked. "That's going to be some airlift."

"Especially if we have to ship them there in explorers," I said. "If Washington is serious about invading that planet, they're going to need to come up with something."

"When do we leave for Fort Houston?" Thomer asked me.

"Pretty soon—1100."

"When do we deploy?" he asked.

"I don't know. I think they plan to send us out as quickly as possible," I said around a wad of bacon. I finished my first cup of orange juice in one long drink. "It just depends on how quickly they can figure out the logistics."

"But they know how to find the Mogat planet?" Thomer asked.

"They seem to. I'm guessing they lifted the information off the broadcast computer on that ship we took."

Thomer nodded again.

I had withheld a lot of information. My boys did not know that the Unified Authority and the Confederate Arms had signed a treaty and that we would likely ship out in battleships like the one we had captured. I neglected to mention that the entire Mogat fleet, which was still nearly four hundred ships strong, was moored around the target planet. I said nothing about our unarmed ships needing to slip in, drop us on the hostile planet, and get out before the Mogats shot them down. I also neglected to mention that the Mogats' ships had some new shield technology that rendered our weaponry useless.

Three hours after breakfast, we all boarded an explorer and flew to Earth.

It took less than an hour for us to arrive at Fort Houston, a small training base in the southwestern portion of the old United States. Fort Houston had once been attached to an orphanage. Young clones ages twelve and up once had run its obstacle course and bivouacked in its fields. The Mogats destroyed the orphanage after defeating the Earth Fleet. Thirty-six thousand clone children fried in their beds as a Mogat battleship hit the orphanage with a laser from above the atmosphere.

Bastards.

Over the next two days, a hundred platoons moved into portable barracks buildings set up around the Fort Houston parade grounds. That gave us four thousand five hundred Marines. If they'd had a hundred more forts with a hundred platoons, we might have had enough Marines to hold a beachhead while we waited for reinforcements to arrive.

Within an hour of landing in Fort Houston, we began training. I found comfort in this. There was something nostalgic about doing calisthenics in the blazing-hot noonday sun, sweat rolling down my face and back, while another platoon ran laps around the field. We finished our calisthenics and headed for the firing range, passing men on the obstacle course crawling across a field while their sergeants fired live rounds over their shoulders.

Hearing the swearing of sergeants and the explosions of grenades, I realized that I had returned home. Semper fi, Marine.

* * *

One of the great benefits of being stationed back on Earth was the mediaLink. On the *Obama,* the only news we received was prerecorded information released by the Department of the Navy. It wasn't much. Before I logged on to the mediaLink, however, I had important business to take care of. I had a call to place.

At 1600 hours, the base commander announced that we had the rest of the night to ourselves. My men went into a nearby town called Austin. I stayed back.

We had our own barracks building. With the platoon gone, I dug through my gear and found the pair of disposable shades I'd bought in DC. After one last glance to make sure that no one would see me, I logged on to the mediaLink and placed the call.

The picture that appeared on the screen was a pretty little girl with long blond hair and startling blue eyes. She sat on a blanket in a field of daisies holding a dandelion in her hands. Looking at me through the screen, she smiled and in the sweetest of voices said, "We can't beat the Mogats."

"What do you mean?" I asked.

"I tried to break into their compound," Freeman said through his little girl avatar.

"Let me guess, the building has impenetrable shields," I said. My trip to Mogatopolis was highly classified. I could barely wait to share the details.

"Have a look," said the little girl.

The picture of the little girl disappeared from the screen. Video of a large building that took up an entire city block replaced it. There was an explosion. I saw a flash of fire followed by a cloud of smoke. Cars parked near the building flipped in the air and tumbled away. There was no sound.

When the smoke cleared, the building looked exactly as it had before the explosion. Then the image on the screen returned to the little girl as she blew on her dandelion, and the air carried its fluff toward the camera.

"Something big is going on in there. I took energy readings from my station. They're off the scales," Freeman said. On the screen, the little girl, who could not have been older than five and probably weighed all of fifty pounds, picked a daisy and started playing He Loves Me, He Loves Me Not.

"It's almost like they have a broadcast engine running in there."

"They do have a broadcast engine," I said. "That is exactly what they have."

"Sounds like you've been busy," Freeman said. He was using a short video loop. The dandelion magically reappeared in the little girl's hand.

"I went down to Mogatopolis," I said.

"Mogatopolis?"

"That's the name they're using for the Mogat home world," I said. "The Mogats have some new kind of shield generator on their planet. They're broadcasting the shield. If you give me a location on that building, Brocius can send out the hounds of war."

"They still have to deal with those shields."

"We're shutting the shields down at the source," I said. "Now that we have the Mogats' address, we're going to pay them a visit. I think you should come with us as a civilian advisor." I knew that Freeman would never accompany us any other way.

"Why would I do that?" Freeman asked.

"Crowley should be there." The first time I met Freeman, I was stationed in an armory on a backwater planet called Gobi. Freeman, who made his living as a mercenary, had come to investigate a report that Amos Crowley, a former U.A. Army general who had converted to Mogatism and defected, was on that planet. Crowley attacked the armory and almost took us with it.

"What's Crowley worth these days?" Freeman asked.

"I'm guessing two or three million."

On the screen, the little girl blew her dandelion fluff.

42

Word came around the camp to look smart; Admiral Brocius had come to Fort Houston to review the troops.

It was our second week on the base. A captain and three lieutenants woke my platoon and three others at 0500. We dressed and fell in for an early-morning hike that would last sixteen hours and end with a bivouac. We ate MREs in the field and drank only the water we brought with us as we hiked in the 110-degree weather.

None of this would have mattered had we worn our climate-controlled armor, but we hiked in fatigues. My men were more acclimatized to the chilled air on the U.A.N. *Obama* than the heat in Texas. They suffered the entire way.

Philips, who had no trouble staying ahead of the rest of the platoon, bellyached more than the rest of my men combined. He must have asked "Where the hell are we going?" five times an hour as we tromped through plains and over foothills. In the midafternoon we entered a marsh. Philips grimaced as his feet sank in the mud, and he asked, "What is the point of running through this shit?"

In the marshland we ran through ankle-deep mud, crushing reeds and scaring ducks as we went. That lasted for three hours. At 1500, the officers steered us to a makeshift firing range they had constructed in the middle of the swamp. They sat in the backs of their Jeeps and ate MREs as we fired M27s and other small weapons.

Of the 168 Marines on the hike, I scored highest on the range with a perfect score—three hundred shots fired, three hundred hits scored on targets three hundred yards away. In Marine jargon, I had just pulled off a "three-by-three."

I took more than a little pleasure when I noted that Private Philips came in second with a score of 283. No one else scored over 250.

We spent two hours on the firing range, then continued our hike. Mud sucked at our boots. The air smelled of sulfur and decay. Clouds of mosquitoes formed around us. The hot sun glistened on the water and shone in our eyes. The air was hot and wet and thick as perspiration. The crickets and cicadas buzzed so loud it nearly drove some men insane.

When we finally reached the far side of the swamp, we were met by two trucks. The captain over the exercise climbed into the back of a truck and dumped out our gear. "We're here for the night," he said. "You might as well set up your bivouac." As he grabbed a pack, Philips mentioned something about using their Jeep as a latrine once the officers settled down for the evening. I seriously toyed with the idea of joining him.

We had tents, but whoever'd planned the hike wanted us to rough it. Instead of a plasticized tent with an elevated floor and inflatable cots, we slept in an old-fashioned canvas tent. Groundwater soaked through the floor of our tent and our blankets.

Had we been planning to invade a swamp, I would have called this bivouac an ideal proving ground; but I had never seen so much as a drop of groundwater on the Mogat home world. Unless the brass wanted to invade their planet through its plumbing, the hike made no sense.

That night, as we doused our lanterns and went to sleep, one of the lieutenants called in through the tent door. "Harris, Captain Moultry wants to see you in his tent."

A bright full moon hung over the campgrounds. We had set up our bivouac on the edge of the swamp lands. As likely to Inhale mosquitoes as oxygen with every breath, I trudged to the captain's tent.

I knocked on the door.

"Enter," the voice growled back.

There sat Admiral Alden Brocius, looking tired and grim in the bleaching white light of a lantern. "This hike was not my idea," he said as I stepped in.

"It certainly wasn't my idea," I said.

"Your base commander didn't want me fraternizing with enlisted men," Brocius said. "His replacement is arriving tomorrow.

"You're welcome to come back with me and spend the night in the commandant's quarters. They're vacant and a lot more comfortable."

Compared to my canvas tent in the swamp, this plasticized tent with its dry interior and hardened floor was a five-star hotel. It had climate control and folding chairs.

"Sounds nice, sir, but I would prefer to stay with my platoon," I said.

"I had a feeling you would say that," Brocius said. "This hike was a very bad idea. We need you rested."

"Big plans for us?" I asked. I already knew the answer. If we didn't launch an invasion soon, we'd be defending, not attacking.

"Briefing the day after tomorrow." Brocius pulled a book with a black leather cover from a table by his seat. He tossed it to me. The book was unread and its cover stiff. Its pages did not flutter as it flew through the air. I caught it and looked at the cover. The title was printed in gold leaf: *Man's True Place in the Universe: The Doctrines of Morgan Atkins.*

"Have you read this book?" Brocius asked.

I shook my head. "No, sir."

"Have you ever wondered why you haven't read this particular book?"

"It's against regulations," I said.

"Yeah, they don't want to take a chance on any of you enlisted men becoming converted. I always wondered who came up with that rule," Brocius said. He took a bottle of Scotch from the table and poured himself a glass. Then he tossed me the bottle. "You can share it with your platoon. Tell them it came compliments of Fleet Command."

"Thank you, sir," I said, turning the bottle in my hand so I could read the label. I did not recognize the name.

"They made us read the Space Bible in Annapolis. It always seemed like a fairy tale to me. Atkins claims he found an underground alien city in the center of the galaxy." Brocius waved his hand. He made a sour face as if he had just smelled garbage. "Strictly Jules Verne stuff. You know what I mean? It's like *Journey to the Center of the Earth*.

"I've read your report a dozen times, Harris. Every time I read it, I think about Atkins. That city you described, it sounds just like the one in his book. Right down to the transparent ceilings,

Atkins described it all just the way you did.

"There's something else, too. We tracked down the location of that planet using the broadcast computer on the battleship you boys stole. You know where that planet is located? It's in the inner curve of the Norma Arm. It's the very rock the Liberators invaded fifty years ago. The difference is that back then no one ever thought about looking under the covers. This time we know better."

"Admiral, how can we possibly invade their planet?" I asked. "Even with the Confederates and the Japanese, the Mogats have ten ships for every one of ours, and they have those shields. They'll pick us off before we land a single platoon."

Brocius laughed. "Come on, Harris. You don't think I'd send the Marines into the meat grinder without leveling the field? Atkins isn't the only one with secret technology. The boys on the Golan came up with something good."

"Did they figure out how to get through the Mogats' shields?" I asked.

"We already know that," Brocius said. "You turn them off at the source.

"No, they came up with something better. They came up with a way to get through the Mogats' radar. They've invented a new cloaking technology that makes our capital ships invisible to radar detection."

"What about transports?" I asked.

Brocius shook his head. He was not drunk, just morose. He sat there looking craggy and old, his skin showing not a hint of color in the bleaching light from the electric lantern. He sat silently for several seconds. I had no idea what he might have been thinking about. Finally, he said, "I'll send a truck by tomorrow morning. No more hikes for you and your men."

"Thank you, sir," I said.

I saluted. Admiral Brocius returned my salute. I started to

leave, but he stopped me. "Your friend Freeman turned himself in to Navy Intelligence last night. I don't suppose you had something to do with that?"

"I spoke with him," I said.

"He had a crazy story about a Mogat base," Brocius said. Maybe he had forgotten our conversation back on the Golan Dry Docks, or maybe he thought I had.

"We checked into his story. He was right. The energy readings coming out of that building are off the scale. Did you know they were there?"

"Yes, sir," I said.

"We've set up round-the-clock satellite surveillance. They slipped an entire broadcast engine in under our noses. Who knows what else they brought with them.

"Freeman said something about going out with our invasion force."

"Oh, yeah, can he come?" I asked.

43

The rules changed when we returned to camp the next day. We did not drill all day, nor did we get to go into town that evening. Instead, we had a quiet night on base, lights out at 2200.

They called Reveille at 0600 the next morning. Our briefing was at 0800. The sergeants from every platoon filed into the mess hall. In my platoon that included Thomer, Evans, and a guy named Greer, whom we shipped in to replace Sutherland. I went, of course. There were almost five hundred of us sprinkled across a cafeteria built to serve as many as two thousand men at a time.

A small ten-foot-by-ten-foot dais sat on one side of the cafeteria. In the time that I had been in Fort Houston, no one had ever used it. Now I saw a podium on that stand. Three empty chairs formed a short row behind the podium.

When the officers in charge came into the cafeteria, everyone snapped to attention. The officers, all Marines in Charlie Service uniforms, marched up to the stand without so much as a sideward glance. One of those men was a colonel—probably our new camp commandant. One was a major. He'd been around all along. The third, also a major, was a briefing officer who had most likely flown in from Washington.

The briefing officer stood straight and tall. He was a Marine who had seen combat; I could see it in his demeanor. We all could see it. Something about the way he carried himself commanded instant respect. Even the way he scowled at us commanded respect.

"At ease," the colonel said. Then he followed up with, "Gentlemen, make yourselves comfortable. We have a lot to discuss."

With this he stepped back and gave the mike to the briefing officer.

"Gentlemen, we have an enemy; and as you know, the Unified Authority Marines do not take kindly to enemies. Our enemy is Morgan Atkins. Now, gentlemen, we could try to reason with Mr. Atkins. We could try to negotiate with Mr. Atkins. We could even offer to play nice with Mr. Atkins, but that would not be the Marine way.

"Do I make myself clear?"

"Sir, yes, sir!" we yelled.

"What was that?" the major asked. "I don't believe I heard you clearly."

"Sir, yes, sir!" we all shouted at the tops of our lungs.

"That's better," the major said.

He was a short man with a shaved head and glasses. He had a scar on his forehead. That scar might have come from an old skiing injury, but I had the feeling he'd earned it in battle. Sitting as close as I was, I could also see that he was missing some teeth.

"You," the major called to one of us, "shut down the lights."

"Aye, aye, sir," the man called back as he raced to the switch.

A screen lowered from the ceiling, and a familiar image appeared. It was a planet called Hubble, certainly the ugliest piece of real estate I had ever seen. The planet had a smoggy, brownish black surface that had not seen sunlight in thousands of years.

"Gentlemen, this here is Hubble. Hubble does not have oxygen in its atmosphere. The gases that surround Hubble are humid with oil. If you breathe that shit, you will die, Marines. I suggest you take good care of your armor so it can take good care of you."

The picture changed to a surface view of the planet. Several of the men in the cafeteria groaned. The landscape looked like a desert at night except that the soil sparkled like fresh coffee grounds. The cliffs looked like they were made of volcanic glass.

"This is the surface of Hubble. This is what happens when a sun expands and bakes a planet, gentlemen. It turns to shit.

"Hubble is made of one kind of shit and one kind of shit only. That shit is in the air. It is in the ground. It is in the rocks. It is nasty shit, gentlemen.

"Should you visit Hubble, do not shoot the rocks or dig a hole, gentlemen. In the rocks and ground you will find the nastiest shit of all. The boys in the science lab have labeled this an 'extreme-hydrogenation elemental compound distillation.' At the Pentagon we call it 'distilled shit gas.'

"You may not know this, Marines, but we lost a lot of good men and equipment on Hubble because distilled shit gas eats through armor and machinery."

The scene changed to show a corpse. It was a Marine in combat armor. The outside of his armor was intact. The camera came up to his visor, which normally had tint shields but was now entirely transparent. The face behind the visor was stripped down to skull and muscle, with the muscle disintegrating right before our eyes.

I'd fought on Hubble. That was before the Confederate Arms declared independence. We massacred a Mogat settlement on that planet. I always wondered why the Mogats had chosen to hide on such a hideous planet. I was about to find out.

"Gentlemen, you learn something new every day. Today we have learned that the corrosive elements in distilled shit gas can be used to produce energy. If you strip those corrosive elements out of the shit gas compound, you are left with highly malleable chemicals that carry an electrical charge and are easily transformed."

"Nanotechnology," somebody whispered in the audience.

"You are almost correct, Marine," said the briefing officer. "Not nanotechnology." He stretched the first syllables—*Nan-oh-technology.* "Atomic conversion." *A-tomic con-versh-shun.* "This is alchemy, Marines. Morgan Atkins is an alchemist. He is taking shit and turning it into plastics, metals, fuel, and fertilizer. For all we know, the Morgan Atkins Separatists even eat food made of distilled shit gas.

"It turns out that distilled shit gas is useful stuff. Morgan Atkins has based his entire civilization on the use of distilled shit gas. He fuses the noncorrosive compounds with an electrical charge and converts them into plastic to build his cities. He condenses it and strips the acids out to fuel automobiles. The man has an endless supply of distilled shit gas at his fingertips, and he is specking Albert Einstein when it comes to the many uses of that gas.

"When you invade his planet, gentlemen, you will be underground. Be aware, Marines, that everything around you will be made of distilled shit gas.

"Do you hear me, Marines?"

"Sir, yes, sir!"

Manipulative or not, I had to admire the way this briefing officer personalized the war. He never referred to the Mogats. Everything focused on Morgan Atkins himself, as if he personally had attacked Earth, killed Marines, and declared war.

The screen reverted to an orbital shot of Hubble. "The good news is that we no longer need to invade Hubble. There are no Mogats on this planet, we already killed them," the briefing officer continued.

Across the cafeteria I heard sighs and nervous laughter.

"The bad news is that you will be invading a planet that is exactly like Hubble, right down to having distilled shit gas in the dirt.

"The distilled shit gas will be the least of your worries. You Marines will invade a planet that is home to an estimated 200 million Morgan Atkins Believers. Those men and women will not welcome you into their home, Marines.

"Leading their forces is one General Amos Crowley. You may have heard of this man. You may be ignorant of him. Amos Crowley was once a general in the Unified Authority Army. His having deserted the Unified Authority makes this dickweed our enemy, Marines. His having swapped sides to join the Mogats makes him a treacherous dickweed.

"Do not underestimate this dickweed. When he was our dickweed, he led the Unified Authority Army through many great battles. He may be a dickweed, but he is a dickweed who knows how to fight."

On the screen, the white-bearded face of General Amos Crowley smiled down at us. Crowley had a smooth, kind face with a generous smile. He had shown that same smile to me as I lay on a table waiting to be tortured. He was the reason I'd invited Freeman to join the invasion. Whether we won or lost, Freeman would make sure that General Crowley did not survive the battle.

"I have more good news for you, gentlemen. Morgan Atkins has developed shields that protect his ships and his buildings from any weapon we possess. We have not seen his tanks in action, but we have reason to believe that his tanks and battle vehicles may have those shields as well.

"Their shields are the real specking deal, Marines. Do not bother shooting Morgan Atkins tanks with laser weapons. Do not bother shooting his buildings with particle beams. You will not hurt them with grenades or mortars.

"If this invasion goes as planned, we hope to shut those shields down before you have to deal with them. If it does not go as planned, gentlemen, you may find yourselves in a battle against an invulnerable enemy. If that becomes the case, Marines, you will be expected to employ hit-and-run tactics until those shields are brought down. You are not to engage the enemy in a head-on war. Do you understand me, Marines?"

"Sir, yes, sir." The chant was not especially enthusiastic.

Clearly hearing the lack of enthusiasm, the major said, "Gentlemen, this is the Unified Authority Marine Corps. We do not send our own off unprepared."

That was not the case in my experience, but I did not quibble. In my experience, officers did not think twice about wasting clones.

"The Navy is sending SEALs to visit Morgan Atkins and disable his shields. We are not sending you to invade Morgan Atkins's planet. We are not sending you to kill Morgan Atkins or his followers. We are sending you Leatherneck Marines to distract Mr. Atkins's army while the SEALs persuade him to shut down his shields.

"Once the SEALs have turned off his shields, the Navy plans to send his fleet a message. Once that message is received, you will be joined by three million soldiers from the Unified Authority Army. Gentlemen, as you know, the Marines capture the fort, then the Army holds down the fort.

"Do you read me, Marines?"

"Sir, yes, sir."

"Let's try that again. Do you read me, Marines?"

"Sir, yes, sir."

"I'm glad to hear that, Marines. You and your men ship out at 0930."

44

What they did not tell us at the briefing:

After we landed on Mogatopolis, the Navy would send three teams of SEALs. One of those teams would go after the Mogats' shield generator, likely the most closely guarded spot on the planet. The second team would go after the broadcast engine that the Mogats used to transmit their shield signal. The third team would attack the Mogat power grid on the off chance that having failed to shut down the shields or engine, they might still be able to shut down the power.

I would have judged this a suicide mission if they weren't sending one thousand Adam Boyd clones. This was their element. If anyone could slip in under the radar and find those targets, it was the Adam Boyd clones.

Never once did the major mention modes of transportation. Except for me, none of the Marines knew of the alliance with the Confederate Arms. As far as everyone in the camp knew, we would fly our transports from Earth to the Mogat planet. What more did they need to know, I suppose.

"Holy Moses on a rope. What the speck is that?" Private Philips asked as we waited to board the transport.

I followed his gaze. There, nearly eighteen inches taller than the armor-plated clones around him, stood Ray Freeman. He wore full battle armor that he must have bought custom-made. Because I knew Freeman, I also knew that the armor was the right size to fit over his enormous shoulders and torso. Had I never seen him before, as the Marines around him had not, I would have thought he had a jetpack or maybe a luggage compartment inside that huge armor. There was no jetpack and no hidden compartment, just a giant of a man.

So here came Freeman, tall, dark-skinned, bald, and muscled to extra-human proportions. He carried a rifle case in his left hand.

"That is Ray Freeman," I said.

"Okay," Philips said, "as long as he's on our team."

"Ray only plays on his own team. This time he happens to be on our side."

"Does he ever change sides?" Philips asked. "If he does, I don't want to be nearby when that happens."

We were issued special gear for this battle. Everything worked the same, but instead of the dark green camouflage we generally wore, this time we had desert beige.

Since Freeman brought his own armor, his was more gray than beige. It was a light silvery gray that stood out against his dark skin. As he silently moved through the ranks, Marines quickly stepped out of his way.

"Ray, I didn't recognize you without the dandelion," I said.

Freeman did not say anything. He might have caught the reference to the little girl he used for cover on the mediaLink, but I doubt it. Humor did not register with him.

"You don't need to bring us the corpse," I said, trying to move on from my failed joke.

"I don't plan to. Brocius says the video record from my scope will do."

"How much is he paying?" I asked. I felt envious even before he answered. The only money I would see from this action was a sergeant's combat pay.

"Five million," Freeman said.

"That's a lot of money," I said. "How did you work him up to that?"

Freeman shrugged. "That's what he offered."

Around the deck, the grunts in my platoon eyed Freeman nervously. He was huge and different. He radiated danger. He had cold, dark eyes, and his face betrayed nothing but indifference to everyone around him.

Ahead of us, the doors of the transport slid apart. "Fall in," I called to my men. We jogged forward as a platoon, our armored boots clanging against the steel ramp that led into the kettle. Freeman stayed beside me at the front of the group. Standing beside him, I flashed back to our four-billion-mile trek from Little Man. Back then we'd wanted to reenter the war. Now we might possibly play a role in ending it.

Once my platoon settled in, a second platoon joined us. Normally a sprinkling of officers would come along for the ride, but this time we clones traveled alone. My platoon was still shy some men from hijacking that battleship, so we came nowhere near filling the transport to capacity.

I had each of my squad leaders take a roll call. They reported every man present and accounted for. A moment later we got the all clear sign, and the kettle door closed.

We did not know how long it would take to get to the target. It took three minutes to fly to our base ship. Between the Japanese Fleet, the Confederate Arms Fleet, and the battleship we stole, we had thirty-seven self-broadcasting battleships. The Confederate Arms had an additional twenty-five self-broadcasting destroyers.

Battleships had two launch bays, each of which was designed to accommodate four transports. Each destroyer had a single launch bay. Crews had worked around the clock to prepare the ships for attack, not only adding a stealth device, but expanding every launch bay so that it could handle six transports instead of four. In theory, our landing force included 59,400 Marines.

We were a force of nearly 60,000 men being dropped among an enemy with a population in the hundreds of millions. The brass wanted us to distract the enemy; but if the real forces did not land soon, any distraction we provided might be short-lived.

"Five million seems awfully generous," I said. I remembered Admiral Brocius's house and the casino on the second floor. He liked house odds. Maybe he was betting Freeman would not live to collect.

Freeman sat silent for a moment. He opened his rifle case and pulled out a magnificent sniper rifle with a computerized scope. Returning the rifle, he pulled out his gear and sorted it. He had rope, grenades, and a knife. He pulled the knife half out of its scabbard, looked at the blade, then pushed it back in.

Around the kettle men stood or sat in silence. A few well-trained Marines stripped and tested their M27s. Most of the men wore their helmets. If they spoke among themselves, I would not hear it unless I located their frequency.

"So what is that guy doing here?" Philips asked over a platoon-wide frequency.

"Just so you know, Philips, Ray Freeman is the best friend you can have on this mission. In the entire Mogat Empire, there is only one great military mind, and Freeman came to put a bullet through it," I answered on a private band.

"He came to assassinate Crowley?"

"He did."

"So he's a sniper?" Philips asked.

"A sniper? Philips, snipers are guys who sneak around with rifles waiting for someone to shoot. Freeman doesn't wait."

"No shit? A specking corpse factory," Philips said. He sounded impressed.

"Just keep out of his way."

Freeman had his helmet on. Since he was not a Marine, and his armor was of civilian make, he could not legally access the frequencies we used on the interLink. "Freeman, you on?"

"Yes," he said.

"Did you and Admiral Brocius discuss any other work he might have for you after you've collected on Crowley?"

"No," Freeman said.

"You do know that civilians are not allowed to listen in on communications on this frequency?" I asked. Then, without waiting for Freeman to answer, I added, "If you listen in on my communications, we won't need to waste time updating each other."

Freeman did not respond.

We touched down on our base ship. We would step off of our transport, tucked away in the launch bay. Once all of the transports checked in, the battleships would broadcast to a spot 100 million miles from Mogatopolis, where no one would detect the electrical anomaly. Then we would fly the four-hour trip into Mogat space under the cloak of the new stealth engines.

Once every last destroyer and battleship was in place, we would launch our transports. There was no way to cloak or protect our transports, so we would scramble down to the planet as quickly as possible.

Standing there, in the dim and anxious atmosphere, I comforted myself by looking for things that would make me feel safe. I did not come up with much.

I thought about the Mogats... the Believers. They might know we were coming. They had to know that we hijacked their battleship and that we now knew how to find them, but they would think we had no way of striking them. Since they did not know about our alliance with the Confederate Arms and the Japanese, they would not know that we had access to a self-broadcasting fleet. The more I thought about it, the more I realized that the alliance was both our best-kept secret and our greatest strength. Even the men in my platoon did not realize we were riding in a Confederate Arms ship.

Time passed slowly now. We could not hear what happened outside our sealed world. Had our host ship already broadcasted itself? Were we nearing enemy space? What if the Mogats spotted us? We could die in a flash, never knowing the battle had already begun.

Then, after hours of sitting, we received our warning. Lights flashed in the cabin as our pilot prepared to launch.

The invasion had begun.

45

"Sergeant Harris, do you want to come up to the cockpit?" the pilot asked.

"On my way," I said.

I looked up at Freeman. "I have to go to the cockpit," I said. He continued checking his gear.

"Where are you going?" Private Philips asked, as I started toward the ladder.

"The pilot wants to see me," I said. I thought for a moment, then radioed back to the pilot. "Can I bring one of my men?"

"We have room for a fourth." That might not have applied if I tried to bring Freeman.

"Philips, you want to come?"

"Sure," he said.

I had a reason for taking Philips. He might have been old and irreverent, but he was a leader. When the bullets started flying, and bombs started to burst, the guys in the platoon would forget all about who wore stripes and who wore clusters. Despite his antics around the barracks, Philips kept his head under fire. During an extended campaign, the rest of the platoon would look up to a Marine like him.

We climbed the ladder and removed our helmets before entering the cockpit.

The inside of the cockpit was dark except for the light from the dials and gauges. We had a pilot and a copilot for the flight. Both men wore combat gear without helmets. The pilot looked back, and said, "Which one of you is Harris?"

"Me, sir," I said. He was a lieutenant.

The transport had just entered the planet's atmosphere. Below us, an endless plain stretched ahead. Special gear under our transport shone a blinding light down on the landscape.

"I hear you've been down here before," the pilot said.

"Once," I said.

"Think you can find one of those gravity chutes?" the pilot asked.

"I might recognize one if we passed close to it," I said.

"Good enough," the pilot said. "They sent an explorer yesterday to scout the place. The pilot mapped a path for us, but I want you up here just in case."

I nodded. "The gate we entered was in the mountains," I said.

"Oh, man, that's one shitty-looking planet," Philips said.

"We're not landing on this part. The place we're going has air," I said.

There was a radar scope beside the pilot's seat. My gaze strayed toward it, and I froze. If I read that display correctly, hundreds of ships had gathered behind us. Then I realized they were other transports. "Those are all ours, right?" I asked.

"Every last one of them," the pilot said. "Believe me, you'll hear alarms if the Mogats show."

"Transport pilots, this is Fleet Command. Be advised that enemy ships are approaching. We are going to evacuate orbit in twenty seconds. Repeat, we will evacuate in twenty seconds."

"Now that's just specking great," the pilot said.

Below our ship, the plains ended at the foot of a tall, sheer mountain range. The peaks looked like they were made of obsidian. They were as black as deepest, darkest space and reflected the transport lights with all the clarity of mirrors.

"There's your entrance," I said, pointing toward a particularly tall and jagged peak ahead and to the left. The entrance itself was not lit, and the mountain looked like a shadow against a night sky, but blue-and-white marker lights flashed on its face.

"We're going there?" Philips asked. He did not sound scared, he sounded incredulous.

"That's just the doorway," I said. Having not been admitted to the briefing, Philips had no idea what to expect.

"You know we'll drop straight down like a rock if the Mogats cut power to that gravity chute?" the pilot said.

"Let's hope they don't," I said. Could they cut the power to a gravity chute? They knew we were coming. If they could cut the power, they would.

We slowed to a crawl and dropped several hundred feet until we pulled parallel with the mountain. Then we hovered toward the entrance at a very slow speed. Our searchlight shone all the way across the entrance. It looked like a giant tunnel. A short way in, the floor suddenly disappeared.

"So that's a gravity chute?" the pilot asked.

"That's a gravity chute," I agreed.

"Do you remember how your ship approached it?" the pilot asked.

"We flew in. I think I felt the engines cut..."

"I was afraid you would say that," the pilot said.

I shrugged my shoulders. "Everything else was automatic. The pilot came into the cabin and stood around talking to passengers."

"I hope we're not missing anything here," the pilot said. We inched ahead. The light from our searchlight reflected and refracted from the walls. Its glare seemed to multiply and fill the cavern around us; and yet, the cavern still seemed dark.

We hovered ten feet off the deck as we ambled forward. I looked down and saw the shimmering black floor below us. Then we dropped over the edge.

"Here's your leap of faith," the pilot said.

"Damn, why'd you ask me up here, Harris? I'd rather be back there and ignorant with the rest of the grunts," Philips complained.

At first we hung in the air. With our spotlight shining on the walls around us, I could see dozens of spotlights as hundreds of transports followed us in. The beams of light looked like spokes as they cut through the darkness.

One moment we seemed to hang in the air, the next we dropped at least fifty feet. Not a peep came from the kettle where eighty Marines probably thought we'd hit an air pocket. In the cockpit, we braced ourselves and held on for the ride. Then the transport found its equilibrium.

"Good thing I have one of them siphon lines attached to my pecker," Philips said. "I'd hate to have all that piss running down my leg."

We were in the chute for nearly one minute when a synthetic voice spoke over the radio. "Transport pilots, be advised that enemy ships have entered this orbital space." The message came from a cloaked satellite.

"Can we all make it into the chute that quick?" Philips asked.

"There are six hundred transports," the pilot said.

The frantic messages started a moment later. Pilots screamed at the transports in front of them to hurry. Someone yelled, "Oh, God!

They got the transport behind me!" Another pilot yelled, "We're going to run for it! We're going—" and his radio went dead.

Our pilot looked over to his copilot, then switched off the radio. We went the rest of the way in silence. I could not tell how anyone else felt, but I agreed with what Philips had said right before we entered the chute. I wished I was back in the kettle, unaware of everything.

46

We started the invasion with 582 transports. By the time we reached the target, we were down to 461. The Confederate Arms Fleet evacuated the area long before the Mogats arrived, leaving their ships to pick off one-fifth of our transports as they waited to enter the gravity chute.

"Line up! Move it! Move it! Move it!" I shouted into the microphone in my helmet. The circuits in the receiving helmets would filter out my volume, but the intensity and voice would still resonate. We were going to war. No time for questions. No time for thinking. These clones were designed to respond.

With the exception of Ray Freeman, who sat in a far corner sorting his gear, every man stood at attention. My platoon moved to the rear of the kettle, ready to charge the moment the doors opened. They held their M27s across their chests. From here on out, we would act like war machines, not men.

The heavy metal doors of the kettle started their slow swing apart. They seemed to move at the speed of an ocean tide. I noticed my fingers squeezing and relaxing along the butt and barrel of my gun. The neural programming inside my brain had already sent my nerves into their clockwork movement. The combat reflex had not taken effect yet. That highly engineered gland was back in sync. It would not secrete its euphoric mixture until the enemy closed around us. With the bullets would come peace of mind. With the killing would come warmth. It was the Zen of the deranged.

When the opening was large enough for two men to run out side by side, I sent my men out. "Move it! Move it! Move it!" I screamed, prodding them in the backs with the butt of my M27.

We knew the drill, and we ran it by the numbers. First we would secure the area. We would not encounter resistance, of course. Not on this level of the planet. It was just for landing and taking off.

We might run into some hostility one deck down, but we had landed in the civilian sector, and the military had not yet had time to mobilize. In the meantime, we would make ourselves a thorn in their side by disrupting their home world. I had my platoon break into squads and my squads break into fire teams. Only when we were ready for battle did I observe my surroundings.

The topography of the civilian sector looked no different than the top layer of the military district. The space was flat and open, with elevator stations spaced miles apart. We had landed in a spaceport that was probably identical to every other spaceport on the whole specking planet.

I heard a whining siren that sounded like it was coming from hundreds of miles away. The wailing was just a whisper in the air that the audio equipment in my helmet registered and amplified. If I removed my helmet, I might not hear the siren at all.

Hundreds of transports landed around us. They dropped out of the gravity chute, engaged their boosters, and hovered until they found clear spots on which to land.

Clearly the brass had done a poor job of planning for this part of the invasion. The transports should have landed in some sort of order that arranged their shields into a protective picket line. Instead, they dropped down here and there, some with their cockpits facing me, some offering their broad sides, some pointing their asses in my general direction.

Two hundred feet above me, the gravity chute kept spitting out transports. Every five seconds another one fell from that hole in the sky. But I did not have time to watch. "Platoon one-zero-three, move out!" I yelled.

"Where is he going?" Thomer asked. He pointed across an open stretch. I turned and saw Freeman tromping toward an elevator station, his rifle case in one hand. "Do they call it 'absent without leave' when civilians abandon their platoon?"

"Just you worry about your own men," I said. "If that man does what he came here to do, this battle is going to go a whole lot easier."

"That guy scares me," Thomer said.

"He ought to," I agreed.

I had my platoon move double time toward the nearest elevator station. Other platoons followed. Hundreds of men in desert beige armor lined up behind us.

"Harris, what is this place?" The colonel called on his direct frequency so that no one would hear us. He could not afford to sound confused; he was the ranking officer.

"This is the foyer," I said.

"The what?" he barked.

"We're on the top floor. The Mogats only use this floor for spaceports. From what I saw, nothing happens up here. Those buildings around us, those are elevator stations," I said. "Didn't they brief you on this, sir?"

The colonel did not answer immediately. "Yeah, they did. I just didn't believe them." A moment later, he yelled, "Secure that elevator station!" on a command frequency.

My men reached the station first. A four-man fire team lined up with two men on either side of the door. The automatic rifleman, Private Mark Philips, peered in the door then gave the all clear sign. The siren blared through the open doorway, but the audio filters in my helmet censored the sound to a hum.

"I think they know we are here," Thomer said.

"I get that feeling," I said.

"I hope them Mogie boys weren't planning on using this little elevator station, because I claim this in the name of the Unified Authority," Philips radioed from inside the elevator station.

"Stow it, Philips," I said.

Across the flatness of the man-made plain, tens of thousands of armor-clad Marines captured five elevator stations. By taking different stations, we spread ourselves over a several-mile area. We would need to regroup before the enemy arrived, but we had no choice. The elevator stations were a bottleneck. It could take hours to funnel forty-eight thousand Marines through them, and we had minutes, not hours.

I followed my men into the building. Ahead of me, one of my men stared down to the lower levels through the opening in the center of the floor. The virtual dog tag identified him as Evans. "It's like we're invading a specking anthill," he said, as I stared down as well.

It was like invading an anthill, except all of the ants had run for cover. The ground below us looked like a bedroom community. I saw buildings that looked like apartment complexes. I saw stores. What I did not see was people.

"Welcome to Planet HomeMo," I said.

"HomeMo?" Evans asked.

"It's short for Planetary Home of Morgan," I said.

"That sounds like something Philips would say," Evans said.

I laughed.

We stationed snipers around the railing to fire at anyone they saw on the level below. Then we forced the doors of the elevators open and sent men rappelling down the shafts to the next level. Other Marines lowered themselves from the balcony using rappel cords that created magnetic links with their suits, eliminating much of the muscle work. We needed to secure the area around the station and hold it. Nearly ten thousand Marines would have to pass through that elevator station. Even if we sent one hundred men through every minute, it would take us over an hour; and the Mogats were not going to wait around.

My men were among the first to drop to the next level. We hit the deck below and looked for enemies. We found the area abandoned. The sirens still blared their doleful warning. The people must have run for cover.

This was the civilian district. I saw four-story tenements in every direction. I saw roads and storehouses and medical clinics. The Mogats had built churches with steeples that stood thirty feet in the air.

With the exception of the landing, we had executed our invasion in an orderly way. The officers leading the attack knew their objectives and signaled them to their platoon leaders. A message signal flashed. As I turned toward the nearest tenement, a blue frame appeared around the building in my visor. A simple message appeared along the bottom of my visor: "CAPTURE OBJECTIVE."

My men received the same message.

"Why the hell should we waste time capturing an apartment building?" Sergeant Evans asked.

"Stevens, hand me that rocket launcher," I called to one of my men.

PFC Stevens, a grenadier, did as asked. He selected a handheld rocket launcher from his gear and gave it to me.

"Boys, this is the best-built home you will ever see," I said as I hoisted the launcher to my shoulder, turned toward the tenement, and fired. There was a jolt to my shoulder and the rumble of the rocket. A moment later the smoke from the rocket hung across the open area like a fluffy white feather. The rocket's contrail formed a shallow arc, then the rocket slammed into the target with a thunderous bang.

Smoke and flames flashed from the side of the building. There was no debris and the smoke cleared in seconds because the rocket did not so much as smudge the tenement.

"Harris, what happened?" the colonel barked.

"Just showing my men what we're dealing with," I said.

"We need that building in one piece," the colonel warned me.

"Yes, sir," I said. "One piece, sir."

That rocket, which would have destroyed several city blocks back on Earth, had not so much as broken a window on the tenement. The building stood untouched.

"What the hell?" Evans asked.

"Shields," I said. "They have shields protecting every building on this planet."

"Every building?" Evans asked.

"So how the speck are we supposed to take a building with specking missile-proof shields?" Philips asked.

"I don't think we'll have much of a problem," I said. "The shields are only on the outside walls. Once you get inside, everything is breakable."

We moved as teams, taking corners, making sure every corner was secure, then moving ahead to the next. One of my fire teams flanked the rest of the platoon. If we entered a firefight, one team would pin the enemy down while the flanking team came around and attacked from the side. But the enemy had not yet arrived. They were not coming from across town. They were coming from the other side of a continent, possibly the other side of the planet. We would have time to dig ourselves in.

The apartment building had an open doorway, just like the spaceports and elevator stations. The Mogats had never been invaded. They did not expect an invasion. Until the moment we landed on their planet, they did not believe their enemies could reach them. As far as they knew, the Unified Authority was landlocked.

"Is it shielded inside, too?" Evans asked.

"No, just on the outside," I said. I remembered the armory Illych and I blew up as we left the planet. "Hard on the outside.

"Evans, secure the first floor. Thomer, you've got the second floor. Greer, take your squad and secure the third. Got it?"

Evans's squad ran in first. One of the men tossed a smoke grenade through the doorway. All three of Evans's fire teams stormed into the building under the cover of the smoke.

"Evans, run a heat-vision sweep. What do you see?" I asked.

Moments later, he said, "This is a civilian dwelling."

"Yeah," I said, trying to sound as caustic as possible, "that's who you find in civilian sectors."

"There are people in the apartments, Master Sergeant," he said.

"Flush them out," I said. "We want the building to ourselves. Do you read me?" I was prepared to kill anyone who would not leave. We had come here to kill. But I did not relish the idea of killing women and children as they cowered in their apartments. I wanted minimum breakage.

As we cleared the apartment building, other platoons prepared in other ways. Demolitions teams placed mines on the train wells and traffic ramps. We hid snipers and grenadiers along the roads.

We had time to burrow in, but I did not hold much hope. The same shields that protected the building would protect the trains and armored transports. We might derail a train or knock over a transport, but we had no prayer of defending ourselves until the Mogats' shields were down.

I entered the tenement lobby. The last remnants of smoke still hung in the air. My men had trampled the lamps and smashed furniture on their way in. As I looked down a hall, I saw a Marine rifleman kick a door open and step back as his automatic rifleman charged in. A moment later a woman carrying a baby with three young children came galloping in my direction. All of their mouths hung wide open in panicked screams. Fortunately, the audio filters in my armor dampened the sound of their shrieks. I stepped out of their way, and they ran screaming through the lobby and out into the street.

The woman and her children were the first Mogat refugees. Over the next few minutes, dozens of people followed. Men, boys, women, girls, children alone, children with adults—I felt more like a bully than a Marine.

Gunfire echoed down the hall. There was a single shot followed by the rapid fire of an M27.

Those shots were a wake-up call. I ran down the hall and stopped by an open door in which one of my men stood pointing his weapon. Inside that apartment, a man lay sprawled on the ground in a kidney-bean-shaped puddle of blood.

"Report!" I shouted into the interLink.

"The guy had a gun," the Marine said. Near enough to the corpse to be covered with blood, an old-fashioned automatic pistol lay on the floor.

"That was a bad choice on his part," I said.

"Thomer, Greer, stay alert. Evans already found one Mogat packing a gun. There may be more in the building."

Oh, there would be more guns in the building. The problem was, I felt bad for the dead guy. He was not an enemy soldier hunting my men. He was just someone protecting his property... just a guy with an old pistol trying to stand up to armor-clad Marines... a casualty of war.

I looked back at the body—an old man with gray-and-white hair dressed in an old T-shirt. There might be 200 million more like him on this planet. *Why did these assholes ever pick this war?*

47

I stood by a window on the third floor watching a steady flow of Marines pour out of the elevator station. Nearly twenty minutes had passed since we landed on the planet. I wondered how much time we would have before the Mogats would arrive.

Below me, former tenants of the building poured out into the street. Some ran for cover. Some stood just outside the entrance in a forlorn circle. Some walked away huddled together. A middle-aged man walked with his arm across his weeping wife's shoulders. Their children dragged behind. They were refugees now, but at least they were alive.

We found two or three hundred people living in the building and turned them out. Some screamed at us. One woman tried to attack one of my Marines with her bare hands. In anger, her face contorted with hate, she shrieked like a wild animal and beat on his chest. Her husband dragged her back and thanked my Marine for not shooting her. I could not believe it. He actually thanked the man who had just evicted them from their home.

The woman was short and chubby, with six screaming children. Shooting her might have been an act of kindness. I stood in her tiny two-room apartment now. Judging by the mattresses stacked along the wall, four of her children slept in a room that doubled as the family room, living room, and kitchen.

On their wall was a family portrait and a picture of Morgan Atkins. They had a bookshelf with storybooks, a small bin of toys, and eight copies of *Man's True Place in the Universe,* the Space Bible. The entire apartment was twenty feet wide and maybe thirty feet across, about the size of a doctor's office—and eight people lived in this hole.

Atkins, what good did you do for these people? I thought to myself. They lived in a plasticized city. Growing up in Orphanage #553, I played in fields and forests. The Mogats provided their people with apartments but not so much as a blade of grass on the entire planet. All the buildings and streets were made of the same material. I could see schools and stores from up here. Everything was made from distilled shit gas. That was why the Mogats tried to establish a colony on Hubble, too. They planned to turn the distilled shit gas into a city.

From where I stood, I had a clear view of the city around us. Blocks away, the traffic ramps rose out of the ground like attic doors. The Mogat Army would use those ramps as they came to retaliate. Just a half mile away, the magnetically charged lines of several train tracks funneled into a train station. Normally we would destroy the tracks and traffic ramps, but these had shields.

"Sergeant Harris, we have a small situation," Greer called in to me over the interLink.

"I'm on my way," I said.

Taking one last look at the city below, I left the apartment.

I don't know if all Mogats lived as these families did. Looking around on my way out, I saw three child-sized mattresses stacked along the wall. Maybe that was how the Mogat population grew so quickly—pregnancy spread through them like a virus. The small kitchenette in the corner of the room included a hot pad, a sink, and a single pot.

I had no trouble finding the altercation, it was just down the hall. Most of Greer's squad stood staring into the door of an apartment. I pushed my way through.

In the eye of this gathering stood Sergeant Greer, my newest squad leader, along with two teenage boys, both barely five feet tall. The boys looked to be friends, not brothers. They had long hair and pimples. One had oily blond hair to his shoulders, the other had red hair that only covered the tops of his ears.

"Specking clone," the redhead sneered.

"This boy doesn't seem to like you, Greer," I said.

"They attacked one of my men with knives," Greer said. He held up two kitchen knives for me to inspect.

I tried not to laugh, but could not help myself. Our armor would not stop lasers or particle-beam weapons. Bullets glanced off our armor if they hit it at a shallow angle. Kitchen knives, on the other hand, would break long before they could so much as scuff the polish. They might as well have attacked the Marine with a pillow.

"You called me about a couple of kids with knives?" I asked. I said this using the microphone so that the boys would hear me.

"Get specked, clone," one of the boys said.

"Their buddy in the next apartment says he has a gun," Greer said.

I nodded. Without saying a word, I pulled a grenade from my belt.

"Chris, he's got a specking grenade!" one of the boys screamed.

The door of the apartment opened and another old-fashioned twenty-four-shot pistol flew out. "Don't shoot, man, I'm unarmed." A boy who could not have been a day past twelve stepped out with his arms up, his fingers sticking up in the air.

"Somebody take these boys out of here," I said, still using the mike.

Chris, the rebel without the gun, stopped in front of me and spat on my armor. I shot out my hand and grabbed him by the collar of his shirt. "You got something you want to say to me, boy?" I said.

"Yeah, I'm going to kill you, you specking tube-for-a-mother clone."

I pulled off my helmet and stared down at the kid. "The term is, specking tube-for-a-mother Liberator clone," I snarled. All three boys stared up at me in panic, but only Chris wet himself. They knew Liberators. They probably grew up hearing horror stories about us in school.

"Get these children out of here," I said. "We've got work to do."

"Let them go?" Greer asked me.

If the boys found real weapons, they might come back. Ray Freeman would have killed them and not thought twice about it. So would Illych and his SEALs. I suppose I should have as well; but deep in the back of my mind, I did not think we belonged on this planet. Killing Mogat soldiers and destroying Mogat battleships were one thing, landing an invasion in a residential sector and terrorizing kids was something else.

"Unless you have a better idea," I said. I knew he did. We should have shot the boys; but coming after a platoon of Marines with kitchen knives and an old pistol did not seem like capital offenses.

I watched Greer and two of his men lead the boys down the hall at gunpoint. One of them stopped and turned to face me. "Devil!" he screamed. Greer grabbed him by the hair and kept on walking without breaking stride. As they stepped onto the elevator, I replaced my helmet.

"Any other problems, gentlemen?" I asked over a platoon-wide band.

The colonel, the highest-ranking Marine to accompany the invasion, called me over the interLink. "Sergeant Harris, are you and your men comfortable in that cozy little hotel you've captured?"

"Just dandy, sir," I said.

"Sergeant, I have it on good authority that the first wave of Mogats will be here in less than ten minutes. I would like to offer you and your men front-row seats if you're feeling up to it."

This was neither a friendly offer nor an order. It was a challenge. "Scared we'll miss the action?" I asked.

"I just thought you'd want to be in on it. Your choice, train station or traffic ramp," the colonel offered.

"You know, sir, I've always had a thing for trains."

48

Two other platoons replaced us as we left the building. They would fight from behind the shielded walls we had captured. Leaving the tenement gave me the same feeling I sometimes got when I parachuted out of a transport. I had the uneasy feeling of leaving safety behind.

Watching my men, I saw that they knew the countdown had begun. We might have three minutes, we might have seven, but the Mogat Army was coming with its shielded tanks and vehicles and its endless supply of men. Leaving the shielded safety of the tenement, we entered the street. To our right was an elevator station from which a steady stream of Marines continued to pour.

The neighborhood around us looked like a ghost town. No one stood in the streets. By this time everyone had found cover, even the people we evicted from the apartment building. No one stood in the doorways or courtyards of the three- and four-story tenements we passed on the way to the station. Running alongside my platoon, I scanned those buildings and occasionally saw Marines peering through open windows. If the Mogats wanted this neighborhood back, they would have to take it floor by floor.

"Harris, you and your platoon better hurry if you want to catch your trains," the colonel called to me.

"Yes, sir," I said.

The colonel transmitted virtual beacons to guide us to the station. The beacons led us through alleys rather than along main streets. Unless we got very lucky stopping the Mogats, we would need to retreat. The colonel's path would let us fall back more safely, leading the Mogats through gauntlets in which our men would already have high ground.

We ran another three blocks, crossed an open square that was probably the Mogat version of a commons. The park had benches and sculptures of people, but when it came to plant life, it had not so much as a single bush.

Then we arrived. The train station had a roof but no walls. Weather was not an issue in this artificial environment.

Another platoon had already set up. The lieutenant in charge came out to greet us. "Sergeant Harris, am I ever glad to see you," he said.

"Find cover," I told my men, then I turned to the lieutenant. "What's the situation, sir?" I asked.

"We've mined the tracks," he said. "I have snipers on every roof."

"Do you know how much longer till they arrive?" I asked.

"How could I know that?" the man asked.

"Evans, search the station. There should be a computer monitoring which tracks are in use. I want men with rocket launchers watching each of those tracks," I said.

"Got it," Evans said.

Turning back to the lieutenant, I said, "My men and I will have a look. I'll let you know if we find anything."

A moment later Philips called me. "Hey, Master Sarge, ain't those trains shielded?"

"They are," I said.

"So what's the use of shooting rockets at them?"

"We're going to shoot at the front car," I said. "Let's see if we can derail a train or two."

"Derail the suckers; I like it," Philips said.

"Thomer, keep a leash on Philips, will you?" I asked.

"I found your control system," Evans called back a moment later.

"Open band," I told Evans. "We need everyone to hear you. Where's the first train?"

"Track number seven. It arrives in thirty-eight seconds."

"I got this one," Philips called over the interLink. He trotted off toward a track carrying a rocket launcher in his right hand and his M27 in his left.

"I'll watch him," Thomer said.

"No, I'll go with Philips," I said. "Take care of the rest of your squad."

"There are trains coming down tracks one, three, eight, nine, and eleven," Evans radioed me.

"Did you get that, Lieutenant?" I asked.

"Got it. My men can take eight, nine, and eleven," the lieutenant said.

The tracks were trenches with plasticized edges and metal floors. They were five feet deep and fifteen feet across, and they seemed to worm their way under the horizon. The trains used magnetic levitation. The Mogats had undoubtedly shielded the tracks and the trains floating inside them, but the men inside those trains would be as vulnerable as eggs in a carton.

I ran to join Philips. At the edge of our vision, the train sped toward us. At first it was nothing but a tiny spot of light. Soon I saw the massive wedge of its engine, then I could identify the dome on its nose and the airfoils along its top. A mine blew up beneath it, and the train seemed to wriggle in the track. Another mine exploded. A small burst of flames erupted under the heavy engine; the cars kicked from side to side in the track.

"Steady, Philips," I said. Now I was calm. My combat reflex had begun, and warmth spread through my veins. I knew I could have made the shot, but I trusted Philips to shoot as well as me.

"I hope they shut down those shields soon," Philips said.

"Hit the train low," I said. "Let's try to upend it."

"Damn it, Master Sarge, I know that," Philips snapped. He fired the rocket. A long rope of smoke appeared three feet above the floor of the track. The rocket reached the train so quickly that the smoke and the explosion seemed to all happen at once. A star-shaped flame exploded beneath the base of the train. Philips had fired a damn-near perfect shot.

What happened next was as beautiful as any ballet. The train veered toward the edge of the track as its nose kicked up. Magnetic levitation had placed that train in a nearly frictionless environment, so its bulk and momentum continued forward despite the upward thrust of the rocket.

Barreling forward at hundreds of miles an hour when the rocket struck, the engine bounced nearly three feet on its magnetic cushion, enough to leap the edge of the track. The rest of the train followed, twisting over on its side as it did. The track sort of ejected the train.

The rear cars slid over three more mines as they threaded their way out of the magnetic tracks. I expected sparks and a trail of destruction to follow the derailed train, but it did not happen that way. The shielded train slid across a shielded street, hitting a couple of shielded walls. The train gave off no sparks; but smoke rose from its windows as its cars slid along the street, rebounding against walls before skidding to a rest. The outside of the train went undamaged; but liquid, maybe blood, maybe oil, maybe both, slowly seeped out of the wreckage.

The cheer started spontaneously. Marines stood up from behind cover, waved their rifles in the air, and shouted at the tops of their lungs. You had to have your ear to the interLink to hear them, of course, but I imagined the noise ringing through the air. In that moment, I imagined us as the Israelites watching David slay Goliath. I imagined us as the Union soldiers on Cemetery Ridge after Hays's men stopped Pickett's Charge. Our armor and interLink technology did not fit into my image of this battle.

"Nice shooting, Philips," I said as I slapped him on the back.

For the first time, maybe in his whole entire life, Philips had nothing to say. He stood staring at the carcass of the train absolutely silent. Perhaps he was in awe of what he had accomplished.

Our revelry ended quickly when we heard men firing rockets a few tracks away. One of the Marines from the other platoon fired his rocket too early. It struck the track more than a hundred feet ahead of the oncoming train. The train continued to barrel toward us. Mines blew up beneath it, creating small geysers of flames that flashed and disappeared.

Rushing because he knew his life depended on it, the Marine slipped open the back of his launcher and reloaded it. He brought the tube up and rested it on his shoulder. By this time the train was only a quarter of a mile away. I could read the numbers printed along its cab.

The Marine fired his second rocket. It struck the engine head-on but too high. The train buckled and continued on. Then a Marine two tracks down fired a rocket that slammed into the side of the train, just behind the "gills"—the flexible corridor between the engine and the first car. The front of the train leaned over precariously. It would have righted itself, but another Marine fired a second rocket into the side of the engine, tipping the heavy car over.

The train had come close enough to the station that it had already begun to slow for its stop. With so little momentum, many of the rear cars did not follow the engine off the track but sat upright just behind the cars that had tipped over.

Trains started coming down other tracks, but I no longer had time to watch. A Mogat soldier climbed from the wreckage of the train that Philips derailed. The train had come to a stop less than a hundred yards from us, so I could see blood smeared on the man's face and tunic. The train was lying on its side, and he popped out of a door, headfirst, like a prairie dog popping out of its hole.

He had a gun in his right hand. He laid the gun on the side of the train, then used both hands to push himself up. Once he was out of the door, he picked up the gun and stood on the side of the train, a shaky, dizzy survivor. I shot him in the head, and he fell behind the train.

"Shit, here it comes," said Philips.

One of the cargo doors opened on the train that other Marines had knocked over. There was a moment of silent mystery, then three Targ Tanks rumbled out of that compartment.

Targs were an old model, antipersonnel tanks. They had smaller cannons and carried light armor, but they could scoot at speeds of up to 170 miles per hour. They were only five feet high. When they got going, their low-slung profile reminded me of spiders. These particular tanks would not need heavy armor, not with those Mogat shields.

In our rush to nail that first train, Philips and I had separated ourselves from the platoon. It didn't seem important at the time; but seeing those Targs rush toward the station, I knew we were cut off.

"Philips, give me the launcher," I said.

He handed me the rocket launcher, then took up his M27. "Master Sarge, I don't like the look of those tanks."

I fired a quick shot at one of the tanks. It was a perfect shot. The arc of the contrail ended right at the middle of the turret on the tank. There was a massive explosion. Flames and smoke filled the air, and the tank rolled through them untouched. The turret turned in our direction as the tank driver looked to return fire. Philips and I lay flat on the ground, hiding behind a waist-high wall.

"Should we hold the station?" Evans called in.

"We've got to get out of here," Philips said.

Marines fired a hailstorm of rockets and bullets at the three tanks, but the situation was getting worse. Another cargo car opened, and three more tanks spilled out. Down the alley I could see more tanks off-loading.

"We can't stop the tanks!" Thomer yelled into the interLink. "The other platoon is clearing out."

"Go with them," I said. "You got that?" I added for Evans and Greer. I sent the communication over the platoon-wide frequency. "Fall back. Get back to the apartment building."

"Got it," Evans said.

"Yes, Sergeant," said Greer.

"What about you?" Thomer asked.

"Fall back. You read me, Thomer? Fall back."

"Yes, sir," he said.

"Safest place for us is in that train," Philips said, pointing to the wreck he had made.

I knew he was right. "Stay down," I said, as I pulled a smoke grenade from my armor and tossed it into the open area between us and the train. We would need to wait another twenty seconds for the smoke to spread. More survivors climbed out of the wreck. Someone back in the station shot a man as he rose out of a doorway. They shot another as he popped out of a window and started to aim his gun. Then a tank fired a round at the station. I could not tell if the shell hit anyone, but no one fired back. By this time the smoke from the grenade had formed a fairly thick cloud.

"Let's go!" I yelled as I leaped from behind the wall and dashed into the cover of the smoke. "You there, Philips?" I asked.

"Right behind you," he said.

"Run for the train," I said. Once you start talking in battle, it's all too easy to repeat the obvious.

"And here I was thinking I should run for the Mogat tanks," Philips said.

A Targ fired into the smoke. It was a blind shot that missed us completely, but the force of the shell's explosion sent me skidding just as I reached the train. I flew forward five feet and spun to the ground. The upended engine lay on its side, its roof facing in my direction just a few feet ahead. I lunged forward and hid behind its mass.

"That was close." Philips said.

"It's going to get a lot more exciting around here," I said. I found a handhold and scaled the roof of the engine. We needed to find a way inside.

One of the tanks spotted me and fired a shell that struck the base of the train. The whole thing slid. I dropped flat against the engine and held on. Philips, who was trying to climb up behind me, fell off.

"Philips, you all right?"

"Yeah, just dandy," he said.

I had climbed to the top of the train. Several cars ahead of us, a Mogat popped out of a doorway. His head, chest, and rifle stuck out of the train. He spotted me and started to bring his gun to bear, and I shot him. Another followed him. Philips nailed that one before I could get off another shot.

I found an open doorway just behind the gills of the train and jumped in. What a mess we'd created. With the train on its side, rows of seats hung horizontally in the air like padded shelves. Some bodies lay slumped in the seats. Others were thrown across the car. The ceiling of the train car was to my left. All the light fixtures along the ceiling had shattered.

Scores of men lay bleeding along the side of the car. Some were dead and lay as still as sardines in a can. Others squirmed. If they squirmed enough, I shot them. If they lay still with their hands on their weapons, I shot them—the logic of the battlefield: Only when an enemy truly looked dead did you spare him.

In some spots the bodies were stacked two and three men deep. I suppose I could have pushed them out of my way. Instead, I had to stretch my legs and step over them. An inch-deep stream of blood ran along the side of the car.

I saw a man lying facedown in a puddle of blood so deep that he could have drowned. His hand was wrapped around a gun, and his finger was on the trigger, so I shot him. Another man sat limp in a corner of the train. His hair was matted with blood, but he sat vertically and had a gun on his lap. He looked dead, and I saw no sign of breathing as I fired a shot into his chest. Either of them might have been alive enough to shoot me in the back as I passed.

I heard a crash, pivoted around and aimed my M27, then saw that it was Philips. "Don't shoot, Harris, it's me," he said, holding his hands in front of his face.

I lowered my gun and started for the next car.

"I heard gunshots," Philips said.

"I'm making sure there aren't any survivors," I said.

"You think any of these guys are alive?" Philips asked. He prodded a pile of bodies with the barrel of his M27. The man on the top slid over the other side showing no more signs of life than a sack of potatoes.

"Not in this car," I said. "What's going on out there?" I called to my squad leaders.

"It's getting ugly," Thomer shouted. "They parked two trains out of range and off-loaded tanks. There's a column headed right for us." I could hear gunfire in the background.

"Targs?" I asked.

"Bigger. I think the Targs were meant to pin us down while they waited for the real guns to arrive."

"Where are you?" I asked.

"We're still in the station," Evans said. "They sent Targs around the building to cut us off."

The door to the next compartment fell open and machinegun fire sprayed across the wall above my head. I dropped to one knee and fired back, knowing I would not hit the gunman.

I snatched a grenade, pulled the pin, and tossed it through the open doorway. The grenade exploded, blowing out most of the wall between our car and the next one. Nothing stirred when I got a look in the next car. I climbed over the remains of the door. With the train on its side, the doorway formed a horizontal stripe. It looked more like a window than a door.

"I'm not sure how long they'll hold up against those tanks," Philips said as he followed me into the next car.

I sighed. Maybe all of the bodies were bothering me. So much blood and carnage and no one left to shoot.

"Good news, gentlemen," the colonel called over an open frequency. He had to be calling about the shields. If they were down, we could shoot our way out of this killing bottle. A rocket or two would take care of the Targs once the shields were down, and our grenadiers had plenty of rockets. If the shields were down, all we would have to do was hold out for a few more minutes, then the reinforcements would arrive—wave upon wave of soldiers.

"Navy SEALs have touched down on Mogat territory," the colonel said. He spoke in a cheerful tone that radiated his utter ignorance about the fight. He was probably tucked away safely in a transport, a million miles from the action.

"Speck," I hissed. "They've only specking touched down?" I asked. They'd barely begun their damn mission. "That's great, sir," I said. "Why don't you call me when they shut down the specking power."

"Watch yourself, Sergeant," the colonel said. For a moment, it occurred to me that the spirit of the late Colonel Grayson had returned to haunt me through that fool.

"Sorry, sir," I said.

"You and I are going to have a conversation when this is over, Harris," he said over an open frequency that every Marine on the planet could hear.

Several Mogat survivors fired at us from inside the next car. I took cover behind the metal walls of a storage locker and radioed back to Philips. "Can you go up top and flank these guys?" I asked.

"I've got 'em, sir," Philips answered. He called me "sir." Enlisted men never called other enlisted men "sir." That kind of respect was reserved for officers. By reprimanding me, the colonel had won me respect that I could never have earned on my own.

Bullets clattered against the metal and ricocheted around the compartment. The firing stopped for a moment. I looked around the locker and fired shots through the open door. I had nothing to shoot at, but I wanted to distract the Mogats on the other side. It did not work. When no one fired back, I ventured for a closer look and peered into the next car. I saw a Mogat trying to shoot through the windows along the top of the train. He must have been shooting at Philips, but his bullets would never get through the shielded glass.

One of the Mogats spotted me. I rolled back behind my cover

as he shot. Then I heard the creaking of metal. I rolled out and fired at the man as he tried to climb onto my side of the door. I missed, and he ducked back for safety.

"How's it going, Philips?" I called over the interLink.

"Keep your panties on, Master Sarge," Philips sneered back. So much for respect.

"They're expecting you," I said, warning Philips.

"I know… I know."

The gunfire continued, but now it was farther away. I rolled for a quick look, shot the Mogat who was supposed to be covering me, then rushed the door of the next compartment, where I got the drop on one of the three men tracking Philips. I shot him. As the other two turned on me, Philips shot them.

"Harris, are you there?" Thomer called in over the interLink.

"I'm here," I said. "What's going on out there?"

"They're closing in on us," Thomer said.

"Did the other platoon make it out?" I asked.

"Some of them," Thomer said. "Those tanks caught a bunch of them in the open. Half of them did not make it across."

"Squad counts," I ordered.

"I'm down to nine," Thomer said. One of those nine would be Philips, who was in here with me.

"Seven," said Evans.

"Five," said Greer.

Of my original forty-two men, I now had twenty-three remaining, including myself. If I did not find some way to get my men out of there, the roll call might only find two.

"Hold on," I called over the platoon-wide band. "I'll find a way to draw some of the heat off you. Just hold on."

"You want to draw some heat?" Philips asked. "You should see what we have in here."

49

The Mogats had only launched the first wave of their counterattack and already our invasion was unraveling around us. I wondered how long the platoons guarding the traffic ramps would hold out. I wondered if the Mogats would send gunships across the planet to attack our transports. Probably not. Why should they? Their Navy ruled orbital space. If they waited for us to surrender, they could take our transports intact.

Everything hinged on the SEALs. Our invasion was meant to draw Mogat forces away. Well, we'd pulled that one off. If the SEALs could just accomplish their objectives, some of us might survive.

"Harris, over here," Philips called excitedly, as I came across the car.

Along the left wall, which had become the floor when the whole train tipped on its side, lay stacks of clear canisters filled with some sort of swirling brown gas. The canisters were strapped down tight. Nothing short of a grenade would have shattered them; the Mogats did not take any chances with this cargo.

Stacks of a different sort hung from the top of the train—canisters filled with gray, glittering gas. Seeing these lethal weapons, I could not help but smile.

"What is this shit?" Philips asked.

"The brown ones are distilled shit gas," I said, borrowing that briefing officer's parlance. "This is the most corrosive stuff you'll ever see. Eats anything soft—skin, wires, rubber."

I pointed to the canisters on the other wall. They were filled with compressed silver gas. They looked like they might have contained mercury. "You know what this is, right?" I asked.

Philips shook his head.

"That's noxium gas. You've heard of noxium gas before?" I said.

"Oh, yes, I've heard of it." Terrorists favored noxium because it was cheap and scary. It bored into people and turned them to jelly, then dispersed into the air. You could shoot it into a building, kill everyone inside, then enter the building yourself five minutes later. The air would be clean.

"How are you holding up out there?" I called on a frequency that reached only my squad leaders.

"Rumsfelds," Evans said. "They've got specking Rumsfelds!"

Of course there were Rumsfelds. I should have known there would be Rumsfelds. That explained the gas canisters. Rumsfelds were designed to spew supercharged gas. They also packed the standard machine guns and cannons.

Despite all the weapons and armor, the Rumsfeld was obsolete before it rolled off the assembly line. It moved too slowly for practical use in battle. Other battlefield units could outmaneuver Rumsfelds and ultimately cut them down. The government had labeled them obsolete thirty years ago, but they should have been discontinued long before that.

"Are they on you?" I asked. I worked as I spoke, hoping to find the guns that foot soldiers used to shoot gas canisters. I found a rack of compressed-gas shooters near the door. These were breech-loading rifles with barrels as thick as baseball bats.

"Bearing down," Evans said.

"Just hold on," I said. "Help is on the way."

Rumsfelds had a closed circulation system with filters that could weed out noxium gas—a biogas that quickly evaporated into the environment. I did not think the tanks' filters would hold up against distilled shit gas, however. That long-lasting corrosive would eat through the filters. Shit gas hung around for hours as it seeped into the ground. The Rumsfelds would probably fire the canisters in one direction, then drive off in the other.

I pulled off my helmet and placed four canisters of shit gas into it. The canisters were about three inches tall and two inches in diameter. I removed three of the other canisters as well, the ones with the gray-colored gas.

Philips removed his helmet and did the same.

Strapping a shooter to my back, I climbed to the top of the train. Up ahead, I saw at least twenty Targs facing into the station. Rumsfelds lurked in the distance, rumbling in like dinosaurs. I sat on the edge of the doorway with my feet dangling down as I unstrapped that shooter. "Philips, pass me my helmet," I said.

Each of the tanks had brown camouflage paint and a golden crown painted on its turrets. The Targs had formed an elliptical row about forty feet from the station. They fired cannons into the station in rapid and unordered succession. I saw the flashes, then heard the rumble of their guns a split second later.

Hoping to create an uncrossable puddle, I planned to fire distilled shit gas into the street behind the station. Distilled shit gas was heavy, and that puddle would last for hours. I would shoot canisters of noxium gas in front of the station to clear a path. In the open air, the noxium would do its work and evaporate in a minute.

"If you see gas floating in your direction, run," I said over the platoon-wide band.

"In case you haven't noticed, they've got tanks out there," Greer said.

"Not for long," I said as I loaded a canister of noxium gas into my shooter.

"When I give you the signal, I want you to run," I said.

"They'll hit us," Greer said.

"Take my word on this one, Greer," I said. "Getting hit by a shell would be a lot better than waiting around for this shit." I fired. The canister sailed through the air so slowly that I could actually watch it as it hurtled toward the target. The shot lobbed over the roof of the train station. A moment later, the top of a silver-white cloud appeared in the air.

I quickly loaded a canister of distilled shit gas and fired behind the train station. The canister flew into the center of the tanks, where it vanished in a rapidly spreading cloud of brown haze.

"That gas won't hurt those tanks," Philips said, as I loaded another canister of shit gas. "They have shields."

"It won't hurt the outside of those tanks," I said, and squeezed off the next shot, lobbing this canister deeper into the tank column. "Those boys have to breathe something. It's like spraying insects."

Philips handed me the next canister. It was gray—noxium gas. I loaded it into the shooter and fired over the roof of the train station.

"Get running!" I yelled to my squad leaders.

Philips handed me another canister of distilled shit gas. I

raised my trajectory and fired at the Rumsfelds in the distance. Dinosaurs that they were, the first of the Rumsfelds charged straight ahead, directly into the spreading cloud. Philips handed me another canister. I loaded it and fired deeper into their lines. I did not want any stragglers to escape.

One of the Rumsfelds fired back.

"Incoming," I yelled, bracing myself in the door of the train for cover.

The shell hit the train like a giant hammer. Standing below me, Philips lost his balance and fell, his arms cradling the canister-filled helmet. The canisters did not break. They were designed not to break until fired, but I did not want to test the quality of their manufacture.

"Give me a brown one," I told Philips.

Tanks were now coming in our direction. I reached down without saying a word, and he slapped the canister into my hand. I loaded and fired at the tanks, and they fired at us.

"Duck!" I yelled, as I dropped into the train.

Philips placed his helmet top down on the floor and laid over it, cradling it in his arms. If he'd seen what those gases could do to a man, he would not have been so brave.

One shell hit the train, followed by a second, then a third and a fourth, in rapid succession. Then there was silence.

I emptied the remaining canisters out of my helmet, then pulled my helmet down over my head. I called my squad leaders. "Report."

"What was that?" Thomer asked.

"What is your status?" I asked.

"Safe for now," Evans said. "We made it to an apartment building."

"What did you hit them with?" Thomer repeated.

"Bug spray," I said. "Be ready to make a quick exit from your building. The reason they brought that shit out here was to feed it to you."

General Crowley, I thought to myself. The son of a bitch was always ahead of the game. He knew that if we made it to this planet, we would hide in buildings with tank-proof shields; and he found a way around it. Gas the buildings, and the occupants would die. Bastard.

50

“What are you doing?” Philips asked, as I headed back into the car with all of the gas canisters. The shelling had stopped but more Rumsfelds were undoubtedly on the way. The last place he wanted to be was in a train car carrying canisters filled with deadly gases. I didn’t want to go back there any more than he did.

I had not worked with Ray Freeman for two full years without learning a trick or two. The man did not talk much, but he knew the angles for every situation. He knew how to find winning solutions to desperate situations and how to turn traps to his advantage.

“The Mogats know we’re here,” I said as I pulled a grenade from my armor. Grenades were all-purpose devices. You could pull the pins and toss them, or you could program them, then pull the pins. In this case, I programmed the grenade for maximum yield and set it to explode on impact, then I pulled the pin and laid it to rest between two canisters of distilled shit gas. Then I set three more grenades the same way.

"They know we're in the train, and they're coming after us," I said. "They're probably going to shell the train to shake us loose, right?" I patted the second grenade to make sure it was snug. Those canisters were designed to not explode until fired from a shooter, but I had the feeling that a grenade might do the trick.

Looking around the car, I did not find what I wanted. I rushed to the next car and found it—a small airtight case for carrying canisters. As I pulled it off a shelf, a Mogat moaned and stirred on the floor. I shot him, then went back and fitted eight canisters of noxium gas and four canisters of distilled shit gas into the case.

Satisfied that I had the right load, I headed for a doorway through which I could leave the train. I had the canister shooter strapped over my shoulder. I carried my M27 in my right hand and the case of gas canisters in my left. I also had two canisters of noxium gas tucked into my armor. If anything broke those canisters...

"Where are you going?" Philips asked.

"That way," I said, pointing to my left. The Mogats were coming from the right. Using the telescopic lens in my visor, I could see two waves of tanks on the way. The rear guard were Rumsfelds, slow, vicious machines. The first wave were Targ Tanks. They were still five miles back, but they would close that gap quickly. There were hundreds of them this time. These guys could tell what I had done to the first wave. They would skirt around the gas.

"I'm headed that way and going as fast as I can." I swung my legs over the edge of the train and hopped off.

"Why left?" Philips asked.

"Do you want to head right?" I asked.

"Guess not," Philips said. The ground was still covered with distilled shit gas in that direction. If he used his telescopic lens, he would have seen the next column of tanks coming from behind us. He slid down the roof of the train and landed next to me.

"Those tanks back there are going to start shelling this train in another minute," I said. "That will set off my grenade, gas will leak..."

"That gas is going to leak out of every orifice," Philips said. I was going to say doorway, but I preferred his description.

"Harris, you better beat it out of there," Evans called over the interLink. "The whole frigging Mogat Army is headed in your direction."

"Where are you?" I asked. "Give me a beacon on your building."

"Just up the street. I can see you from the window." The virtual beacon turned the building blue in my visor.

"Are the streets clear?" I asked.

"Not entirely. I sent my snipers up to the roof to clear a way for you."

I heard sporadic gunfire. The crack of rifles echoed through the streets.

"Call your boys in," I said. "We'll catch up with you, but for now, I want everyone tucked in safe."

"Harris, those tanks are getting closer."

"I got it," I said. "Just bring your squad in."

"Philips, let's move out," I said. Feeling a little awkward with a gun on my back and both hands full, I hunched over and sprinted as best I could up the street. We ran one block, then another before the shelling started. When I looked back, I saw searchlights from the tanks. Then, hearing another shell fired, I ducked against a storefront. It was a three-story Laundromat, of all things, with an all-glass fascia, but it was the only choice we had. At least I knew it was empty.

"Philips, in here!" I yelled. I pushed the door open and ran for the stairs. Philips and I climbed to the top floor and hid behind a row of washers.

"Oh, shit," Evans said. "Look at all those specking Mogats."

At that very moment, the tanks fired a barrage of shells. The Targs fired at the train. They pounded it.

I could see the whole thing from the third floor of the Laundromat. Shells and rockets slammed into that train, sending it sliding, jostling the cars back and forth. It reminded me of shooting at an empty can to see how long you could keep it in the air. Eventually, several cars rolled upside down.

The gases did not mix. Brown and gray gases began oozing from the windows and doors of the train. The brown gas crept along the streets like a tide, swelling nearly two feet in the air. Targs might have been fast, but they were not built for sharp turns at top speeds. The first row of tanks on the scene cut sharp and managed to avoid the gas. The tanks that followed did not. Line after line of Targs stampeded into the deadly fog and stalled.

From my third-floor vantage point, I saw dozens of tanks stall in the distilled shit gas mist. I could also see hundreds beyond them that the gas would never reach.

Around the train station, I saw the carcasses of the tanks that I'd gassed. They sat totally immobile, looking like stones. No, not stones. With their curved backs and squat, low-slung profiles, and their green camouflage, they looked like gargantuan frogs. At least the Targs looked like frogs. There were twenty Rumsfelds in the mix. From up here, they looked more like armadillos.

The distilled shit gas I'd fired at the Rumsfelds would have dissolved the wiring in the tanks as well as the drivers. I shot the Targs with noxium gas. They would still work, so long as you didn't mind sitting in the puddle of what once was an enemy soldier.

A half mile away from the train station, the nearest traffic ramp spewed out a river of green personnel carriers. Our men had put up a fight there. Beside the ramp, a couple of trucks lay on their sides; but the men we sent to hold that ramp were dead or in retreat, and now tens of thousands of Mogats poured out.

From here, I could also see the nearest elevator station. When the reinforcements came, they would funnel through buildings like that one. I imagined ten thousand soldiers storming through each station, M27s raised, grenades in their hands. Sooner or later they would need to destroy the elevator stations so that they could lower their tanks and gunships.

Lord, it would be a beautiful sight to behold, I thought. I had begun to doubt whether any of us would live to see it.

"Talk to me, Evans," I called on the frequency for squad leaders.

"They stopped shooting," Evans said.

"Can you see the street around your building?" I asked.

"I can't see the street from here," said Evans.

"No windows?" I asked.

"I've got a window," Evans said. "I just can't see the street. There are too many specking Mogats on it. Those speckers are everywhere."

"How long can you hold out? I'm going to try to make it over to your building," I said. Not much had changed since I left Little Man; I was still committing passive suicide.

"We barricaded the entrance," Evans said. "They might be able to bash through with their tanks, but I'd hate to be the first man to come through that door. We may go down, but we are not going down easy."

"Is Philips with you?" Thomer broke in.

"He's here," I said.

"And he's okay?"

"Not a scratch on him," I said.

Thomer did not answer. I figured that he probably switched bands and called Philips directly.

"Master Sergeant, there's no point in coming here," Evans said. "We're cooked."

I laughed. "Evans, we're all cooked. I don't know about Philips, but I'd rather go down with my platoon.

I'd lost a platoon a few years ago. I still remembered every man in that platoon by name. Sometimes I heard them in my sleep. "We'll find a way to reach you, Evans. Just hold on."

"What about your friend, the giant with the rifle?" Evans asked.

"His name is Freeman. He came here hunting Crowley." I said this more to myself than to Evans.

"You mean Amos Crowley, the Mogat general?"

"Crowley is a field general. He likes to go down to the field to fight with his men. He's down there somewhere right now. At least he should be. He'll be sleeping with Napoleon and Caesar if Freeman spots him." I did not believe what I'd just said. In truth, I regretted bringing Freeman on a suicide mission.

"Are the Mogats outside your building, too?" Evans asked.

I looked out the window. The path back to the train station was almost clear. Most of the tanks and troops had gathered around the tenements. The street around the building in which my platoon had hidden looked like a parking lot.

"Nope," I said, trying to sound cheerful. "All's clear."

"You should stay put," Evans said.

"Are you shitting me?" I asked. It might have been the combat hormone speaking by then. If someone had shot me in the head at that moment, I think I might have leaked out more hormone than blood or brains. "Just keep some men by the back door. Philips and I are on our way."

I switched frequencies. "Philips."

"Thomer says I should shoot you. He says I should shoot you and lie low until the Army comes." Thomer must have listened in on part of my conversation with Evans.

Philips stood in front of the window staring down at the street. The sky had turned dark during the time that we hid in the Laundromat. Bright lights shone all over the city, and fires blazed near the train station and some of the traffic ramps.

Philips removed his helmet as he viewed this panorama. He stood still as a tree holding his M27 by the butt in his limp right hand, its muzzle pointing straight at the floor. "Look at all those specking Mogats. Hell, with that many men, they don't need to shoot us. They can just wait till we run out of bullets, then trample us to death."

I pulled off my helmet and stood beside Philips. Neither of us spoke for a time. Then I pointed to the building where the rest of the platoon was waiting. "They're only six blocks away."

He said, "Damn, Master Sarge, you can't possibly think we'll survive those six blocks."

"You know what, Philips, I really hate being called Master Sarge. The rank is master sergeant, not master sarge."

He smiled but did not answer.

Still glaring at Philips, I replaced my helmet. It was at that moment that the lights went out.

51

The city lights did not stutter. They did not blink on and off. They went out. In the pitch-darkness, my visor automatically switched to night-for-day vision. I stared out the big glass window down at a cityscape painted in blue-white and black.

I looked over at Philips as he put on his helmet. "The power is out," I said.

"I can see that," he growled.

"You don't get it," I said, and I fired my M27 into the window, which shattered into tire-sized pieces of jagged glass and dropped to the street.

"Evans, Thomer, Greer," I called. "The shields are down."

"Harris," a familiar voice interrupted my conversation with my squad leaders. "You out there?"

"Nice to hear from you," I said.

"I'm the only SEAL with any time on this planet," Illych

said. "They had to send me.

"I'm in their capital sector. You should have seen this place. It's wild. It's half government, half religious shrine. Too bad it's all going away."

By this time Philips and I had already started down the stairs. The rows of washing machines did not glisten or reflect light. There was no light for them to reflect. This world had become that dark, as black as any hole.

"You guys pulled off a coup turning out the lights," I said, full of admiration for the SEALs.

"Not just the lights," Illych said. "We sent two teams into the military sector. Alpha Team took out their broadcast engine. Tango just knocked out their shield generator. Considering all the trouble these guys have caused, we wanted to shut them down for good."

Philips and I ran into the street. Seen through the night-for-day lens, the scene had no more depth than an old black-and-white photograph. I saw it in the ghostly blue-white. I could see details clearly enough. I could see clearly enough to know I was staring into an empty street. I looked both ways, then switched to heat vision to make sure that no one was hiding. The walls gave off no heat, but tanks, men, and weapons all had heat signatures. The block ahead of us was clean.

"When are you pulling out?" Illych asked.

"We're not," I said. "We're going to hang around until the Green Machine arrives." The "Green Machine" was a Corps name for the Army.

I didn't really need my visor to know that the coast was clear. Mogat soldiers typically did not wear armor. They would have needed torches to see anything. With the power out, Mogatopolis was nothing more than a big specking cave. I felt the excitement of a battle won. We had the advantage now. We had better armor.

Once the Army arrived, we would have comparable numbers and better equipment.

"Harris, what are you talking about?" Illych asked.

I ran through an alley using a building for cover, not that anyone would be able to see me without some kind of vision enhancement. The tanks and trucks had spotlights—big specking deal. I'd see the spotlights a mile away.

"The second wave," I said. I stopped and parked myself against a wall. "They're sending the Army in to occupy..."

"What are you doing?" Philips broke in.

"Quiet," I snapped.

"Harris, the Army isn't coming. The Confederate Arms Navy is engaging the Mogat Fleet right now. Once we chew through their Fleet, the Mogats will be landlocked. All we need to do is pin them down on this rock for another two hours and..."

"No Army?" I asked.

"Why would they send in the Army? Now that the power is out, everything down here is going to revert back to elemental gas."

"Distilled shit gas," I whispered. The briefing officer had told us that everything down here was made of the stuff.

"They'll all be dead," Illych said.

"We'll all be dead," I repeated. I felt stunned. I felt like I had received a knee in the groin. This was pain and confusion that even the combat reflex could not mask. I thought of Samson, blinded and captured by the Philistines. In a final show of faith, he killed himself and the Philistines by toppling their temple down upon his head.

Only Samson volunteered to pull the temple on his own head. And then it struck me: the Unified Authority might have been God; but the clones were the sacrifices, not the high priests. Those speckers were offering me up to die.

"Harris, you have to get out of there," Illych said.

"And go where?" I asked. "Where the speck are we supposed to go?" Even if we made it topside and boarded the transports, who would pick us up? If it were not for my programming, I would have shoved the muzzle of my M27 in my mouth and pulled the trigger. I felt numb. I felt dizzy. The Unified Authority had betrayed us. I should have known they would. And by leading my men into the trap, I had betrayed them.

"Master Sarge, what is going on?" Philips said.

"The battleships are still up there," Illych said. "If you make it up before they leave, they'll take you."

"No, they won't," I said. "They came to kill Mogats, not rescue Marines."

"Harris, you need to hurry," Illych said. "Without their shields, those Mogat ships won't last long against the fleet."

We were a distraction, I thought. *They sent us here to clear the way for the SEALs. That was all they wanted us for, and now we've outlived our purpose.* "Those specking assholes. Ah, shit," I said as I rested my gun on a the ground. "Bloody hell."

"Harris, you need to get your men topside," Illych said.

"Harris, what the speck are you doing?" Philips asked.

So we are still the bullet. We are still a commodity. Even if I can lead my men out, why should I? This will just happen again. Even as I considered this, I knew that I had to try to escape. They programmed survival instinct into my being. They also gave me aggression, and I found reason enough to live in the idea of revenge.

"How long do we have?" I asked Illych. I had picked up my gun and begun running to the next corner. Philips remained a pace behind me, gun ready.

"Till the Navy leaves or the whole city reverts back into elemental gas?" Illych asked. "You have two hours until everything down here melts. The Navy will be long gone by then."

"Harris, can you get to a transport?" the low resonant voice of

Ray Freeman asked. I had forgotten about Freeman.

While we were back on the transport, I'd suggested that he listen in on my communications. Back then I said that he should listen in so he could keep an eye on our troop movements. "Freeman?" I asked.

"Are you pinned down?" Freeman asked.

"I've got to go," I said, more for Freeman than Illych, though they both heard me. I was so angry and ashamed that I could barely think. The combat reflex protected me against fear, not humiliation. I had to get my men out. I had to get them to a transport. I knew this, but my actions were as mechanical as my breathing and heartbeat. All that ran through my head was anger and embarrassment.

"Semper fi, my ass," I whispered. I was a faithful servant to an unfaithful master. I was a fool. If I made it off this planet, I would turn my back on the Unified Authority once and for all. My programming might prevent me from fighting against bastards like Brocius, but I did not have to die as one of their pawns.

"Get moving," Illych shouted, before signing off. Freeman said nothing. He had offered to help; now he was already on his way to the transport.

I changed frequencies to call to the colonel commanding the operation. This asshole must have had more enemies than friends. He was the highest-ranking sacrifice sent out here to die. Some general back in Washington, DC, had probably asked, whom should we screw on this one, and everyone agreed on this jerk. I should have known something was wrong when they sent an asshole colonel to command a sixty-thousand-man landing. Where was the boatload of generals trying to claim the victory for themselves?

Now that I thought about it, I should have spotted the whole plan from the start. The combined Navy only had sixty-two self-broadcasting ships. Sixty-two ships would not have enough space for all of the men and machines. Then I thought about the elevator shafts. It would take days to funnel one million men through those shafts.

"What is it, Harris?" the colonel asked.

"Call the men back to the transports, sir," I said.

"What are you talking about?" the colonel asked. "Hold your position."

"We've accomplished our mission," I said.

"We're supposed to hold our position until reinforcements arrive," the colonel said.

"There won't be any reinforcements," I said. "The Army's not coming."

"You're full of..." The colonel paused. "Harris, give me a minute."

"We don't have a minute," I said, but the colonel was already gone.

I switched frequencies so that my entire platoon could hear me. "Boys, we're in trouble." I did not have time to explain everything. I would not have explained it all, even if I had. They would need whatever fight they had in them.

"We need to make a run for the transports," I said. "When I give you the signal, fire everything you have at the Mogats in front of your building; then when I clear you, run out the back door and keep running. Do you read me, Marines?"

"What about the ones in the back?" Evans asked.

"I've got them," I said. "You just start shooting when you get my signal."

"Where are you?" Greer asked.

"I'm two blocks out the ass of your building. You hit them from your side, and I'll hit them from back here."

"There are too many," Greer said.

"We don't need to kill them, they're already blind," I said. "Just run on my command and keep running until you are topside and harnessed into your transport. You got that, specksucker? That is an order."

It was in their programming. These boys could not disobey a direct order.

Peering out from behind a wall, I saw that the street was filled with enemy soldiers and tanks. Most of the tanks had searchlights. The trucks had headlights, and the soldiers held flashlights. Soldiers sat on the turrets of the Rumsfelds shining spotlights down into the street. Foot soldiers milled around the beams of the lights, talking and drinking. They looked confused, not blind. These men could not have realized the extent of what had happened to their world. They had the enemy trapped, but no one had given them their next orders. Without their power grid, they could not communicate with their commanders.

Philips and I crouched behind a wall and watched the Mogats for a moment. "Hold this," I whispered, handing the case with the gas cartridges to Philips. I was wearing my helmet. I could have screamed the words at the top of my lungs and the Mogats would not have heard me, but I whispered. It was a natural reflex. There might have been ten thousand Mogats around us.

Philips took the case without saying a word. He was not afraid, but the smart-ass style had run out of him. He was serious now. He wanted to walk away from this battle with his skin intact, and he wanted to make sure the other members of the platoon went with him.

I leaned my M27 against the wall, then pulled the canister shooter off my shoulder. I broke it open at the hinge and loaded a canister of noxium gas in its chamber.

Once I fired the shooter, it would take three minutes for the gas to dissipate. I aimed the shooter so that it would spit the canister deep into the Mogats' ranks and fired. The muzzle of the shooter did not flash like a gun, it simply emitted a quiet belch. The darkness remained total as the canister spiraled through the air and struck a tank no more than twenty feet from the back door of the building.

There was a crash and a moment of silence, followed by screaming and yelling. They wanted to run, but they could not. Panic and death came too quickly.

I had my second cartridge loaded before the first even hit the ground. This time I aimed at the Mogats in the rear, the ones closest to Philips and me. I fired again.

The Mogats had already begun to panic when the second canister dropped. By now they were screaming in pain as well as panic. The men near spotlights might have seen the gas seeping in around them, but most only heard the shouting caused by an undefined death. I fired the third canister right in the middle of the crowd. Each canister unleashed enough gas to cover hundreds of square feet.

Someone else might have described the scene as pandemonium, but to me it spoke of entropy. The Mogat troops fell into disarray from which they would never again organize. They ran, they panicked, they dissolved into the street.

On the other side of the building, the other Mogats must have heard the noise. They must have wondered what had happened. I waited a few more moments before radioing up to Evans. I wanted to make sure the noxium gas evaporated before he came running out.

"Light 'em up!" I shouted at Evans over the interLink.

In the street before us, all was still and quiet now. Any Mogat who was going to escape had escaped. The rest had died. I could see the bodies by using my night-for-day vision. The dead men still looked human, more or less. The bodies, strewn along the ground like toys thrown in a pile, had limbs and hair. Their faces had no more distinct features than a giant blister; and they would squash like overripe melons if you stepped on them. Given another hour, the bodies would burst under their own weight.

Quick flashes of light that reminded me of sheet lightning broke and faded on the other side of the building. Evans and his squad had begun firing their rockets at the tanks. The flashes followed each other quickly, with less than a second's separation. The audio equipment in my helmet picked up the explosions and played them as ambient noise.

The rockets made a sizzling sound when they launched. Their explosions reverberated and echoed through the dark city. I imagined millions of civilians around me, scared, huddled like mice in their apartments, hearing the explosions and praying to whatever god the Mogats believed in for the battle to end. I thought about those three boys who had tried to stand up to my platoon with a knife. I spared them. Big specking deal. I'd bought them a few more hours and a more painful way to die.

For the Mogats, the universe was ending. They would all die. I could not save them if I wanted to. I might not be able to save any of my men. I might not be able to save my own sorry carcass, not that it deserved to be saved. Friend, foe, soldier, civilian... if we did not escape this very moment, we would all die as one. The men, women, and children would certainly die. They were innocents, but they could not be saved.

Exploding rockets and firing cannons make different sounds. To the untrained ear, it all sounds like a big bang. Once you've been in combat, you learn to listen for pitch, intensity, duration, and volume. I heard the sound of the tanks returning fire.

"Evacuate the building. Now!" I yelled. "Now! Now! Now!" Without shields, those shells would tear right through the building. In another minute, the entire building would come down.

"They got Evans," Thomer called back.

"Out of there!" I screamed. The planet was dissolving, the building was crumbling, and Thomer was taking roll. "Move it!"

"Are there Mogats out the back?" Thomer shouted. I could tell he was running. He sounded winded.

"The street is clear!" I yelled.

I'd started to say something else, when the colonel's voice sounded over the interLink. He shouted, "Everyone, fall back to the transports. Anyone who does not make it back to the transports in fifteen minutes will be left behind."

Had he somehow reached Washington or just gotten the lowdown from an officer in the Confederate Arms Fleet? Somehow, he now knew the truth.

52

Marines understand exactly what it means when they receive the order to fall back. It means that your invasion has gone to shit. Fall back means that you cannot hold your position, and the situation has become critical. It means that the enemy is on your heels. It means stragglers will be captured or killed. Marines are trained to lead the way into battle. They don't much care for the order to fall back.

Of all the Marines that landed on the Mogat planet, only my platoon had begun its retreat when the colonel gave the order to fall back. The rockets my guys fired from the building crippled a lot of Mogat hardware, and my gas had opened a route for them to escape.

The back door of the apartment building flew open, and out ran my platoon, or what remained of it. A twenty-man stampede. They ran straight ahead, straight into the clutter of bodies that filled the street. By this time the noxium had largely accomplished its purpose. Without so much as a glance at the ground, Sergeant Greer stepped into a corpse. He should have tripped over that dead soldier. Instead, he kicked through him.

Philips and I saw the scene from two blocks up the street. Our boys dashed out of the building. Moments later, another platoon followed. They could follow us if they liked, but I would not waste time waiting for them.

I jumped into the street, making a pinwheel motion with my arm to direct my men on. "Philips, take the lead," I yelled. He knew the way to the elevator station. I had shown it to him in the Laundromat.

"You heard him," Philips called over the interLink. With the platoon under fire, the lowest-ranking man took the lead. "This way... now move it!"

I had just joined Thomer at the back of the pack when the first of the Targs rounded a corner ahead of us. Its spotlight cut through the darkness. Its beam looked as hard and pale as a marble pillar. The light never found us; and inside the tank, the driver only saw what his spotlight showed him.

A moment later, one of our grenadiers fired a rocket at the Targ. After the explosion, the jagged remains of the turret looked like an enormous crown. Small fires danced on the top. I saw spotlights and headlights cruising back and forth on the streets around us. Those tanks should have had radars; but for some reason, the drivers were hunting for us by sight.

By this time we had almost reached the elevator station. The road we were on came to a dead end at the door of the station—which towered above everything around it. The elevator station reached all the way to the ceiling, a hundred feet above us. With the power down, I could now see a rough rock ceiling instead of a sky overhead.

Three Rumsfelds rolled out onto the street a thousand feet behind us. Their searchlights sniffed along the ground until they located Marines from the other platoon. Machine guns opened fire.

"Light 'em!" I yelled over the interLink.

My last remaining grenadiers spun and fired rockets at the tanks. One actually hit his target. The other two missed. At a thousand feet, a shot from the hip was too much to ask. They fired again and hit a second tank. Seeing the wreckage of the tanks on either side of it, the third Rumsfeld ambled for safety.

"You shouldn't have done that," Philips called back to me. He had already reached the door of the elevator station. He stood in the doorway, letting other men pass him, his M27 pointing up the street. "Now they know we're here."

My training told me to stay on the street and clear the way for the other Marines. My programming ordered me to survive. The Mogats used Targ Tanks like wolves. They dodged in and out of alleys and streets, picking at groups of Marines, herding them away from the elevator station. There must have been thousands of tanks rumbling around the city. I might get some of them, but I would never get all of them. The most I could accomplish now was saving my men. By waiting and trying to save another platoon, I would only endanger the few men I had left.

I ran in the door of the elevator station and turned to see the street. I saw searchlights, tanks, and Marines in retreat. "Philips, Thomer, get them topside."

There were no stairs in the elevator station. With the power down, the elevators would no longer work. Since we did not come with jetpacks, the only way up was using ropes. Fortunately, the magnetic link between our armor and the rappel cords would make the climb easier. Any man who could not climb those hundred feet would stay behind and die.

With the power out, I did not know if the gravity chute would work. All I could do was hope that it ran on a natural convection created by the distilled shit gas. On the other hand, I did not want to know what the gas might do to a transport.

A searchlight shone across the entrance of the elevator station. It was from a Rumsfeld at least a hundred yards away. The light formed a blinding circle that scoured the road outside the station, then shone on the door. I stepped back and hid behind a wall as the light played past me.

I looked back at the men. A few had started the climb. Most stood in front of the shaft, waiting their turn. "Any of you have rockets?" I called.

One of the men came over and handed me a launcher and three rockets. They were small, no bigger than my fist.

"Thanks," I said. "Now get topside."

Outside, the Rumsfeld moved toward the door of the station. I fired a rocket into it, and the tank somersaulted forward and landed on its turret.

I looked back again. All but three of my men had started up the shaft. Philips, Greer, and Thomer were still down, but I knew they could handle the climb. Seeing Philips grab a cord, I had to smile. We were going to make it out of this shit hole. More than half of my platoon would survive this mission.

A scattering of Marines saw the explosion and headed in our direction. Spotlights roved up and down the side streets. Gunfire and tank engines rumbled in my audio. I started to head toward the cords; but just as I did, I caught a glimpse of something that made me freeze.

At first I thought the Mogats had turned the power back on. In the distance, the civilian sector glowed brightly. The light that filled the sky was so bright that the lens in my visor switched from night-for-day to standard tactical. Tint shields clouded my visor when I looked directly into the glare.

The light did not come from the city, it came from behind it. It wasn't just light. It wasn't like the glow of a searchlight or even a thousand searchlights.

The light above the city constantly changed hues and pattern as if the reds, yellows, and blues separated and remixed with each other. Patterns of color rose like smoke out of the glow. It looked something like the aurora borealis, only enormous sparks flashed in it. For a moment I thought the light might be coming from the city itself. Maybe light happened when buildings made of distilled shit gas decomposed; but I did not have time to waste reasoning it out.

"Harris, you seeing this?" Freeman called over the interLink.

"Where are you?" I asked.

"One floor up," Freeman said. "You better get climbing."

"You can see that light?" I asked. I took one last glance out the door. The light had a slow gelatinous property about it. It seemed to seep over the city like viscous oil. As soon as I turned from the door, the night-for-day lens resumed in my visor. The glow from that strange light had not yet reached the elevator station, but it would soon.

I ran to the elevator shaft, grabbed a cord, and started up.

The shaft looked like a gigantic tunnel turned vertical. Dozens of rappel cords dangled from the top.

"Thomer, where are you?" I called over the interLink.

"In the elevator station." Thomer said.

"Can you see any transports?" I asked.

"There's a transport just outside," Thomer said.

"I requisitioned us that one," Freeman said.

"What happened to the pilot?" I asked.

Freeman did not answer.

The area inside the shaft would have been black as coal if not for the glow that started to pour into it. It gushed in like a flood of water, shining on the opposite wall. I had never known a man could climb as quickly as I now scaled my way up that shaft.

"Load the men in the transport," I called to Thomer.

"They're in," Thomer said.

"And you're in?" I asked.

Thomer did not answer.

"Get in the transport!" I yelled.

I looked up to see how much farther I had to go, but I did not pause. I had another twenty feet. Below me, the light in the shaft became blinding. It was like looking into the sun. The tint shields in my visor blocked out some of the brightness, but when I tried to look up again, I found that my eyes would not adjust to the darkness.

I looked back down. That was when I saw it. There was a creature in that viscous light. Whatever it was, the creature I saw was nearly as bright as the light around it. It looked like a six-foot, canary yellow smudge in a field of glare that had the startling silver-white clarity of an electrical spark. I only saw it for a moment, and I mostly concentrated on the two silver-black eyes. They were too large for that head, the size of my fists, and they seemed to be made of smoky black chrome. For a brief moment my eyes met that creature's eyes and I saw no pity in him. Then I saw that the creature held a rifle of some kind.

"Oh, shit," I moaned, and managed to climb even faster.

A bolt of white light flew past me. It might have been some sort of white laser, if there can be such a thing. It might or might not have been any more powerful than our particle beams, but the bolt cut through the cords around me and struck a wall. The spot it struck glowed white and orange, and distilled shit gas gushed out of it like blood from a bullet hole.

The men above me must have seen the shot, too. One of them leaned into the shaft, lowered an M27, and fired a continuous ten-second burst. "I can't hit it!" Freeman yelled, but he did not say if his bullets missed or failed.

Two sets of arms grabbed me and pulled me out of the shaft. Philips and Thomer pulled me to my feet as Freeman dropped a grenade down the shaft. We sprinted out of the elevator station. Outside the station, the strange, gelatinous light continued to creep toward us. It was less than a mile away and moving at a slow pace. Running as fast as I could to the transport, I did not have time to stop and check.

"Can anybody fly this thing?" Thomer asked, as we rushed the ramp.

Freeman did not bother answering. He climbed the ladder and entered the cockpit with all the dexterity of a spider checking its web. A moment later the boosters sounded. We were already off the ground when the doors at the rear of the kettle banged shut.

I looked around the kettle and tore off my helmet. "Get harnessed," I growled at my men. From here on out, we had to rely on luck, Freeman, and God. Of the three, Freeman was the only one who had not abandoned us so far. Leaving my helmet on the bench along the wall, I crossed the deck and climbed up to the cockpit.

Freeman sat at the controls, holding the yoke with one hand and hitting switches with the other. Through the windshield, I could see the landscape ahead of us. The tide of light continued to move toward us. I did not see tanks or gunships or armies moving inside it. Then Freeman rotated the ship toward the gravity chute.

Staring out of the cockpit, I saw Marines running out of elevator stations and transports taking off. We might not be the only ones who made it out, if we made it out. There was still the question about the gravity chute.

Freeman slowed down as he approached the chute the way Mogat pilots did. "Do you know how it works?" he asked.

"You just fly into it," I said. "It's like an elevator."

We approached the chute so slowly that we seemed to inch toward it. I felt like we would simply drop. And then the updraft caught us, and we rose. I peered over the nose of the transport. I saw another transport below us; and then I saw the strange light spreading over everything below.

"Did you see that thing that shot at me," I asked, then added, "in the elevator shaft?"

Freeman shook his head.

"It wasn't human," I said.

I could not shake the image of those metallic eyes watching me as I climbed up the dark elevator shaft. For the first time since I entered the Marines, I had felt real fear, mortal fear, fear undiluted by the delirious effects of the combat reflex. Even the hormone in my blood had not kept me calm. And now, standing behind Freeman, I realized that I was still trembling.

We rose more quickly up the gravity chute than I had expected. Whatever was happening in the Mogat city below had accelerated the natural convection. It was probably consuming thousands of Marines and millions of Mogats as well. Glare as bright as sunlight shone up the shadowy length of the chute. Rainbow colors spiraled on the rock just below us. At some point, the light faded, and a minute later we emerged on the dark surface of the planet. There was no hint of whatever was happening below.

Freeman flew us out of that hollowed-out mountain and straight up, out of the atmosphere. A few moments later, we received the message I think we both doubted would come: "U.A. Transport, this is the battleship *Sakura*. Please prepare to dock."

EPILOGUE

"Wild Bill" Grace, the senior member of the Linear Committee, stood at the podium smiling at his audience. Gordon Hughes, the chairman of the Confederate Arms, stood behind him. Both men smiled so freely you would never guess that they had recently sent navies to annihilate each other. Behind them, two flags hung from crossed staffs—the Unified Authority stars and bars and the Confederate Arms map of the galaxy.

Seated at the back of the podium were Admiral Brallier, General Smith, and several other officers I recognized. An empty seat marked Admiral Brocius's place. He was in exile back on the Central Cygnus Fleet. He had sent Freeman to die along with me and my platoon. He had deceived Ray Freeman just as he had the rest of us; but there was no programming in Freeman's natural-born brain to cause him to overlook the indiscretion. Freeman would take his revenge. Once he learned that we had survived, Brocius fled to the safety of his ships.

Admiral Brallier looked particularly pleased with himself, sitting beside Brocius's empty seat.

Brocius's obsession with house odds had done him in. He tried to hedge his bets against the Mogats by sacrificing the Marines. Afraid that Freeman might try to avenge me, he improved the odds against Freeman by sending him to die on a wild-goose chase. Crowley was never on the Mogat planet; he died fighting his former allies when the Mogats attacked the Confederate Arms as they battled for control of the fleet. Yoshi Yamashiro gave us that scrap of information on our way back to Earth.

"Wild Bill" held a single sheet of paper. "Perhaps we can get started," he said. "I'd like to start by introducing my colleague for this occasion, Mr. Gordon Hughes, chairman of the Confederate Arms."

The reporters in the gallery obviously recognized the former Speaker of the House and chairman of the Confederate Arms Treaty Organization, but the introduction drew anxious whispers from the crowd.

"This afternoon at 2:30 Washington, DC, time, the Unified Authority and Confederate Arms launched an invasion into Mogat space," Grace continued.

Judging by the gasps of the reporters in the audience, you might have thought that Grace had tossed a live grenade into the gallery. Some people merely raised their hands to signal questions. Others tried to push right up to the dais.

Grace ignored the pandemonium and continued.

"We sent an invasion force of sixty thousand Unified Authority Marines and two hundred Navy SEALs to the home world of the Morgan Atkins Movement. At the same time, the Confederate Arms sent its forty-ship self-broadcasting fleet to support the invasion.

"I am pleased to announce that the invasion was an

unqualified success. The Mogat threat has been eliminated. We have destroyed their base of operations, and we have destroyed their self-broadcasting fleet.

"I think it is safe to say that we have closed the door once and for all on the Morgan Atkins uprising.

"Are there any questions?"

Reporters pushed and shoved to climb in front of each other. One man actually grabbed another by the back of his collar and yanked him out of the way.

Grace selected a pretty female reporter and pointed to her.

"When did you create an alliance with the Confederate Arms, and does this mean the Confederate Arms will be rejoining the Republic?"

"Perhaps I could answer that," Gordon Hughes said, stepping up to join "Wild Bill."

"Ambassadors from the Unified Authority approached us several months ago. As you may know, our alliance with the Mogats ended quickly..."

This might have been the hundredth time I replayed the briefing. It was a work of art that mystified me. Grace and Hughes put on a splendid show. They never hinted that the invasion had ended in the total annihilation of an entire planet. They never mentioned the Japanese Fleet. They sure as hell never mentioned that they'd left tens of thousands of Marines stranded or that they annihilated 200 million civilians. To listen to those two prophets, you would have thought that we won a conventional battle on Mogatopolis and that the long-dead Morgan Atkins handed over his sword from his grave.

"You're not watching that briefing again?" Freeman asked as he stepped into the courtyard.

Including the question-and-answer period, the briefing lasted two full hours, and no one ever bothered to ask the most important question: "Who was helping the Mogats?"

If their performance was any indication, Grace and Hughes did not believe the Mogats had any help. The Confederate Arms ships circling the planet did not see any bright lights or alien ships.

I removed my shades. I was sitting on a deck chair, in an open-air courtyard, in a villa on the Hawaiian island of Oahu. I'd stayed here four years earlier, shortly after I was promoted to sergeant. When I received my honorable discharge three months ago, I marched off the base and boarded a plane to Hawaii. I rented the villa and had been staying here ever since.

I liked the sun and the warm air in Hawaii. I liked it when it rained, and I liked the sweet smell in the air following the rain. I liked going to the beach. Most of all, I liked the feeling that I was out of the picture.

"You think I spend too much time watching the briefing?" I asked as I picked up the Space Bible I'd placed beside my chair. The book was six hundred pages long. I'd read it five times now.

"You spend too much time with the book, too," Freeman said. "If you wanted to become a Mogat, you should have done it before you helped kill everyone on that planet."

Freeman telling jokes... what a world.

His joke struck a nerve. I had helped kill 200 million people. Two hundred million. I didn't feel bad about the soldiers, but the faces of the civilians still haunted me day and night. I was obsessed. I was obsessed with that briefing and everything Grace and Hughes did not divulge. I was obsessed with the Space Bible and everything Morgan Atkins had told the world.

When the book first appeared, people dismissed it as a hoax. As far as the public knew back then, Atkins had died during the Liberator invasion, and that was all they knew. When evidence emerged that Atkins had not died and that the book was authentic, everyone dismissed his book as the work of a crackpot.

Now that I had read the book, I did not blame them. In it, Atkins talked about uncovering an alien city buried in the core of a planet in the center of the galaxy. He referred to the "radiant being" who guarded the city as a "Space Angel." The angel, he said, warned him that his race would soon invade our galaxy. Atkins said he created an alliance with the creature. He would unite the galaxy under his control, and the radiant aliens would leave mankind alone. That was why he needed to subvert the government, so he could set up a government of his own. He wanted to save us. Morgan Atkins was actually the good guy—no wonder no one believed it.

It sounded ridiculous. From what I had seen, Atkins told the truth about some things, but I had trouble envisioning that "Space Angel" as a benevolent partner. I did not think the Unified Authority would be able to stand up to those aliens. I abandoned the Christian Bible and began studying the Space Bible because Morgan Atkins had a more powerful God.

"You think I should stop reading, I'll stop reading," I said. I tossed the Space Bible back on the table.

"You can't stay here forever," Freeman said. "You're not going to be able to sit this one out."

Now Freeman, a man who never swore allegiance to anything or anyone, was lecturing me about patriotism and civic duty.

"If we cannot stop them, they're going to kill everybody," Freeman said. "You might as well commit suicide as sit this one out."

"Stop them? Are you joking? We barely beat the specking Mogats. These guys will eat us alive."

Off in the distance, waves rolled in and out of the bay below the villa. I heard the sound of the waves. A breeze blew off the ocean and rustled the leaves around the garden. The sun burned hot and bright overhead.

Part of me actually believed that Freeman was talking to me. Sometimes it was Freeman who came to talk me into rejoining the war, sometimes it was Philips, and sometimes it was Thomer; but it was all in my imagination.

Philips and Thomer and the rest of my platoon remained in Washington, DC. Given the option to retire, they'd all reenlisted. Some young lieutenant now commanded my platoon. Yoshi Yamashiro and the Japanese returned to Earth. The Unified Authority allowed them to settle on the original islands of Japan. His four battleships now orbited the Earth.

I did not know where Ray Freeman was. He simply vanished while we orbited Earth. He said he would join this fight, but he had no intention of fighting it as a Marine or a soldier. Not Freeman. He was a mercenary.

But I had no intention of fighting or of rejoining the Marines. The U.A. had betrayed me too many times. Yes, I would die, too; but at least I would not die protecting a government that had tricked me and left me to die. One thing seemed certain, we were all going to die.

Yet deep inside I knew I was just fooling myself. Sooner or later, I would get sucked in again. After all, I was a military clone. Like it or not, I was government property, and the final battle was coming.

AUTHOR'S NOTE

My efforts to write this book were sabotaged!

A company called VG Pocket released a handheld game system called Caplet, with really excellent versions of the arcade classics *Burger Time* and *Bust a Move*. You may not have guessed, but I am an avid video game addict. When a Caplet landed on my desk, I often found myself struggling to reach the elusive fifth level of *Burger Time* when I should have been writing.

Caplet pried its way into my life sometime in August 2006, ten weeks before a finished manuscript was due to my publisher. That act of Caplet sabotage came toward the end of a rather rushed chronology that began on May 31, when I got a call from my agent, Richard Curtis, letting me know that he had sold Ace Books two more books in the Wayson Harris series.

Ace asked for nothing more than titles and story lines in May, but drafts of the books were due in October and April. At the time that Richard called, I was working on a book from an unsold series of young adult books. Switching gears in mid-book was not easy.

At first the words for this book came slowly. I try to write two thousand words per day. As I began this project, I had days in which I wrote seven hundred words and days in which I wrote five hundred. Thus, while I expected to finish the first draft before August, I did not finish until September 13. That left me roughly fifty days to finish and proof a story that would clearly need a lot of polish—which would not have been much of a problem in a Caplet-free world.

These are the people who helped me with that job. My parents read *The Clone Alliance* as I went along in weekly installments. My dad, an *Analog* fan from the first days of the magazine, was particularly helpful.

Once I finished that first draft, I ran copies of that very rough draft to Mark Adams and John Thorpe for suggestions on improving the story line. John was diplomatic about his reservations, Mark was not. The alarms go off when a soft-spoken friend like Mark Adams says he is afraid to send you his comments because he does not want to endanger your friendship. Mark, friends don't let friends go out in public with their pants down. Thank you, Mark, and thank you, John; many of your suggestions have been added.

I started the third draft of this book before finishing the second—mostly because the biggest problems were in the first half of the book. Once things seemed almost presentable, my wife gave this book its first proofing. With the spelling and punctuation in hand, I finished my half of this project by handing the book off to Rachel Johnson, a family friend who has a great eye for spelling, punctuation, and story suggestions. You may have noticed the dedication—Rachel Johnson is that "Rachel." Dustin and Dillan are her husband and son.

The second half of this project happened at Ace, where an editor named Anne Sowards cut and cleaned my work. She and her team are the final eyes. She tells me to cut scenes to make the pace faster or to add to scenes to get the point across.

One point I did not spell out adequately in prior novels was why Harris came out so different than the Liberators before him. I could not come up with a satisfactory explanation. Marcelo Sanjines (if the name sounds familiar, it is because Father David Sanjines, the priest in *Rogue Clone,* borrowed his family name from Marcelo) rescued me from this conundrum. One night while I was grappling with that question, I went out for hot chocolate with Marcelo and he said, "Harris is so different than the other Liberators. Is that because he was raised in an orphanage?"

"Of course," I said, acting as if I had planned that all along. Thanks, Marcelo. Next time we hit Starbucks, the hot chocolate is on me.

Back to my publisher... There are a lot of benefits that come from being published by Ace Books. The best perk, though, is having my covers created by Christian McGrath.

I wish to thank everyone I have mentioned for their help with this project, except VG Pocket. VG Pocket, your little handheld game system is diabolical in nature.

ABOUT THE AUTHOR

Steven L. Kent is an American author, best known for *The Clone Rebellion* series of military science fiction and his video game journalism. As a freelance journalist, he has written for the *Seattle Times*, *Parade, USA Today,* the *Chicago Tribune,* *MSNBC*, the *Japan Times*, and the *Los Angeles Times Syndicate*. He also wrote entries on video games for *Encarta* and the *Encyclopedia Americana*. For more about Kent, visit his official website www.SadSamsPalace.com.

BEHIND THE BOOK

The Clone Rebellion author Steven L. Kent finds inspiration in the unlikeliest of places...

HOW I RAN INTO ARTHUR DENT ON A DESERTED ROAD IN THE MIDDLE OF IDAHO

In *A Study in Scarlet*, the first Sherlock Holmes novel, Sir Arthur Conan Doyle describes the United States as something akin to a landlocked black hole once you head east of San Francisco or west of New York. (Please note the lack of quotation marks, I may have taken a few liberties.) This description, of course, is patently absurd. America's societal black hole starts just west of Chicago and it includes Los Angeles and San Francisco. It's been many, many years since I read *A Study in Scarlet*, but I wasn't entirely impressed with Doyle's understanding of all things Americana.

The black hole does in fact exist, and its locus is a large vacant square in the bottom center of Idaho. This is what visitors to this particular spot should NOT expect to find: mountains, hills, forests, castles, recognizable airports, indigenous grass, planetariums, or French restaurants. Here is an incomplete list of the things that visitors are likely to find in this vicinity: the ramp Evel Knievel used in his ill-fated attempt to jump a rocket (not a motorcycle) across the Snake River Canyon, potato farms, wheat farms, beet farms, dairies, fast-food restaurants, truck stops, some of the hardest working and most honest people in America today, churches, and an occasional tree. The main tourist attraction in one town is a crosswalk sign with a stick figure of a drunk. Not surprisingly, it's outside of a bar.

My point is this, if you are looking for beautiful vistas, Sir Arthur Conan Doyle pretty much nailed this little section of the States.

In 1990, I graduated with a master's degree in Communications. I packed up my meager belongings into a few boxes which I hoped to haul from Utah to my new home in Oregon, following the very route that takes unwary travelers through Doyle's black hole, or as I call it, "The Burley Triangle." (Burley is a town along the route.) I had a long drive ahead of me, but I didn't have a pickup truck, which I didn't consider a problem, not in Utah. If there is one place on Earth where pickup trucks abound, it's Utah.

Afflicted by the typical graduate student's lack of funds, I went to a used-car lot. When I told the salesman how much money I had, he told me he had just the thing. We walked to the front of the lot, where beautiful brand new trucks sat in perfect rows like Emperor Qin Shi Huang's terracotta soldiers. When I saw that these trucks cost more than my education, he assured me that he had just the financing solution for me. I said, "No." So we crossed the lot and there stood another not-so-neat row of trucks. These looked a bit older, but they weren't bad. Sadly, the salesman then unlocked the chained gate at the back of the car lot and led me into an open field with grass as high as my belt. There, parked in the grass, were the trucks that the Egyptian slaves drove as they delivered the stone blocks used to build the pyramids.

There was an entire fleet of 'em, each looking dirty, sturdy, powerful, and ancient.

"Will they even start?" I asked the salesman.

"Sure they will," he assured me.

I picked the cleanest, neatest one and had a look. It didn't start, but that was because the lot attendants had pulled the batteries out. Once they placed a suitably dirty battery back in the truck, the engine turned.

The truck was a 1984 Ford. A lot of people mistakenly believe the name Ford has something to do with Henry Ford, the legendary founder of the Ford Motor Company. A quick Google search reveals that FORD is actually an acronym for "Fix Or Repair Daily."

The only work that my not-so-new truck needed, however, was aesthetic. The paint had faded from years of sitting in a field. As I cleaned the cab, I found a sandwich bag containing a badly infected hotdog stashed under the driver's seat. Don't worry, I won't describe how the hotdog looked or tasted; I save that kind of thing for my novels.

The other problem with the truck was that it had an ancient AM-only radio. Even back in 1990, there was not much to listen to on AM radio, especially when you were driving past towns with names like Pocatello, Glen's Ferry, and Hell's Canyon. The one and only thing I insisted on before signing on the dotted line was that the lot install a tape deck. Yeah, yeah, CD decks made the retail scene in 1983 and I was still playing cassette tapes in 1990, I never claimed to be an early adopter. As my family will tell you, I still do not own a cell phone. That fad is going away sometime soon, and I don't want to embarrass myself by being the last person caught carrying an iPhone.

I suspect the salesman grabbed my tape deck from the same shed that held the batteries.

So, armed with a few good tapes, I set off for my new home at approximately five in the evening... which meant I entered the Burley Triangle, the black hole of lost souls, at about 10.00 P.M. Here is what I found when I entered the desolate stretch: lots and lots of open blackness. There were farms and streets in the distance, I saw the lights. Those lights, however, seemed as distant and alien as the stars in the skies. It was like entering outer space, only I wasn't completely alone. I passed truck stops and gas stations regularly. In the beginning, I passed an endless supply of eighteen-wheel rigs—the big trucks. As the night wore on, however, the roads became empty. I saw signs for Declo and Malta, but the towns themselves were nowhere to be found. Burley, the biggest berg between Pocatello and Boise, was only on the south side of the freeway. Everything to the north was buried in blackness.

After Burley, there's Rupert and then Twin Falls, where Evel Knievel's long-forgotten ramp still stands. Rupert is a few miles off the highway, but you can still see the lights. Towns like Twin Falls and Mountain Home are far from the highway, sparkling on the horizon like distant galaxies. It was in all of that darkness, distance, and despair that my tape deck decided to make a meal of my cassette of The Cars' *Candy-O*. I tried another cassette. The tape deck munched it as well. Quick study that I am, I stopped feeding tapes to the satanic deck after four more cassettes, and found myself relegated to one of Dante's innermost rings of

Hell—the one in which you are less than halfway through the Burley Triangle late at night with no form of entertainment except an AM radio.

I searched the radio as I drove. Mostly I found static. Occasionally, I found weak signals with Mexican or country music. I'm not much of a country music fan. And then, somewhere in the darkness between Kimberly and Jerome—that's Kimberly, Idaho, a small town just east of Twin Falls, and Jerome, Idaho, a town one hundred miles east of Boise—I picked up a crystal-clear signal of a program that made no sense because the people talking were saying the damnedest things. I heard someone say something about an archaeological dig. As I listened more closely, I realized that I was hearing a wimpy sounding guy speaking with several women, all of whom appeared to have the same voice. Here is what they said:

Man: "Why are you all exactly the same as each other?"

Woman II: "Well, you're exactly the same as yourself aren't you?"

Man: "This is true."

Woman III: "Well then."

Man: "But unhelpful."

Woman: "We're clones."

Man: "Ah! Clones! I've heard of that! You mean there was one of you to begin with and then exact copies were made, and now there are three of you?"

Woman: "Yes, except that there are now nearly five hundred and seventy-eight thousand million of us."

Man: "Huh?"

Woman: "It's alright. The others aren't here at the moment. Can we get on with the work?"

Man: "That's rather a lot isn't it?"

Five hundred and seventy-eight thousand million sounded like a lot to me, too. Fortunately, a narrator came on to explain the situation: it seemed that the Brandisvogon Escort Service decided to clone a beautiful, intelligent, vivacious woman named Lintilla—a good idea, but in the hands of the Vogons, good ideas inevitably go awry. As their cloning machine began making the next clone before finishing the last, it became impossible to shut down the contraption without committing murder. (For a complete explanation, go to http://hitchhikers.wikia.com/wiki/Lintilla)

That wimpy sounding man, of course, was none other than Arthur Dent, with whom I was somewhat acquainted, having read Douglas Adams's *The Hitchhiker's Guide to the Galaxy* my senior year in high school. I didn't recognize him on that evening, mostly because I got to spend so little time with him.

The signal didn't last all the way to Mountain Home—let alone Boise, Nampa, Fruitland, Baker, Weezer, Pendelton, and ultimately Portland—but the humor stayed with me. I barely had time to hear why there were so many women named Lintilla before static obscured the dialog, and soon the strange man with all the carbon-copy women was gone. I spent the next thirty minutes trying to relocate the radio signal and the next twenty years trying to locate the story. I told friends about the girl who was cloned five hundred and seventy-eight thousand million times and asked if they had any idea just who she might be. Fortunately for me, I eventually came to know a gentleman from Wales named Andrew Perry. Andrew had not only read *The Hitchhiker's Guide to the Galaxy*, as many Americans have, but he'd also listened to every BBC radio broadcast and owned a published version of the script (and not too many Americans can claim all of that.)

Check out the next book in the series, *The Clone Elite*, for more bonus material from Steven L. Kent!

ALSO AVAILABLE FROM TITAN BOOKS

STARK'S WAR

BY JACK CAMPBELL

(WRITING AS JOHN G. HEMRY)

The USA reigns over Earth as the last surviving superpower. To build a society free of American influence, foreign countries have inhabited the moon, where Sergeant Ethan Stark and his squadron must fight a desperate enemy in an airless atmosphere.

STARK'S WAR

STARK'S COMMAND

STARK'S CRUSADE

"A gripping tale of military science fiction, in the tradition of Heinlein's Starship Troopers and Haldeman's Forever War… The characterization is right on… the plot is sharp and crisp…Give this one a try." *Absolute Magnitude*

"The *Stark's War* trilogy has great action scenes, interesting characters and an original concept." The British Fantasy Society

"Solidly written, action-packed mil-SF… a good page-turner that will amply satisfy fans of John Scalzi's *Old Man's War* series, Jack McDevitt, David Weber or John Ringo." SFF World